Critical acclaim for Linda Lael Miller's marvelous *New York Times* bestseller

ONE WISH

"[A] story rich in tenderness, romance, and love. Her protagonists are adorable, with a strength and courage that touched my heart. . . . Ms. Miller reminds us of a simpler time in which determined men and the strong women by their sides forged our future. An excellent book from an author destined to lead the romance genre into the next century."

—*Rendezvous*

"An author who genuinely cares about her characters, Miller also expresses the exuberance of Western life in her fresh, human, and empathetic prose and lively plot."

—*Booklist*

"I loved this book! Ms. Miller touches our hearts again in a very special way. Do not miss this wonderful story!"

—*Old Book Barn Gazette*

"Another triumph. . . . *One Wish* is an entertaining Americana romance that shows why Linda Lael Miller has remained on of the giantesses of the industry for the past decade. The story line is crisp and filled with family conflict."

—Harriet Klausner, Barnesandnoble.com

Acclaim for Linda Lael Miller's irresistible novels of love in the Wild West

SPRINGWATER

"Heartwarming. . . . Linda Lael Miller captures not only the ambiance of a small Western town, but the need for love, companionship, and kindness that is within all of us. . . . *Springwater* is what Americana romance is all about."

—*Romantic Times*

"A heartwarming tale with adorable and endearing characters."

—*Rendezvous*

A SPRINGWATER CHRISTMAS

"A tender and beautiful story. . . . Christmas is the perfect time of year to return to Springwater Station and the unforgettable characters we've come to know and love. . . . Linda Lael Miller has once more given us a gift of love."

—*Romantic Times*

THE VOW

"The Wild West comes alive through the loving touch of Linda Lael Miller's gifted words. . . . Breathtaking. . . . A romantic masterpiece. This one is a keeper you'll want to take down and read again and again."

—*Rendezvous*

"A beautiful tale of love lost and regained. . . . A magical Western romance . . . that would be a masterpiece in any era."

—Amazon.com

Also by Linda Lael Miller

Linda Lael Miller

Courting Susannah

POCKET **STAR** BOOKS

New York   London   Toronto   Sydney   Singapore

An *Original* Publication of POCKET BOOKS

A Pocket Star Book published by
POCKET BOOKS, a division of Simon & Schuster, Inc.
1230 Avenue of the Americas, New York, NY 10020

ISBN: 0-671-00400-X

First Pocket Books printing October 2000

10 9 8 7 6 5 4 3 2 1

POCKET Star Books and colophon are registered trademarks of
Simon & Schuster, Inc.

Front cover illustration by Gregg Gulbronson

Printed in the U.S.A.

For the grandparents I never knew,
Selma and Horace Bleecker
and
Dora Purtee Lael,
with love

Courting Susannah

Chapter

1

~

1906

When no one answered her ring, Susannah McKittrick gathered the last frayed ravels of her courage and, in an act of unprecedented boldness, let herself into Aubrey Fairgrieve's grand house high on one of Seattle's seven hills. Shoulders straight, satchel in hand, glancing neither left nor right lest she lose her nerve and flee like a thief discovered, she mounted the grand staircase, marched along the imposing hallway, and selected a modest but adequate room at the rear.

From the one narrow window, she could see the mountains in their mantillas of white and the unsettled waters of Puget Sound, charcoal beneath a glowering October sky. A muddy patch of neglected garden fell within the range of her vision, as did the churchyard on the other side of a high stone wall, a patchwork of gold, yellow, and crimson leaves tucked round about its slabs, wooden crosses, and statues like a quilt.

She wondered which stone marked Julia's grave, and sudden, weary tears pricked the backs of her eyes. She braced up, as best she could, given that she'd been traveling for more than ten days, having left Nantucket as soon as Mr. Fairgrieve's telegram arrived, and tried to turn her thoughts in a more constructive direction. It was no mean endeavor, considering the rigors of her journey and the weight of sorrow in her heart. She was exhausted, half starved, a stranger in a strange land, and probably an unwelcome one at that, for while Julia's husband—now widower—had sent a terse wire to inform her of his wife's death, he certainly had not invited her to join his household and serve as his daughter's guardian. That had been her own idea, and Julia's.

Lingering at the window, she lifted her gaze to the mountaintops again, sighing as she shed her dusty, mud-speckled cloak and let it fall over the back of a plain wooden chair. Although Seattle's climate seemed similar, she missed Nantucket very sorely in those brief moments of reflection; at a distance, home seemed a far gentler place, and it was easy to discount the isolation, the moody winter skies, the fierce Atlantic storms that battered the island in all seasons.

With a twinge, Susannah turned at last from the vista before her, resolved to make the best of the situation, for the sake of Julia's child. In the mirror over the bureau on the other side of the room, she caught a glimpse of herself, fair-haired, gray-eyed, neither plain nor beautiful, clad in a practical brown sateen gown with a matching bonnet, embellished only by a tufted lining of satin inside the brim. Everything she wore, including her camisole, petticoats, and drawers, had been carefully mended in a stalwart effort to hide the evidence of long use, and although she still felt as though she'd reached the end of her tether, an innate sense of dignity sustained her.

After untying the wide ribbons beneath her chin as she approached the looking glass, Susannah removed the bonnet and set it on the bureau top. She was definitely not as pretty as Julia had been, she thought without the slightest flinch, though her skin was uncommonly clear and glowed with vibrant good health, the seemingly endless sojourn from the east notwithstanding. She wanted a hot bath, a meal, and a good, long sleep, in just that sequence, but there were other matters that must be attended to before she could indulge.

First, and her heart quickened measurably at the thought, she would see Julia's baby—the infant girl meant to be Susannah's own namesake. Then, inevitably, she must confront Aubrey Fairgrieve, for this was his house after all, and the child, the precious child, was his, too.

Susannah sank down onto the edge of the unadorned iron bed, overwhelmed at the enormity of the task that lay before her. She allowed her mind to drift again, her thoughts wafting back through time like smoke dissipating in a breeze.

Julia, a romantic at heart, had met Mr. Fairgrieve in Boston, where she held a post as governess to the children of one of his friends, and had eloped with the man only weeks after that first innocent encounter, despite frantic letters from Susannah, begging her to be cautious, take her time, *think* about what she was doing.

Julia's letters had been lengthy and effusive in those early months following the marriage, describing her bridegroom as nothing less than a paragon. He was "gloriously" handsome, she'd written, a vital, witty man, thirty-three years of age, with a ready smile, mischievous hazel eyes, and a head of wavy brown hair that gleamed in any degree of light. He stood just under six feet tall, and though he was lean, he had broad and powerful shoulders. He had been reared in the timber camps, where hard work made him muscular, but he was a wealthy man now, and polished; he owned a mansion, wore fine suits, kept magnificent horses, and enjoyed a good cigar every night with his brandy.

Susannah had read her friend's written rhapsodies eagerly, if a bit enviously, for at the time she herself had been employed as a companion to an imperious widow with a dwindling fortune, and though she had lived in shabby splendor in a gray-shingled Nantucket house, she was, as ever, an outsider. When Julia had written that she was with child, Susannah had been overjoyed, but the news had also intensified the loneliness that had always plagued her.

Then, over the course of half a dozen letters, Julia had gone from ebullient delight with her lot in life to bitter uncertainty, followed by rising defiance and, finally, rage. The Fairgrieves' fairy-tale marriage had not merely fallen apart, it had exploded in flaming pieces, yet for all Julia's fury, the precise cause of the destruction remained a mystery.

Of course, Seattle was a rambunctious place when compared with staid Boston. Both Julia and Susannah had practically grown up within the sheltering, if austere, confines of St. Mary's Institute for Wayward and Unfortunate Girls, where they had been educated in music, Latin, stitchery, and literature. Raised with the graces of a lady, if not the means, Julia had seemed overjoyed by her good fortune, thriving in the warm light of her husband's love. What had happened to change everything so drastically?

Susannah's stomach churned. She'd been over and over that question, like someone crawling over sharp stones, trying to find a way out of a dark cave, and all she had to show for the effort were a lot of emotional scrapes and bruises. Still, she couldn't let the matter go; Julia, with all her faults, had been the only "family" she had, and the bond between them was not easily severed, even by death.

Mr. Fairgrieve, for his part, surely had counted himself equally fortunate to land such a prize as Julia, at least in the beginning, for all his money, position, and purported good looks. Julia had been a rare beauty with creamy white skin, enormous green eyes, and a wealth of auburn hair that grew in a tumbling riot of curls. She had been exuberant, full of laughter and mischief, whereas Susannah tended toward shyness and intro-spection, and yet the two were fast friends from the start. Mere days after Julia's unceremonious arrival at St. Mary's—she had been dragged there, screaming and kicking, by her mother, a stage actress fallen upon hard times—the ten-year-olds had adopted each other as "blood sisters," pricking their index fingers to seal the pact.

Just then, the soft, tentative cry of a baby reached Susannah, prodding her out of her private reverie. Julia's child. A nurse or maid must have taken the little one from the house earlier and just now returned.

Heart racing a little, Susannah stood and ventured out of the tiny bedroom into the wide corridor beyond, listening from the deepest parts of herself, opening every pore and fiber to the sound. Closed doors lined the hallway like sentinels, set to keep out the unwanted visitor. Fancy gas fixtures adorned the wainscoted walls, unlighted but shining in the gloom, and here and there a table stood, bare and polished. The scent of beeswax gave the place a mystical aspect, like a passage in some pharaoh's private temple.

The baby's lament had risen to a furious wail by that time, and Susannah's agitation grew each time she paused to press one ear to a door. She was in just that position when the tall double doors at the end of the hallway sprang open and a man appeared, shadow-draped, a small, furious bundle squalling in his arms.

"Damn it, Maisie," he shouted, "where are you?" In the next instant, his eyes found Susannah, standing paralyzed in the hallway. He wore high black boots, well-fitted trousers of some soft leather, a tailored white shirt, and suspenders, and his hair captured what little light there was. "Who the devil are you?" he demanded without preamble.

Susannah stood still as an ice sculpture, though her very organs seemed to flail within her in a kind of sweet panic. Her first attempt to speak failed; her second was a dismal croak. She had hoped to introduce herself and explain her presence in a reasonable manner, rather than simply appear in a hallway like some passing wraith, but that opportunity had already come and gone.

"You must be Mr. Fairgrieve," she managed at long last, and flushed.

"And you are?" he prompted after a distracted nod of acquiescence, stalking toward her. The baby had ceased its pitiful cries and burbled against his shoulder now, sounding calm, almost contented. Idly, he patted the little back with one powerful woodsman's hand. His eyes did not look friendly as he glowered down at her; she saw none of the mirth and mischief Julia had described in her early letters.

She swallowed, then straightened her weary shoulders. "My name," she uttered with hard-won grace, "is Susannah McKittrick. Your late wife, Julia, was my dearest friend."

"Ah," he said. She saw in his eyes that he remembered, although Susannah had no reason whatsoever to think he approved of her presence. "What are you doing here?"

She drew upon all that remained of her composure. What she'd done was impulsive, perhaps even foolish, but it was, indeed, *done*. Nothing to do now but go forward. "I've come to attend to the child."

He arched one eyebrow, still comforting the baby

with an inattentive proficiency that might have been comical, given his size and the sheer impact of his personality, if Susannah hadn't been in the awkward position of a trespasser. "What?" he asked, as though she'd spoken in a language he didn't comprehend.

"Julia asked for my promise—that I would look after her baby if anything happened to her. When I received your telegram—"

His frowned deepened. "I see," he said, though he plainly didn't. "Maisie must have let you in."

She swallowed hard, raised her chin a notch, and shook her head. The name, Maisie, was not a familiar one; Julia had never mentioned the woman. No doubt she was a servant.

"I turned the bell repeatedly, and when no one answered, I simply came in." She paused, and color pulsed in her cheeks. "I felt I had no choice, you see. I'd come so far, and in a state of extreme urgency."

She thought there might have been a grin lurking in the depths of those remarkable eyes of his, though there was no knowing for certain. "Do you make a habit of walking into people's houses when nobody comes to the door, Miss—er—?"

"McKittrick," she reiterated. It was all she could do to hold his gaze, but she would not, *could* not allow herself to be intimidated. She had no acceptable option except to follow through with her grand gesture and find a way to keep her heart's vow to Julia's memory by tending the child. "I do not," she said coolly. She had, of course, admitted herself to the Fairgrieve house out of desperation, not audacity; she had no friends in Seattle, no prospect of employment, and virtually no money. She would find herself in dire straits indeed if this man turned her away.

Susannah felt fresh panic stir within her and attempted to stem the tide by biting the inside of her lower lip.

"You say you were a friend of my wife's," he reflected soberly.

Susannah let out her breath, nodded. Surely Julia must have told him about their shared childhood at St. Mary's, and he had, after all, written to tell her when his wife passed away. For all of that, he seemed surprised by her existence, let alone her presence in the upstairs hallway of his house.

"I've—I've taken the smallest bedroom—the one overlooking the churchyard," she said, resisting an urge to twist her hands. Her gaze was locked on the baby; she longed to reach out, cradle the infant in her arms.

Fairgrieve's brows arched, and once again she thought she saw the beginnings of humor far back in his eyes, but the impression was gone as quickly as it had come to her. "I don't guess I object, since nobody else is using it," he allowed. "All the same, I'd still like to know what you want."

She ached to hold the child. "I told you," she said, speaking as forthrightly as he had. "I'm here to take care of Julia's daughter. What is her name?"

He looked down at the babe with a curious frown, as though expecting to be advised in the matter, then met Susannah's gaze again. "I don't believe she has one," he replied, and Susannah would have sworn he had never so much as considered the oversight before that moment, though she had to admit he held his little girl with an ease that seemed to belie some of her preconceptions where his character was concerned.

For a few moments, Susannah was rendered speechless. When at last she found her voice, she sputtered, "No name? But the poor little thing is four months old!"

"Yes," Fairgrieve said, without apology. Then he held

the infant out, like an offering. "Here. If you want her, take her. She's hungry."

Trembling, Susannah accepted the precious child. How could an innocent baby be allowed to go *four months* without a proper name? The warmth of the babe brought tears springing to her eyes, and she blinked rapidly, in the hope that Fairgrieve wouldn't see. She took a deep breath or two, in the effort to recover, all the while holding Julia's baby close against her bosom.

"Take her? Where?" she asked, bewildered, when she could trust herself to speak moderately.

"Well, to the kitchen, of course. I believe she needs a bottle."

Susannah stared at him. "Then I can stay?"

He answered briskly, already turning away, heading back toward the gaping doorway through which he had come. "For the time being," he said in dismissal.

Susannah stood there briefly, in the middle of the hallway, and then made for the stairs. She moved in cautious haste, lest Mr. Fairgrieve appear again, having changed his mind, and order her out of the house.

She found the kitchen after some exploration and was impressed to discover that it boasted a real icebox with a crockery pitcher of cold, buttery milk inside, along with a plenitude of cheese, eggs, and other supplies.

Ignoring her own ravenous hunger, Susannah laid the infant in a wicker bassinet set before a bay window, searched for and found a bottle and nipple in one of the cupboards, built up the fire in the cookstove, and put the baby's meal on to heat.

She was seated in a rocking chair, feeding the child, when Mr. Fairgrieve entered from a back stairway and stood watching for a long moment, his expression unreadable.

"You've had practice with babies," he said at some length.

She smiled. "Yes," she said. "There were a lot of children born at St. Mary's, and I helped to take care of them until they were adopted."

He frowned. "St. Mary's?"

Surely Julia had told him about the school, about the nuns and the troubled young girls who often took refuge with them, and yet he seemed genuinely puzzled. "Where your wife and I met," she added, in an attempt at clarification.

He drew up a chair and sat down facing her, their knees almost touching. "St. Mary's," he repeated, as though to extract some private and elusive understanding from the phrase.

Susannah continued to rock gently back in the chair, the baby resting warm and solid and milk-fragrant in her arms, though something had quickened within her. Julia, in her eagerness to belong, had been known to tell the occasional small and generally innocuous lie, and she could be self-serving when it suited, but she certainly must have told Aubrey about her childhood. Hadn't she? Before Susannah could think of a response, Mr. Fairgrieve spoke again.

"Tell me," he said. "Exactly who *was* my wife?"

Susannah was stunned. "I beg your pardon?"

He folded his strong arms. "I'd like to hear a description—from your perspective."

So he *had* cared, despite Julia's protestations to the contrary. Susannah's heart softened, and she smiled, a little sadly, to remember it all again. She sighed. "Julia *hated* being left behind at St. Mary's—I think she knew her mother was never coming back for her."

Mr. Fairgrieve leaned forward, listening intently, but said nothing.

"She was an actress on the stage—Julia's mother, I mean—and I suppose that's where Julia got her temperament. She was—well—somewhat *high-strung*."

Aubrey raised his eyes briefly heavenward. "That's an understatement."

Susannah felt a little defensive on her friend's behalf. "If you'd been there—if you'd seen how she cried, how she flung herself against the iron gate and called for her mother to come back—" She closed her eyes against the image, but it was as clear as if it had happened only moments before, though, of course, nearly fourteen years had passed. "The nuns practically had to drag Julia inside. She carried on until she was sick. Finally, a doctor was summoned. He gave her a dose of laudanum to make her sleep, and she was still in such a state that they kept her in the infirmary for days."

Mr. Fairgrieve did not flinch. "St. Mary's is an orphanage, then?"

Susannah nodded. "As well as a school and a hospital."

He sat in silence for some time, absorbing what she had said. "And you?" he asked finally.

"Me?" she replied, confused.

"How did you wind up there? At this—school, I mean?"

Susannah bit her lower lip. "I was raised there." She looked down at the baby and rocked just a little faster in the sturdy wooden chair. Speckles of sun-washed dust twinkled in the air. "One of those children you read about in penny dreadfuls—left on the doorstep in a basket—except that I was in an old fruit box."

"I'm sorry."

She bristled slightly, although there had been a note of gruff kindness in his voice. "Don't be. I was very happy at St. Mary's. The nuns were good to me, and I was given an education of sorts."

"You never married." It might have been either a question or a statement, he spared so little inflection for the words.

Susannah felt the old hollowness inside and quelled it quickly. The baby was asleep now, sweet and sated. "No," she said softly, and at some length. "I worked as a companion after I left school, and there never seemed to be time for anything else."

He sighed heavily, shoved a hand through his lustrous hair. "Until you left your work to come here. To Seattle."

Susannah wanted to weep, though she did not allow herself that release, fearing she might never stop crying. "I felt I could do nothing else. Julia's letters—"

"I can well imagine Julia's letters," he said wearily and with some disgust. He spread his hands, started to say something else, and bit back the words.

"I won't be a burden, Mr. Fairgrieve," Susannah said, perhaps too quickly. She was a proud woman, but she was prepared to beg if that was what she had to do. "I can give music lessons, if you will allow me the use of Julia's piano, and, of course, I will pay room and board."

"All this," he asked, rising to his feet, "for a stranger's child?"

"Julia was not a stranger," Susannah said.

"No," Aubrey answered. "I don't suppose she was—to you. But I am." He paused. "Aren't you afraid to live under the same roof with the sort of monster Julia must have made me out to be?"

She met his fierce gaze, held it. "I can look after myself," she said evenly. "My concern is for this baby. I'd like to call her Victoria, if you don't mind. She should have a name."

"Call her whatever you like," Aubrey replied, his voice cool.

"Poor Julia," Susannah muttered aloud, quite inadvertently.

Fairgrieve leaned forward until his nose was barely an inch from Susannah's. "*Poor Julia*," he replied with quiet mockery, "*God rest her soul*, cared for nothing and no one but herself. Her greatest worry, where this child was concerned, was that the pregnancy might spoil her figure. Therefore, whatever you do, please do not waste your sympathy on the likes of my late wife."

Susannah blinked, shocked by the cold fury of such a reply. Yes, she'd known that Julia wasn't happy in the marriage, at least not in its latter days, but even then she had never guessed that the situation had deteriorated into such bitterness and rancor as Mr. Fairgrieve was displaying now. "I do not wish to argue the quality of my friend's character, with you or anyone else," she said. "But Julia looked forward to the birth, and she loved you very much, at least in the beginning. I know that from her letters."

Fairgrieve's expression was one of exasperated contempt, and for all that, he was still very attractive, a contradiction that unsettled Susannah to no small degree. "Julia wouldn't have known *love* from the grocer's lame horse," he snapped. "From the moment she knew she was pregnant, she bewailed her fate and cursed me for a rutting bull with no concern for her delicate faculties." He let out a short, huffing breath. "As though I had anything to do with it."

Susannah's eyes widened as his implication struck home, but she refused to honor such a suggestion with a response. Like everyone else, Julia had not been perfect; she had been quite shallow in some ways, and she could be childish and petulant at times, but she had many good qualities as well. If Aubrey Fairgrieve had been her husband, then he was without question the father of this child, and that, as far as Susannah was concerned, decided the matter.

"We seem to be thinking of two different women," she said in a reflective tone. "You knew one Julia, and I knew another."

"Apparently," he ground out.

She held the child just a little tighter, and she saw in his eyes that he understood the gesture for what it was, a declaration. She was laying claim to a place, a prominent place, in this baby's heart and future. She also saw his tacit resistance to the idea of surrender in any shape or guise.

Julia had been at least partially correct, it appeared, in her bitter assessment of her husband's nature. He was bone-stubborn, a man who liked getting his own way.

He glared at her for a long moment, without another word, and then turned and left the kitchen.

Susannah lingered in the chair for a while, thinking, and then went back upstairs, laid the baby carefully on her bed, securing her on either side with pillows. That done, she fashioned a cradle from one of the bureau drawers, padding the bottom with a folded blanket and the sides with rolled towels. No doubt there was a nursery somewhere in the house, but for now, this arrangement would do.

After moving a soundly sleeping Victoria to the improvised crib, she ventured out long enough to locate the splendid bathing room Julia had written her about, took a hasty bath in the giant copper tub with its tank of hot water, dried herself off, pulled on a wrapper suspended from a hook on the door, and dashed back to her own quarters.

Victoria was snoring, and Susannah smiled, feeling restored. After unpacking her brush, fresh undergarments, and a not-too-wrinkled cotton dress, she sat on the edge of the bed, took down her hair, groomed it thoroughly, and pinned it up again. A cup of tea, she decided, would be just the thing, and some bread and butter wouldn't hurt, either. Her hunger, in abatement after the encounter with Aubrey, was back in full force.

She dressed, ventured down to the kitchen to set a tray for herself, and returned to eat cheese and bread and drink delicious hot orange pekoe in her room. In good time, Victoria awakened, waving her fat little arms and fussing. Feeling completely happy, despite her grief for Julia and her deep misgivings about Mr. Fairgrieve, Susannah changed the infant, using a damask towel for a diaper, washed her hands in the green and black marble sink in the bathing room, and then wrapped the child in a fresh blanket, purloined from the linen cabinet in the corridor.

Descending the back stairway to the kitchen, Susannah found herself in the presence of a plain, plump woman, just shrugging out of a heavy woolen cloak. Maisie, no doubt.

"Well, now," she said, assessing Susannah with a smile of ingenuous welcome. "You came, then. Good."

Susannah blinked. Suddenly, though she could not have said precisely how, she knew that it had been this woman who had sent the wire that brought her to Seattle, and not Mr. Fairgrieve. "Susannah McKittrick," she said by way of introduction, putting out one hand while holding little Victoria securely with the other.

"Maisie," was the reply, with no last name given. The two women shook hands, and Susannah noticed the little boy then. About three years of age, he huddled shyly in the voluminous folds of Maisie's skirt.

"This is my Jasper," Maisie said proudly. "Say a proper howdy to the lady, Jasper."

Obediently, the boy executed a slight bow, though Susannah still had the sense that he wanted either to melt into his mother's limbs or to bolt.

Once she'd dispensed with her bonnet and cloak and divested Jasper of his jacket, Maisie extended competent arms for the baby. "Here, let me have the precious little critter. She must be plumb starved. I don't know as Mr. Fairgrieve thought to give her a bottle, though mercy knows I reminded him. Got back as quick as I could."

Jasper took an apple from a bowl in the center of the table and made for another room.

Susannah hesitated before giving up the baby, even though she liked and trusted Maisie already. "She's had a bottle," she said as the other woman took Victoria into her arms, bouncing her affectionately. "A nap, too." Susannah blushed when Maisie uncovered the infant and spotted the fancy embossed towel tied loosely into place. "I didn't know where to find a diaper."

Maisie smiled. "You did just fine. Didn't she, sweetums?" She made a face, and Victoria gave a chortling gurgle in response. "Miss Julia said you was a resourceful type, and she was right. Now, set yourself down and tell me, how was your trip?"

With that, Maisie took a seat herself, still holding the baby, in the rocking chair where Susannah had sat earlier, and Susannah drew up a short stool. "Long," she said in belated reply. "Maisie, Mr. Fairgrieve—did he— well, did he know I was coming?"

Maisie chuckled. "Nope," she said. "I see he didn't throw you out, though."

Susannah put a hand to her breastbone in a mingling of surprise, consternation, and amusement. "Then it *was* you who sent that wire? Why ever—?"

"I promised Mrs. Fairgrieve," Maisie said, and looked away into the distance for a long moment. "She wanted you here to look after the little one. I reckoned the mister would let you stay if you showed up."

"Thank heaven he did," she replied. "I'd have nowhere to go if he'd turned me away."

"Oh, you'd have been all right. This is a big house. Lots of hidey-holes to tuck you away in, with Mr. Fairgrieve none the wiser. Why, me and Jasper, we rattle around in this house like two pinto beans in the bottom of a bucket and hardly ever run into another soul."

Susannah closed her eyes for a moment, imagining herself haunting the place like a ghost, living a shadow life, avoiding contact with "the mister" at all costs. It was enough to make her shudder, for she was a creature of sunlight and fresh air. "You and Julia—Mrs. Fairgrieve—were friends, then?"

"I wouldn't say that," Maisie said, rocking. "She was the mistress of the house, after all, and I was here to cook and clean. Neither of us ever forgot that. All the same, I felt mighty sorry for her, especially there at the end."

"How—how did she die?" Susannah ventured, realizing she had been holding the question at arm's length ever since she'd received the wire nearly two weeks ago in Nantucket.

Maisie dashed the back of one work-reddened hand against her cheek. "It was a fever," she said. "Came on sudden, right after this little angel here was born. She was gone, the missus was, before the baby was a day old."

Susannah bit her lower lip, imagining the sorrow and shock of such a thing only too clearly. At St. Mary's, she'd seen many a mother and child perish, sometimes separately, often together. She braced herself. "Did she suffer? Julia, I mean?"

Maisie gave Susannah a long, measuring glance. "Yes," she said. "She was a tiny thing, wasn't she, and she had a hard time."

Susannah blinked back a rush of scalding tears. "And Mr. Fairgrieve? Was he kind to her?"

"He paced the hallway, like any daddy would do, but by the time sweet'ums here came along, Mrs. Fairgrieve had gone right out of her head. She didn't know any of us. Kept calling for her mama."

Susannah sighed. Yes, she thought sadly. The mother who left her at St. Mary's all those years before and never looked back.

"Little while after midnight," Maisie went on, her voice soft with sympathy and sadness, "Mrs. Fairgrieve passed on to the next world, and the mister, well, he left the house and didn't come back till the day they buried her. That was when I reckoned I ought to send for you, like the Missus asked me to—spoke up right after the first pain came, she did. Said I had to get you to come, no matter what."

Susannah struggled to retain her composure. "Well," she replied at some length, "The message took its sweet time reaching me."

Maisie smiled. "You're here," she said. "That's what's important. You take this baby to Mr. Fairgrieve's room to sleep, and then you go and rest up till supper. You look all done in."

Susannah stood automatically and took Victoria from Maisie's arms. "The crib is in Mr. Fairgrieve's room?" she asked.

Maisie nodded, unfazed by the question or by Susannah's bewilderment, which must have been obvious. "Big room at the front of the house," she confirmed. "The one with the double doors."

Susannah climbed the stairs yet again, carrying the infant, and found her way to the master chamber. Sure enough, the crib was there, among towering, heavy furniture, so masculine in character that she knew immediately that Julia probably had never actually resided within these walls.

A trancelike weariness overwhelmed Susannah as she placed Victoria gently in the elaborate crib, with its drapery of gossamer silk, and she lingered there for a time, forgetting her surroundings, trying to make sense of the situation, the place, the man Julia had loved, and then hated, with such passion.

It all caught up with Susannah then, the pain of loss, the confusion, the effects of a long and difficult journey. She turned from the sleeping baby—she would return to her room and take a brief rest, as Maisie had advised—and then the floor and ceiling exchanged places. She stumbled, got as far as the bed, and lay down, her head reeling. Although she had every intention of rallying, she dropped off into a fathomless slumber instead and fell end over end into the sweet refuge of darkness.

The next thing she knew, the room was draped in evening shadows, and a strong hand rested on her shoulder. She looked up and was startled into complete wakefulness, between one heartbeat and the next, to see Aubrey gazing down at her. Because of the relative gloom, she could not make out his expression.

"I'm sorry," she blurted, mortified beyond all endurance to be found lying prone on a man's bed—particularly *this* man's bed. "I must have—I don't know what—"

"Shh," he said, and she heard amusement in his voice, and something more tender. "There's no harm done."

Susannah bolted upright, and Aubrey stepped back, giving her plenty of room. She pressed the fingertips of both hands to her temples after setting her feet on the floor, trying desperately to reorient herself. She went immediately to the cradle and saw that the baby was gone. She panicked a little.

"She's downstairs with Maisie," Aubrey said gently. Susannah had no right to be soothed by his tone, but she was. Oh, heaven help her, she was. "There's a fine supper waiting for you in the kitchen."

Susannah could not face him, not then. He made light of finding her sleeping, no doubt with abandon, on his bed, but in many quarters, such an infraction, however innocent, was enough to lay even the best reputation to ruin. "Thank you," she said, keeping her head down and hurrying toward the doorway at top speed. Thus it was that she compounded her offense by colliding with Aubrey with such momentum that she surely would have fallen had he not grasped her shoulders and held her upright.

"Susannah," he said, *"it's all right."*

Oddly, she found his kindness more difficult to endure than simple annoyance would have been, or even skepticism. "Yes," she replied, with a sort of tremulous aplomb, addressing herself as much as him. "Everything is all right."

He let her go then and stepped back rather quickly. For once, he was the one to sound awkward. "I'll carry the cradle to your room," he said. "Then I'll see you downstairs at supper."

She tried to speak and could not. Nodded and fled.

She felt his smile like a kiss on the nape of her neck.

Chapter

2

*S*usannah McKittrick was nothing like Julia, at least on the surface, Aubrey decided as he watched his uninvited houseguest trying to eat her supper slowly and with a measure of decorum. His late wife had been fashionably plump, even before her pregnancy, and never one to deny herself any sort of pleasure for the sake of appearances.

Susannah, on the other hand, was thin, almost angular. Her perfect skin was pale, and it was obvious that she was half starved by the way her fork trembled as she raised it to her mouth. He wondered when she'd last taken a decent meal, but he had no intention of inquiring. Judging by the state of her clothing, she was practically destitute, and her pride might be all she had.

Most likely, she wanted to take Julia's child home to raise, though she hadn't said so straight out. She was, if he recalled correctly, from Nantucket. Perhaps, he reflected, drawing his brows together and watching as Susannah cautiously speared a second portion of Maisie's fried chicken, she expected a financial settlement of some sort. Provided that she was who she represented herself to be—a caring friend of Julia's—such a bargain might be an expedient solution to the problem. But suppose she was a swindler instead? He had no real knowledge of her character. She might abandon the child—or worse—once she had the money, and he would never know the difference.

Common decency prevented him from taking such a chance; he'd have her investigated before he made a final decision, and he knew just the man for the job.

For the present, she was attempting, without much success, to cut the drumstick on her plate with her knife, and the pinkening of her neck indicated that she knew he was watching her.

"Out here in the wild west," he said, taking pity, "we eat fried chicken with our fingers."

She glanced at him uncertainly, as if she thought he might be mocking her, and he took up a wing with his hands, to prove his contention, and took a bite. He thought he saw a tentative smile lurking in her gray eyes, though he couldn't be sure, for she lowered her heavy lashes right away, like a veil. But she set aside the knife and fork and nibbled at the drumstick with delicate restraint.

He felt something stir in the depths of his belly, watching her, and shifted uncomfortably in his chair. "How long have you been traveling, Miss McKittrick?" he asked, in an effort to distract himself as well as to make conversation.

She looked at him solemnly, as if to determine his reasons for asking even so innocent a question. "I left Nantucket ten days ago," she said after a moment's consideration.

"You don't seem to have much baggage," he commented, refilling his wine glass. She had already refused his gestured offer to pour some for her with a shake of her head.

She lifted her chin, and her eyes darkened to a

stormy shade of charcoal. "I have very few encumbrances," she replied flatly.

He'd said something wrong, though he wasn't sure what it was. Women could be very prickly creatures. "Julia owned a great many dresses," he ventured to observe, hoping he wasn't insulting her. "They're in the armoire in her room. Help yourself to whatever you want." He paused, cleared his throat. "You'll want to alter them, I suppose. Julia was—bigger."

She surprised him with a wan but genuine smile that left him shaken and even more off-balance than before. He wasn't sure he'd ever recover from the sweet, fiery shock of finding her asleep on his bed. "That is very kind, but I don't suppose Julia's garments would be appropriate for a child's nurse. As I remember, her tastes ran to silks and laces."

Aubrey frowned, recalling without admiration how delectable Julia had looked in her elegant, costly clothes and how she had used her singular charms to make a fool of him before the whole city of Seattle. "There might be a few more practical garments. Please—help yourself. She would want you to have her things."

She continued to assess him, and though there was nothing untoward in her expression, he felt increasingly unsettled, as though in some unaccountable way she might be seeing far more than he would have chosen to reveal. A splotch of color blossomed on each of her cheeks. "You and Julia didn't—didn't share a room?"

He laughed, and the bitterness of the sound surprised even him. "That is an audacious question," he remarked, provoked in a way that could not have been described as even remotely unpleasant, "for a woman who was wildly embarrassed to be found sleeping on someone else's bed."

The blush intensified, then drained away, leaving pallor behind. "I have never been wed, Mr. Fairgrieve," she said evenly, "but I am not ignorant. I know that most husbands and wives share a chamber, at least in the early years of their marriage."

"Julia enjoyed social engagements. She did not like to disturb my sleep, coming home at all hours of the night as she did, and so she asked for her own room. I was only too happy to oblige."

"I see." She spoke coldly, her food forgotten.

"I don't think you do," Aubrey answered. He pushed back his chair and stood. What the hell was happening to him? He'd always kept his own counsel, and now here he was, airing his private grievances to a stranger. "Sleep well. You might get some noise from the alley in that back bedroom, but I'm sure the mattress is comfortable enough."

She looked down at the half-eaten piece of chicken on her plate, longingly, he thought. "What shall I do if the baby awakens in the night?"

He thrust a hand through his hair. "Feed her and change her diaper," he said. "If that doesn't work, fetch Maisie. She and the boy sleep downstairs, in the little room off the kitchen." He let out a long breath. "Good night, Miss McKittrick," he said, and, with that, he turned and left Susannah alone at his table.

A door closed in the distance, and Susannah realized, with a surprising sweep of loneliness, that Mr. Fairgrieve had left the house. She sat still for a few moments, there in that grand and gleaming dining room, trying to sort through the storm of emotions that seemed to assail her whenever she was in his presence, then rose resolutely to clear the table.

In the kitchen, working by the bluish-gold glow from the gas fixtures, she washed the few dishes left undone and put the leftovers in the wooden icebox. Maisie was apparently one of those cooks who clean up as they go

along, a trait Susannah admired, and there was very little work to do. The meal had been excellent, not that
she would have complained in any event. Beggars, after
all, could not be choosers.

Gratefully, Susannah turned down the lights and
mounted the rear stairway. Several lamps burned in the
upper corridor, and she found her way easily to the
room she had chosen and looked in on the baby, who
slept peacefully in her cradle, moved there by Mr. Fairgrieve, her tiny form bathed in the glow of an autumn
moon.

She kissed the tip of one finger and touched it to the
tiny, furrowed forehead. "Sweet dreams, little one," she
whispered. "Shall I go on calling you Victoria? You're
not a Julia, I can plainly see that." She frowned and
shook her head. "Your mother was going to name you
after me, you know. It's just as well she didn't, though,
for you aren't a Susannah, either."

The child gave a sigh as soft as a fairy's heartbeat,
and a feeling of such poignant tenderness overtook Susannah that tears came to her eyes once again. She
hadn't wept, outwardly at least, since the news of Julia's
death had reached her. She'd been too busy, first resign-
ing her post, over vociferous protests from her elderly
charge, then packing up her few belongings and settling
her affairs, and finally traveling.

She laid aside gloomy thoughts and stiffened her
spine. The baby needed her to be strong, and she would
not fail in this or any other duty.

She tucked the soft blankets gently around the tiny
infant, lest the night chill reach her.

A flannel nightgown, far too fine to be her own, lay
across the foot of the bed, along with a soft towel and a
new cake of lavender soap, still in its painted tin. Blessing Maisie for an angel in disguise, she went to the bathing

room to wash, change, and brush her teeth. While there, she admired the grand tub yet again.

Back on Nantucket, Susannah had taken all her baths in the kitchen, setting the wash tub in the center of the floor and filling it with water laboriously heated on the cantankerous old cookstove. What a wonder it was simply to plug the drain, turn a couple of knobs, and sink into luxury.

After inspecting everything for a second time, rapt as a country bumpkin gone to the fair, she crept back to her own room, checked on Victoria once more, and climbed into bed.

She did not expect to sleep, after her long rest on Mr. Fairgrieve's bed, and promptly dropped off into a world of nebulous, troubling dreams.

She awakened before the child, deeply saddened. All her life, she had yearned for a husband, a child, a home, however modest, of her own. Julia had had those things, and yet she had not been happy. What could have happened to change her from an exuberant bride to the angry woman who had written those final letters?

With a sigh, she got up, pulled on the borrowed wrapper, and crept down the rear stairs, intending to heat a bottle for Victoria.

She found Maisie already there, up and dressed, her thin, flyaway hair groomed, her eyes bright with prospects all her own. Jasper sat at the table, dallying over a bowl of butter-drenched oatmeal.

"Mornin'," Maisie greeted her with a smile. "You look some better, I don't mind sayin'."

Susannah smiled. "Thank you," she replied, amused by the unassuming bluntness of the remark.

"Is my sweet'ums awake yet?" Maisie asked. "I've got her bottle started."

Susannah shook her head. "She'll be awake any moment, though. I'll need diapers, pins—"

"Set them right there for you," Maisie said, pointing to a bureau near the back stairway. "Fetched them from Mr. Fairgrieve's room just this morning."

"He isn't—here?" Susannah asked, and then could have bitten off the end of her tongue.

"Bed ain't been slept in," Maisie replied matter-of-factly. "Here, now. Sit down and have some coffee and a bowl of this oatmeal. You'll hear sweet'ums right enough when she wakes up."

Susannah hesitated, then accepted the offer. Maisie promptly brought the promised breakfast.

"Was Mr. Fairgrieve unkind to Julia?" she dared to inquire after several minutes of silence. There were men who abused their wives, both physically and verbally. Perhaps the handsome Aubrey was such a one, for all his charms and graces.

Maisie took a few moments weighing her answer. "They shouldn't have married up in the first place, the two of them. They was too different, one from the other. Mrs. Fairgrieve, she liked parties and dancing and fancy clothes. As for him, well, I think he thought she was somebody else entirely from who she really was. He wanted her to be home at night, readin' and sewin' and waitin' for him. It got to be a real sad situation."

"He seems to believe—" Susannah swallowed, started again. "He seems to believe that Julia was unfaithful. Even promiscuous."

"I ain't sure what that last word means; the first one's clear enough, though. She tended to her own business, the missus did, and I tended to mine, and we sure never talked about such as that." Maisie made a sound that might have been a chuckle, though it held more sorrow than humor. "Oh, no. Mrs. Fairgrieve never confided in me, 'cept to ask me to send for you." She sighed. "She was a fragile little thing, homesick for the life she knew in Boston."

"Did she have other companions? Women, I mean?"

The older woman gave a forceful sigh. "Not many, truth to tell. She had a way of lookin' down her nose at folks that didn't win her much in the way of admiration."

Susannah closed her eyes for a moment, exasperated even in her grief. Julia had always thought well of herself, or pretended to, at least, and she had never had many friends. Still, when she fell so wildly, romantically in love with Aubrey Fairgrieve one spring day and soon after eloped to Seattle, Susannah had dared to hope that her friend's happiness would inspire her thereafter to take a more generous view of the world. Instead, something had spoiled her joy, turned her love for Aubrey to bitterness.

Maisie lingered at the stove, raised one of the lids, stirred the embers with a poker, and added two hefty logs from the basket on the hearth. A lovely, crackling blaze rose, casting light onto the whitewashed walls. "Mind you, if you go out, take a warm cloak," she instructed Susannah. "I've seen the pneumonia take them that was careless in such things."

Susannah nodded, touched by the woman's concern. They were, she suspected, more alike than different, for, like Maisie, Susannah had taken care of others for the better part of her life. "I'll be careful," she said. She wasn't planning to go out, at least not that day, but she would need to put up fliers soon, offering her services as a piano teacher in order to have money of her own.

"You hurry yourself, young feller," Maisie said to the boy. "School'll be startin' right quick."

Jasper made a face. Like his mother, he was unremarkable in appearance, but Susannah had a sense that he shared Maisie's determined, kindly nature. Then he proceeded to finish his oatmeal, and Susannah did likewise.

A feathery snow was just beginning to fall when Jasper and Maisie left the house, both of them bundled against the cold, and Victoria summoned Susannah with a furious shriek of hunger.

After a number of days spent sitting upright on a noisy, filthy train, surrounded by strangers, it was utter bliss to move about a warm, clean house, attending to ordinary tasks. She hummed as she took the warm bottle from its pan next to the stove, grabbed up the diapers and pins, and hurried up the stairs. Victoria began to scream with the lust of an opera singer.

She was changing the baby's diapers, amidst the din, a difficult proposition when she did not dare uncover the infant to the chill, when an impatient knock sounded at her half-open door and Mr. Fairgrieve stuck his rumpled head into the room. He was fully dressed, though in need of a shave, and Susannah wondered where he'd passed the night, recalling that Maisie had said he hadn't slept in his bed.

"Is that kid dying or what?" he demanded. "For God's sake, do something before she raises the dead."

"She's hungry," Susannah said, somewhat testily. Victoria was in fine form, wriggling and kicking both feet. "I'll attend to that as soon as I've finished with the diapers."

He thrust out a martyr's sigh. "Well, hurry it up. I'm getting a headache."

"Perhaps," Susannah pointed out, irritated not, oddly enough, because he was behaving impatiently but because he had been out all night, "if you went elsewhere, the noise wouldn't bother you so much."

The baby continued to kick and flail and scream at the top of her tiny lungs, as if to put in her two cents' worth. Muttering, Aubrey closed the door. Susannah finished with the diaper, made a quick trip to the bathroom to wash her hands, and returned to give Victoria the bottle.

Fifteen minutes later, sated at last, Victoria nodded off to sleep again. Smiling, Susannah kissed her smooth little forehead and laid her gently in the crib. Then she simply stood there, watching the baby sleep; the sight was infinitely beautiful to Susannah, and she was filled with a kind of joy she had never known before. Victoria was not hers, she had no illusions on that score, and yet, in the brief interval since her arrival in the household, Susannah had formed an enduring attachment to the child.

She went to the chair near the window, sat down, and leaned forward slightly, resting her forehead on her palms while she struggled to rein in her emotions. She was normally level-headed; it was not like her to feel so deeply, and she was frightened.

Maisie found her there minutes later. Although she had shed her cloak, her cheeks were bright from the cold outside. "Here now," she said in a gruff whisper. "The little mite's dropped off to sleep. Let's you and me head downstairs and have ourselves some tea."

Gratefully, Susannah nodded and rose to follow Maisie out of the room and down to the kitchen.

"That Jasper," Maisie remarked fondly, setting the kettle on to heat with a clunk of metal against metal. "He don't much care for school."

Only then, in the warmth of that spacious kitchen, with snow drifting past the windows, did Susannah recall her first impression of Jasper—that he was three or four years of age. Surely he was too young for school.

"How old is Jasper?" she asked.

"Six," Maisie answered. Her gaze was discerning, though she was obviously a woman of simple means and background. "He's a bit small for his age. Smart, though. Smart as a whip."

Susannah smiled and nodded. "Have you any other children, Maisie?"

Maisie's strong, plain features teetered on the brink of something, then assembled themselves into a stalwart expression. "Nope. No husband, neither. It's just me and my Jasper."

Susannah devoutly hoped Maisie wasn't feeling defensive; it was nothing new for a woman to be left alone with a child. "How long have you worked for Mr. Fairgrieve?"

"Nigh onto a year," Maisie said, spooning dried tea leaves into a crockery pot while the kettle chortled on the range. "My man done got himself sent off to prison, over yonder in Montana somewheres, and me and Jasper wound up here in Seattle after knockin' around this way and that for a spell. The mister hired me to do for his new wife." She assessed Susannah. "What about you? You ever been married?"

Susannah had always kept her hopes and dreams to herself, for all were fragile as butterfly wings, not to be shared with the other students at St. Mary's, with the nuns, or with Mrs. Butterfield, her crotchety employer. Somehow, though, in the presence of this unassuming woman, it was easier to let down her guard. "No," she said, shaking her head. "I've never had a husband, or a child."

"Are you plannin' to stay on here?" Maisie asked, meeting Susannah's gaze squarely in the snow-dampened morning light. The fire made the room warm, fogged the windows with steam. "That baby needs you. Mr. Fairgrieve, he cares for the child right enough, whatever he'd like folks to think, but he's a man, and they don't know chicken scratch about raisin' up a little one."

Susannah spoke moderately. "I came to Seattle to look after Julia's baby, and I mean to stay."

"And the mister?"

"What about him?" Susannah retorted, wary.

"He's a good man, miss. He can look after himself out there in the world, and better'n most, I'd say, but when he comes back here, he needs to have somebody waitin' for him. He didn't build this here house just for himself, you know. I reckon he was powerful lonesome. And the reason there's lots of bedrooms is because he hopes to have lots of babies to fill them up."

Susannah hoped the hot blush rising around her cheekbones wasn't visible on the outside. "I'm sure there are many women who would marry such an at-tractive—such a prosperous man," she said stiffly.

"Not out here there ain't," Maisie countered. "Oh, there's the tawdry ones, down on Water Street and thereabouts—he don't hold with such as them, but they say he's got himself a fancy lady down at the Pacific Hotel. Thing is, a mistress ain't the same thing as a wife. Ain't the same thing at all."

It nettled Susannah mightily—for poor Julia's sake, of course—to think of Aubrey Fairgrieve keeping such a woman. Why was Maisie telling her all this? "Perhaps he is the sort who expects to have both," she said uncharitably. "Wife and mistress, I mean."

But Maisie laughed, rattling stove lids again. "He's the sort that wants a woman, all right. That's normal, ain't it? But he never strayed from his promises until Mrs. Fairgrieve turned him out of her bed."

Susannah could make no reply to that. Beyond the basic mechanics of intercourse, she had no idea what would be considered normal. She bit down hard on her lower lip and dropped her voice to a scandalized whisper.

"Why are you saying these things?"

"I reckon I want you to understand Mr. Fairgrieve

better'n you most likely do. Mrs. Fairgrieve, too, for that matter. You know one side of her, I think, and the mister, well, he knows another."

"It's hardly necessary for me to 'understand' Mr. Fairgrieve, and I knew Julia very well, thank you. Probably better than anyone." But had she? Although her experience with people was limited indeed, Susannah knew people had many different facets to their natures and presented varying faces to varying friends, relations, and acquaintances.

"Don't get all tetchy now," Maisie said good-naturedly. "Things ain't always what they seem. That's all I'm tryin' to say."

Susannah nodded. "I'm sorry. It's just—it's just that Julia seemed so very unhappy."

"And you can't help thinkin' that was the mister's fault?"

She hesitated, nodded again. Something about this woman, something about the cozy warmth of the kitchen and the snow falling beyond the windows, made Susannah feel safe. "I've heard," she ventured, then stopped and started again. "I've heard that it hurts terribly, what men and women do together. Maybe Julia just couldn't bear it."

Maisie's eyes held a sort of pitying humor as she watched Susannah. She served the tea. "There's some hollerin' that goes on, I'll grant you that," she said, "but I don't reckon it's pain that makes a woman cry out. Not with a man like Mr. Fairgrieve."

Susannah was fascinated; she felt her eyes go wide. "She—she cried out?"

Maisie merely smiled and served the tea.

After they'd shared the tea, and a confidence or two, they set out to accomplish the housework. Although Mrs. Butterfield had referred to Susannah as a companion, she had, in effect, served as housekeeper and cook into the bargain. She found a welcome distraction in dusting, sweeping, making up beds, and doing dishes.

By mid-morning, the work was done. She returned to her room, and to Victoria, who was still sleeping. Although Susannah was not one to place great store in her appearance, she caught a glimpse of herself in the mirror above her bureau, and she was nonetheless pleased to note the silver-blond shimmer of her hair, the stormy, changeable gray of her eyes, the trim agility of her figure.

No, she was not beautiful as Julia had been beautiful, but she was pleasing to look upon, a person of distinction and value. She could make a difference in Victoria's life.

She got out a book and sat down to read.

Luncheon was served in the kitchen, and Maisie was there, seated in the rocker close by the stove, a pile of knitting in her lap. "There's my sweet'ums!" she cried, catching sight of the baby as soon as Susannah carried her into the room. "Let me have that darlin' thing."

To Susannah's surprise, Aubrey was at the table, looking considerably more cheerful than he had earlier, when he'd complained about the noise Victoria was making. He had already pushed away his plate, but there was a cup of coffee steaming in his hand, and he seemed in no hurry to finish it.

He was dressed for business—high time, Susannah thought uncharitably—in a well-cut tweed suit with a waistcoat, now draped over the back of an extra chair. His brown hair gleamed, still damp from brushing, and his eyes showed a brief flicker of amused admiration before he forced a frown into them.

"Good morning, Miss McKittrick," he said, rising momentarily out of simple good manners.

She took a plate from the table and went to the stove to fill it. There was corned beef hash in a skillet and baking powder biscuits in the warming oven. "Hullo, Mr. Fairgrieve," she answered, pointedly omitting the expected "good morning." It was, after all, nearly twelve-thirty.

"I would like you to call me Aubrey," he announced.

She joined him at the table. "I would like you to call me Miss McKittrick," she replied.

He laughed. "What makes you so prickly?"

"What makes you so bold?" she countered.

He grinned.

"You want me to fetch you more tea, Miss McKittrick?" Maisie put in.

"Call me Susannah," she answered, and Aubrey laughed again. He had a wonderful laugh, low and masculine and yet somehow innocent. She could picture him as a mischievous boy, even though he was unquestionably a man.

He stood and carried his plate, utensils, and cup to the iron sink, a gesture that intrigued Susannah. She had never once seen a man clear away after himself, but then, she hadn't dined with many. Only Mrs. Butterfield's two fussbudget sons, who had visited from Boston on rare occasions and expected to be waited upon. "I'd better get to the store," he said. "If there's anything you need, *Miss McKittrick*, make a list. And have a second helping of that hash. You've got all the substance of a sparrow, and you look pale enough to swoon."

Susannah, buoyantly cheerful only minutes before, took the remark to heart and was deflated. She had thought she looked, well, almost pretty. "A pram would be nice," she said. "If there isn't one in the house."

Her injured feelings must have shown. "What did I say?" Aubrey asked, frowning.

"Susannah looks right pretty this mornin', if you ask me," Maisie put in helpfully, laying Victoria to her shoulder and patting her little back.

"I didn't ask you," Aubrey said. "Make that list," he added for Susannah's benefit. Then, after giving her one last look, half bafflement and half annoyance, he got up, put on his coat, and pulled a gold pocket watch from an inside breast pocket. Flipping open the case, he frowned again, and then he was gone, slamming out the back door into the cold, shifting fog of a snowy Puget Sound morning.

"There's a pram up in the attic," Maisie said into the echoing silence that followed his departure. "Mr. Fairgrieve's brother Ethan gave it to the missus for a baby gift. When she died, the mister made me put it away, out of sight."

Susannah's attention was caught. She remembered Ethan from Julia's letters, though she hadn't thought of him even once since her arrival. Over the last six months of her life, in fact, it had seemed to Susannah that Julia had had more to say about him than about her husband. "She liked Ethan very much."

"You could say that," Maisie allowed, and while the remark had a point to it, there was no malice in her words.

Susannah backed off, mentally at least, unprepared to explore the subject of Mr. Fairgrieve's younger brother any further. She already had a great deal to assimilate as it was, and she had not begun to align her thoughts into any sensible order, at least where the affairs of that household were concerned.

"You sure you won't have more tea?" Maisie persisted.

"Thank you, no," she said, struck once again by sorrow, and crossed the room to collect the baby, so that Maisie, who had worked hard all morning, might have a moment's peace.

She'd find that pram, she decided. When the weather warmed up a little, she and Victoria would go out and take some air.

Chapter

3

~

$\mathcal{T}$he store was full, as usual, when Aubrey reached it, but he didn't pause to slap the shoulders of his rough-hewn customers or to consult with the sales clerks as he normally would have done. His mind was elsewhere; specifically, with Miss Susannah McKittrick, his late wife's friend and the newest member of his household. She had not, in fact, been out of his thoughts since her unexpected appearance in the upper corridor of his house the day before, though he had tried mightily to dismiss her.

She was not classically beautiful, not in the way Julia had been, and yet her face, her shape, her manner and movements were all etched into his memory as effectively, as inexorably, as if he had always known her. At the same time, she was an intriguing mystery; he sensed that there were unfathomable depths of intelligence, indeed whole worlds to explore, hidden behind those large gray eyes. He wanted to learn her every secret, even those she had kept from herself, but it seemed unlikely that he would attain this objective. Susannah was a universe unto herself, and even a lifetime would not be long enough to unfold the many layers of her mind and heart and spirit.

A lifetime. Halfway up the stairs that led to his office, Aubrey stopped, shaken. After Julia, he had sworn never to think in such terms again, where a woman was concerned, at least, yet here he was, a mere four months after burying the wife he'd thought he loved, pondering the claiming and charting of Susannah McKittrick's soul. Such fancies would not do; far better to confine himself to the shallow but artful Delphinia, awaiting his pleasure in her suite at the Pacific Hotel.

He'd fully intended to go to her the night before; instead, he'd spent the night upstairs in his office, brooding.

He was scowling as he gained the upper floor and strode past Jim Hawkins, his bespectacled secretary, toward the open door beyond. Until the day before, he'd enjoyed a consuming passion where Delphinia was concerned, but suddenly, without warning, and just since Miss McKittrick's invasion of his home and his thoughts, he had lost interest in the woman as well as the affair.

Crossing the threshold into his private domain, he slammed the door behind him, no doubt causing Hawkins and the bookkeeper to start in their chairs. Hellfire and damnation, he thought, why hadn't Susannah stayed on Nantucket where she belonged? Just by showing up that way, by falling asleep on his bed, she'd spoiled a perfectly tenable arrangement for him. In one corner of his mind, he was already calculating what it would cost to pay off his mistress and send her packing.

He remembered his resolve to make sure Susannah was who she seemed, went back to the door, and wrenched it open. "Hawkins!" he barked.

The clerk jumped to his feet, nearly overturning his wooden swivel chair in the process. "Yes, sir?"

"Get me a Pinkerton man."

Hawkins swallowed. The autumn sunlight pouring in

through the windows struck his spectacles in a dazzling flash. "A Pinkerton man, sir?"

Aubrey had no intention of explaining his request further. "Damn it, Hawkins," he said, "you heard me!" With that, he slammed the door again and strode to his desk. Of course, he assured himself, that was the thing to do. Hire a detective. If Miss McKittrick was indeed the dear friend Julia had been corresponding with all during their brief, tempestuous marriage, as she now claimed, and a fit guardian for the child, he would settle an ample sum of money on her and ship the pair of them straight to Massachusetts. The whole problem would be solved, leaving him with a clear conscience. For the most part, anyway.

The pram was hidden away in the attic, where Maisie said it would be, as shrouded with dust as if it had been there for years. It seemed a sad summation of Mr. Fairgrieve's basic attitude toward both his wife and his child.

With a sigh, Susannah began to brush off the pretty wicker carriage as best she could, before bumping it carefully, awkwardly, down the steep folding staircase. Maisie was waiting at the bottom, looking fretful, with the baby at her shoulder and little Jasper beside her, home from school, slate clasped in both arms.

"I don't know that you ought to take her out afore spring," the older woman said. "Suppose she takes a cold?"

Susannah smiled. The snow had stopped, and the sun was out, however briefly. "Of course, I'll bundle her up warmly," she said. "And we won't be out for long." With that, she wheeled the pram down the rear staircase, through the kitchen, and out into the backyard, where buckets of hot, soapy water awaited. While Maisie gave the infant another bottle in the rocker beside the stove, Susannah scrubbed and rinsed the carriage until it had been restored to its former glory.

When that was done, she dried it carefully with strips of flannel Maisie had provided, then went back inside for a fluffy blanket, which she folded carefully and placed in the bottom of the pram to serve as a mattress. Maisie surrendered her charge somewhat reluctantly when Susannah went back inside, and, after wrapping Victoria carefully, Susannah laid her in the carriage. The air was starch-crisp that afternoon, like a fine linen sheet. The snow hadn't stuck, and the sunlight, though cool, brightened Susannah's spirits considerably.

Although the little bit of Seattle she'd seen upon her arrival had seemed downright unprepossessing, there were wooden sidewalks in Aubrey's neighborhood and trees growing behind whitewashed fences. The sky cast ice-blue reflections onto the sparkling waters of the sound, and beyond them loomed the snowy mountains of the Olympic Peninsula. Now and then, a buggy clattered by, or a well-made carriage, and Susannah returned neighborly waves with a nod of greeting, while pretending not to notice the curious looks she inspired. She continued her stroll, intending to follow the sidewalk around the block, and hummed softly to reassure the baby.

Perhaps not by accident, though she hadn't consciously made the choice, she found herself at the gateway of the large church that stood on the lot behind Aubrey's mansion. She stopped, admiring the simple stained-glass windows and bell tower, the well-kept grounds and enormous arched doors. Several minutes passed before she allowed her attention to stray to the cemetery, with its crop of crosses and monuments. She had known it was there, of course, having glimpsed it from her bedroom window the day before, but actually confronting the place was another matter.

Julia was buried there.

Something tightened in her throat. Julia's grave. She

felt compelled to find her friend's final resting place, if only to ascribe it a place in her mind. She fumbled with the gate latch and finally pushed the pram through the opening.

An elderly pastor came out of the church, one hand extended. "Welcome," he said. His blue eyes were wise and merry, his thin hair white and flyaway. "I'm Reverend Johnstone," he said. "And you would be—?"

"Susannah McKittrick," Susannah answered. She indicated the Fairgrieve house with an inclination of her head. "Julia was my closest friend." *My only friend.* "I'd like to pay my respects."

Reverend Johnstone's smile was gentle. "Certainly," he said. "Pity you missed the funeral. It was very sad indeed. Come, I'll show you to the grave, not that you'd have much trouble finding it." With that, he led Susannah along a stone pathway, between simple headstones and elaborate ones, bringing her to a grand tomb of pink marble, overseen at head and foot by enormous alabaster angels. Here, then, was the place where Julia lay.

Tears burned in Susannah's eyes, and she sniffled, fumbling for her handkerchief. The reverend waited in easy silence until she had recovered herself a little. *JULIA*, proclaimed a bronze plaque, set into the ground, though there were no dates, no words of mourning or even farewell.

"Was Mrs. Fairgrieve a parishioner here?" She had never known Julia to be religious, but perhaps in her unhappiness she had found comfort within the walls of Reverend Johnstone's church. Susannah devoutly hoped so.

The holy man hesitated only for a moment, but it was long enough. "No," he said quietly. "Regretfully, no." He bent over the pram and peered benignly down at the well-wrapped baby. "I suppose this would be her child?"

"Yes," Susannah replied. She was still thinking about the expensive monument marking Julia's grave, undeniably beautiful yet strangely sterile, meaninglessness, even in all its grandeur. It was as though no one had truly grieved for her, not here, at least.

"A girl, I'm told. What is her name?"

Susannah averted her eyes, then met the pastor's kindly gaze again. "I'm afraid she doesn't have one, officially, at least. I've been calling her Victoria."

"Then she has not been christened." There was no judgment in the reverend's tone, no reprimand. It was merely a concerned observation of the sort one might expect from a man who had spent his life overseeing such details.

"No," Susannah admitted.

The pastor raised feathery white eyebrows as a soft breeze played in his hair. "Mr. Fairgrieve has approved this choice, I assume. The name, I mean?"

Again, Susannah sighed. Then she shook her head. "I don't believe he's interested—" Color suffused her face, and misery thickened in her throat. "I don't think he believes the child is his."

Reverend Johnstone placed a tender hand on Susannah's shoulder. "Aubrey is a good man, Miss McKittrick. I feel certain of that. But like the rest of us, he has demons all his own."

The wind was taking on a chill, and Susannah was concerned about keeping the baby out too long. She cast a final, sorrowful glance at Julia's resting place and turned the carriage back toward the gate. "Thank you, reverend," she said quietly. "Might I come and speak with you again?"

"Of course, child," came the response, accompanied by a tender smile. "Our Sunday services begin at eleven."

Susannah nodded and hurried away. She would return soon, she promised herself, and alone, to sit on the stone bench near Julia's grave and say a proper farewell. In the meantime, it seemed imperative to give the child a formal name and, therefore, an existence. An identity.

"What do you think of Victoria?" she asked half an hour later in Maisie's kitchen, her cheeks still pink with cold, a cup of strong tea steaming before her. The baby was sleeping peacefully in a basket within the warm radius of the stove.

"Victoria who?" Maisie asked with a frown. She was up to her elbows in bread dough, and the front of her plain calico dress was covered with flour.

Susannah smiled and took a sip of the savory tea, generously laced with milk and sugar. She was sure she'd mentioned the name to Maisie, even referred to the child by it, but maybe she'd only used it in her own head. "That's what I think we should call the baby."

"That's a lot of name," Maisie reflected solemnly, "for such a little scrap of a thing. I reckon it's as good as any other, though. Pretty, too. I always thought if I ever had a girl-child, I'd call her Bertha, for my ma."

Susannah was careful not to let her expression change. "That's an idea," she said gamely. "Julia's mother's name was—" She paused, trying to remember. "Lilith, I think."

Maisie's distaste was plain. "Weren't she a bad woman, that Lilith, mentioned in the Good Book someplace?"

Susannah hid her amusement behind the rim of her tea cup. "She might be in the Bible, but I think she's more a creature of legend. Supposedly, she was Adam's mate, before Eve came along."

"Oh," Maisie said, still nonplussed. She gave the bread dough a punch that would have felled an ox.

"What about Mr. Fairgrieve's mother? What was she called?"

"You'd have to ask him that," was the answer. "I don't know much about the boss. He's a private man, Mr. Fairgrieve is."

"But he keeps a fancy woman?" Susannah prompted, lowering her voice, remembering what Maisie had told her the day before. For some reason, the idea stung.

Maisie looked disgusted. "Delphinia Parker," she said. "Used to be an actress. That's how Mr. Fairgrieve took up with her. She got herself left behind, here in Seattle, after one of them travelin' shows passed through."

"You certainly seem to know a lot about her," Susannah observed moderately. "Surely, if Aubrey—Mr. Fairgrieve—won't speak of his family, he wouldn't talk about his lover, either."

"Everybody knows about Delphinia," Maisie said. "She don't make no secret about where she got that shiny new carriage she rides around in, or all them French gowns made out of velvet and silk, either. She's got more jewelry than that queen you want to name the baby after."

Susannah felt a combination of intrigue and fury. "I suppose he was carrying on with Miss Parker while Julia was still living?"

It was then that the door to the dining room swung open, and Aubrey appeared in the chasm. "If you have questions about my mistress—and it's *Mrs.* Parker, by the way—why don't you ask me directly?"

Maisie reddened and gave the bread dough a pummeling but said nothing. Susannah, caught in gossip, a pursuit she had always abhorred, was mortified. Only bravado kept her from dissolving. "Very well," she said, "I will. Did you betray Julia with this woman?"

A muscle leaped in Aubrey's jawline, and his left temple pulsed ever so slightly. "No," he growled. "Not that it's any of your damned business. I will ask you, Miss McKittrick, to confine your efforts to looking after the child from now on. I'm quite capable, I assure you, of tending to my own affairs."

Susannah's blood was pounding, but she wouldn't allow herself to look away from Aubrey's face; it was a point of honor. "I'm sure you are," she answered, leaving him to take whatever meaning from those words that he wished.

He glared at her for a long moment, then his gaze sliced to Maisie, who looked as though she wanted the floor to open up beneath her feet and swallow her whole. "I'll be bringing guests home for dinner," he said calmly, though there was still an edge to his voice. "If you'd rather not cook for them, I can have something sent over from the hotel."

Maisie was beginning to recover herself, wiping her hands on her apron. "There's a smoked ham in the pantry. I can serve that, along with some potatoes and the like. How many places should I lay out?"

"Six," Aubrey said, glancing only briefly toward Susannah. The way he spoke, she might not even have been in the room. "Including Miss McKittrick. See that she has something decent to wear."

Susannah was on her feet. "I don't want—" she began, but he was gone before she could finish the sentence.

"Best do as the boss says, if there's to be any peace around here," Maisie put in sagely.

"I don't care to have supper with strangers," Susannah argued. Nor did she care to dress herself up in Julia's clothes, which would certainly be all wrong for her. "Besides, I'm not a houseguest. I'm a nurse. Why on earth does he insist—?"

"This town is his home, miss. The baby's, too. And you were the missus's good friend, which makes you more than a nurse. If you're goin' to look after that little smidgen, then you got to make a place for yourself right here in Seattle."

Maisie was right; for the time being, at least, she must make every reasonable effort to belong. Meeting Aubrey Fairgrieve's friends and associates was apparently a part of that process, whether she liked the idea or not. Susannah finished her tea in a reflective silence, then, leaving the baby in Maisie's charge, went upstairs to assess her wardrobe.

The four worn, unfashionable frocks she and Maisie had hung in the armoire the day before had undergone no magical changes in the interim. They were still drab and unsuitable for any formal occasion, and the sight of them filled Susannah with a kind of grief that bore no relationship at all to the loss of her friend. As a young girl, she had dreamed of dances and fetes and eventually marriage, and if she was no great beauty, she was attractive in her own way. She was intelligent and quite accomplished—she had read virtually every book in the library at St. Mary's, and then in Mrs. Butterfield's considerable collection, and she played piano well enough to teach—and yet somehow she had been left standing on the sidelines, on onlooker instead of a participant.

She squeezed her eyes shut for a moment. Then, for the child, she sought out Julia's sumptuously furnished bedchamber, which adjoined Aubrey's. Upon entering, Susannah was surprised to find her friend's things laid out on the vanity and bureaus, as though she had just stepped out and would surely return at any moment. The place was neatly kept, and the faint scent of Julia's perfume lingered in the air, like the last shadowy remnants of a vivid dream. An open book rested spine-up on the nightstand, and Susannah traced the title with the tip of one index finger, frowning slightly. She had never known Julia to read for pleasure; she had always been too impatient, too restless to concentrate. Yet here was the latest of Sir Walter Scott's novels, half read.

Along the far wall were two enormous, intricately carved armoires, stuffed with a profusion of gowns. Straightening her backbone, Susannah examined the lovely frocks one by one, finding the rich, colorful fabrics and exquisite designs much more appealing than she cared to admit. These were the garments of a princess in a fairy tale, not a mortal woman.

Holding her breath, she drew a sedate black velvet from its padded hanger, went to the mirror, and held the dress up in front of her. Although simple, the gown was also dramatic, trimmed at the high collar and cuffs with tiny white pearls.

She turned to one side, then the other, imagining herself clad in such a garment. It wouldn't fit, of course, for Julia had been plumper and not so tall, but with a few judicious nips and tucks, it could be made to suit her.

Even as she longed to wear the dress, Susannah found her pride, always her besetting sin, rebelled against the idea. She had loved her friend, her "blood sister," and she would cherish Julia's child as her own, but it galled her to take the other woman's castoffs, however attractive they might be.

In the end, however, she was left with no choice. She cared nothing for Aubrey Fairgrieve or his friends, but the baby had already claimed her heart. She would do whatever she had to do to protect the little one's interests.

After both Jasper and the baby had had their early suppers and been tucked into their beds, Susannah donned the black dress, and Maisie pinned it to fit. The bosom and waist had to be taken in, the hemline lowered, but Susannah had done her share of sewing, both at St. Mary's and with Mrs. Butterfield, and she made short work of the alterations. When, after a leisurely bath, Susannah put on the gown again, it looked as though it had been made expressly for her. With her hair swept up and the high color of shyness and indignation in her cheeks, she looked almost, well, *pretty*. Emboldened, she returned to Julia's room and helped herself to a delicate pair of pearl-drop earrings.

When she descended the main staircase, of necessity leaving the child in Maisie's care again, she encountered Aubrey, who was just coming through the doorway of his study. He stopped at the sight of her, and she saw something glitter in his eyes, though whether it was bitter exasperation or admiration she could not tell. She assumed it was the former.

"Well," he said. His voice sounded hoarse, and he hadn't moved from the threshold of the study. Indeed, he seemed to be frozen there. "Well," he repeated.

Susannah was secretly pleased to know that she had unsettled him so. "You did tell me to wear one of Julia's dresses," she reminded him.

He nodded, swallowed. "Yes."

"I've been giving some thought to the child—"

Aubrey managed, at last, to break whatever inertia had overtaken him. He frowned. "And what conclusion have you reached?"

"She must have a name. We can't keep calling her 'she' and 'the baby' and 'the child.' She should be properly christened in any case. I've spoken to Reverend Johnstone, and—"

The frown intensified to a glare. "Do as you like," he snapped, and started past her, moving toward the dining room, where Maisie had laid a spectacular table, complete with silver candlesticks, fine china, and sterling utensils.

"But *you* are her father," Susannah persisted, following close on his heels. "You should be the one to decide—"

"Call her anything you like. Except Julia, of course."

Susannah felt a stab of pain. "Did you hate her so much?" she asked quietly.

"Yes," he replied without hesitation or kindness. "I did hate her. And kindly remove those earrings. They were a gift from one of her lovers, and I can't stand the sight of them."

"If you hated Julia," Susannah pressed, pulling off the ear bobs at the same time, "why do you *care* if she took lovers?"

"Because I loved her once," came the answer.

Susannah was silenced by his admission, though only briefly. When the doorbell chimed, she followed Aubrey across the entry hall. She couldn't resist a little barb. After all, it wasn't as though he had been a model husband to Julia. "Perhaps we could name your baby—let's see—Delphinia?" she chimed.

"I would advise you not to plague me, Miss McKittrick," he warned in a harsh whisper. "I am not a patient man." With that, he wrenched open the door, and in those few seconds, his aspect changed from one of anger to one of smiling good humor.

A handsome gentleman with chestnut-colored hair and a waxed mustache stood on the porch, bowler hat in hand. It seemed to Susannah that the visitor's eyes narrowed slightly when Aubrey made his introductions. Clearly, John Hollister was as curious about her as the neighbors had been during her walk earlier that day, even though Aubrey had already explained that she was his late wife's childhood friend, come from far-off Nantucket to look after the child.

"We're considering names," Susannah said cheerfully as the three of them retired to the parlor to await the other guests and Maisie's eventual signal that supper was ready. "For the baby, I mean. I suggested Delphinia."

Aubrey sliced another warning glance in her direction, and Mr. Hollister smiled almost imperceptibly. It was obvious that he knew about Aubrey's illicit affair with Mrs. Parker—no doubt the whole city was enjoying the scandal. On Julia's behalf, Susannah felt a flash of fury. She was behaving shamelessly, she knew, and yet she couldn't seem to help herself. The whole concept of Mr. Fairgrieve keeping a mistress galled her.

"Don't tell me you haven't named the poor little mite after all this time," Hollister scolded. Aubrey had given him a snifter of brandy, and he gestured with the glass as he spoke. "I declare, Fairgrieve, that's downright negligent of you. Personally, I've always favored Elisabeth. That was my mother's name."

The doorbell chimed again, and Aubrey hurried off to answer it. When he returned, he was accompanied by two more gentlemen, both older, with balding heads, large bellies, and heavy gold watch chains. Susannah guessed before the introductions were made that they were bankers. No doubt both of them had names to suggest, but the topic had changed to the situation in the gold fields and the "Chinese problem," whatever that was.

After fifteen minutes or so, the last guest arrived. This one looked more like a cowboy than a businessman, and Susannah liked him immediately. His eyes were a mischievous blue, his fair hair sun-streaked and slightly too long, lending him a rakish appearance. He presented himself to her without waiting for Aubrey to do the honors. "I'm Ethan Fairgrieve," he said, taking her hand briefly. "My brother probably hasn't mentioned me."

"No," Susannah said, almost stammering the word. Julia had, of course, but it didn't seem like a good time to bring that up. There were a lot of undercurrents flowing through that house, too many for her comfort.

"I'm Susannah McKittrick—Julia and I were at school together. It's—it's good to meet you."

"Likewise," Ethan replied, his eyes twinkling with a merriment that made Susannah want to know him better. "If I weren't already taken, I swear I'd come courting you, Miss Susannah." He glanced at his brother, who was taking in every word of the conversation and, at the same time, doing his best to look disinterested. "My Rosa," Ethan went on with mock solemnity, "weighs three hundred pounds and packs a pistol. If I dared to stray, she'd have my hide nailed to the barn door quicker than you can say so long."

Susannah laughed. "And where is Rosa tonight? I would like to meet her."

"She's keeping the home fires burning. I'm only here because word got back to me that Julia's favorite correspondent had arrived. I wanted a look at you."

"What was your mother's name?" Susannah whispered, leaning close.

Ethan barely missed a beat, though it was plain that the question had caught him off-guard. "Jenny," he said. "Why?"

"Jenny," Susannah repeated, savoring the name. "That's lovely."

Just then, Maisie rang the fancy supper bell, and Aubrey started toward Susannah. Before he reached her, however, Ethan offered his arm, and she took it, allowing him to escort her into the dining room.

Maisie was a gifted cook, and the meal was one to savor. Susannah said very little but listened instead, sorting and assimilating what she heard. It soon became obvious that Ethan and Aubrey were not on the best of terms, brothers or not. Every time Ethan flung one of his taunting grins in Aubrey's direction, Aubrey glared as though he'd been formally insulted.

The bankers were Aubrey's business associates rather than his friends, Susannah quickly discerned, but Mr. Hollister was harder to place. Despite his remarks about the baby going unnamed for so long—that certainly indicated some degree of familiarity on both his part and Aubrey's—he didn't quite fit into the pattern of things. While the conversation swirled around him, he ate sparingly and watched Susannah whenever he thought she wouldn't notice. Because his manner was thoughtful and not unfriendly, she was not troubled but rather intrigued.

The meal ended, and the gentlemen retired to Aubrey's study, ostensibly to smoke cigars and drink brandy. Susannah was tremendously relieved when Maisie bustled into the dining room and began to clear the table.

"You didn't tell me Aubrey and his brother were barely speaking," she challenged.

Maisie gave her a level look. "I don't tell everythin' I know," she retorted. "And put down them dishes. You ain't dressed for clearing up."

"Nonsense," Susannah protested, scraping and stacking plates.

"Mr. Fairgrieve won't like it if he sees you doing that."

"He doesn't mind my changing diapers. I hardly think it would disturb him to find me helping you with a routine household task. I'm only a nurse, after all." A maiden aunt, she added to herself. A poor relation who wasn't really even a relation. "Frankly, I don't even know why he wanted me to join him for dinner tonight. He didn't say one word to me."

Maisie smiled. "But his visitors had plenty to say, didn't they? Especially young Ethan. Did he tell you his wife weighs three hundred pounds and carries a pistol?"

"Yes," Susannah said.

That time, Maisie laughed outright. "Well, *he* ain't changed since he was here last, anyhow."

"What's wrong between those two?" Susannah ventured, heading toward the kitchen door with an armload of plates and silverware. "Ethan was cordial enough, but Mr. Fairgrieve was downright bristly. If he didn't want him here, why issue the invitation?"

"I doubt that he did," Maisie said. "They've had their differences, Aubrey and Ethan," she went on when the two of them were standing side by side in front of the sink. Maisie elbowed Susannah deftly aside, poured steaming water from the kettle on the stove over the soiled dishes, and pushed up her sleeves. "Now that Miss Julia's gone, God rest her soul, I reckon they might just start in to mendin' fences."

Susannah sat down, suddenly weary. "What did Julia have to do with it?"

Maisie turned and looked at her over one sturdy shoulder. "You want to know that," she said, "you're gonna have to ask either Mr. Fairgrieve or his brother. It ain't my place to say."

Susannah felt a sick sensation in the pit of her stomach, recalling parts of Julia's letters, parts in which she'd described Ethan as a gentleman with the heart of a poet. She'd recounted buggy rides in the country with Ethan and picnics by a lake, though at the time the interludes had sounded innocent. Julia had merely said that Aubrey was too busy with his store—he'd gotten rich selling picks and shovels to miners headed north, she liked to boast—and Ethan had "taken pity" on her.

She let out a long sigh.

Maisie set a cup of tea in front of her. "Don't be frettin' about what can't be changed now," she said. "That makes a body crazy."

Chapter

4

~

"Your brother is quite charming," Susannah remarked to Aubrey the next morning, when by accident rather than design they ended up in the kitchen at the same time. Perhaps it was because she was unprepared for the encounter that she spoke without thinking first.

Seated in Maisie's chair near the stove, the sleeping child resting against her shoulder, she watched as his jawline tightened. Resentment flashed fierce in his eyes, like lightning striking in some far-off and inaccessible place, and was quickly quelled.

For her part, Susannah was utterly content, there in the warmth of the fire, the child warm and sweet-smelling in her arms.

Aubrey went to the stove, coffee mug in hand, and poured a full cup. "My brother," he answered in his own good time, "has a way of barging in where he doesn't belong."

While Aubrey was absorbed in the task, Susannah took the opportunity to admire the fine muscled breadth of his shoulders, the way his powerful back tapered to a lean waist. All of this was highlighted rather than hidden by the crisp fabric of his white linen shirt.

In addition, he wore suspenders, tweed trousers, and highly polished boots and no doubt would don a proper coat before leaving the house.

Guilt struck her with the impact of a charging bull. Whatever their problems might have been, Aubrey had been her best friend's husband. What had possessed her to think such untoward thoughts?

She tried to make light conversation. "Do you have other family?"

Aubrey turned after a moment's hesitation and regarded her over the rim of his cup. His expression revealed precisely nothing, and so did his tone of voice. "You are a meddlesome creature," he said, and suddenly she glimpsed that light kindling in his eyes again, just before he smiled. "Why should you care whether I have one relative or a tribe of them?"

"I was merely attempting to be pleasant," Susannah said in a stiff tone. His rebuff, framed in good humor though it was, had stung her, for all that she should have expected it, and she could only hope the hot ache in her face was not accompanied by a vivid blush. "You needn't be so rude, Mr. Fairgrieve."

He raised the coffee cup in a sort of mocking salute. Susannah wondered just then why Julia had never picked up a gun and shot him. "Not rude, Miss McKittrick," he countered. "Blunt. There is a difference."

"If you say so," Susannah allowed ungenerously. Then she sighed and stroked the tiny, flannel-covered back with one hand as the child stirred fitfully against her bosom, perhaps sensing the discord. It seemed only prudent to change the subject. "There are things I need for little Victoria," she said. "I should like to visit the store later today, if that is convenient."

"Nothing in my life is convenient these days," he replied, "but I'll send a carriage for you around ten o'clock. Of course, you may select whatever you feel *little Victoria* requires."

"Thank you," Susannah replied primly. What she felt was nothing so noble as gratitude, and she suspected Aubrey knew that, but there was no use in their jibing at each other. What was needed was some sort of arrangement between them. "I believe we can—tolerate each other, Mr. Fairgrieve, if we simply make a civilized effort toward that end."

She thought she saw a smile dancing in his eyes again, however briefly, though it did not reach his mouth. "A civilized effort, is it?" he retorted, straightening his string tie. "I must say I thought I was already doing that, simply by not showing you the road." He set his empty cup in the iron sink and headed back toward the inner door. "Good day, Miss McKittrick. I'll let the clerks know you'll be visiting the store later."

With that, he was gone.

Half an hour later, Maisie came in, cheeks reddened from the brisk autumn air. She'd walked Jasper to school, then gone down to the pier to buy fresh fish for the evening meal. She kicked the door shut behind her with one heel and set her marketing basket on the counter.

Susannah had been reading—or attempting to read—but proper concentration had eluded her. Her mind kept straying to Aubrey Fairgrieve and the enigma he represented. He spoke so brusquely, when he spoke at all, and yet she'd seen him show uncommon tenderness toward Victoria. He disliked his brother, and yet he was willing to suffer the presence of a virtual stranger in his household, a woman he had not invited and could have turned away without being blamed.

"There'll be a carriage coming for me at ten," she told her friend. "Can you look after Victoria while I'm gone?"

"Sure." Maisie beamed, bending to pat the baby, who lay in a bassinet at Susannah's side, gurgling and kicking. "We're the best of friends, aren't we, sweet'ums?"

"Tell me about Ethan," Susannah urged. She was on her feet—the carriage would arrive in a short while, and she wanted to change her clothes before venturing into the heart of Seattle—but curiosity restrained her.

Maisie was bustling about the kitchen, building up the fire in the cookstove, pumping water into the tea kettle, emptying and rinsing out the coffee pot. She seemed, to Susannah, to be everywhere at once, moving and doing and being. "He's Mr. Fairgrieve's younger brother, but then you knew that. Lives outside Seattle, on land of his own."

"And his wife? What is she really like?"

Maisie laughed fondly. "He don't have one. He just likes to stir things up a little now and then. We've missed him around here, Jasper and me, I mean." Her expression became solemn. "It don't seem that Mr. Fairgrieve has, though. I don't believe they'd been in the same room, the pair of them, since Mrs. Fairgrieve's funeral, until dinner last night. And even on the day they buried that poor woman, there was some harsh words and some door slamming afore it was all over."

The distant buzzing clang of the doorbell interrupted the discussion before Susannah could think of a way to extract more information from Maisie. "I'll answer it," Susannah said, because her friend was still flashing about the kitchen, moving with a strange, hasty grace between one task and the next.

She had expected to find the carriage driver waiting on the porch when she peered through the glass oval in the front door, but instead Mr. Hollister was there, wearing a practical suit, a bowler hat, and a polite, slightly pensive smile.

Susannah admitted him. "Good morning, Mr. Hollister," she said. "I'm afraid Mr. Fairgrieve is out—"

Hollister took the knob gently in hand and closed the door, removing his hat in almost the same smooth motion. "I'm not here to see Fairgrieve," he told her. Westerners, Susannah was fast learning, could be very frank, despite their stubborn propensity for guarding their privacy. "Forgive me, Miss McKittrick. I shouldn't have come uninvited like this."

Susannah was embarrassed for the man and touched his arm lightly, hoping to reassure him somehow. The face of the long case clock dominating the entryway loomed behind his right shoulder, like a numbered moon, ticking away the time she'd allotted to putting on another dress and making sure her heavy hair would not come tumbling down around her shoulders the first time the carriage struck a rut.

"Do come in," she said, for the mores of the day afforded little other choice, and, besides, she liked Mr. Hollister, for all that she knew almost nothing about him.

Hollister stood fast. "Oh, no, I can't stay," he said. Color surged past his tight collar to pulse in his neck. "I was hoping that—well—you might consent to join me for dinner one night soon. Tomorrow, for instance?"

Susannah was taken aback and not a little flattered. She had lived her life as a spinster and had never been invited to dance, let alone to go out in a gentleman's company. "Why, Mr. Hollister, I don't know what to say," she confessed, placing one hand to her chest.

He shifted his feet, almost imperceptibly. "Say yes," he urged. "Unless I was mistaken in concluding that you are—unattached?"

Susannah caught her breath. "But I don't even know you."

"I'm trying to remedy that," he replied. His smile was

benign and wry and quite winning, and if he wasn't as compellingly handsome as Aubrey, well, that was probably a good thing. Like Ethan, Mr. Hollister had a charm entirely his own.

She smiled. Julia had always been the sought-after one. It felt good to be wanted, even desired. "Yes," she said. "I mean, yes, I'll have dinner with you."

He regarded her appreciatively for a long moment. "Splendid," he said. "I'll come for you around seven o'clock, then."

Susannah nodded, a little dazed. Her life had changed so quickly, from a dull procession of days to an adventure of sorts, and she would need a little time to adjust gracefully. "Seven o'clock," she affirmed with another nod, and then Mr. Hollister took his leave. Only after he'd gone did she realize that she did not even know what he did for a living.

Susannah stood in the entryway so long, pondering the turn her fortunes had taken, that she was barely ready when the carriage arrived, a sleek, imposing thing, shining in the fall sunlight.

Clad in one of her own dresses, over which she wore a blue woolen cape purloined from Julia's wardrobe, her hair plaited and pinned up into a bright coronet at her nape, Susannah allowed herself to be handed into the costly vehicle. The scent of some flowery cologne lingered amidst the smells of leather and cigar smoke, and she began to wonder, uncharitably, if this was Mrs. Parker's carriage, temporarily conscripted for the transport of an otherwise indigent and wholly self-appointed nurse.

She straightened her spine as the coach jostled and pitched over the rutted streets leading down one of Seattle's steep, raw-boned hills, already feeling defensive. When the driver brought the team to a halt in front of an imposing structure with an elaborate brick facade, bearing the legend A. *Fairgrieve, Proprietor and Founder* in giant brass letters, she was downright uncomfortable.

She got out of the carriage without waiting for the driver to climb down from the box and open the door for her. She was no more important than anyone in Aubrey's employ, and it wouldn't do for people to go treating her as though she were.

She could not help being aware of glances from passersby as she mounted the wooden steps to the sidewalk, crossed the splintery, weathered boards, and pushed open the door. A bell chimed overhead, in stalwart brass notes, and she paused on the threshold for a few seconds, assessing her surroundings and charting her course before shutting out the cool wind that swept uphill from the waters of the sound.

The store was even larger than it looked from outside, and there was so much merchandise that she was, for a moment, dazzled. Besides the inevitable picks and shovels—Julia had written that Aubrey owed his fortune mainly to the seemingly endless procession of miners streaming north in search of gold—there was a whole wall of fabric and ribbon, another of books and periodicals. The establishment offered patent medicines of all sorts, as well as farm equipment and tools, ready-made garments, boots and shoes, and a surprisingly comprehensive array of toys. The aromas of fine tobacco, rich coffee beans, and fresh tea filled the air, along with a twinge of smoke from the large metal stove in one corner.

A clerk came forward immediately, smiling. "Miss McKittrick?" he inquired. "We've been expecting you. Please—come in."

Mercifully, the spell was broken, and Susannah managed a faltering smile. She wanted desperately to appear confident, but in fact she had never been in such an emporium before. At St. Mary's, there had been no cause and certainly no funds. Nantucket boasted only a few small shops, and islanders grew what vegetables they could, ate the fruits of the sea, and bartered for the goods they could not supply for themselves.

"I should like to look at baby things, please," she said, squaring her shoulders a little and raising her chin.

The clerk smiled. "Indeed. Mr. Fairgrieve said you might want some personal items for yourself, as well. You are to select whatever you need—books, linens, toiletries, the like—without consideration of cost."

Susannah lowered her eyes for an instant, absorbing the self-evident fact that Aubrey saw her as a pauper, then met the young man's pleasant gaze again. "Thank you," she said. "The baby things?"

He led her into the midst of a bewildering selection of tiny gowns, bonnets, booties, and blankets and left her to choose what was needed. She took her time picking out an extensive wardrobe for the child, including a beautifully made christening gown of snowy white cotton and Irish lace. Where Julia's baby—and Aubrey's, she was sure—was concerned, she had no compunction about spending lavishly.

When the little one was properly outfitted—Susannah added a few items for Jasper before she was finished—she chose three muslin camisoles for herself, along with matching drawers and a petticoat. She was admiring the books, not quite daring to take one down from the shelf and hold it in her hands, when another sudden rush of chilly air filled the store, heralded by the now angry clamor of the bell over the door.

"Where is he?" a feminine voice demanded, imperious as a queen's.

Susannah, like the other customers and the clerks, turned to see a slender, dark-haired woman, dressed in green velvet from head to foot. Her garments were wondrous, trimmed in gold braid and fitted precisely to her figure, and the fabric matched the color of her eyes precisely. She was, beyond a doubt, the loveliest creature Susannah had ever seen, for all that her manner and expression were venomous.

No one needed to tell her that this was Delphinia, Aubrey's mistress. A paramour. A kept woman. Susannah, impressed, could not help goggling a little.

"I said *where is he?*" Mrs. Parker cried. Except for the sounds of wood crumbling to embers inside the stove and the inevitable noises from the street, the store was quiet as a tomb.

Then there came the echo of boot heels on the stairs, and Aubrey appeared. His countenance suggested bleak annoyance, and his face was like granite. Susannah wondered, with a sorrowing heart, if he had ever turned that soul-withering look upon Julia.

"Delphinia," he said with a small inclination of his head. "We've settled everything there is to settle. We're through." He paused. "I don't suppose it will do any good to tell you that this is neither the time nor the place for the sort of scene you clearly have in mind?"

The breathtaking creature raged toward him, like a small, scented storm. The air crackled around her, and Susannah looked on in helpless fascination, feeling admiration for the other woman, as well as pity and a number of other, less easily identified things into the bargain.

"How dare you?" Delphinia simmered, standing at the foot of the stairs and glaring up at her lover. Her temper made heat, but his anger was cold enough to freeze the rest of the room; all, including Susannah, stood unmoving, unspeaking, without bothering to pretend they weren't listening.

"We'll discuss this in private," Aubrey said in a voice that probably wouldn't thaw before spring. With that, he closed the distance between them, took Delphinia's arm, and "escorted" her up to the second floor. Only when a door slammed, probably that of his office, did the customers and clerks begin to stir, like so many statues coming to life in an enchanted garden. There was much clearing of throats and straightening of neckties, and the old men gathered around the stove to whittle and gossip chuckled among themselves and reminisced in low tones. An angry discussion ensued upstairs, like distant cannon fire.

Susannah completed her shopping and made haste for the carriage, still waiting in the street. Very possibly, it had been the presence of that coach that had drawn Delphinia's attention in the first place, and Susannah did not want the woman's fury to turn in her direction.

Upon her return to the Fairgrieve house, looming against an overcast sky like a stone fortress, Susannah had nothing to do but find places for all her selections, since the baby was sound asleep. The task was a pleasant, homey one, and by the time she went downstairs for a cup of tea, she had forgotten the tempestuous scene at the general store.

Maisie was snoozing in her rocking chair, and Jasper was still at school.

Moving as quietly as she could, Susannah brewed a pot of orange pekoe, smiling softly to herself, and was on her way to the main parlor, which afforded a view of the mountains and the blue-gray waters, when the front door burst open and Aubrey blew in, like a great rush of wind. The door crashed shut behind him.

"Please be quiet," Susannah said moderately. "Your daughter is asleep."

Aubrey thrust a hand through his hair and emitted a heavy sigh. To Susannah's great surprise, he actually looked chagrined. "I'm sorry," he said, amazing her further. There was a beleaguered expression in his eyes that aroused a tenderness she did not wish to feel—was not *entitled* to feel. "You were there?" he asked briskly. It was plain that he was referring to that morning's drama and already knew the answer.

Susannah held her tea cup with both hands, for the sake of steadiness. "Yes," she said.

"It wasn't the way she made it sound."

Opposed to the use of ardent spirits all her life, Susannah suddenly wished with all her heart that her cup contained whiskey instead of tea. She could have used some bracing up. "There's no need to explain, Mr. Fairgrieve. Not to me."

"Aubrey, damn it," came the growled response. "When you call me Mr. Fairgrieve like that, it makes me feel like my own grandfather."

Susannah was bewildered—and secretly a little pleased—by this confession. She liked knowing that she could make this man feel something, anything. Was she turning into a loose woman?

"If you'll excuse me—" She started toward the main staircase. She had, after all, selected one book from the shelves at Aubrey's store, paid for out of her own scant funds, just as her more personal purchases had been, and planned to put her feet up and read a few pages before the baby awakened.

He stopped her with a firm but painless grasp on her arm. "Susannah, about Hollister—"

She summoned up a shy smile. "He's a very nice man," she said sincerely. "And he's invited me to have dinner with him tomorrow night. I accepted, of course."

Aubrey frowned. "Of course," he repeated, looking distracted. "What do you know about him?"

Susannah wanted to laugh, perhaps hysterically, though she could not have said why. "Why, nothing, except that he is well mannered and makes pleasant com-

pany. I assumed he was a friend of yours, since you en-
tertained him at your table."

Aubrey was still distracted and rubbed his chin between thumb and fingers. "So I did," he muttered. Then,
with no further elaboration, he wandered off into his
study, like a somnambulist, and closed the door softly
behind him.

"Damn it," he snapped, glowering at Hollister over the
green felt gaming table in the back room of one of Seattle's best gambling establishments. "I told you to investigate Miss McKittrick's past, not make a conquest of her."

Hollister had been winning all evening, and from the
cool way he assessed the cards in his hand, it appeared
that his luck was holding. "Getting to know her seemed
like a good idea," he mused. His eyes flashed with
humor as he looked at Aubrey. "And it's not unpleasant
work. Not at all."

Aubrey leaned forward in his chair. "By God, Hollister, it had better not get *too* pleasant."

The Pinkerton man laughed and slid a stack of chips
into the center of the table. "Taken with her, are you?
Now, that's interesting. Though not surprising, I must
admit. Ante up, or lay down your cards."

Aubrey tossed yet another worthless hand onto the
table, galled. "I am not 'taken' with anyone," he said. "I
merely want to know whether or not Susannah McKittrick is a fit guardian for the child."

"Why don't you use the child's name?" Hollister
asked mildly. "Or do you begrudge the poor little creature even that much?"

There was an ominous pause, during which Aubrey
felt both fury and shame. While it was true that he had
closed himself off from Julia's daughter—indeed, he
had not dared to open his heart—there was very little

he would have denied her. Wasn't she the whole reason he was putting up with Susannah McKittrick and all her interference? Why, if it wasn't for that woman, his arrangement with Delphinia might not have turned sour quite so soon.

"The child is well looked after," he said at great length. "You needn't concern yourself with her well-being."

Hollister cleared his throat, then leaned forward and scooped up a considerable pile of poker chips. He had lit a cigar, and it was clamped between his teeth as he pondered his winnings. "What, precisely, am I supposed to tell Miss McKittrick about myself? She's bound to ask how I earn my living, for instance, and I'm not comfortable with lying to her."

"Tell her as little as possible," Aubrey warned. There was a stir at the other end of the room, and he saw with a pang of irritation that Ethan had just come in.

"She's a proper female, our Susannah, and none too experienced in the ways of men and women," Hollister observed, following Aubrey's gaze across the span of crowded card tables to Ethan, who was now moving toward them. "She'll want to know my history."

It figured that after the scene with Delphinia at the store and heavy losses at cards, he would have to deal with his younger brother, too. Some days, it just didn't pay to put on pants and leave the house.

Ethan stood tableside, easy in his skin. "Losing, I hope?" he asked with an amicable smile.

Hollister finished gathering his chips. "Hullo, Ethan," he said. "My sister Ruby is home from school. Why don't you stop in and say howdy?"

Ethan grinned. "How is little Ruby?" he asked.

Hollister grinned back. "Not so little," he said. "What was she the last time you saw her, thirteen or so?"

Ethan nodded, held one hand roughly at the height

of a sawhorse. "She was about that tall," he said. "All eyeballs, knees, and freckles."

Hollister laughed. "Times change," he said. Then he spared a nod of farewell for Aubrey, got up, and left, trailing cigar smoke as he walked away. Ethan swung one leg over the back of a chair and sat down, reaching for the scattered cards and deftly shuffling them. He had spent more than his share of time in saloons and gambling halls, although he was not yet thirty years old.

"What do you want?" Aubrey asked bluntly. No sense in pretending brotherly affection when he didn't feel any.

Ethan dealt, arranged his hand, and pondered the cards therein before replying. "An answer," he said, meeting Aubrey's gaze squarely. "You like straight talk, brother, so here it is. It's all over Seattle that you and Delphinia have split the sheets. I guess what I want to know is, precisely what do you have in mind for Susannah?"

Aubrey sorted his own cards and tossed a chip into the pot, for all that his luck seemed to be worthless that night. Whenever he and Ethan tried to talk—and the effort was rare enough—they both had to be doing something else, whether playing cards, saddling or grooming a horse, or slinging their fists at each other.

"If you want to know Susannah's plans," Aubrey reasoned, "why don't you ask her yourself?"

"I don't need to," Ethan answered evenly, frowning at his cards. That probably meant he had a royal flush or a straight with aces high. "It's clear enough that Susannah wants to look after the little girl. I asked about your intentions, Aubrey, not hers."

Aubrey leaned forward in his chair. "My *intentions* are none of your damn business."

"Susannah is a lady, Aubrey. Don't get her mixed up with Delphinia and the others."

"Others?" Aubrey echoed furiously. He resented the

implication that he had been that much of a rounder. He'd been a faithful husband to Julia, until several months after she'd barred him from her bed.

Ethan forced out a sigh and closed his eyes for a moment in plain exasperation. "All right," he said. "Let's forget our differences for a little while and talk like grown men, shall we? I know you, Aubrey. If you showed Delphinia the road, it means you have your eye on someone else. It doesn't take a scholar to figure out that it's Susannah you want."

Aubrey couldn't quite bring himself to deny that he wanted Susannah, but at the same time, he wasn't ready to admit it, even in the privacy of his own mind. It outraged him that Ethan thought he would stoop to seducing an innocent like his present houseguest. Assuming she *was* innocent, of course. He'd thought Julia was a delicate flower, and look how she'd fooled him.

"If you came here to deliver a lecture on morality," he said, "I'd advise you to take to the road before I knock your teeth down your throat."

Ethan threw down his cards and glared across the table. He was making an effort to restrain his temper, that was clear by the bulging vein in his neck, but they were probably attracting attention anyway. Their feud was well known in Seattle, which, for all its rambunctious, bounding growth, was still a small town in most ways.

"Damn you, you pig-headed son of a—" He paused, began again. "I didn't sleep with your wife. I don't have plans to take Susannah to bed, either. For God's sake, *I'm your brother.*"

Aubrey felt a rush of emotions, savage in their force—rage, grief, and wild hope, all entangled with one another. Then he remembered Julia's taunts, her derisive laughter. And he considered the baby's fair hair and blue eyes—eyes like Ethan's.

"Exactly," he snapped. "I trusted you. I trusted her. What a damn fool I was." With that, Aubrey pushed to his feet, turned, and strode away. He needed fresh air and open space.

Ethan didn't follow.

When he reached the house on the hill minutes later, Aubrey turned his horse over to a stable hand and stood for a while in the cold, damp night air, looking up at the darkened windows on the second floor. He imagined Susannah in her small room at the back, perhaps brushing her hair, or reading a book, or holding the baby.

A painful lump filled his throat, and a sense of loneliness seized him, greater than any he had ever known. His right hand knotted into a fist, and only by the power of his formidable will was he able to open his fingers. He swore under his breath, pushed open the gate, and strode up the walk.

Susannah heard footsteps in the hall, heard them pause outside her door.

Her heart pounded, not from fear, she concluded with some mortification, but with a sort of sweet, breathless anticipation. She waited there at the vanity table, hair brush in hand, clad only in a flannel nightgown. After a few moments, she heard the footsteps again, retreating slowly down the corridor.

Unaccountable tears filled her eyes; she blinked them back, unsure whether she was relieved or disappointed. She did not know if she would have welcomed Aubrey or turned him away, and the mystery was difficult to live with. It made Susannah feel as though she were a stranger to herself. And what about Julia? Susannah had been a loyal friend to her, and she would be just as loyal to her memory.

In her cradle near the hearth, Julia's child gave a

small, whimpering cry, and Susannah, grateful for the distraction, hurried over to her. Victoria looked up at her, so resembling Aubrey that it nearly took her breath away.

How could he distance himself from this child? How?

Susannah held out a hand, and the baby gripped one of her fingers, chortling with the pleasure of accomplishment and holding on tightly.

"Whatever happens," she promised Victoria in a whisper, "I'll look after you."

The baby laughed again and kicked her tiny feet.

Susannah's eyes burned, but she laughed, too. Then she sang softly until Julia's daughter drifted back to sleep.

"Good night, little one," she whispered, but her thoughts had strayed to the opposite end of the corridor, in search of Aubrey.

Chapter

5

~

$\mathcal{M}$r. Hollister arrived promptly at the stroke of seven the following evening, at the reins of a smart buggy drawn by a dapple gray gelding, both brought to a smooth and graceful stop within the glow of a street lamp. Peering at her gentleman caller through the lacy curtains of the front parlor, Susannah felt serious trepidation, and not for the first time since she had agreed to join him for dinner. She had no earthly idea what sort of man he was; he might well be a rounder and a rascal, promised to someone or even *married*.

She laid splayed fingers to her bosom in silent consternation.

"Oh, stop your frettin'," Maisie scolded. She was standing beside Susannah, taking as much pleasure in the evening's engagement as if it were her own. In those moments, Susannah wished that were the case. She'd have been more than content to stay home with the baby and a book and let Maisie do the socializing. "He's fine to look at, and it ain't every day a gal gets an invite to eat somebody else's cookin'. Just smile at everything he says, no matter how stupid it might be, and make sure he don't press you for a kiss afore you're good and ready."

"Here I am," Susannah lamented in a whisper, "twenty-four years old, and I've never had a man come to call. I don't have the first idea what to say or how to behave."

"I just told you," Maisie answered, underscoring her assertion with a light jab of her elbow. "You just listen like he's smarter than Solomon, and he'll fall in love with you. If he ain't already done as much, that is."

Susannah was horrified. "But I don't want him to fall in love with me!" she protested in an anxious whisper.

Mr. Hollister had gained the porch by then, and the bell rang forcefully. After giving Susannah a rather smug look, Maisie swept out into the entryway and answered the door with all the dignified flourish of an English housekeeper presiding over the gates of some grand manor.

"Hello, Mr. Hollister," she said, and from her gruff exuberance, Susannah concluded that her friend liked this visitor very much, though she did not seem to know him personally. "Miss Susannah's all ready, and she looks mighty pretty, too. A body'd never know she was a spinster to look at her."

Susannah, lurking behind the parlor door, blushed and squeezed her eyes shut for a moment. As much as she liked Mr. Hollister, she would have given anything just then to pass the evening at home, perhaps sitting by the fire, while Aubrey read his newspaper nearby . . .

"Come on out here," Maisie all but brayed. "The man ain't got all night, and besides, there's no use in bein' shy."

Susannah was weak with embarrassment, but somehow she made herself walk, smiling and dignified, out of her hiding place. She extended her hand to Mr. Hollister, and he kissed it. Merriment twinkled in his blue eyes. *Don't be frightened*, they seemed to say. *You are safe with me.*

"You'll want a warm wrap," Hollister said as he released Susannah's hand. "It's crisp outside."

"Winter's comin' on," Maisie put in, still relishing her part in the occasion to the fullest.

Susannah reached for the blue cloak she'd worn to the store the day before; it was still hanging on the oak coat tree next to the door. Mr. Hollister, ever the gentleman, took the heavy garment from her and laid it gently over her shoulders.

"We'll be home around nine o'clock," Hollister told Maisie, opening the door and standing back to let Susannah precede him onto the porch. Even though it was early, darkness had long since fallen. She smelled salt and smoke and pine pitch in the air.

Susannah's instincts about Mr. Hollister proved sound over the course of that quiet, innocuous evening. His first name, he told her, was John, and he would like to be called that, if she was amenable to the idea. He had been born and raised in Missoula, Montana; he had once been married, but his wife had been gone a long time. She'd perished, with their unborn child, when their wagon overturned while crossing the Missouri River. He had a younger sister, Ruby, just back from school in San Francisco, and he beamed proudly when he spoke of her.

"Tell me about you," John urged over the main course of thick steaks, each of which would have been ample fare for a whole family, let alone one person.

Susannah knew—had known from the first—that she would never fall in love with this man, whatever Maisie's fanciful hopes in the matter might be, but she liked and trusted him and counted those things better than reckless sentiment. Such as she was beginning to feel toward Aubrey, for instance.

She told John about her childhood at St. Mary's, about leaving Boston to serve as an elderly lady's companion on Nantucket, where she had lived a worthwhile, if lonely, life. She explained her closeness with Julia and her hope that Mr. Fairgrieve would allow her to raise the child.

John studied her, his wine glass in one hand. "But you were never even betrothed? A lovely, intelligent woman like you?"

Although flattered, Susannah sighed inwardly. Would that love were an easy thing to control, something she could summon in the face of favorable circumstance. "I had many duties," she said with a little shrug. "Mrs. Butterfield—my employer—wasn't well, and giving piano lessons took up what little spare time I had." She thought sorrowfully of her small savings, which had been spent on a train ticket to Seattle.

"Hmmm," John remarked thoughtfully. "And who taught you to play piano?"

Susannah sighed. "One of the sisters at St. Mary's." Suddenly, she yearned to play the dusty grand she'd glimpsed languishing in the rear parlor of Aubrey's house. She needed to start giving lessons as soon as she could. Perhaps tomorrow, after she'd gone to see Reverend Johnstone about Victoria's christening, she would have time to play awhile and plan a campaign to recruit a half-dozen music students.

"Ruby used to play a little. Perhaps you might teach her."

The attention made her feel warm and a bit giddy, as she had always thought champagne might do, should she ever be depraved enough to taste the stuff. "I'd like that very much," she said. She sat up a little straighter. "How do you earn your living, Mr. Hollister, if I'm not being too forward in asking?"

He cleared his throat, looked away, looked back. "I

have a private income," he said, and while Susannah knew he wasn't lying, something didn't ring true.

She withdrew into herself a little way, feeling wary.

John smiled reassuringly, and she remembered that she liked him, that he was her friend. "I hear they have fine lobster off the shores of Nantucket," he said. "Do you miss such delicacies?"

Susannah looked down at the remains of her meal, ordered for her, as custom dictated, by Mr. Hollister. Her mouth watered just to remember eating steamed lobster, bought at the pier and drenched in butter got from a neighbor down the road. "Oh, yes," she said, wondering if she would ever see Nantucket again. She did not miss Mrs. Butterfield, but her rare walks along the beach were a bittersweet recollection. She told him about the sailboats skimming over blue seas, about the lighthouses and the sand dunes and the spiky grass.

The remainder of the evening seemed to have wings, and soon Susannah was back in John Hollister's buggy, being driven back to the grand but solemn house where her best friend had lived and died.

"Did you know Julia?" she dared to inquire just as they reached the cobbled driveway in front of Aubrey's mansion. Beyond were the gate, the yard, the lighted windows. "Mrs. Fairgrieve, I mean?" she added, lest her question be unclear.

John shook his head, drawing back on the reins and setting the brake with one booted foot. "No." He sighed and looked at Susannah squarely, though his face was in shadow beneath the brim of his hat, and she couldn't read his expression.

Susannah wanted to weep, thinking of Julia, and of her baby, and the man who could not admit that he'd sired the child. "But you are obviously acquainted with Mr. Fairgrieve."

"We've done business together before," John said with a moderation in his tone that made Susannah think he was speaking guardedly. "I would like to see you again, Susannah," he told her moments later as he helped her down from the buggy. "Perhaps you might be willing to attend church with me on Sunday? We could picnic near the water afterward, if the weather allows."

Because she liked John, and because she knew he had more to say to her, Susannah nodded. "That would be very pleasant," she said.

He did not attempt to kiss her at the front door but simply tipped his hat and bowed slightly before turning away to take his leave.

Maisie was waiting on the other side of the threshold, the baby asleep on one shoulder and Jasper entangled in her skirts like a wiry little monkey. "Mr. Fairgrieve was fit to be tied when he found you was out takin' your dinner with that Hollister feller," she hissed, delighted to convey the news.

Susannah felt a frisson of satisfaction and was immediately chagrined. Aubrey was her friend's widower, and he had not been kind to Julia. It made no difference that he was as handsome as Lucifer before the Fall, that it made her lightheaded and breathless just to stand close to him, that a glance from him could set her heart to wild fluttering. Of all the men on earth, he was the last one she could afford to love.

"I don't see why he should be upset," she said, shrugging out of the cloak and returning it to the coat tree. "I am a grown woman, after all, and quite capable of looking out for myself." She started to reach for Victoria, but before Maisie could hand the infant over, the study doors swung open and Aubrey towered in the chasm like an archangel come to pronounce judgment.

"May I speak with you in private for a moment, Miss

McKittrick?" he asked. His jawline looked ominously hard, and there was a glitter of dark challenge in his eyes.

"I'll put the babe to bed for you," Maisie told Susannah, and abandoned her in the entryway, just like that.

Susannah swallowed, though her shoulders were straight and her chin was at a deliberately haughty angle. "It is late," she said evenly, "and I am quite tired."

Aubrey simply stepped back and gestured for her to precede him into his inner sanctum. She swept past him, all pretense and bravado, feeling much as Anne Boleyn must have done on her way to the chopping block.

"Sit down," Aubrey instructed.

Susannah wanted to flout his command, but that would only prolong the interview. She sat, folding her hands daintily in her lap.

"What do you know about Hollister?" Aubrey took the leather chair opposite her, behind his large, cluttered desk.

"That I like him very much," Susannah replied honestly. "We are going to church on Sunday, and perhaps for a picnic afterward, if the weather holds."

From Aubrey's expression, one would have thought she'd said she planned to run away with the man and live in flagrant sin for the remainder of her days. "I was under the impression you came here to look after my—Julia's daughter. Maybe you were looking for a husband instead."

A wash of color scalded Susannah's cheeks, but she managed to hold on to her composure, for all that no suggestion had ever stung her so deeply before or made her angrier. Words crowded into her throat, but she could not force them out, and perhaps that was a good thing, because she wouldn't have been civil, let alone kind.

Aubrey sat back in his chair and cupped his hands behind his head. In the glow of the lamp, the masculine grace of his arms and shoulders seemed to be accentuated by a craggy tracery of shadows. His rich brown hair shimmered, even in that dim light, and it was in disarray, which only added to his roguish appeal. "Of course," he began airily, "if you *have* set your cap for a husband, you could hardly have come to a better place than Seattle. There's still a dire shortage of marriageable women here, you know—you could be a bride tomorrow if you wanted."

The change in his manner took Susannah very much off-guard. He'd seemed profoundly annoyed when confronting her in the entryway minutes before, but now his aspect was quiet and calm. "Let me assure you," she said when she found her voice, "I had no such intention, at any time. Nor have I changed my mind—however plentiful the prospects might be."

He made a steeple of his fingers and rested his chin on the tip, smiling a little. His eyes were narrowed, but Susannah could not tell whether he was conveying suspicion or merely pondering her statement. "Why," he asked after some time, "would you wish to remain unmarried all your life?"

The question was plainly intrusive, and yet, strangely, Susannah's irritation had ebbed away, and she could not seem to revive it. She sat up a little straighter. "That should be obvious," she said. Surely Julia had told him, when things were still good between them, that her dear friend Susannah had been left on the shelf, for all that she was passably pretty.

"It isn't," he replied. Obdurate man.

"No one asked," she said.

"Would you have accepted, if someone had?"

She paused to consider her reply. "That depends. I would have had to love the man very much."

He was leaning forward in his chair now, looking at

her intently, turning a pencil from end to end on the surface of the desk. "Love is an unreliable measure, in a matter so practical as marriage, Susannah. Far better to be wed for sensible reasons."

"Sensible reasons, Mr. Fairgrieve? And what would those be?"

He shrugged. "Money. Property. Heirs. Companionship in old age."

Susannah's fingers tightened on the arms of her chair. "Julia could never have given you property or money," she pointed out evenly. "You deny your child, and Julia will never see her old age, let alone provide comfort in yours. Why, then, did you marry her?"

The strong brows drew together for a moment, but when Aubrey met her gaze, she saw misery in his eyes. "And so we come back to the point. I married Julia because I loved her—and I thought she loved me in return. As things turned out, that was a misconception on my part. I paid a high price for my foolishness."

"So did Julia," Susannah said quietly and without rancor. Aubrey flinched at her words, all the same, though almost imperceptibly, and she regretted causing him pain.

"Do you think I ever forget?" he asked. "I came to despise her in the end, I admit that. I fully intended to divorce her. But I would never have wished her dead."

Susannah knew he spoke the truth. "I'm sorry," she said with a deep sigh, rubbing her temples. "I'm very tired, and that tends to make me short-tempered."

Aubrey rose from his chair and indicated the study doors with a gesture of his hand. "By all means, go to bed. I merely called you in to tell you I'm leaving for San Francisco tomorrow. I'll be away a week. If you need anything, you have only to contact Hawkins, my secretary, and he'll see that your requirements are met."

She should have been relieved, she supposed, to

learn that she was to have a respite from Aubrey Fairgrieve and his overwhelming presence, square in the middle of her life, but instead the news of his departure saddened her. She would miss him, even worry about him until he was safely back in Seattle. She wasn't about to admit to anything of the sort, of course.

She rose from her chair and nodded coolly. "Very well. Enjoy your travels, Mr. Fairgrieve, and rest assured that I will look after your daughter while you are away."

He thrust his hands into the pockets of his finely made trousers. "When did I become Mr. Fairgrieve again?" he asked.

Susannah paused at the door, one hand resting on a brass knob. "Good night, Aubrey," she said, and left him to himself.

The following morning, when Susannah brought Victoria downstairs for breakfast, she knew without being told that Aubrey had left. The vast house seemed to pulse with his absence, as though every room had been stripped bare of furniture and all adornment.

"Mornin'," Maisie greeted her, taking the child and carrying her to the rocking chair near the stove for a bottle. Jasper had already been delivered to the schoolhouse, evidently.

Susannah set about brewing a pot of tea and slicing thick wedges of bread to toast in the oven of the cookstove. "Good morning," she grumbled, grimacing at the frost-covered windows. It would be too cold to take Victoria out for a walk, that much was certain, and yet the idea of staying inside was almost more than she could tolerate. She craved fresh, salty air, blue skies, and the smell of garden soil turned up for planting.

She wanted spring, with all her heart and soul, and it was months away.

"He'll be back right quick," Maisie put in, and while her voice was gruff, the words were gently framed.

Susannah stiffened. "Who will?" she countered, though she knew full well, of course, that her friend had been referring to Aubrey.

Maisie chuckled, stroking the baby's downy head with one work-roughened hand as she rocked the chair back and forth. The infant drew hungrily from the bottle. "You don't need to pretend with me, miss," she said. "I ain't lived all this while 'thout knowin' a thing or two. Until last night, when Mr. Fairgrieve waited for you in his study the way he did, I had Hollister in mind for your match. Now, though, I've started seein' things from a different angle."

Once more, heat filled Susannah's face. She slammed the tea canister down on the work surface beside the big cast-iron sink. "And what angle is that?" she asked, more tersely than she had intended.

Maisie was unfazed. In fact, she looked downright smug. "I reckon you're the reason the mister got shut of his fancy woman. You could do a lot worse than Aubrey Fairgrieve, you know."

Aghast, Susannah stared at her friend. "You can't be serious! This is my *best friend*'s widower we're talking about—why, it would be—it would be—"

"It would be what?" Maisie prompted. "Mrs. Fairgrieve was your friend, but she's dead and gone, and you're alive. She wanted you here, begged me to send for you. Maybe she knew—"

"Stop," Susannah pleaded.

"Like I said, Mr. Fairgrieve would be a mighty good catch. Even in Seattle, there's plenty of women who'd bless their stars if he wanted them."

Susannah regained control of her outward manner, though still swept up in the confusing maelstrom of emotion Maisie's remarks had aroused in her. "They can have him," she said, perhaps too hastily, "with my blessings."

Maisie only laughed.

An hour later, the weather had not cleared, and the baby was sleeping soundly in her basket. Susannah, always ready to snatch any opportunity for a walk, rain or shine, kept going to the steamy windows, wiping with her apron, and peering out.

"Go on with you," Maisie said, busy chopping vegetables for a supper of stew. "I'll look after the little one till you get back."

Susannah flung her friend a grateful glance and fled toward the front of the house, grasping the cloak and swirling it around her as she went. Outside, the sun struggled behind a curtain of clouds, and there was a distinct chill to the atmosphere, yet she was jubilant with excitement.

She strolled the neighborhood for some time, at a brisk and bracing pace, before winding up in the churchyard, beside Julia's bleak, elegant grave. There was no sign of Reverend Johnstone or anyone else, which was just as well.

Susannah sat down on the stone bench nearest her friend's resting place and held the cloak closed with a tightened fist. The wind was rising, stinging her skin, and the cold seemed to reach past flesh and fiber to hollow out her bones. She had shed many tears for Julia. Now, she was left with a sort of emptiness, and she had to practice remembering the other woman's features, the same way she made her piano students go over and over the scales, in order to keep herself from forgetting.

"I've come to look after your baby, Julia," she said quietly, although she knew the essence of her cherished friend, the life force that had animated her and made her an individual, was not in this grimly beautiful place. "And I've got to admit, I'm not sure I understand why you found your husband so objectionable."

There was no answer, of course—just the wind whispering in the dried and falling leaves of the churchyard's few deciduous trees. Most were evergreens, venerable and pungently scented.

"I'm going to give your daughter a name," Susannah went on presently. "Victoria. I've bought her a christening gown, and lots of new clothes as well. She's growing so fast, Julia! Why, Maisie told me she's three times the size she was when she was born. Pretty soon, she'll be walking and talking and going to school." Sudden tears stung her eyes, and she paused to dry them with the back of one hand. "I'm so sorry you won't be here to see her. It isn't fair, that you have to miss even a moment—"

Behind Susannah, someone coughed diplomatically, to let her know she wasn't alone. She turned on the bench and was startled to see Ethan standing there, cattleman's hat in hand, ears red with the cold. He looked every inch the cowboy, in his boots, denim trousers, and fleece-lined leather coat. Between the lapels, she glimpsed the blue chambray of his shirt.

"I didn't mean to disturb you," he said.

Susannah was relieved, if anything. She had been getting a bit maudlin before he arrived, and that never did anyone any good. "Not at all," she said with a smile, patting the stone bench beside her. "Sit down."

He grinned. "I reckon I'd rather go out to the ice house and settle myself on a big lump of last year's lake water," he said. His expression turned serious. "You all right, Miss Susannah? You look a little flimsy to me."

She smiled and stood, dusting off her skirts, more out of habit than necessity. "It's just that I miss Julia so very much," she said, glancing back at the monument. She paused, studying Aubrey's younger brother, then spoke her mind. "Did you know Julia well?"

He looked away for a moment, then settled his hat on his head with a movement so brisk that it was almost harsh. "Not as well as I thought I did," he said. He brought his gaze back to hers then and regarded her un-flinchingly. "I came here looking for you, Susannah. I've already said all my good-byes to Julia."

She was honestly puzzled. "What do you want with me?"

"I thought we could talk. I was driving past, about to return a rig I borrowed from Aubrey, and I saw you, so I stopped. I guess I shouldn't have interrupted you—I'm sorry." He started to turn away, but Susannah found her-self at his side, taking hold of his arm.

"Wait," she said. "Don't go. Please. There are things I want—I need to know. About Julia's life and—and about her death."

Ethan gave another sigh, then crooked his elbow. "I'll tell you what I can," he promised, "but I'd rather we had our chat someplace warm. How about the dining room at the hotel? We could take some refreshment and thaw ourselves out at the same time."

Susannah felt a little surge of pleasure. She was be-coming quite the woman about town, first having din-ner out with Mr. Hollister and now tea with Ethan Fairgrieve. "That sounds fine," she agreed, hoping the delay wouldn't worry Maisie.

Ethan helped her up into the box of the wagon, then climbed up beside her and took the reins. His grin was boyish, a reminder that he was very young and probably much less sophisticated than his elder brother. Within a few minutes, they had made their way over bare streets and cobbled ones and reached the Washington Hotel.

Inside, Ethan removed his hat and coat and helped

Susannah out of her cloak. The garments were left in the charge of a clerk at the front desk.

The dining room, where Susannah had eaten with John Hollister only the night before, was a spacious place, with a Persian carpet and a plethora of potted palms. Ethan looked somewhat out of place in his rough, practical clothes and scuffed boots, but he was clearly at his ease; he might have been relaxing in his own parlor, for all the self-consciousness he showed.

They were given a table next to the fireplace, where a cheerful blaze crackled and snapped, and a Chinese man came to greet them. With Susannah's approval, Ethan ordered a pot of hot chocolate, some sandwiches, and a selection of sweets.

"You wouldn't have found Aubrey at home, you know," Susannah said, referring back to the mention Ethan had made earlier of borrowing his brother's wagon.

Ethan grinned again, and even though Susannah was not moved romantically, she could imagine female hearts breaking all over the west. "That's why I took the rig," he retorted. "Because Aubrey's on his way to San Francisco, I mean."

Susannah didn't know if he was teasing or not, the mischievous grin notwithstanding. "Surely he wouldn't have minded lending it to you," she said.

He sat back in his chair and heaved a great sigh. "My brother has little or no use for me these days," he admitted. "At the moment, it's my niece I'm concerned about. The poor kid hasn't even got a name yet, has she?"

Before Susannah could answer, the waiter returned with a tray, and she waited until the cups, pot of chocolate, and various plates of sandwiches and cookies had been set out and they were alone again before speaking. "I call her Victoria," she said. Then, after taking a deep breath, she plunged into deeper waters, like a resolute swimmer. "I suppose you know that Aubrey believes Julia was unfaithful to him," she said, taking care to keep her voice low.

Ethan looked distinctly uncomfortable and busied himself pouring hot chocolate into both their cups. He was surprisingly graceful at it, considering his rugged appearance.

"Ethan?" Susannah prompted when the silence went on too long to suit her. She had an odd, sick feeling in the pit of her stomach.

"Julia was—unhappy," he said at long last. He was a study in polite misery.

"You don't mean she actually *did* take a lover?"

He cleared his throat. "Yeah," he said. "That's what I mean, all right. That was her business, I guess. But it happens that she told Aubrey that I was the other man. He believed her."

Susannah's heart stopped, then lurched back into motion again. She felt all the color drain from her face, and the sickness grew to the point where she could not have touched the food and drink before her for any reason. "Was he right?" she dared to ask after a long time, wondering at her own audacity the whole while.

It was then that she saw the resemblance between Ethan and his older brother. He glared at her, looking for all the world like Aubrey, and sounding like him, too, when he snapped, "What do you think?"

Chapter

6

~

$\mathcal{S}$usannah kept her gaze level with Ethan's, though her voice faltered a little. "I don't know what to think," she said, keeping her voice down lest the other diners overhear. "That is why I'm asking you. Were you and Julia—improperly close?"

For a while, there was no reply. Ethan's cup rattled dangerously as he set it down on the tabletop. "I've loved one woman in my life," he said in quiet, even tones, leaning forward in his chair. His resemblance to Aubrey was still greater than before. "Her name was Su Lin. Before we could be married, her father sent her back to China to marry a distant cousin."

The news made Susannah catch her breath. Ethan's grief was acrid as smoke between them, and it brought a brief, stinging sheen of tears to her eyes. "I don't know what to say."

"Neither did I," Ethan rasped. " 'Good-bye' just didn't seem to be enough." After a few moments, he relented a little. His features relaxed visibly, and his impressive shoulders, stooped a moment before, were square again. He thrust a hand through his hair. "I'm sorry, Susannah.

None of this ought to concern you, but I'm afraid it does, if only because of the baby."

Susannah was still deeply troubled, for she knew, in her heart of hearts, that Julia *was* capable of vengeance and deception, if her private purposes were served. A rift between brothers, and all the damage it could do, might not have worried her overmuch. She had been a fully faceted human being after all, not a one-dimensional image painted on canvas or caught by the lens of a camera. Funny, intelligent, pretty, and adventurous, Julia also had been somewhat reckless and selfish at times. She had had vain moments, and spiteful ones as well, and Susannah had loved her without illusion, loved her for her whole self, not merely her admirable qualities.

"The baby." She sighed, steering the conversation back to its center of importance. "Aubrey has given me permission to have her christened. I mean to have that done before he returns from San Francisco, since it's doubtful he'll want to participate. Would you agree to be her godfather?"

Ethan was quiet—and expressionless—for so long that Susannah began to fear that she had committed a serious error by asking. "You are aware that Aubrey might interpret that as a sort of claim on my part?"

Susannah scraped her teeth over her lower lip, a habit she had been trying to break for years. The sisters had reprimanded her for it repeatedly, and Mrs. Butterfield had called it "common."

"Aubrey," she said presently in measured tones, "has made it clear that he does not wish to be involved. And it seems to me that he's already drawn the worst possible conclusion."

"Yeah," Ethan agreed, somewhat wearily. "But he did give you permission to do this, right? He doesn't take kindly to interference in his affairs, so you've got to be sure."

Aubrey certainly hadn't given his blessing to the idea; he'd just tossed off an all-right-let's-be-done-with-it sort of remark the last time the topic was discussed, and Susannah had chosen to translate that as consent. A child could not be let to grow up without a Christian name, after all. "He made it clear that he doesn't care," she replied honestly. "Therefore, it falls to me to take action, as the person Julia depended upon."

Ethan looked doubtful. "Whatever you say. A word of warning, though—don't name that kid after Julia. Aubrey will never accept her if you do."

Susannah was still fanciful enough to hope that Aubrey would eventually see reason and had immediately ruled out "Julia" for the reason Ethan had given and several others as well. "I mean to call her Victoria," she said. She paused. "Will you be her godfather?" she asked again, frankly hopeful.

Ethan hesitated, then nodded. "All right. When's the ceremony?"

She recalled, with some agitation, that she had not spoken to Reverend Johnstone about the christening, as she had intended to do. She would see to the task before returning to her duties at the house. "Sunday, if that can be managed." She needed confirmation of his promise. "Will you be there?"

"Yes," he said, with little enthusiasm. Then a wicked grin flashed across his face. "You might want to stand in a doorway, though, in case lightning strikes and the ceiling comes down."

She laughed. "Are you such a sinner as that?"

"Yes, ma'am," he replied with another grin. After that, they talked about the gold rush in Alaska and the hardships and perils of crossing the Chilchoot Pass with the supplies required by the Canadian government. There was no further mention of Aubrey, of Julia, or of the innocent, beautiful child they had made together.

True to her promise to herself, Susannah asked Ethan to drop her off at the church, where he'd found her earlier, and spoke to Reverend Johnstone before hurrying home. The christening was officially scheduled for Sunday morning, after church services were held.

That would leave little or no time for a picnic with Mr. Hollister, but Susannah was convinced he would understand. He was, after all, a reasonable man, quite unlike Aubrey Fairgrieve in that way.

The intervening days were busy ones. Susannah kept Victoria by her side almost constantly, whether she was helping Maisie with the cooking and housework, drawing posters advertising her musical skills, or playing the splendid piano in the rear parlor. The child loved the sound of music—twinkling, dancing Mozart, thundering, ponderous Beethoven, it didn't matter what sort— she would coo and chortle in her basket, waving and kicking like a ladybug on its back.

Susannah's protectiveness and concern for little Victoria deepened into a desperate love, an emotion as intense as if she'd carried the infant inside her own body. As the wind heightened and the sky turned grayer, as the last leaves of the maples and oaks scattered in a shower of crimson and gold, while the fir trees stood fast against the onslaught, she thought often of Aubrey and wished him gone from her mind, not just from the house.

On Sunday morning, a drizzling, icy rain fell, beginning at dawn. That would put a finish to Mr. Hollister's plans for a picnic, Susannah thought, with no great degree of disappointment, but he arrived promptly in a rented surrey to drive her and Victoria around the block for church. Maisie walked, hand in hand with Jasper, both of them dressed up in their best clothes.

The service was long, the sanctuary was cold, and Victoria was fitful in her magnificent christening gown, but at last the time came to carry the child to the front and stand before the altar. Ethan, who must have been seated in a rear pew, came up the center aisle when summoned by the reverend, clearly enjoying the whispered speculation that swelled around him like foam in a tide pool.

The full name Susannah had chosen for Julia's daughter was Victoria Elizabeth, and there was a murmur of approval from the congregation, most of which had remained to watch and wonder. No doubt some of the members had expected a wedding rather than a baptism; if so, they were disappointed.

Mr. Hollister seemed oddly subdued when the ceremony was over. There was no choice but to cancel their picnic, of course, and he did not offer another suggestion. Neither did Susannah, who wanted only to take Victoria home.

All the same, Hollister drove them both to the house and saw them safely inside. Ethan came, too, driving Aubrey's wagon again, with a proud Maisie sitting stalwartly on the seat beside him, Jasper on her lap, all three of them apparently oblivious to the incessant rain.

"So it's Vicky, is it?" she boomed when she and Susannah and Ethan were all in the kitchen. Jasper was evidently playing in another room, for there was no sign of him, and Maisie made haste to build up the fire in the cookstove and put coffee on to brew. On such a day, she commented, tea simply wasn't enough.

Susannah smiled, happy except for a hollow place tucked away in a corner of her heart.

"Vicky," Ethan repeated quietly, drawing back a chair

to sit down at the table. "That's a real pretty name. Has some backbone to it."

Susannah nodded, her mind wandering a little, now that one important task had been completed. "Julia liked that name. One year there were dolls at Christmas—at St. Mary's, I mean—and Julia named hers for the queen of England."

Maisie and Ethan exchanged an unsettling look, but neither of them spoke.

"What?" Susannah prompted.

Maisie crossed the room, took little Victoria from her arms, and headed up the rear stairway, presumably to change her diaper and put her down for a nap. In the meantime, Ethan dropped into the chair, quite lost in thought.

"Ethan?" Susannah demanded, going to stand opposite him, behind her own chair.

He raised his eyes, and she saw amusement there. "Aubrey is going to be furious," he said.

She sat down with a sinking motion, all the starch gone out of her knees. She didn't have to ask for any further explanation; Ethan supplied it readily.

"My brother can be real cussed. No matter what name you gave that kid, he'd find a reason not to like it." His face hardened. "He's like our daddy that way. Nothing makes him happy, especially when it's over and done and can't be changed."

"But I mentioned—"

"He'll forget," Ethan said flatly.

Susannah was rigid and, at the same time, weak with confusion, frustration, and worry. "What kind of man—?"

"Forgets? Or what kind of man was our daddy?"

Susannah waited.

"Our ma lit out when we were little," Ethan said,

"and we were brought up rough in the lumber camps—
we passed a month or two in every one between here
and San Francisco, I reckon. Dad was a hard man, with
a tendency to drink too much, and he probably never
had an easy day in his life. Sometimes he took that out
on us."

Despite Ethan's calm way of outlining the tale, Susannah's thoughts were fixed on the image of two small,
frightened boys, abused by their father, abandoned by
their mother. No wonder Aubrey found it so difficult to
trust. Her heart seized painfully. "That's terrible."

Ethan squeezed the bridge of his nose between his
right thumb and forefinger. On the stove, the coffee
began to perk, fragrant and welcoming. "Plenty of people have had it worse," he said.

"Maybe Reverend Johnstone could do the ceremony
over—when Aubrey gets back from San Francisco—"

Ethan looked wryly skeptical. "Seems like a lot of trouble to go to, for something that's over and done with."

"Ethan, why didn't you tell me this before?"

"Seemed like you had your heart set on it," he said, as
though that explained everything.

The coffee boiled over, sizzling on the stovetop, and
Ethan got up, hurried over, and burned himself in the
process of trying to remove the pot from the heat.

Susannah pumped cold water into a bucket at the
sink and stood beside Ethan while he plunged the injured hand into it, expelling a long breath in relief. "That
was a very stupid thing to do," she said.

Ethan laughed. "Thanks for the sympathy," he retorted.

"What good would sympathy do?" Susannah reasoned, still distracted. Victoria's name had already been
penned onto a page of the church record, along with
those of other children of the community. Fussing
would serve no purpose at all; it was, as Ethan had said,

too late for that. Still, she couldn't help being a little upset.

Ethan cupped his good hand under her chin and made her look at him. "Listen, Susannah. It's behind you, this naming business, I mean. If Aubrey objects, let him solve the problem himself." He smiled and let her go, clearly noticing, as she had, that there had been no charge to the contact between them. "Besides, Victoria is a perfectly acceptable name. Maybe that little girl upstairs will make it count for something special."

Susannah was developing a headache. "Maybe," she confirmed, and pumped more water into the bucket.

Aubrey had been gone a full ten days when he returned to Seattle, one dark and gloomy afternoon in early November. Things had not gone well in San Francisco, and the sea journey back up the coast had been unusually rough. He had one thing to look forward to, by his own reckoning, and one thing only: the prospect of a little verbal sparring with Susannah McKittrick. During his travels, he had come to terms with the fact that he wanted much more from her, which partly accounted for his sour mood. She wasn't the sort of woman he could alternately bed and ignore; she was a lady, with every right to expect marriage from any man who sought her favor.

Not that she would marry him, even if he asked. Which, of course, he had no intention of doing.

He might have slammed the front door when he came in, chased and buffeted up the walk by a seaborne wind, had it not been for the faint, sweet refrain of the piano. The sound, so unexpected, paralyzed him for a few moments; he stood there on the threshold, his hat and coat dripping water while more rain blew in to pool around his feet.

The word *stop* swelled in his throat, and yet he was enchanted by the music, drawn by it, like a sailor summoned to his doom by the songs of sirens. Slowly, ever so slowly, he closed the door behind him, shed his hat and coat, and tugged at the cuffs of his shirt. He found himself at the entrance of the rear parlor, where he had not intended to go.

Notes spilled over him like the crystalline drops of a waterfall, and he shut his eyes tightly, in pleasure. In pain.

"Stop." He had barely breathed the command, she could not have heard it, and yet the wellspring of sound ceased. She turned on the piano stool, wide-eyed, to regard him in bewilderment.

"You've come back," she said. It broke the spell, and for that, at least, he was grateful.

"Obviously," he replied, because at the moment sarcasm was the only defense left to him. The pain was still with him, though slowly ebbing away, and he was vulnerable.

She moved her fingers lightly over the piano keys, just once more, leaving a sparkling trail of sound in her wake, then sighed. A brave little smile faltered on her lips, just briefly, then fell away. "I see your disposition has not improved," she remarked in tones of cheerful resignation.

He crossed the room, for something to do and no other reason, and poured brandy from a decanter on the bureau. The painting of Julia, commissioned just after their impulsive marriage, while they were still in Boston, loomed above him in all its glory, and he wondered why he hadn't consigned it to the attic. Gazing upon it, he felt no vestige of the consuming passion his late wife had roused in him when they were courting— there was nothing left, not even rancor.

He took another sip from his brandy. Alas, that assessment wasn't quite true. He felt sorrow, he felt pity, and he felt a peculiar sort of anguish that had more to do with his sense of betrayal than anything else.

"She was beautiful, wasn't she?" Susannah spoke wistfully, and she was standing right beside him. He had not heard her approach.

"Yes. So, they tell me, was Lucifer, before they threw him out of heaven."

"You are too hard on her. She was flawed, certainly, but she was not a monster."

Aubrey looked down into Susannah's eyes and wanted, suddenly, desperately, and unreasonably, to kiss her. He reminded himself that he knew even less about her than he had about Julia, and look where *that* state of blissful ignorance had taken him. "Perhaps you didn't know your friend as well as you thought you did," he said with the slightest lift of his glass.

She did not miss the subtle impudence of the salute; her eyes flashed, and it was plain that she would have slapped him if she'd dared. Instead, she folded her arms tightly against her middle, her hands bunched into fists. "No one knew her better than I did," she countered. She indicated the painting with a nod of her head, and fragments of gaslight caught in the tendrils of fair hair curling loosely against her cheeks. "I would like to have this painting, if you don't want it. For Victoria."

It was as though a ram had butted him in the stomach; for a few seconds, he couldn't breathe, let alone speak. The brandy splashed in its glass as he set it aside. "Who the hell is Victoria?" he rasped, though he had a terrible feeling that he already knew the answer to that question.

"She is your daughter."

As he was absorbing her words, he quite literally saw red, was temporarily blinded by it. Had she been Ethan, the only other person on earth who had ever been able to bring on that particular phenomenon, he would have struck her. Because she was a woman, because she was Susannah, violence did not even occur to him. "You went ahead and christened that child while I was gone?"

"You said I could do what I wanted—"

He retreated a step, but she had the temerity to follow, even to take hold of his arm, and he did not pull free, even though he was rigid with anger.

"She's a child, Aubrey. An innocent little baby. She'd gone without a name long enough."

He rubbed his eyes with a thumb and forefinger, weary to the center of his soul. "You're right," he rasped. "You're right. I'm sorry, Susannah. I don't know what—"

She looked up at him with sympathy, and he supposed he would have preferred scorn to that, or even outright contempt. "You were so furious with Julia," she said gently. "Did you ever allow yourself to grieve for her? For the woman you believed her to be?"

He turned away from her to gaze out into a dark, leaf-strewn corner of the garden Julia had so cherished. It had been the one thing she seemed capable of nurturing, that crop of roses and shrubs and small trees. Soon enough, he would have Hollister's report on his investigation of Susannah. He would know whether or not it was safe to turn the baby over to her for good, to send them both away, once and for all, out of his sight, with nothing to connect them but a monthly draft on one of his bank accounts.

"I did all my grieving *before* she died," he ground out.

"Why do you hate the sound of the piano?" Was there no end to her infernal questions? He wished she would go away, and, at one and the same time, he drew a kind of heated sustenance from her presence. "Julia didn't play, at least not well, so it couldn't be—"

"You're wrong, Miss McKittrick. Julia became quite accomplished, in lonely hours, which were, for her, relatively rare. All the same, she played until I thought I would go mad. Played and wept and yearned for her lover."

"Maybe it was you she was yearning for," she suggested. She had brass, Susannah McKittrick did, there was no denying that, and no apparent idea when to hold her tongue. "Julia adored you—early on, at least. I have letters from her, extolling your virtues."

"And later?"

Her eyes darkened. "She became more and more unhappy as the months passed. She wished she'd never married you."

"God, that was certainly mutual. Tell me, did she mention my brother?"

"No," Susannah shot back immediately. He saw in her eyes that it wasn't true.

"I suppose he told you that it was all a lie. That Julia had accused him out of spite." He could not hide his derision, not now. He was too thoroughly caught, a man flailing in a web. "If you believe that, you are a fool."

"I do believe it. Julia was capable of that sort of deception, when she was angry or hurt. However, it would have passed with her fit of temper."

Upstairs, the baby—*Victoria*—began to squall. Aubrey felt a wry, weary sort of envy for the child. What a luxury it would have been, to bellow, again and again, until all the pain was gone. To have Susannah McKittrick rush to one's side, bearing comfort.

"Excuse me," Susannah said primly, and swept out in a flurry of skirts and conviction. He went to the doorway and watched as she hurried up the stairs in reply to that imperious summons. Oh, yes, he was envious, all right.

Miss Victoria Fairgrieve was one lucky baby.

Even during the brief time Aubrey was away, Victoria had grown significantly. Delighted by every task, Susannah changed the child's diaper, washed her hands, and then lifted the warm, plump little bundle out of the cradle.

"There, now," Susannah said, patting Victoria's tiny back as she headed down the corridor toward the rear stairs. "Your papa is home, safe and sound." Some consolation that is, she thought with sad frustration. He thinks you're his brother's child.

In the kitchen, she prepared a bottle while deftly shifting Victoria from one arm to the other. The baby fussed and tugged at Susannah's hair, nearly causing it to fall from its combs, and settled down only when the milk was ready. Rocking Victoria in Maisie's chair, Susannah felt deeply calm, despite the recent confrontation with Aubrey in the rear parlor.

She rested her cheek against the baby's downy head, humming softly, and went to sleep. That was how Aubrey found her, some time later.

"Susannah." He touched her shoulder gently. "Susannah, wake up."

She sat up very straight, groping for the child, finding her arms empty. Panicking.

"It's all right," Aubrey said in a quiet voice. "I put—Victoria to bed."

She was first relieved, then befuddled. "You did?"

He smiled, and she was shaken by that, as always. "Go and get some sleep, Miss McKittrick," he said. "You are plainly exhausted."

She nodded and took his hand when he offered it. As she rose, her fingers curved around his palm, and a shiver of sweet fire raced through her. Why, she wondered, did she have to react to Aubrey Fairgrieve in such a way, when it would have been so much more convenient to be so affected by Mr. Hollister?

She was still pondering the question when either she

tripped on the hem of her dress or Aubrey pulled her close. Whatever the case, she collided with his chest, and when she would have righted herself, he bent his head and caught her mouth with his own.

If the touching of palms had set Susannah's senses ablaze, Aubrey's kiss fairly consumed her. He was very skilled; she had only to receive and accept, it seemed, which was a good thing, because she would not have known how to do more.

After a thorough introduction to the intricacies of the form, Aubrey drew back, looking bemused. "Have you ever been kissed before?" he asked. She blushed, mortified that her inexperience was so obvious, and tried to flee, but Aubrey held her firmly by both arms. "Susannah," he insisted.

"No," she cried in an indignant whisper. "*No*. Are you satisfied?"

He tilted his head back and laughed softly, and the sound was wholly, implicitly masculine. "Far from it," he replied, and his chameleon eyes, now green, now amber, now clear as water, glittered with pleasure. "We have a problem, Miss McKittrick."

She stepped back, and he released his physical hold on her, though his gaze held her just as effectively. "And what is that, Mr. Fairgrieve?"

"I believe I just demonstrated the difficulty."

Susannah squared her shoulders. "You kissed me," she said. "I forgive you."

He laughed again. "Ah," he parried. "That is magnanimous of you. But I did not ask for your pardon, did I?"

She drew herself up, incensed—and secretly excited—by the utter impropriety of his attitude. "I think, sir, that you are drunk," she said, although in truth she thought nothing of the sort. Even though he'd taken brandy earlier in the rear parlor, he was anything but intoxicated. For all her lack of experience in such matters, Susannah knew that much.

"I never get drunk," he replied, a little smugly. "Believe me, I've tried many times, but no amount of liquor will drown my damnable good sense. I am condemned, more's the pity, to a life of raw-nerved sobriety."

Susannah did not know how to respond. She smoothed her skirts, patted her hair, and realized too late that the gesture had displayed the lines and form of her bosom in a most provocative way. "Good night," she said. And this time, when she started toward the stairs, he made no move to stop her.

When she came downstairs the following morning, carrying a freshly bathed and dressed Victoria and feeling frazzled for lack of rest, there was a place set for her at the table. Beside it was a volume, bound in fine leather.

She frowned. "What's this?"

Maisie took Victoria and set her on the blanket in the center of the room, alongside Jasper, who was home from school that day because of the sniffles. The two children studied each other with wide, curious eyes. "Mr. Fairgrieve left it for you," Maisie said with a shrug, and went back to the kettle of corn mush on the stove. "You want some toast?"

"Yes, please," Susannah said distractedly, taking her chair and reaching for the book. The name on the inside cover was Ethan Fairgrieve.

Maisie brought coffee and went back to prepare the toasted bread. Susannah turned the first page and found herself immersed in line after line of spare yet vivid poetry. The verses were a tribute to a love so deep, so total, that reading them was tantamount to eavesdropping on the author's very soul.

Susannah read on, ignoring her breakfast, one hand

pressed to her heart, her eyes blurry with tears. She was three-quarters of the way through when Victoria demanded her attention. Reluctantly, she put the volume away and carried her charge back upstairs, for a change of diaper and the addition of several layers of warm clothes.

She and Victoria were returning from their third turn around the neighborhood with the pram when Aubrey rode up on a handsome black gelding.

"Are you trying to give that child pneumonia?" he demanded, dismounting and tossing the reins to a waiting stable hand.

"She is bundled up like an Eskimo baby," Susannah said, undaunted. She was a great believer in fresh air. "Why did you want me to read Ethan's poetry?"

A muscle flexed in his jawline, and for a few moments, his gaze was fixed on something far away, beyond the sound and the snowy mountains framing it. "Because he wrote it for Julia," he said.

Susannah felt sick. She was going to be terribly disillusioned if Ethan turned out to be a rascal; she liked him and did not want to change her opinion. If she'd had to hazard a guess, she'd have said the lines were written for Su Lin. "I read most of the verses, and there was no mention of her name."

"She kept the book in her bedside table," Aubrey said, as though she had not spoken. "She asked me to read aloud from it the day she died. Really very romantic, don't you think?"

"Aubrey—"

He stepped back, holding his hands at his sides, palms out. "No, Susannah. The words in that book are Ethan's, and Julia was their subject. Nothing you can say will change it." With that, he turned and strode toward the house, leaving her to stand watching him in consternation and despair. Only when Victoria began to cry did she push the pram through the open gate and up the walk.

Mr. Hollister arrived just in time to help her maneuver both baby and buggy up the steps onto the porch and through the doorway. She was relieved, if anything, when, instead of inviting her on another outing, he asked to see Aubrey.

Susannah gathered up Victoria and made herself scarce.

Chapter

7

~

The contingent of church women came to call the following morning, moving in single file up the walk, through a wispy fall of snowflakes and the pluming fog of their own labored breath. They resembled a train of freight cars, steaming determinedly along behind the engine.

"Oh, lordy," breathed Maisie, who had seen them gather into a flock at the end of the street when she was returning from taking Jasper to school, and summoned Susannah from the piano with a hissed, "Come quick!" and an excited gesture of one hand.

Even before Maisie gave their official title, Susannah had known who the women were. Their black sateen dresses and bonnets, their grim and implacable expressions, said it all. Each carried a Bible; they had clearly put on the full armor of God before making their assault upon the house of sin.

"Bunch of fusty old crows," Maisie muttered.

Susannah smoothed her skirts and patted her hair. "Let them in, please," she said. "I shall receive them in the parlor. And make tea, if you wouldn't mind."

"Hell, yes, I mind," Maisie retorted, "but I'll do it for

you. Can't say as I understand what you're up to, though. Them old biddies ain't here to welcome you to town, you know. They want to find out whether or not you're the mister's new fancy woman."

Susannah let out a sigh as the doorbell chimed. "I know," she said, and, assuming what dignity she could, turned and swept into the parlor to receive her grim-faced guests. Had it not been for the circumstances, she might have been a little flattered by their suspicions. She was not sophisticated in such matters, but she knew that not even Delphinia Parker would have dared to live openly with a man who was not her husband. The good ladies saw themselves as guardians of Seattle's morals, at least in the stratum they occupied.

There were six of the visitors, and not one spared so much as a smile when Susannah, stirring the fire to warm the room, offered a cheerful greeting.

"I," announced the leader, "am Mrs. Charles Fielding Shimclad. President of the Ladies' Christian Benevolence Society. I believe you know our pastor, Reverend Johnstone, and have even attended our services." There was a faint note of recrimination in the woman's words, as though she believed Susannah might have over-stepped her bounds merely by crossing the threshold of their church but was reserving judgment.

She recalled all of the women from Victoria's christening but made no mention of the fact. "Susannah McKittrick," she said with a cordial but reserved nod. "Julia—Mrs. Fairgrieve—was my schoolmate and friend. Won't you sit down? Maisie will serve tea in a few minutes."

The Benevolence Society, having paraded through the icy morning air, was not quite stalwart enough to refuse tea and seats near the fire, although it was plain from their manner that they would have preferred to state their mission, issue their demands, and depart in a blaze of Christian indignation.

"Thank you," said Mrs. Shimclad with the utmost reluctance. At her signal, the other ladies found places around the room, while Susannah remained standing, just to one side of the fireplace, wanting to keep the slight advantage of being on her feet.

"I suppose you know why we're here," submitted another delegate, a skinny creature with a spray of pockmarks down one side of her face and a pair of protruding front teeth.

"I haven't the faintest idea," Susannah lied airily. She was an unmarried woman, living in the home of an unmarried man, and such arrangements were not looked upon with favor by Mrs. Shimclad and her ilk. Not in Boston, not even in frontier cities like Seattle.

The formidable leader cleared her throat. Her many chins quivered, and Susannah was momentarily—and unkindly—reminded of a turkey's neck. "We are here on an errand of the Lord," Mrs. Shimclad said.

Susannah nearly laughed but managed to restrain herself. "Oh?" she asked, with as much innocence as she could summon up.

"It is sinful," Mrs. Shimclad pressed, "for you to reside, unchaperoned, in this house."

Unfortunately, Maisie entered the room at that precise moment, a tray full of tea and crockery rattling in her hands. "Don't see 'em out lookin' after those poor women that's been left behind by their miner husbands to starve, do you?" she muttered, but loudly enough for everyone to hear.

Susannah suppressed another smile, and among the Benevolence Society, there was much harrumphing, and well-I-nevering.

"It is our responsibility to set standards for the bene-

fit of the community," Mrs. Shimclad insisted after tossing Maisie a look that would have cured leather. The
former would serve the Lord whether he required her
able assistance or not, that much was clear. In point of
fact, Susannah doubted that he had any real say in the
matter. "If you wish to become a member of our church,
you will have to do something about these scurrilous
circumstances, Miss McKittrick."

Maisie stomped out, still muttering, and Susannah
found that her own amusement had abated a considerable degree. "Scurrilous?" she repeated. "I have done
nothing wrong, and neither has Mr. Fairgrieve."

The Society exchanged glances, but they helped themselves to tea and to the plate of cookies—no doubt baked
for Jasper and Aubrey—that Maisie had added to the tray.

"We must think of appearances," Mrs. Shimclad said
loftily.

"Why?" Susannah asked.

"—like that woman from Boston—" she heard someone murmur.

"—better if she weren't so pretty—" put in another
visitor.

Mrs. Shimclad set aside her tea cup with a righteous
clatter, though she did not, Susannah noted, forsake her
cookie. "I have already explained our position in the
community, Miss McKittrick."

"Mrs. Shimclad," Susannah said with labored patience, "I am a nurse to the child. That's all."

Mrs. Shimclad might have been deaf for all the note
she took of Susannah's statement. "We must insist that
you either marry Mr. Fairgrieve, move out of this house,
or cease attending our church!"

"That's a fine idea," Aubrey put in cheerfully from
just inside the parlor doors, thoroughly startling everyone, including Susannah, who had thought him well

away, occupied with the business of running his store. "Will you marry me, Susannah? That way, we can have all the pleasures of sin without incurring the wrath of these fine ladies."

Susannah's heart began to pound against her breast-bone, while, at one and the same time, she had to stay herself from flying at Aubrey in a temper for making such an ill-advised and audacious remark. These women didn't have a sense of humor among the lot of them; they did not know that he was merely joking.

They began to buzz, like so many plump bumble-bees caught in a jelly jar.

"Well?" Aubrey prompted, spreading his hands and beaming.

Susannah was red from her toenails to the roots of her hair. "This is hardly the time or place—" she protested.

"Is there a better time?" Aubrey asked expansively, bending over Mrs. Shimclad as if putting the question to her. "A better place?" he demanded of another woman.

Mrs. Shimclad actually simpered. "I think it's a very romantic notion," she said.

Susannah stared at her in confoundment and felt her heart soften a little, though she would have preferred to keep it hard. "*I* think it is insane," she said. "Mr. Fair-grieve and I barely know each other, and we have not made an especially auspicious beginning."

Aubrey looked like the hero of a tragic road show. He even went so far as to press one hand to his heart as he declaimed. "See?" he asked of Mrs. Shimclad and the others. "No matter how fervently I declare my passion, this is how it's received."

The women sighed.

"That," Susannah said through her teeth, "will be enough. I mean it, Aubrey."

He crossed the room and wrenched her to his

bosom. "You drive me mad with desire," he declared, and the ladies, chilled to the bone only moments before, began to fan themselves and chirp out a chorus of oh mys. "I can't stand it any longer. Say you'll be my wife before I'm forced to carry you off over one shoulder like spoils after a battle!"

Susannah was speechless with mortification, while Aubrey's hazel eyes twinkled with mischief as he watched her reaction to his performance.

"I shoulda sold tickets," Maisie commented from the doorway that led to the dining room and the kitchen beyond. "This here is better than that fella who could play 'Clementine' on a crosscut saw. You remember that, Mr. Fairgrieve? He had a mangy old bear, too, trained to dance to the music."

Aubrey's eyes never left Susannah's. It was as though they were locked together in some private challenge, one that no one else was privy to, for all the witnesses and all the tomfoolery that had gone on in their presence.

"I remember," he said.

Susannah swallowed hard, found her voice at last. She would deal with Aubrey later, when she could speak to him alone. In the meantime, she fixed her attention on the Benevolence Society, sweeping them up, one by one, with her gaze.

"You must all have a great many things to do," she said evenly. "Being the gatekeepers of the city's conscience cannot be an easy task. And then there is the matter of those destitute women Maisie mentioned earlier. I'm certain you will all want to go straight out and take charge of the situation, good Christian ladies that you are."

There were, to their credit, a few blushes among the members of the Society. They finished their tea with hasty slurps and their cookies with quick nibbling and rose to depart.

Maisie saw them out, leaving Susannah and Aubrey standing in the center of the main parlor, staring at each other.

"Are you *mad*?" Susannah burst out in a furious whisper. "I don't want to marry you, and you don't want to marry me. Why in heaven's name would you suggest such a thing?"

For the first time since his entrance, Aubrey's expression was serious. "Am I? Mad, I mean?" he asked quietly. "I need a wife, if for no other reason than to entertain my business associates and offer me a place of refuge at the end of a long day. You need a husband, to support that child you are so determined to raise."

Susannah took a step toward him, hands resting on her hips. "*That child*," she pointed out, "has a name. It's Victoria. And she is your daughter."

"Whatever you say," he answered. "I'll accept her as my own if you'll marry me."

She felt her eyes widen, and not for anything in the world would she have admitted to the strange, dizzying sense of hope welling up inside her. "That is very noble of you, Mr. Fairgrieve, considering that she *is* your own."

"Stop hedging," he said. "I require an answer."

"You came home to ask me to marry you?" She was incredulous.

"No," he answered in his forthright way. "I came home because I forgot some important papers when I left the house this morning. Finding you directly in the pathway of a band of Christian soldiers, bearing torches and on the march, I decided to come to your rescue with a proposal. Take it or leave it."

"Suppose I leave it?"

"Then you might as well leave the baby—Victoria— too. The good ladies who've just graced us with their presence will make life intolerable for you—and for me—if you stay after they've warned you. Worse, they'll eventually shun Victoria as well." He paused to let the pronouncement sink in. "In the eyes of the law, if not of God and creation, Victoria is indeed my child. I'll keep her here until she's five or so, then send her back east to boarding school."

"You wouldn't do such a callous thing!" She cried. But she knew he would. He did not hate Victoria, but he did not love her, either. Never lacking for anything material, she might nonetheless be raised by strangers, utterly without the more tender affections.

"Marry me," he said flatly.

Susannah was once again stricken to silence. It was a long time before she could speak again. "Would you— would I—?"

"We would," Aubrey confirmed.

Heat surged into Susannah's face, and for an awful moment, she thought she might actually swoon into the parlor chair now pressing against the backs of her knees. Oddly enough, the sensation wasn't entirely unpleasant. "What—what about Mr. Hollister?" she asked. Although the other man had not declared himself, he had intimated that his intentions toward her were serious ones.

"He won't," Aubrey said with a grin. "Not with you, anyway."

She collapsed into the chair recently occupied by Mrs. Shimclad, which was still warm from that good woman's ample bottom. She ought to leave, Susannah thought, just pack up her belongings and go, before she made some irretrievable mistake, but Aubrey would never let her take Victoria, and she could not leave her behind.

"This is merely some whim," she accused.

Aubrey came to stand before her. Bending down, he gripped either arm of her chair and looked straight into her face. He smelled pleasantly of soap and salt air, and the very proximity of him caused an aching heat inside her. "It is no whim, Susannah," he replied. "Believe me. I've been pacing my study half the night, thinking about it."

"But it would be a loveless marriage."

"I have told you what I think of love," Aubrey answered. "It's a fable, for fools to break themselves to pieces upon. Our union would be practical, serving both our purposes. Think of it, Susannah. You would be the mistress of this house. You would have all the money you ever wanted. And when you've given me a son or two, you may feel free to do as you like—travel the world, take up a separate residence in New York or London or San Francisco, wherever you like."

He had not moved, and Susannah felt paralyzed by his nearness, rather like a mouse faced with a snake, although, strangely and much to her surprise, she wasn't the least bit frightened. "Would you be faithful?" she asked. It was the first chink in her armor, and he knew that, damn him, and smiled.

"If you were," he countered, not unpleasantly. "God help you, though, if you make a cuckold of me the way Julia did."

Susannah wet her lips nervously with the tip of her tongue. It scared her how much she wanted to agree, and shamed her a little, too. Aubrey had been *Julia's* husband, after all. "But you would swear not to take a mistress?"

He raised one hand, though he still loomed over her, strong, coatless, and hard-muscled in his crisply ironed, starch-scented shirt. "I swear," he replied.

"Julia was my—my friend—"

"You were hers. She was no one's. Susannah, don't you see? By giving her daughter the best possible life, you'll be settling any debt to Julia, real or imagined."

She hesitated for a long time. "I must think this through," she murmured, at last, and left the room.

Aubrey tried his damnedest to get drunk that night, but the more whiskey he consumed, the more clear-headed he became. The stuff affected him like day-old coffee, souring his stomach and giving him more energy than any man in his right mind could ever need.

Not that he was in his right mind. He hadn't been able to make that particular claim since the day he found Susannah McKittrick standing in the upper hall-way of his house, looking at him as though *he* were the intruder. When, precisely, had she descended upon him like the plagues of Egypt? It seemed to him that he had known her longer than Julia, longer even than Ethan . . .

Idiocy. That's what it was.

He slammed his glass down onto the surface of his desk, and the sound drew Maisie—she stood peering around the edge of the study door, bristly eyebrows wriggling.

"Congratulations," she said.

Aubrey glared at her. "None are in order."

She approached him, undaunted. She glanced from the half-empty bottle to the glass in his hand and shook her head. "It ain't natural. You could soak in that stuff for a month, and it wouldn't even wrinkle your skin."

In spite of his gloomy mood, Aubrey laughed. "I trust there is some reason for this interview?" he said.

Maisie drew up a chair and sat down. "You're doin' a smart thing by gettin' yourself hitched up with Susan-nah. She's about ten times too good for you—might mean your salvation, if you play your cards right."

Aubrey leaned back in his chair. "My salvation, is it? Have you taken up with the Benevolence Society, Maisie?" She was, in point of fact, the best representation of Christian dedication he had ever known, but he didn't tell her that because she wouldn't have listened.

She gave a gruff chuckle. "They'll irrigate the devil's back forty and plant corn afore that happens."

"I don't suppose you'd care to join me in a drink? Merely for purposes of celebration, of course."

"You know I don't take spirits," Maisie answered with a sniff. "What do you think they use to keep them fires of hell burnin' so hot?"

He took a cheroot from his shirt pocket, held it in his teeth, and lighted it with a wooden match. Watching Maisie through the smoke, he raised one foot onto the surface of the desk, then another. "What brings you in here at this hour?" he asked, ignoring her rhetorical question. He drew out his watch, flipped open the lid, and frowned at it. "Great Scot, it's after midnight. Think of your reputation."

"Everybody knows I'd never take up with the likes of you," Maisie shot back, but she was grinning her gapped, mischievous grin. "Now, Miss Susannah, well, I do believe she's sweet on you. She'll make a fine wife."

Aubrey said nothing but simply watched his friend and housekeeper through the thickening haze of cheroot smoke.

"I reckon what I want to say is this," Maisie went on, as he'd known she would if he gave her adequate space. "You've got a lot of bitterness in you. If this weddin' is some kind of joke to you, then you better just leave that young woman alone. There's plenty of other men wantin' to make her acquaintance—I've got 'em comin' to both doors all the day long, just hopin' for a look at her. She deserves to be happy, and if you get in the way of that, you and me, we won't be friends no more."

It was no rash pledge; Maisie wasn't capable of an idle promise. What she said was precisely what she meant, whatever the subject. And Aubrey felt a pang of sorrow at the prospect of losing her regard. "You don't have much confidence in me, do you?" he countered.

She frowned. "Truth is, I don't know *what* to think. When you found Miss Susannah here, you were civil enough, but you sure weren't friendly. You ain't had but a few kind words to say to her from that day to this. And now, all of the sudden, because a bunch of old bats came in here beatin' on the Good Book and prophesyin' a rain of hellfire, you ask her to marry you! Sounds a little too much like dallyin' to me."

Aubrey was touched by Maisie's devotion to Susannah, and a little envious of it in the bargain. "If Miss McKittrick keeps her part of the agreement, I will keep mine. Was I such a bad husband to Julia?"

Maisie sighed. "She was troubled, that one. You judged her harshlike. When you come right down to it, I believe you think ever'body's out to do you in, 'cause of your pa and Miss Julia and all."

Aubrey lowered his feet to the floor and sat forward. "What do you know about my family?"

"What Ethan told me," Maisie said staunchly. "That your pa was a mean-spirited man, and your mama lit out when the pair of you were hardly bigger'n my Jasper."

He was quietly furious that Ethan had betrayed a family secret the likes of that one, but then, he shouldn't have been surprised. With his brother, betrayal was a way of life. "You'd better get yourself to bed," he said, rising. "Morning will come around early."

Maisie got up. "Don't you hurt Miss Susannah. That's all I'm sayin'. Don't you hurt that girl. She's had pain aplenty in her life, and she's gone on despite it, and I won't see you punishin' her for some other woman's sins." She jabbed at his chest with one index finger. "You hear me?"

"Very clearly," Aubrey replied, ready to retire himself, before the drinking made him any more sober than he already was. "No doubt, the neighbors did, too."

Maisie harrumphed and trundled out of the study without replying.

Aubrey followed her as far as the kitchen, where he drew himself a glass of water to take upstairs, and she hesitated on the threshold of the small room she shared with her son.

"You're a good man," she said when he simply waited for her to speak, "but you got demons chasin' you. You gotta stop runnin', turn around, and face 'em down."

With that, Maisie turned and disappeared, closing her door behind her.

Aubrey stood there in his kitchen for a long moment, looking inside himself and not particularly liking what he saw.

Finally, he climbed the rear stairs and stood in the hallway looking toward Susannah's faraway door. He wanted to make peace with her, to tell her that he truly wanted to marry her, and that he wanted that marriage to work, but every time they spoke, he just seemed to make matters worse.

He didn't sleep at all well that night, and the first thing in the morning, he had Hawkins send for Hollister.

Hawkins went to do his bidding right away. It was a quality Aubrey appreciated in other people, and it was all too rare these days, if you asked him.

He had barely settled down to go over a contract with a wholesale merchant in San Francisco—the negotiations had been the reason for his trip down the coast, and his interests had not been served in the matter—when Hollister burst in without even waiting to be announced.

"I'm off the case," he said.

Aubrey laid down his pen and looked up at the other man, who was chomping at the bit and red in the face. In fact, the skin above his tight celluloid collar looked as though it were going to burst. "What?"

"I want to court Susannah McKittrick," Hollister said. He made no move to sit down, and Aubrey neither rose nor offered the visitor a chair. "I can't do that, in good conscience, if I am prying into her past."

"I beg your pardon?"

"I think you heard me," Hollister blustered. "I don't care if she's an ax murderer or a typhoid carrier. Susannah is a very special woman."

"Very true," Aubrey agreed. "What do you think her opinion of you will be after she finds out that you're a Pinkerton, hired expressly to investigate her?"

Hollister wavered slightly, then got hold of himself. "No doubt she will be disturbed. I should think her reaction to the news that you were the one to hire me in the first place would be equally interesting."

Aubrey had already thought of that. He'd been up half the night; he'd already thought of most everything. "Susannah knows I'm a son-of-a-bitch. As for you, well, she thought you were a gentleman."

"Damnation," Hollister muttered. Aubrey almost felt sorry for him. Almost, but not quite. The Pinkerton gathered himself together and braced up. "I'll just have to go to her and make a clean breast of things," he said. Then he flushed purple.

Had they been discussing any other woman on earth, Aubrey would have laughed. As it was, he found himself grappling with a ridiculous urge to work violence on a man he considered a close associate, even a friend. At last, he did Hollister the courtesy of standing. "You're fired," he said evenly.

"I quit," Hollister replied.

"I've asked Susannah to be my wife."

That news got through to Hollister as nothing else had. His eyes bulged a little, and his neck turned a shade of mingled lavender and pink. Aubrey wondered if he should summon a doctor.

"And her response?" the detective asked quietly. For all the discoloration of his flesh, he held himself with manly dignity.

"She hasn't given one," Aubrey said with a sigh he had not meant to release. He sat down again, suddenly weary. "But she'll agree, Hollister, if only because that's the only way she can stay with the child. Sit down. You look as if your jugular is about to rupture."

Hollister hesitated a few moments, then dragged over a chair and sat. Only then did he think of removing his bowler hat, which he held in both hands, turning it round and round by the narrow brim. "You *are* a son-of-a-bitch," he said, "if you'd use that little baby to get the woman you want."

"I generally get what I want," Aubrey answered, but he sounded rueful, even in his own ears. Oddly enough, he'd never been so serious about any enterprise as he was about taking Susannah to wife. "And I should tell you that the Ladies' Christian Benevolence Society is on my side."

At last, Hollister laughed, though the look in his eyes held nothing of humor. He'd been done an injury—he truly cared for Susannah—and Aubrey was sorry that it had come to this. On the other hand, it wasn't his fault that the other man had developed tender sentiments for a woman he was supposed to be investigating. Come to think of it, it was downright unprofessional.

"If she hasn't agreed," the Pinkerton said at some length, "that means I still have a chance to win her. I do not intend to give up until the lady herself tells me there is no hope."

Aubrey spread his hands in acquiescence and tried to look unconcerned, but deep down he wasn't at all certain that Susannah wouldn't choose Hollister over him. She had to know that he wouldn't really keep her from seeing little Victoria—didn't she? That was a bluff, the only ace in his hand. He made a steeple of his fingers and rested his chin on it. "Fair enough," he said.

"Do you love her?" It was a personal question, even coming from a detective, and Aubrey bristled a little.

"I think love is a fatuous concept. Susannah is well aware of my opinion in the matter."

Hollister stood again and reached across the desk. The two men shook hands, in the way of duelists about to turn back to back and walk their ten paces before firing at each other, and then the detective left the room.

Aubrey was immediately on his feet. "Hawkins!" he yelled, fussing with his string tie.

The young man burst into the room. He was a scrawny fellow, too prissy for the timber camps and too smart to go running off to the Alaskan Territory looking for gold. "Yes, sir?"

"We're having a party. Start planning it."

Hawkins swallowed visibly. "A-a party, sir?"

"You know," Aubrey replied impatiently, "one of those affairs where people dance and eat fancy food."

"Where would we hold this festivity, sir?"

"Stop calling me 'sir.' At my house, of course. What do you think I built it for?"

"I didn't exactly know why you built it, s—Mr. Fairgrieve. Surely you don't expect me to arrange—?"

"Never mind," Aubrey snapped. "Maisie will handle

it. Just pay the bills when they come in, and make sure everybody who should get an invitation does. Can you manage that?"

"Yes, s—er—yes." Hawkins looked earnest and straightened his own tie. "Do I understand you to say that money is no object?"

"That," said Aubrey, his hand on the door knob, "is exactly what I'm saying."

Chapter

8

~

*S*he sat propped up on her bed, fat pillows plumped at her back, reading while baby Victoria slept nearby in the cradle. Snowflakes wafted past the high, narrow window, light as a fall of fairies' wings, but Susannah, who loved extreme weather of any sort, spared them only the occasional glance. She was immersed in Ethan's poetry, ostensibly composed in tribute to Julia, and while certain passages caused her to blush, she could not bring herself to put the book aside before the last page.

What must it be like, to be loved so powerfully, so well?

She sighed. It wasn't so much that the verses were explicit in any unseemly way; they weren't, and yet by their very intimacy, by their startling honesty, they conveyed a passion of truly mythical proportions. Were a man—especially one so winsome as Ethan Fairgrieve—to woo her with such chivalrous words and images, under other circumstances, of course, she might not be able to resist temptation. Had that been Julia's dilemma? Honor an empty, foundering marriage, or give in to the raw, unrestrained adoration of a lover?

But he'd loved a woman named Su Lin; he'd told her so himself. Furthermore, he'd said Su Lin was the *only* woman he'd ever loved.

A tap at the door interrupted her musings. "Yes?" she asked, and wished she'd cleared her throat first, because the word came out sounding hoarse.

Maisie put her head inside the room, beaming. "There's gonna be a party," she said, as breathless as if she were announcing the arrival of a prince bearing a glass slipper in just Susannah's size. "Right here. Next Saturday night."

"Here?" Susannah asked.

"Well, not in your room, ninny," Maisie replied with good-natured scorn. "Downstairs, in that part of the house that's been closed off since the missus passed on. I can spend whatever I like for food and gewgaws, too. Hawkins says I've got 'cart blank.' "

Susannah suppressed a smile, set Ethan's book aside, and stood, straightening her skirts. "I'll be glad to help, of course."

Maisie peered down the corridor, then slipped stealthily into the bedroom and shut the door behind her. "I'll bet my garters that Mr. Fairgrieve means to give you an engagement ring that night. He's had poor Hawkins runnin' all day, sendin' wires from here to Sunday breakfast. The man's near tuckered out—like to meet himself comin' or goin'."

Susannah had hoped that Aubrey would forget his decree regarding their marriage, but at the same time she was ridiculously pleased to know he hadn't. "But I haven't accepted Mr. Fairgrieve's proposal," she said.

"You'd be a fool if you said no to an offer like that," Maisie retorted. "It ain't delicate to say, you bein' a beautiful woman and all, but you're gettin' a little long in the tooth. There'll be bids comin' in right along, I reckon, but the fellers are bound to get uglier and poorer with every passin' day."

Susannah erupted with soft laughter, careful not to awaken Victoria. "Maisie, you are no diplomat," she said.

"Be that as it may," Maisie replied, "you know it's true." With that, she turned and left the room.

For a few moments, Susannah just sat there, motionless, in a state akin to shock. She had no doubt that Maisie's theories on the declining quality of suitors were sound ones, but the implications of being described as beautiful were harder to sort through. She went to the bureau and stood looking at herself in the wavy mirror above it.

She was tall, for a woman, and her hair was a nice, pale wheat color. Her eyes were gray and quite large. She had a good, straight carriage. She frowned critically. But, no, she was decidedly *not* beautiful—her mouth was too wide and her cheekbones slightly too prominent. A faint spray of freckles spattered her nose, evidence of too many summers spent playing kickball in the dooryard of St. Mary's.

Julia—*Julia*—had been the beauty. And that very distinction had destroyed her, in the end.

Susannah turned her back on the mirror and went to stand at the window, looking out, watching darkness gather, while the snowfall intensified. A little old man moved along the street, lighting the wicks of the tall lamps. Their glass doors creaked on metal hinges as he opened and closed them.

She was still standing there, some minutes later, when Maisie sounded the dinner bell from the base of the kitchen stairs. Victoria stirred, cooed, and went back to sleep with a fluttering of lashes and a tiny sigh that pinched the back of Susannah's heart.

After making certain the baby was dry and covered, she washed her hands and face in the elegant bath chamber, tightened the pins holding her hair in a loose bun at the back of her head, and made her way to the first floor. She had discovered that she could hear Victoria from the kitchen if she left the door of her bedroom open.

Maisie was bustling about, setting bowls and platters on the table, and Susannah immediately noticed that there were two places set. One was surely hers, but the other would belong to a visitor, since Aubrey generally insisted on taking the evening meal in the dining room.

She tossed a questioning glance at Maisie, who was pummeling boiled potatoes with a metal masher. The older woman stepped around Jasper and his toy fire wagon without so much as looking down, setting the large crockery bowl on the table, where a platter of fried chicken and a dish of baked squash awaited.

"Ethan's here," Maisie said. "Mr. Fairgrieve sent word that he'll be workin' late tonight."

Susannah felt an unfounded twinge of jealousy; was Aubrey really at the store, or had he already resumed his relationship with Delphinia Parker?

"Don't be lookin' like that," Maisie scolded, evidently as skilled at mind reading as she was at cooking and cleaning, as Jasper came over to the table and assessed the contents of the chicken platter. "It ain't just the store, you know. Mr. Fairgrieve has interests all over the state. Why, he's got stocks and bonds, and he's even a partner in one of them gold mines up north."

Susannah handed the little boy a drumstick, after making sure it wasn't too hot. Before she could think of a retort, Ethan strolled in, the sleeves of his shirt rolled up, his muscular forearms still glistening from a recent washing. His fair hair was neatly tied back, and he wore lightweight woolen trousers and polished boots.

"Evening, Susannah," he said.

Maisie snatched up Jasper and the chicken leg, making a hasty assessment of the table and the state of the kitchen in general. "That's a good day's work as far as I'm concerned," she declared. "Just leave them dishes, Susannah. I'll do 'em up in the mornin'."

Within a few moments, Maisie had retired to her room, taking the reluctant Jasper along with her.

Alone with Ethan, Susannah couldn't help thinking of the hours she'd spent poring over his most private thoughts, and she felt like a sneak thief. At the same time, it wasn't in her to pretend ignorance.

"I have something that belongs to you," she said obliquely, and retreated back up the stairs to her room. Victoria was still sleeping, so Susannah snatched up the handwritten volume of poetry and went again to the kitchen.

Ethan had not taken a seat at the table, though the food was cooling off, but instead waited politely, arms folded, leaning back against the sink. When he saw the book, his eyes narrowed, and the warmth of his manner gave way instantly to a bone-biting chill.

"Where did you get that?"

She surrendered the book. "Aubrey gave it to me."

Ethan held the volume in both hands, as though to lose his grasp would be a tragedy, like dropping an infant or a precious piece of porcelain. "*Aubrey?*" he asked, apparently dumbstruck.

Susannah had certainly not intended to cause more trouble between the two brothers, but the poetry belonged to Ethan—he'd conjured every word in the innermost regions of his heart, after all—and she would not keep it from him. Seeing his reaction to recovering the volume, she knew she had been right to return it, whatever the consequences. "Sit down," she said gently.

"Maisie worked very hard making supper, and, besides, you looked hungry until you caught sight of that book."

He drew back her chair, waited while she took it, then went around to sink into his own. He laid the tome beside him on the table, pondering it with a frown. "Where did Aubrey get this?"

Susannah offered a silent prayer, not only in gratitude for the plentiful food set before her but that she might say the right things, the gentlest things, without betraying the truth. "Julia gave it to him."

Ethan gave up all pretense of eating and stared at Susannah as though she'd just announced that she was growing another index finger. "Julia?" he echoed.

"He believes you wrote those poems for her." She speared a piece of chicken, scooped out a serving of mashed potatoes, helped herself to squash—and touched none of it.

Ethan closed his eyes and sat back in his chair for a long moment, keeping his own counsel. When he looked at Susannah again, he was much more composed. "That little—"

Susannah cleared her throat quickly. Whatever Julia might have done, it wasn't right or fair to speak ill of the dead.

"It's a lie," Ethan said miserably.

"I know," Susannah said. "You were writing about Su Lin, weren't you?"

He gave a taut nod, frowned again. "You've read them?" A raspy sigh escaped him. "Of course you have. And so has Aubrey, if he's convinced himself that they were composed for his wife. Damnation."

Susannah dared to reach across the table and touch his hand, though in a sisterly way. "They're wonderful, Ethan," she said. "I've never seen anything quite like them."

He pushed his plate away, propped his elbows on the table's edge, and rested his head in his hands. "Sweet God," he breathed wearily. Almost brokenly. "How could she do that?"

Susannah waited; she knew he didn't expect an answer, and she wouldn't have had one to give if he had.

After a long time had passed, Ethan met Susannah's steady gaze again. She wanted to look away, but she had pried into his private affairs, and she would not flinch from the responsibilities entailed in such an intrusion. "After Su Lin left for China, I started writing those verses," he said. "It was all that kept me from losing my mind. I had to have a place to put all the things I wished I'd said to her."

Tears sprang to Susannah's eyes, and she was inspired, once more, to touch Ethan, this time taking his hand in her own. She was a romantic at heart, and for all its tragedy, the story was a poignant one. "She must have known how you felt—"

"Isn't this cozy?" The intruding voice, sharp as a freshly ground blade, was Aubrey's. He stood in the inner doorway, still wearing his great coat, snowflakes melting in his butternut hair and on his broad shoulders. He wrenched off his leather gloves, one at a time, and stuffed them into his pocket. "Once wasn't enough, Ethan?"

Ethan shot to his feet, but not, Susannah could see, because he was afraid. No, he was coldly angry, perhaps angrier than Aubrey. His chair tipped over with a clatter, and upstairs Victoria began to wail.

"You should both be ashamed," Susannah cried, rising herself and snatching up her skirts. "You've frightened the baby!" With that, she turned her back on the pair of them and hurried up the stairs to collect and comfort Victoria. Below, in the kitchen, she heard Aubrey and Ethan speaking in more moderate tones, but the whole house seemed to reverberate with their combined fury. It was as though two thunderstorms were about to collide in the middle of an open sky.

"You had no right!" Ethan snarled, tapping Aubrey in the chest with one end of the volume of love poems.

"*I* had no right?" Aubrey countered in a furious rasp. Keeping his voice down was the second hardest challenge facing him at the moment; the first was keeping himself from knocking his younger brother on his ass. "Julia was my wife!"

"Yes," Ethan growled, "God help you." He made for the doorway, and Aubrey stopped him by grasping his arm. He immediately wrenched free. "I will tell you this once, brother, and once only. Your precious Julia was a selfish, scheming little bitch with a mean streak wider than the best vein in the Klondike, and I wouldn't have had her on a bet." He waggled the slender book between his fingers as evidence. "Looks like she was a thief in the bargain."

Aubrey had a sick feeling in the pit of his stomach; the kind he got on those relatively rare occasions when he found out he'd been wrong about something. He hated being wrong. "Ethan—"

His brother replied with an expletive better suited to a saloon than a decent household, but Aubrey didn't blame him. He felt like shouting out the same oath and was prevented only by the sure and certain knowledge that Susannah would have his hide if he did. He watched in silence as Ethan walked out of the kitchen.

Presently, the front door slammed, and the sound caused Aubrey to flinch.

He was still standing there, in the center of the room, when Susannah reappeared, feathers smoothed, baby bottle in hand.

"I hope you're proud of yourself," she said as she

washed the bottle, took milk from the icebox, and poured it into a pan to heat.

Aubrey said nothing. For once in his life, he was at a loss for words.

After setting the pan of milk on the stove, stirring up the embers in the grate, and adding a chunk of firewood, Susannah turned to glare at him, arms akimbo. "Well?"

"Well, what?"

"Have you driven him away, once and for all? Your only brother?"

Aubrey thrust a hand through his hair. Ethan. His brother. What had he done? "I don't know," he admitted, feeling an overwhelming weariness settle over him. Then, again, "I don't know."

"Sit down," Susannah said.

He sat. He'd used up the last of his fight on Ethan.

Susannah crossed to the table and began clearing away the food, removing the platter of chicken just as Aubrey reached for a thigh. He wasn't quick enough.

"If you had any sense at all, you'd go after him," she fumed. "Apologize. Talk this thing through, settle the matter once and for all."

He refused to reply, mostly because he didn't know what to say. His pride was lodged in his throat, dry and scuffed as an old boot.

She had scalded the milk in her earnestness and had to start the whole process over again. Upstairs, Victoria's wails intensified, and in that moment, it came to Aubrey that he loved the child, whether she was his or not.

"Go and get her," Susannah said.

He was halfway up the stairs before he realized he'd just obeyed an order. He couldn't remember the last time he had done that.

Entering Susannah's room, Aubrey was immediately struck by an intrinsic sense of her most private self. Her petticoat lay spilling across the foot of the bed, in intriguing disarray, and there were books, purloined from his study for the most part, piled on every surface. Her soft, unique scent teased his nostrils.

Victoria squalled, effectively regaining his attention. He went to the cradle and lifted the baby into his arms. He'd held the infant fairly often, out of necessity, but never with the certain knowledge that she was his own, whether she was his flesh and blood or not. "Hush," he said awkwardly. "There's a bottle brewing downstairs." They were midway down the rear stairway when she wet on his shirt, a christening he supposed he deserved, all things considered. "Susannah," he said.

"What?" she asked testily.

He reentered the kitchen. "She's wet."

"Then change her."

"I beg your pardon?"

"You know. Take Victoria back upstairs and put a fresh diaper on her. Then bring her back down, and I'll feed her in the rocking chair by the stove."

"Couldn't you—?"

"You," Susannah said pointedly, testing the contents of the bottle on the inside of her left wrist—a place Aubrey wanted very much, all of the sudden, to kiss, "are her father."

Aubrey sighed and did as he was told. Only after he'd presented Susannah with a clean if crotchety baby did he go to his own room to wash and change his shirt. When he returned to the kitchen again, Victoria was snuggled against Susannah's shoulder.

"Are you asleep?" He was filled with a wild, careening sort of tenderness, seeing the woman and child in such an ancient, ordinary pose. It frightened him, how much he might come to care for them, if things progressed as they had been.

Susannah opened her eyes. "No."

He stood with his back to the stove, pretending to warm his hands. In fact, he merely wanted to be near Susannah for a while, near his daughter. "What have you decided?" he asked quietly.

"About what?" Susannah asked, her voice very soft. Not for his sake, he knew, but for Victoria's.

"Our getting married," he said, surprised that she'd forgotten. He knew what Maisie had said was true; there were a great many men in Seattle who would give their last good tooth to have Susannah for a wife, Hollister included. Still, she was a spinster by her own admission, damnably fetching or not, and certainly penniless.

She patted Victoria's tiny back rhythmically, and the baby gave a belch that would have done a lumberjack proud. "I'm going to call your bluff, as they say in the game of poker," she said. "I won't marry you. I'm gambling that you won't part Victoria and me because you know she needs me."

He stared at her. "Do you realize—?"

"How many women would like to marry you? Oh, yes. Maisie told me, and I could have guessed anyway. After all, you are very attractive—er—physically, and it certainly appears that you are more than solvent. But I fear you have no poetry in your soul, and, now that I've read Ethan's verses, I know what I want from the man I marry. Romance. Passion. Steadfastness."

"You want Ethan?" It would be a bitter irony if she did.

She smiled sleepily. "Of course not. He still loves Su Lin."

He frowned. *Who?* he thought, and promptly decided to pursue the question later. "Hollister, then?"

She shook her head. "John Hollister is no more sentimental than you are, I'm afraid. Bless his soul. Anyway, he deserves a woman who truly cares for him, and while I think he is a wonderful man—"

"You needn't extol his virtues," Aubrey broke in. "And what makes you so da—so certain that I'm incapable of ardent emotions?"

She continued to rock, considering him appraisingly, as though he were a plucked chicken hanging in the butcher's window or a sway-backed horse on the auction block. "If you wish to marry me, Aubrey Fairgrieve," she had the audacity to say, "you will have to court me. As of right now, I am receiving gentleman callers."

"Not in my house, you're not!"

She was undaunted. "Furthermore," she went on, as though he hadn't spoken, "I intend to take in piano students. We discussed that, if you recall. You have been very generous, but I must have an income of my own, however modest."

No one, not even Julia, had ever dared to flout his authority like that. And right there, under his own roof. "I could turn you out into the snow, right now—tonight," he said mildly. Reasonably.

"Yes," she conceded, standing slowly in order not to disturb the baby, now nodding against her bosom. "You could do that. But I'm sure Ethan would take me in. So would Mr. Hollister, I think. Or, of course, there's always Reverend Johnstone."

He rubbed his right temple. "All right," he said. "All right. You can stay, for now, at least. But this other matter isn't settled, not by any means."

She smiled sweetly from the base of the rear stairs. "Whatever you say," she replied, and disappeared.

He paced awhile, feeling like a race horse confined in a closet, then found his coat and went out again. It was colder than when he came in, and the stableboy had headed for home. Aubrey saddled his gelding himself, mounted, and made for Ethan's place.

It took an hour to reach the small cabin in the hills above Seattle, but there was light in the windows, which was probably a good sign.

He put the gelding in the stock shed, with Ethan's horse, before approaching the door of the cabin. "Let me in, damn it," he shouted after the third round of knocking failed to rouse a response. "I'm freezing to death out here."

The door creaked open on its rusty hinges. The old place had never been a palace, but it had gone downhill since Aubrey had seen it last. "Go back to your mansion," Ethan snapped, barring Aubrey's way. "I've got nothing to say to you."

"Well, I've got something to say to you." Aubrey pushed past his brother and headed for the fireplace, where a low blaze burned. He remembered frying trout there, when they were kids. Remembered the day their father had taken a horse whip to Ethan, and he, Aubrey, had wrenched the lash out of the old man's hand and sworn he'd kill him if he ever saw his face again. From that day to this, he hadn't caught so much as a glimpse of Tom Fairgrieve, and he had no regrets on that score.

Out of the corner of his eye, Aubrey saw the volume of poetry lying on the large cable spool that served as a table.

"I'm sorry," he said. The price of those simple words was higher than any he'd ever paid in hard currency.

Ethan leaned closer, his blue eyes flashing, even in the dim light of that old cabin, with its sod roof and rough board floors and grim memories. "What was that?" he said. "I didn't hear you, big brother."

Aubrey closed his eyes in a bid for patience. The situation called for humility, and he had that aplenty, but he also had more than his share of pride. Without that, he knew he would not have survived, would not have built an empire, but it was time to set it aside, however briefly. "I said I'm sorry," he replied in a louder voice. "Julia told me you'd given her the book, and I believed her."

Ethan turned his back. His shoulders were stiff, his spine straight as a ramrod. "You know, Aubrey," he said, his voice low and harsh with fury, "that doesn't make a hell of a lot of sense, in view of the sort of woman she was."

Aubrey sighed, shrugged out of his coat, dragged back one of the crude chairs at the spool table, and sat down. "I'm ready to hear it," he said, folding his arms.

"Hear what?" Ethan was facing him now, but his features were in shadow, and Aubrey could tell nothing by his voice.

"The rest of the sordid tale. Julia wanted you, didn't she? In fact, she probably threw herself at you. Am I wrong?"

His brother pushed a hand through his hair, now brushing his shoulders like that of an Indian, and huffed out a sigh of his own. "You, wrong?" he scoffed. "I didn't think such a thing was possible."

"Talk to me," Aubrey insisted.

Ethan was silent for a long time. He stood behind the chair opposite Aubrey's, his hands gripping the top rail, but showed no sign that he intended to sit down. "She came out here a couple of times. She wasn't happy, Aubrey. I don't think it was your fault, or hers, either. She was lonesome for the east, and Seattle wasn't what she bargained for."

"I knew she hated it here," Aubrey said quietly. "She made that obvious, on a thousand occasions. But why didn't you tell me about these—visits?"

"What was I supposed to say? 'Your wife wants to sleep with me'? I didn't know what the hell to do, and I was still real torn up about—" He trailed off, fell silent.

"Sit down," Aubrey urged. "It hurts my neck, looking up at you."

"You aren't used to looking up at anybody, are you, Aubrey?"

"I didn't come here to fight."

Ethan swung his chair around and sat astraddle of it, his arms draped across the back. Once again, he ran a hand through his hair. His gaze, usually so direct, was averted. "Julia thought you'd taken a mistress. Hell, to hear her tell it, you had women from here to the Mexican border. I guess she figured she could get revenge by lying down with me." He met Aubrey's eyes with visible effort. "I swear to God I didn't touch her. I wouldn't have done that to you—or to anybody else."

"I know," Aubrey said after a long pause.

"Then why?"

He indicated the battered volume with an inclination of his head. "Partly because of that. She said I'd never be able to sweet-talk a woman the way you did, and she was right. I never will." He thought of Susannah, wanting romance and all the fairy-tale trimmings, and felt despair settle over his shoulders like a mantle. "Words aren't my gift, Ethan. I like numbers. They make sense to me—you know just what's what when you're dealing with a column of figures. There are rules that apply. But words?" He spread his hands.

Ethan laughed. It was the first time they'd shared a friendly exchange since well before Julia's death. "You've done all right with numbers, brother. Just take a look at your bank accounts if you're inclined to feel doubtful."

"Women don't care about things like that."

"Women?" Ethan prompted. "Or Susannah? I'd say most females have a marked fondness for money, same as men do. But she's different, isn't she?"

"From everyone I've ever known," Aubrey admitted. "Do you keep any whiskey around this place?"

"No," Ethan answered with good-natured gravity. "Are you hell-bent on turning out like Dad, or what? That stuff is bad for you, like those cheroots you're always smoking."

Aubrey forcibly relaxed his jawline. "I don't want to talk about Dad," he said.

"There's a whole passel of things you don't want to talk about," Ethan pointed out. "This is a start, though. Are you sweet on Susannah?"

"You're not going to let that drop, are you?"

Ethan flashed another of his famous grins. "Not real soon," he answered.

Chapter

9

~

It was frosty out the next morning, though the snow had stopped. Susannah, having left Victoria in Maisie's competent care, bundled up in her cloak and struck out for the churchyard around the corner. Given the size of Aubrey's house and grounds, the walk was not as short as one might think.

After letting herself into the cemetery through the icy iron gate, Susannah walked over to Julia's grand monument, drew back one foot, and kicked at the base. "How could you have done such things?" she hissed. "How could you open a chasm like that between two brothers?"

To her surprise, Susannah realized that she was crying. She sniffled and touched the side of her wrist to her nose. Although she hadn't kicked the mausoleum very hard, her toes, already half frozen inside her scuffed high-button shoes, ached from the blow.

"I thought I knew you," she murmured.

Julia didn't answer, of course, and Susannah was at a loss. The whole exercise of confronting her dead friend was, of course, a pointless one. She lingered only a few more minutes, then hurried home to shiver out of her cloak and warm her hands before the kitchen stove.

Maisie walloped a serving of cornmeal mush into a bowl and set it on the table with a telling thump. "You'd better eat," she said. "A person's got to keep up her strength around here."

Susannah certainly couldn't disagree with that. She sat down to take a meal, reaching for the crockery pitcher of milk, then the rough brown sugar that was still a luxury to her. Neither St. Mary's nor Mrs. Butterfield had found room in the budget for sweets of any sort. "Mr. Fairgrieve has left the house already, I imagine," she said between hearty spoonfuls of cereal. Never in her life, until she'd come to live in that house, had she had as much to eat as she wanted. She hoped she wouldn't succumb to corpulence.

"Don't think he came home at all," Maisie answered, her eyes too busy to meet Susannah's. "I went up to his room a little while back—I was after the sheets, this bein' wash day—and his bed ain't been slept in."

It should not matter to her, Susannah thought dispiritedly, that Aubrey had passed the night under some other roof, but it did. She had no claim on him, especially since she had refused his proposal. Still, she wanted more than anything, in those first moments, to push aside her breakfast, lay her head down on her arms, and weep inconsolably. She didn't give in to that cowardly desire, however; long experience had taught her that she must be strong and depend only upon herself, whenever possible.

"I see," she said.

Maisie was distracted, worried-looking. She kept peering out through the window, trying to see through the fans and curlicues of frost coating the glass. Jasper, home from school again, was listless and wan.

"Is something wrong with Jasper?" Susannah asked, ashamed that she had been so caught up in her own concerns that she hadn't noticed Maisie's uneasy manner before then.

"I sent a stable hand for the doc," Maisie answered. "It troubles me, Jasper feelin' so poorly. He's got a little fever, too."

Susannah was alarmed, not only because Jasper was ill but because sickness could so easily spread from one person to another, one household to another. She had a brief, wild, and wholly unrealistic urge to snatch little Victoria from her cradle, wrap her warmly, and flee to somewhere safe. There was no such place, of course, so, instead, she stood and carried her bowl and spoon over to the sink. Water was heating in a kettle on the stove, and she poured some into the large iron basin to wash them.

"It ain't like Jasper to be so quiet," Maisie fretted when Susannah didn't speak.

"Maybe you should put him to bed," Susannah said gently. "He needs rest. I can watch for the doctor and show him in when he gets here."

"There's the wash to do," Maisie said. "And all the cookin', too."

"Never mind that," Susannah told her firmly. "Whatever needs doing, I'll do. You just take care of your son. Please."

"You've got the baby to tend—"

"I'm not helpless," Susannah interrupted, watching Jasper with growing concern. He did not even seem to hear what they were saying; he was just staring off into the beyond with a strange, rapt expression on his face. "I've done my share of laundry in my time, and I'm a proficient cook. After all, I took care of Mrs. Butterfield and her house for nearly seven years."

Maisie's worried eyes settled a moment on Susannah's face, full of gratitude and distress. "What if this is something really bad?" she whispered hoarsely. "They had the scarlet fever down the street, just a month or so back—"

"Hush," Susannah said, taking Maisie's upper arms into her hands. "You're borrowing trouble. We'll just do what lies at hand and wait for the doctor. Right now, all we know is that Jasper doesn't feel well."

Maisie nodded. Her lower lip wobbled. "Thank you," she said.

"I'll make you some tea," Susannah replied. "You go and get Jasper settled in bed."

As soon as Maisie and Jasper were out of sight, Susannah rushed to Victoria's crib upstairs and touched the child's forehead, dreading the very real possibility of a fever, but her flesh was cool to the touch. She murmured a prayer, tucked the blankets more closely around the little form, and hurried back down to the kitchen.

The doctor, a fit man with white hair and dark, insightful eyes, arrived just as Susannah was finishing with Maisie's tea.

"Griffin Fletcher," he said, extending a hand in greeting. "I came in Dr. Martin's place. My friend is out on another call."

Susannah introduced herself, welcomed the physician inside, and took his coat. His manner was brisk but competent, and she found his very presence reassuring. She showed him into Maisie's room, where he was met with relief and one very sick little boy.

Susannah brought in the tea tray without a word and went out again.

Dr. Fletcher and Maisie were a long time returning to the kitchen, and when they did, Maisie's eyes were suspiciously red-rimmed.

"Send word if you need me," Dr. Fletcher said, taking in both Susannah and Maisie in one sweeping glance. "My wife and I are visiting the Martins all this week."

"Thank you, Doctor," Susannah said when Maisie apparently couldn't find her tongue.

He nodded, put on his coat and hat, and left the house, battered bag in hand.

"Maisie, what on earth—?" Susannah whispered.

Maisie sniffled. "He's got the measles," she said.

Susannah's knees nearly buckled. The measles were wildly contagious, of course, and when they weren't fatal, they often left their victims hard of hearing or even blind. She offered up a brief, silent prayer, then sighed, pushed up her sleeves, and set to work.

"Everything is going to be all right," she said, though she wasn't at all sure that was true.

The first order of business was to keep Jasper and Victoria apart, lest the malady spread. She went back upstairs to feed and change Victoria, who was now awake and summoning her quite imperiously, and tucked the pacified baby into a basket padded with a blanket. Then, with the little one nearby, playing contentedly with her toes, Susannah filled the tub in her bathroom with hot water, stirred in some powdered soap, and began to scrub the sheets from Jasper's bed. Maisie had already burned the clothes he'd been wearing in the kitchen stove, along with her own dress, one she could ill afford to lose.

Aubrey found her there some time later, her hair limp from the steam, up to her elbows in yet another tubful of water and soap and soiled laundry. Having gotten off to a good start, she simply continued with the washing.

He grinned. "Very domestic," he said, with only mild sarcasm. "Didn't Maisie tell you that we have a machine for that?"

Susannah was embarrassed that he should catch her kneeling on the floor, with a washboard in one hand and a sheet in the other. "No," she said with what dignity she could manage. "She did not. She's been distracted today." She had not forgotten that he hadn't come home the night before, among other transgressions, but at the moment, that was the least of her concerns.

He peered into the basket at Victoria, who was now sleeping again, still blessedly free of fever and spots, and smiled in a way that softened Susannah's frightened heart just a little. He turned dancing eyes to her. "I must say, Miss McKittrick, you look a sight." He extended one hand. "Stand up. If Maisie is indisposed for some reason, then we'll get someone in to do the wash. Or send it out."

She hesitated, then took his hand, grateful for his help and for the reprieve, although she was indeed accustomed to hard work, had often took refuge in it. Her knees ached as he pulled her up onto her feet. He did not immediately release her fingers and palm from his grasp.

Susannah's heart beat faster, rising until she thought it would choke her, flailing in her throat the way it did. She pulled free and smoothed her skirts, then her hair, knowing all the while that both gestures were futile.

"You are not a housemaid, Susannah," he said quietly. "I expect you to look after the child. Nothing else."

She wondered if he'd been to the kitchen, seen the laundry stretched across it on lengths of twine she had found in a cupboard and secured with considerable difficulty, stringing them between the gaslight fixtures on the wall, suspending them from the backs of chairs. She had had no choice but to hang the wash inside, given the state of the weather, and the room was a steamy maze of wet shirts, towels, and other items.

"Where is Maisie?" he asked patiently, as though speaking to a person who barely understood English.

Susannah felt like weeping, all of the sudden, and wondered if her time of the month was near. She was not good at keeping track of such things anyway, and her life had been in upheaval for a while. "She's with Jasper," she said. "Oh, Aubrey, he has the measles!"

"*What?*"

She couldn't repeat herself, she just couldn't. The news was too terrible to relay a second time.

He crouched beside Victoria's basket and touched her face, a gesture that moved Susannah deeply. "Get your things," he said. "You and the baby can go to a hotel—"

"It's too late for that," she said. "There's nothing to do now but wait and hope."

"Poor Maisie," Aubrey reflected, rising to his feet again. "And you. Susannah, are you all right?"

She nodded. Now, in such close proximity to Aubrey, she saw that he hadn't shaved, and his clothes were rumpled, as though he had worn them for days. "Perhaps I should be asking that of you."

He chuckled, but without humor. "Do you care how I am?" he asked.

"Yes," she answered. Then, flustered, "No. Well, only insofar as you are Victoria's father."

"Ah," he said.

"You do look a little the worse for wear," she allowed.

"I went to Ethan's place, to square things with him. We talked all night."

Susannah believed him. "And did you? Square things, I mean?"

Aubrey sighed. "We made a start. I spent the day helping him saw wood to show I was committed to a truce. As a consequence, I'm hungry enough to eat a side of beef. Come downstairs and have supper with me, Susannah."

It was an ordinary request, really. So why did she feel as though he had suggested something outrageous, something wild, something scandalous? She fussed with her hair again, lowered her reddened hands as quickly as she'd raised them to her nape. "I couldn't take a bite," she said. "But I'll make something for you."

"What good will you be to Victoria or to Maisie and Jasper if you don't keep up your strength?" he asked reasonably.

At last, she relented. "Perhaps a little soup," she agreed.

He hoisted the baby, basket and all, and headed out of the bathroom. Reaching the laundry-draped kitchen, with Susannah just behind him, he gave a low chuckle. "This looks like one of those Chinese establishments down on Water Street," he said.

"Sit down," Susannah ordered, and he obeyed, to her surprise.

She took leftover soup from the icebox, spooned it into a kettle, and set it on the range to heat. Then she made coffee and brought preserved peaches and tinned meat from the pantry.

"How is Maisie holding up?" he asked quietly, taking Victoria from the basket and bouncing her on one knee.

Susannah sighed. "She's terrified, of course. I don't mind admitting that I am, too. For Jasper and for Victoria."

"This one?" he countered gruffly, leaning to kiss the top of the baby's downy head. "She's tough as a lumberjack. So's Jasper, for that matter. It's you and Maisie I'm worried about."

She smiled a little, in spite of herself, comforted by his presence, by his banter, even though it made no sense at all. When it came to the measles and other such diseases, the great Aubrey Fairgrieve was as powerless as everyone else.

"There's talk, you know," he said.

Susannah sighed, opened the icebox again, and

brought out two eggs, which she cracked into a skillet. It would be a hodgepodge of a supper, but it would fill their stomachs. "That's nothing new."

"Because you refused to marry me," he went on as if she hadn't spoken. "The Ladies' Christian Benevolence Society is up in arms."

"Let them fuss," Susannah said. "I have more important matters on my mind just now."

"Still, we could spoil some of the fun by getting married."

A blush surged into Susannah's face; she had no illusion that it went unnoticed. "I have told you," she said carefully, struggling against that part of her that wanted to fling both arms around his neck and surrender to him, "that I will not make sacred vows for the sake of convenience."

He thrust out a sigh, and the lines of his jaw tightened slightly. He was on his feet now, the baby in the crook of one arm. He leaned down, aligning his nose with hers, and she reflected that he smelled pleasantly of wood sap. "You are a contrary female. There is no *better* reason to be married than convenience, and if you weren't such a stubborn bluestocking, determined to counter everything I say, you would admit it."

Victoria began to whimper just then, bless her soul, and Susannah busied herself with the rituals of cooking. "She needs her diaper changed," she said.

"Again?" he replied.

She merely smiled.

He put the baby down in the basket, which immediately got her squalling again, and hurried up the back stairs. In a few minutes, he returned with a tin of talcum powder and stood hovering a few feet away.

"You'll have to do it," she said over the baby's cries. "I'm busy." Although she pretended to be barely aware of Aubrey's presence, in truth she was conscious of him in every part of herself, whether of substance or spirit.

"Do you find me objectionable?" he asked, as if there had been no interruption.

Susannah slanted a look at him. He'd dropped to one knee beside the basket and was now trying to change the diaper. "Yes," she answered. "See that you don't stick her with a pin. And wash your hands when you're finished."

"Why?" he persisted.

"Why wash your hands?"

"Why do you find me objectionable?"

He followed her with his gaze as she worked, moving back and forth among the table, the sink, and the icebox.

"If I'm to go to all the trouble of having a husband, I want one who loves me. Madly. Desperately."

Aubrey laughed outright. "Come now, Susannah. For all your sheltered upbringing, you surely know the truth about such things."

"And that truth is—?"

He was back on his feet, washing his hands at the pump in the sink, then coming to stand directly behind her, a moving wall, hard and warm and full of strength. "That 'love'—the way you're thinking of it, at least—doesn't exist. It's the stuff of pretty stories, told to children and cherished by naive maidens, and you know it. You are too intelligent to think otherwise."

She did not know whether to feel flattered or insulted, and she was well aware that he knew she was confused. That he was enjoying the exchange. She got lost in a flurry of wet laundry and almost started batting at the lines with both hands, out of pure frustration. "If you aren't going to be helpful, kindly just go away."

He paused, took in the array of freshly washed bedding, shirts, and undergarments for a second time. "You have been busy," Aubrey said. "This place looks like an army camp."

Susannah took two chunks of dry pine from the woodbox, opened the stove, and shoved them in. "My options," she said, "were somewhat limited."

"What are you doing?"

"Keeping the fire going," she said, rounding on him with a lofty coolness surely belied by the throbbing heat in her face. "You are starving, and I've just come to realize that I am, too. Would you mind stepping out of the way?"

He looked around at the lines of laundry again, and when he turned his gaze back to her, she saw the shadow of a smile moving in his eyes. "I'm not sure we should separate," he teased. "Not unless one of us leaves a trail of crumbs behind, in any case."

An unexpected laugh escaped Susannah, for all that Jasper was sick and she was terribly worried, about him, about Victoria, about all of them. "I'm beginning to wonder if these things are ever going to dry," she confided, blowing a strand of hair up off her forehead. "And there's still the ironing to do."

His expression had changed in an instant, diametrically opposed to her own. He looked serious, a little sad, and dreadfully, wonderfully competent. He'd taken Victoria out of the basket again, and he held her as easily as if he'd already reared a dozen children. He was comfortable with a baby in his arms, though he did not seem to know this about himself. "Susannah—"

She broke the spell that had held her immobile for several seconds and made yet another trip to the icebox, this time for butter. When she returned, he was right where she'd left him. "You can put Victoria in her basket while you eat," she said.

He stared at her for a few moments longer, then placed his daughter in her improvised bed and took a place at the table. Susannah soon set a large bowl of soup in front of him and brought eggs and toasted bread after that.

He looked down at his food as though surprised to see it there.

Susannah went back to the stove to prepare a plate for Maisie, who was still keeping her vigil at Jasper's bedside.

"Aren't you going to have something?" Aubrey asked when she started toward the door of the small, adjoining bedroom.

"Yes," she said, and her stomach rumbled so loudly then that he heard it and smiled.

Maisie had to be persuaded to eat—there was no change in Jasper's condition—and when Susannah finally returned to the kitchen, she was amazed and more than a little touched to find Aubrey at the stove, taking a loaded plate from the warming oven. He gestured for her to sit, and she obeyed, let him serve her the food, and tucked into it gratefully.

"That was kind of you," she said.

A slight, crooked grin tilted one corner of his mouth. "Even we incorrigible rakes have our generous side," he replied.

She couldn't help smiling. "I'm relieved to hear that."

He chuckled, then, in the space of a heartbeat, turned serious again. "Tell me about St. Mary's."

She chewed, swallowed, sighed. "Julia was—"

"I'm not asking about Julia. I want to know about you. Did you hate the place?"

Her hunger was abating by then, and she ate more slowly. "No," she said. "The nuns were kind. It was a clean place, and we had medical attention when we needed it, decent food if not much of it. There were people who weren't so fortunate."

"What did you do there? Besides learning, staying clean, and having 'medical attention'?"

She knew by the light in his eyes that he was teasing her, knew also that he really wanted to know what St. Mary's had been like for her. "I played the piano whenever I could," she said, "and I helped in the infirmary sometimes. Sometimes there was a rash of new babies, and a few of us helped the sisters care for them."

"You like children," he said. It was a statement, not a question.

"Of course I do," she replied, glancing toward Victoria's basket. "I should think that would be obvious."

"Oh, it is," he allowed, staring at the butter knife in his left hand as he turned it end over end, apparently lost in some ponderous reflection. "Which makes me wonder why you hesitate to marry me. I can give you all the children you want."

A hard lump of longing swelled in her throat, and she attempted, in vain, to swallow. "I want a real *father* for my children, should I ever be so fortunate as to have any, and a husband who truly loves me."

A new silence descended, but it was not an uncomfortable one. There was a certain ease between Susannah and Aubrey, for all that they were so often at odds, and it pleased Susannah to see that he was weighing her words.

When they had finished the meal, Aubrey rose, still without speaking, and carried his plate and Susannah's to the sink. Another demonstration she would not have expected from a man, particularly one of his stature and wealth. There were many things she didn't know about the male of the species, given the life she'd led, and this particular specimen merely added to the mystery.

In time, Susannah collected Victoria, along with the

requisite bottle of warm milk, murmured a quiet good night, and retreated to her room.

In the morning, when Susannah descended the stairs, bringing Victoria with her, Maisie had returned to her usual post in the kitchen. The web of laundry lines had been cleared away, and the other woman was happily pressing a white shirt at a wooden ironing board. Several spare flat irons were heating on the stovetop, close at hand.

"Jasper?" Susannah asked.

Maisie beamed. "He done broke out in speckles from crown to sole," she said, "but he's rallied some. Even took some broth this morning and plagued me to let him go out to the stables to see the horses. Ain't that somethin'?"

Such relief swept through Susannah that her knees went weak. "Oh, Maisie, that's wonderful."

At mid-morning, Dr. Fletcher returned, of his own accord, and examined both children. He was smiling when he sat down at the kitchen table to enjoy a cup of hot coffee before heading back out into the crisp weather. Both Jasper and Victoria, he assured the women, were going to be fine.

He was a quiet, serious man, somewhere in his mid-sixties by Susannah's assessment, and he spoke of his longtime medical practice in nearby Providence, of his beloved wife, Rachel, and their several grown children. They had raised four sons, all of whom were married now, with sons and daughters of their own.

Maisie tried to pay him before he left, from the funds she kept in a fruit jar hidden at the back of a shelf in the pantry, but he refused. He was just doing a favor for his friend, Dr. Martin, he said.

In just three days, the danger of measles had passed, blowing over like the threat of a storm, and both Susannah and Maisie offered up their private prayers of gratitude. They'd been blessed, for the threat to the children had been a very real one, and many other little boys and baby girls lay gravely ill, all over the city.

On the morning of the fourth day, Susannah reached the conclusion that she could delay her plans no longer. Leaving Victoria in Maisie's care, she went up to her room to collect her drawstring purse, which contained a pitifully small amount of money, along with the notices she'd already drawn up offering piano lessons, returned to the ground floor to put on the cloak, and let herself out through the front door.

The air was clear and crisp, and the sun shone high and cold overhead. Susannah felt cheerful as she strolled downhill toward the heart of Seattle, her bag swinging in one hand, her posters under the other arm. She was not anxious to encounter Aubrey, or so she tried to convince herself. He simply unsettled her too much, but it would be a waste of time and effort to search for another mercantile just to avoid the man. She needed supplies—sheet music, stiff paper for making more signs, nails, and a small hammer with which to post them.

When she reached the store—it looked as imposing as a Greek temple, looming against the backdrop of greenery and sky the way it did—she saw no sign of Aubrey. She bought six sheets of good paper, along with the other items, a new pen with a broad nib, and a bottle of India ink. To save herself a trip, she went into the dining room of the Washington Hotel, which she had visited twice, first in the company of Mr. Hollister, then with Ethan, and asked for a cup of China tea. While she sipped, she worked on her placards.

PRIVATE INSTRUCTION IN PIANO, she wrote in strong, dark letters, designed to be seen at a distance.

*REASONABLE FEE. CONTACT MISS SUSANNAH MCKIT-
TRICK AT #8 CHURCH STREET.*

She had consumed three cups of tea when she finally finished her task and left the dining room, satisfied. Affixing the notices to a series of strategically chosen telegraph poles took another hour, and she had barely gotten home and hung up her cloak when her first student arrived. Her surprise at finding not a child waiting in the foyer but a grizzled man of at least seventy, well dressed but still very rough around the edges, was complete.

"I've always wanted to play the pianny," he said with enthusiasm.

Susannah did not want to offend the man. He looked quite earnest and decent, really, for all that his polish was obviously superficial and sketchy. "I'm afraid I was expecting to teach children, Mr.—"

"Just call me Zacharias, if you don't mind," he urged, looking disappointed but still hopeful. He held his hat in one hand, and his salt-and-pepper beard sprang almost straight out from his chin, as if to lead the way for the rest of him. "I ain't heard my first name in so long, I can't rightly recall what it is. I was sure lookin' forward to learnin' all about music, though, ma'am. That I was indeed."

Susannah's hands were knotted together. Zacharias was a customer, and he plainly had the resources to pay for his lessons. "Have you played before?"

Zacharias had one hand on the door knob. "No, ma'am," he said. "It's all new to me. I figured if I learnt the pianny, I might get me one of them fine eastern women for a wife. They like things fancified. But then, you'd know that already, bein' such a lady your own self."

She was touched that this man could want genteel feminine company so much that he would undertake such an endeavor so late in life, and secretly a little amused by his compliment. She was inexperienced, that was true, but she knew when she was being charmed.

"The lessons cost fifteen cents," she said. "I expect my students to be diligent, so you will have to find a place to practice."

Zacharias was beaming as he came away from the door. "I'll pay a quarter," he said. "You never met a harder worker than me, if I do say so, and I got me a pianny of my own, over to the house there." He cocked a thumb to indicate direction. "Came all the way from San Francisco, Californy."

Susannah swallowed. "Come in. We'll get started right now, if that's all right with you."

"It's better'n all right, ma'am. You've made an old miner real happy."

She headed toward the rear parlor, where the piano was housed, and indicated the piano stool. Zacharias sat down, flexing his thick, arthritic fingers eagerly over the keys.

"We'll start with middle C," Susannah said. A quarter was a quarter, after all. Perhaps she'd been undercharging these past few years, asking only fifteen cents for a lesson.

One endless hour later, the miner gave up torturing that splendid instrument, paid his fee, and left. He would be back the following Tuesday, by mutual agreement, and Susannah looked forward to the experience with resignation.

"What the devil is goin' on?" Maisie inquired the minute Susannah entered the kitchen, craving a cup of hot, sweet tea. "Sounded like you were takin' that there piano apart a piece at a time."

"You know very well that I was giving a music lesson," she answered, busy at the task of pumping water into the kettle. "I saw you peeking around the door, Maisie, so you needn't pretend."

"A music lesson, huh?" Maisie scoffed, but she was grinning broadly.

"What else would it be?" Susannah demanded, somewhat impatient. She had not gotten a good rest the night before, and working with her first student had proved to be an unexpected ordeal.

"I'll *tell* you what else it could be," Maisie boomed, delighted. She was still ironing, and the kitchen smelled of clean, starched linens and baking bread. "That old coot came a-courtin'. If you wasn't so darn gullible, you'd have worked that out for yourself."

Susannah, busy until that moment, went still. Looking back, it seemed that Maisie might be right. Mr. Zacharias had worked industriously at his scales, but he'd tried more than once to strike up a conversation, and he'd been dressed awfully well for a miner. "Oh, dear," she said.

Maisie laughed. "I can't wait to see what happens when Mr. Fairgrieve finds out about *this*," she thundered, slamming the iron down onto a white sheet with great energy. "My guess is, you're gonna have more 'piano students' than you know what to do with. What the dickens did you do, anyhow—put up signs?"

The starch went out of Susannah; she sank into a chair in shock, staring blindly into space. Maisie's question echoed in her mind, damning her for a degree of naïveté bordering on outright stupidity. "This is awful," she said.

The other woman shrugged. "That feller wouldn't make such a bad husband," she said, evidently referring to Zacharias. "He lives one street over, in a house nigh as big as this one. He was one of the first to strike it lucky up there in the north country, so he's got a dime or two, and he behaved himself, too. I made sure of that."

Susannah set her elbows on the table's edge and buried her face in her hands. She could not rightly turn her first student away, despite her belated suspicions. He had, after all, conducted himself in a gentlemanly fashion, and she needed the income from teaching if she was ever to have anything at all of her own.

Maisie crossed the room and patted her back hard, offering rough comfort. "Now, now," she growled, "don't take on. If'n one of them fellers steps out of line, I'll drop him to his knees with a skillet to the back of the head. All you gotta do is holler."

"I honestly thought—"

The patting went on, gentler now. "I guess miners've got as much right to pound the piano as anybody else," she philosophized. " 'Sides, one of them is bound to suit you for a husband."

Susannah let out a despairing sigh. "He did give me twenty-five cents," she said.

"See there?" Maisie confirmed. "Pretty thing like you, you'll be rich in no time at all. And it ought to make things real lively around here." She laughed again. "Oh, lordy, but Mr. Fairgrieve is gonna have himself a fine fit when he finds out he's in the match-makin' business."

Chapter

10

~

Three more piano students, all of them male and old enough to shave, vote, and use tobacco, presented themselves at the front door before suppertime, scrubbed and spruced, requesting lessons. All were beginners, and not a one balked at the price of twenty-five cents. By the time the last one disappeared into the snow-speckled twilight, Susannah had earned one dollar, a significant sum of money by anyone's reckoning. Back home, she would have counted herself fortunate to amass that much in a week of teaching; there she'd had to compete for every pupil and then share the proceeds with Mrs. Butterfield.

Of course, she realized by then that Maisie had been right: her students were not really aspiring musicians; they were lonely and starved for decent female companionship, not culture. Apparently, they saw Susannah as a prospect for matrimony, although she suspected it was simply the fact of her femininity that attracted them. In her presence, they were no doubt reminded of the mothers, sisters, and sweethearts they had left behind in their wanderings.

Of course, Susannah had no earthly intention of wedding herself to any one of these men, and that made her feel a little guilty, as though she were taking their money under false pretenses. Still, she *was* instructing them in music, which was all she had promised in the first place. If they had further aspirations where she was concerned, well, that simply wasn't her fault—was it?

Aubrey, although he'd known she planned to teach piano, probably would be less than pleased when he found that she was being courted right under his roof, but there was no turning back now. She even dared to dream that, being paid such exorbitant fees, she might soon have a studio, not to mention a piano, of her own. That would amount to the first real security she had ever known.

Aubrey returned to the house a bit later than usual that evening—it was almost eight—and he was accompanied by several of his business friends. He seemed distracted, his mood strained and weary, and he barely spared Susannah a glance while she served the meal. She had sent a protesting Maisie to her room to put her feet up long before, and Victoria was asleep in her basket in the kitchen.

Having taken her own supper earlier at the kitchen table, Susannah listened attentively, if inauspiciously, to the men's discussions of politics, interest rates, timber prices, and mineral rights. The dollar in her pocket—and those she hoped would follow—was a serious responsibility, one she did not take lightly. She didn't plan to leave Aubrey's house, not without Victoria in any case, but without money of her own she would have no autonomy at all. She listened keenly to the conversation because she wanted to manage her funds as wisely as she could.

She had cleared the table, washed and dried the dishes, and retired to the rear parlor to coax soft, soothing music from that much-abused piano, when she sensed Aubrey's approach, felt him standing close behind her. Once he had asked, nay, practically commanded her not to play, and she normally wouldn't have, knowing he was at home, but she found she couldn't stop. She was like a desert wanderer who has come upon an oasis; she threw the whole of herself into the flowing, silvery strains of Mozart, as though they might quench her thirst.

Even when Aubrey's hands hovered over her shoulders—she felt them there, knew they were trembling—even when he let them come to rest at last, she played on. His touch, ordinary though it was, affected her as profoundly as the notes shimmering unseen around them. She closed her eyes against the emotions welling up from some mysterious inner source, but they consumed her nonetheless.

Finally, Aubrey reached down and caught her wrists gently in his hands, lifting them from the keys. Silencing the storm of music. With uncommon grace, he turned Susannah around and drew her to her feet, and she found herself standing so close to him that she imagined she heard the faint echo of his heartbeat.

"What are you doing to me, Susannah?"

She stared at him. What was *she* doing to *him?* "I'm sorry," she managed, "if the music disturbed you. I was merely—" Only then did she realize that he was holding her wrists again. Or had he ever let them go in the first place?

His eyes seemed haunted, and the flickering gaslights threw shadows across the planes of his face. Beneath the callused pads of his thumbs, her pulse raced, betraying far more than she wanted him to know. "Susannah," he said.

She held his gaze, and it took all her courage not to look away, not to flee the room, for it was in those moments that she first knew she loved Aubrey Fairgrieve as she would never love another man. She had never cared so deeply for anyone before, had never even imagined such powerful emotions as the ones that seized her then, and that was cause for mourning as well as celebration. Aubrey would not, could not return her devotion in equal measure; he had already made that abundantly clear. Furthermore, in a strange way, he still belonged to Julia, in her mind at least.

"Let me go," she whispered. It was a plea.

He released his hold on her, but she did not retreat. "Marry me, Susannah," he said.

She wanted nothing so much as to be his wife, but she shook her head. Somewhere she found the courage to say it. "I can't. You were my best friend's husband."

"Julia is dead. We're not. It's as simple—and as complicated—as that. Are we to live as though we'd been buried with her?"

She knew he was right. Knew that Julia, even in her troubled state, would not have begrudged her Aubrey's attentions now, when she was gone, might even have encouraged the match, for Victoria's sake. She drew a deep breath, let it out slowly. "I don't think she'd want that," she allowed. "But there is the matter of love." It was like leaping off a high cliff into shallow waters, saying the words she had to say. "Do you love me, Aubrey?"

He was silent for a long time, while she hung suspended between despair and hope. Then, at last, he sighed. "No," he said. "But I *do* care for you, Susannah. And God knows, I want you."

She wanted him, too. Desperately. But not at the expense of her self-respect, of her dreams, and she was sensible enough, even in her relative naïveté, to know that once his desire had been appeased, she would no longer interest him quite so much. Loving him could only destroy her in the end, unless he loved her in return, for he would be sure to stray. Many women were willing to share their husbands with mistresses, or at least resigned to their situations, but Susannah wanted complete fidelity, utter devotion. Would settle for nothing less.

"I'm sorry," she said, and slipped around him to hurry toward the doorway.

He made no move to stop her.

Morning brought more snow and more piano students, all of them male. Every time Susannah crossed paths with Maisie, who was busy opening the long-neglected ballroom for the impending party, the other woman looked at her, shook her head, and cackled with amusement. Susannah, still shaken by her encounter with Aubrey the night before in the music room, was distracted and a little irritable. She did not want to love the man—it was inconvenient, to say the least—but she seemed to have no real choice in the matter. He filled her thoughts and senses and made concentration difficult, if not impossible.

She was overseeing the last lesson of the day when the moment she had dreaded was upon her. Aubrey arrived home unexpectedly and strode into the room, jawline set, eyes glittering. Here was another sort of passion, quite different from what he had displayed the night before.

Zacharias, back for another session, ceased belaboring the keys and looked up at Aubrey with a gold-toothed grin. "Well, howdy, Fairgrieve," he said affably.

"Zach," Aubrey responded, but he was still glaring at Susannah.

"Mr. Zacharias was just having his piano lesson," Susannah said, straightening her spine and raising her chin a notch.

"So I see," Aubrey said.

The old man rose from the piano stool and stood between them. "Now, Aubrey, I hope you ain't plannin' to be cussed about this. Nothin' improper about it. Nothin' at all."

Aubrey raised one eyebrow and, in that simple motion, gave the lie to his own words. "Did I say there was?" His tone was dry, and his gaze was still fastened to Susannah's face. A tiny muscle in his right cheek twitched once, twice.

Zacharias remained good-natured. He pressed payment into Susannah's palm and spoke reassuringly. "If'n this here feller gets testy about your havin' callers, you can give all your lessons over to my place," he said. "I got a good pianny, like I told you."

"Thank you," Susannah answered, although her gaze was still locked with Aubrey's. She dropped the coin into the pocket of her skirt and flinched slightly when she heard the parlor door swing shut behind her first and favorite pupil.

"That old coot doesn't give a damn about playing the piano," Aubrey said. "He's looking for a wife, like practically every other man in Seattle."

Susannah folded her arms. "I'm perfectly well aware of that," she replied. Victoria, sitting nearby on a blanket, propped up with pillows, cooed charmingly and held out her arms to her father. He bent to scoop her up, but the look he had fixed on Susannah was no friendlier than before.

"I beg your pardon?"

She sighed. "As of today, I have seven regular students. All of them are yearning for the company of a woman . . ."

Color suffused Aubrey's neck above his starched white collar. "What, precisely, are you selling?"

Susannah might have struck him if he hadn't been holding the child. "I am *teaching music*," she said. "Naturally, I expect to be paid for my services."

"Well, I won't tolerate it. Not under this roof." He didn't raise his voice, but something in his manner alarmed the baby a little; she looked into his face with wide eyes and thrust half of one tiny fist into her mouth.

"Fine," Susannah said, making her voice cheerful for Victoria's sake. There seemed no point in reminding him that he'd already given her permission to teach music using his piano. "You heard Mr. Zacharias. I shall simply set up my studio at his house." She watched with grudging admiration while Aubrey, seeing his daughter's distress, forcibly calmed himself. He bent and set the child back on her blanket, making sure the cushions held her upright.

"Perhaps," he said pleasantly, smiling a wolf's smile, "you should just move into Zach's mansion and be done with it."

"Can't you two stop your bickerin' long enough to figger out that you're meant to be together?" Maisie interrupted, startling them both with her presence as well as her outlandish words. Neither Susannah nor Aubrey had heard the woman come in, but Victoria had; she gurgled in gleeful recognition and held out her chubby little arms to the new arrival. Maisie lifted the child to her shoulder.

Aubrey tugged at the cuffs of his shirt and straightened his shoulders. "Miss McKittrick," he said, "is not interested in being married. At least, not to me." With that, he turned around and stalked out of the room.

"Well, I'll be jiggered," Maisie marveled, and cackled the way she'd been doing all day, like an old hen. "That man's smitten with you, Susannah. Imagine—him bein' jealous of old Zach! I ain't never seen anythin' like it."

"Nonsense," Susannah scoffed, afraid to hope that Maisie was right. That somewhere inside Aubrey Fairgrieve lurked a tender feeling, a seed of sweet regard that might one day grow into love. "He may be jealous, but if he is, it's because Julia betrayed him, not because he cares for me."

"Give things time," Maisie said, with a gentleness so unexpected that it brought tears springing to Susannah's eyes. "He was bad hurt, Mr. Fairgrieve was. But he's a good man." She chucked Victoria beneath the chin. "Why, just look at the way he holds this little mite. He ain't scairt to pick up a baby, like most men would be."

"You're forgetting," Susannah said quietly, rubbing both temples with the tips of her fingers, "that he didn't believe Victoria was his child until he had things out with Ethan. He didn't even bother to name her."

"I reckon he considered her his all along, whether he believed he was the father or not," Maisie insisted, bouncing the delighted infant on her ample hip. "He thought he could keep himself from lovin' her, that's all, so's she couldn't break his heart for him. He tried, and he failed at it."

Susannah sat down hard on the piano stool. The next day was Saturday, and the party Aubrey insisted on giving would be held in the evening, thus forcing her to face a houseful of curious guests. And Sunday morning meant braving the disapproval of the Ladies' Christian Benevolence Society to attend church. The members viewed her as a scarlet woman and would continue to do so until she married respectably, left Seattle, or died of old age. No one, she knew, could be quite so unbending as the devoutly religious.

"There, now," Maisie said, laying a hand to Susannah's shoulder. "You look a mite frazzled. Why don't you bundle up and have yourself a nice walk, whilst I tend to the babe here?"

Susannah welcomed the offer. Although it was surely cold outside, and great flakes of snow were drifting past the windows, there was still enough light for a quick stroll. She thanked Maisie and hurried into the entry-way to collect her cloak from the hall tree.

Curiosity drew her past Mr. Zacharias's residence, a great stone edifice with many windows, a gabled roof, stables, and a carriage house. She stood at the gate, look-ing up at the structure and wishing she could somehow cause herself to care deeply for the man inside. He was a kindly sort, she knew, and clearly generous as well. His rough exterior hid a romantic nature, and he would make someone a fine husband.

She was about to turn away and return to Aubrey's house and her duties there when the front door of the mansion swung open, and Zacharias appeared in the chasm.

"Howdy!" he called out, waving. He looked and sounded so pleased by her visit, however inadvertent, that Susannah couldn't help smiling.

"Hello, Mr. Zacharias," she said. He picked his way through the snow toward her, moving with the light, dancelike steps of a leprechaun. He had left his coat be-hind, and his beard was turning white.

"Come on in, and I'll show you my pianny," he said, with such pleasure that Susannah could not think of a way to refuse him. She was well aware, as she took Zacharias's arm and allowed him to escort her up the unshoveled walk, that members of the Benevolence So-ciety were probably watching her through the windows of the nearby houses.

"I can't stay long," she said. "I've left Victoria in Maisie's care, and she's got her hands full with Jasper and the housework."

Zacharias smiled his understanding. "He's spoken for you, has he? Aubrey, I mean?"

They had gained the gaping front door, and Susan-nah stepped into an amazing foyer with a painted,

Italian-style ceiling and colorful mosaic floors. She had no desire to mislead her friend and student. "Yes," she said, with resignation rather than enthusiasm.

"And you don't want to get yourself hitched up with him?" Zacharias was watching her closely as he helped her out of her cloak.

"The truth is," she admitted, feeling quite miserable, "I believe I care for him." It was hard to say, but she was an honest person, and, besides, she didn't want to give Mr. Zacharias false hope. If he decided not to take piano lessons anymore, she would just have to accept the fact.

The aging miner took her arm and led her into a spacious room with walls papered in gaudy embossed velvet. The fireplace was either painted gold or plated with the real thing, and a spectacular grand piano stood before a trio of towering windows overlooking a garden drifted with powdery snow.

Susannah was drawn to the instrument as surely as a saint would be drawn to an angel. She uncovered the keys, touched them with reverent fingers.

"Had that sent all the way from San Francisco, Californy," Zacharias said, not for the first time. He sounded a little wistful, and Susannah turned to look at him with affection and true regret that she could not care for him in a romantic way. "I know I ain't young and finelookin', like Aubrey is," he said, as though he'd been reading her mind, "but I'd make a good husband." Above the grizzle of his beard, his round cheeks turned bright pink. "You'd have your own bedroom and ever'thin' like that there."

Susannah crossed the room and laid a hand on Zacharias's arm. "I can't marry you," she said. "But it isn't because there's anything wrong with your appearance." Not so suddenly, she wanted to break down and weep. "It's just that I do care for Aubrey, hopeless as that seems. I'd give anything if things were different, but there it is. And I don't know what to do."

Hesitantly, Mr. Zacharias patted her hand. He heaved out a great sigh. "Well, I confess I had my hopes, but never mind that. Set yourself down here, and I'll see if I can rustle up a cup of hot tea. You want a little whiskey in it, too? Sometimes that'll smooth out the road for a person."

Susannah smiled in spite of her low spirits. A glance at the windows told her the sun would soon disappear entirely, but suddenly she didn't care. Victoria was safe with Maisie, and she was safe with Zacharias. "I would enjoy a cup of tea," she said primly. "As for the whiskey—" She let her voice trail away, pursed her lips a little, and shook her head.

Zacharias left the room, and Susannah immediately rose and went back to the piano. It was a superior instrument, better even than the one in Aubrey's rear parlor, and playing it on a regular basis would be a joy.

After pulling off her gloves, she sat down on the long, sleek bench and arranged her fingers on the keys. Soon soft music filled the room, delicate and magical, like something flowing from another, better world.

The rattle of a tea cup somewhere behind her caused her to stop and turn around. Zacharias stood nearby, holding an incongruously fragile teapot in one gnarled and leathery hand. "That was mighty pretty," he said in a reverent voice. "Put me right in mind of my Martha, God rest her soul."

"Your wife played?"

"Not so well as you," Zacharias said, his eyes full of fond remembrance, "but she could coax out a tune if she tried. 'Course, she never had a pianny like that one. She used to go down to the church and use theirs, when she took a mind to make music."

Susannah's heart twisted a little. She joined Mr.

Zacharias at the gilded round table where he'd set the tea service and took one of the two spindly chairs.

"I didn't have nothin' when Martha was alive," Zacharias said, sitting down opposite her. "That sorta takes the frolic outta all this." He gestured with one hand to indicate their rich, if not tasteful, surroundings.

"I'm sure you will find another wife," Susannah said gently and in all sincerity, watching as the older man poured their tea with infinite care. "She'd want you to be happy, your Martha."

Surprisingly, Zacharias laughed. "Oh, no, she wouldn't," he countered, taking his own tea from the saucer instead of the cup. "She told me once that she'd never take another husband if I died afore her, and she expected me to honor her memory for the rest of my days if she was the one to pass first. I've tried, I truly have, but sometimes I jest get so lonesome I dern near can't stand it."

Susannah was careful not to look at Zacharias for a few moments, giving him time to shore up his dignity a little. "Surely there are widows in Seattle—"

"Nary a one," Zacharias lamented. "Why, they get snatched up quicker'n gold nuggets in a creek bed soon as they step off the train or sail in with a ship. And if their man happens to drop dead after they get here, there'll be fellers at the funeral with a ring in their pocket."

Susannah was a little shocked by this statement, but she hid her response for the sake of Mr. Zacharias's feelings. Men, she reflected, in the privacy of her own thoughts, were very odd creatures. Love seemed to matter less to them than convenience.

She took a sip of her tea, which was surprisingly good, before answering. "Have you considered sending away for a bride?" she asked. She knew there were always discreet advertisements in the eastern newspapers—she and Julia had often giggled over them when they were girls—and matrimonial agencies operated in major cities like New York and Chicago. It was entirely possible that something of the sort might be found in San Francisco.

Zacharias shook his head and made a rueful, clucking sound with his tongue. "You just don't know what you might find waitin' for you at the end of the dock if you do that," he said.

This time, Susannah wanted to laugh instead of cry, but she kept a straight face. "You could exchange photographs," she suggested. "Correspond for a time, perhaps."

"I knew a feller did that very thing. Sent a letter and his likeness to a place in Boston, Massychusetts. Got a letter back right soon, 'long with a picture of a pretty little gal with bright eyes and piles o' billowin' dark hair. Good figger, too. They wrote back and forth for nigh onto a year. Then she said she'd marry him. He was all excited and paid her passage. The weddin' was done by proxy, so's they could settle in right away once she got here. Well, now, when she turned up, she was twice the size of the lady in the picture and plain as mud. That wouldn'ta been so bad—Sam hisself had no call to get too picky, you understand—but she had a sour nature into the bargain. Yessir, that woman could strip the hide right off a man with a look, and when she got to ravin' and swingin' a rollin' pin or a chunk of firewood or whatever might come to hand, well, she was downright *dangerous*."

Susannah took another sip of tea. Zacharias's tale was vivid in her mind's eye. "Then you could go in person. To find a wife, I mean."

He sighed forlornly and nodded toward the windows. "Winter's on us, and there'll be no gettin' over the mountains afore spring. I don't care much for ships, truth to tell, so I reckon I'm strapped for a woman. I'd like to keep on studyin' the pianny, though, if it's all the same to you. Women like music, don't they?"

"Indeed they do," Susannah said. She put down her tea cup, all too aware that it was dark out. The street lamps would do little to push back the gloom. "I must go, Mr. Zacharias," she told him, rising from her chair. He stood simultaneously, and once again, she was touched by his eagerness to show good manners. "Are you attending the party tomorrow night at Aubrey—at the Fairgrieve house?"

He beamed. "I got me an invite. Me'n Aubrey are old friends, even though we sometimes exchange hard words." In the garish entryway, he helped her into her cloak, then reached for his own expensively tailored coat. "I'll see you home. Least I can do, when you was so neighborly as to come callin'."

Susannah wasn't about to turn down his offer. "You're very kind," she said in all sincerity.

Less than ten minutes later, she was back in Aubrey's house, hanging up her cloak. Zacharias had taken leave of her at the front gate, though she knew he'd stood watch until the door closed safely behind her.

Aubrey was locked away in his study, engaged in some sort of business meeting from the sound of things, and Maisie was in the kitchen, as usual. She was holding Victoria on her lap, while Jasper played at her feet with a carved wooden horse. The room was warm and fragrant, but Maisie's earlier good cheer had vanished, replaced by a fretful expression.

Susannah was instantly alarmed. "Maisie, what is it?"

"I was gettin' plumb worried about you," Maisie scolded. "Figured you'd been carried off somewheres—"

Susannah smiled. "I'm safe and sound, as you can see.

I was having tea with Mr. Zacharias. That's quite a house he lives in."

"Made him a fortune up in Alaska," Maisie said.

Just in from the snowy outdoors, Susannah shivered a little, just to think of the Klondike in winter, and dragged a chair over close to her friend's. "I'll take the baby from you," she offered in a gentle tone.

Maisie wasn't ready to surrender Victoria. "She's a sweet thing," she responded. "I'd like to go on holdin' her for a while, if'n you don't mind."

"Of course I don't," Susannah said, touching her friend's arm. "Are you sure you're all right?"

"Always sets me to feelin' lonesome, this time of year. A little melancholy, too."

Susannah gave her a hug, careful not to crush the baby. "I understand."

"Makes a body yearn for a husband and a house." Maisie looked around. "Oh, this place is right grand, but it ain't mine. I'd settle for a cabin if I could have me a good man. One who'd be kind to my Jasper, I mean."

An idea niggled into the back of Susannah's mind, out-landish and purely wonderful, but she wasn't quite ready to share it. "Have you a party dress, Maisie?" she asked.

Maisie looked baffled. "Never did," she said. "Not in my whole life."

Susannah assessed her friend. She was bigger than Julia had been, that was certain, but not so much that a few alterations wouldn't suffice. They need only find a gown with fairly generous seams. "Well, it's about time you did."

"What are you up to?" Maisie asked, looking wary.

Susannah smiled, letting the question pass unan-swered. Maisie was a good woman, tender-hearted and hardworking. She attended church every Sunday, with-out fail, and once or twice Susannah had seen her poring over an old Bible at the kitchen table, eyes narrowed in concentration, lips shaping the holy words silently, reverent in her concentration. She cooked and kept a spotless house, and she was a splendid mother to Jasper. Why, if she was gussied up just a little, she'd have herself a husband in no time.

"Susannah?" Maisie prodded.

Susannah looked her over. "I think green is your best color," she speculated. "Come with me."

Maisie didn't balk until they'd reached the threshold of Julia's old room. When Susannah marched in, headed for one of several wardrobes, stuffed to bursting with beautiful gowns, Maisie lingered in the corridor.

"What in blue blazes—?"

Susannah opened the first cabinet and started riffling through its contents, rejecting one dress after another. Finally, in the third and final armoire, she found a dark green velvet, apparently made to accommodate Julia during her pregnancy. A few snips and stitches here and there, and the lovely frock would fit Maisie perfectly.

Of course, Susannah was thinking of pairing her friend with Mr. Zacharias, though she didn't think it prudent to say as much, just yet, anyway. This was Seattle, after all. Wives were a scarce commodity, and Maisie would make an exceptional one.

"Try this on," Susannah said, holding up the dress.

"Are you crazy?" Maisie wanted to know.

Susannah laughed. "Probably. Now, get in here and shut the door. There's no time to waste if we're going to have you ready for the party."

Maisie looked up and down the corridor before stepping, wide-eyed, into the bedroom. Susannah made up her mind to ask Aubrey if she could pack away Julia's things and turn the room into a proper nursery for Victoria.

An hour later, the dress was fitted and basted, and Maisie looked grand. She stared at her image in a cheval mirror, while Susannah, holding Victoria, looked on with smiling approval.

"I thank you, Susannah McKittrick," Maisie said, sounding awed. There were tears standing in her eyes.

"You look beautiful," Susannah replied, and she meant it. She had a feeling Mr. Zacharias and a number of Seattle's other lonely bachelors would agree.

Chapter

11

~

*W*hen morning spilled over the eastern horizon, Susannah arose, attended to Victoria and to her own ablutions, and descended the rear stairway into the kitchen. She found Maisie at her usual duties, humming happily as she prepared a fragrant, sizzling breakfast at the stove.

Victoria, bouncing in Susannah's arms, caught sight of Jasper playing on the floor and strained toward him with the whole of her small, strong body.

"Not until you've had your bottle," Susannah said, holding on tightly and brushing the baby's temple with the lightest pass of her lips. She watched her friend with amused speculation for a few moments. "You seem in good spirits this morning, Maisie."

The other woman smiled as Susannah settled herself and Victoria in the rocking chair, then handed over the customary bottle of warm milk. The household was falling into a routine. She was glad of that, for it made her feel as though she belonged.

"I reckon I'm happy, just to think about the dancin' tonight. I do love my dancin'," Maisie answered, eyes alight. "You pick out a dress to wear to the doin's tonight, or was you too caught up in lookin' after me?"

A suckling sound filled the warm, steamy air of the kitchen as Victoria took her breakfast. Susannah rocked the chair slowly back and forth, taking her time answering. "I'll attend to that later," she said. When she raised her eyes to Maisie's face, she knew her countenance was serious. "I think we should clear away Julia's things and make that room into a nursery for Victoria, don't you?" she asked.

Maisie looked mildly alarmed and intrigued at the same time. "You speak to Mr. Fairgrieve on that account?"

Susannah flushed and shook her head. "Not yet."

Maisie sighed and went on with her stirring and pot-lid raising, while the coffee perked on the back of the stove. "Like as not, he'll be relieved to have those things put away. All the same, you'll want to ask first."

Susannah nodded. She hesitated even to bring up Julia's name to Aubrey, for whatever reason, but she would find an opportunity.

"You've got to wear somethin' fittin' to that party tonight," Maisie persisted. "Folks will be lookin' you over real good, you can bet."

Susannah sighed heavily. "That's precisely why I'm dreading the evening so much. Oh, Maisie, why does life have to be so complicated? Why can't I simply take care of Victoria, teach my piano lessons, and keep to myself?"

"Don't reckon life works that way," Maisie said with a shrug. She frowned thoughtfully, stirring something in a kettle on the stovetop, then brightened. "I know what we can do. You choose two or three of Mrs. Fairgrieve's gowns, and we'll take the sleeves from one and maybe the bodice from another and make somethin' brand new. How would that be?"

"I hardly see how we'll have time," Susannah reasoned, but she was feeling a little less bleak. True, she didn't relish the prospect of facing the curiosity and disapproval of Seattle's aristocracy, such as it was, but she cared even less for the thought of hiding in her room like a coward. After all, she had no cause for shame.

"We're a fine team, you and me. Got my dress ready in a jig, didn't we? Let's get to it."

"What about all the cooking?"

"Mr. Fairgrieve is havin' most of that sent over from the hotel dining room."

That settled it, then. Susannah nodded her acquiescence, though privately she still had her doubts that it was possible to prepare for the party *and* alter one of Julia's gowns so extensively. The work they'd done on Maisie's dress had been fairly simple, and with the two of them working, the job had gone fast.

On the other hand, such hard work was bound to keep her mind off the difficulties she faced, and that was no minor consideration.

Throughout that frenzied day, piano students came to the door, hopeful men with their hair slicked back and their hats in their hands. Rushed and trying very hard not to show it, Susannah politely turned them away, but only after assigning each one a lesson time the following week.

In the intervals, she worked madly on the gown—with Maisie's help, she altered a silk of the palest apricot, attaching full, creamy lace sleeves from another frock, tending the baby as the need arose. Aubrey came home in the late afternoon, found Susannah frazzled but flushed with excitement, and smiled to himself as he went to look at the freshly scrubbed and polished ballroom. She followed in his wake, without meaning to do so.

The elegant chamber looked spectacular—the chandeliers had been lowered on their squeaky brass chains and polished, the heavy velvet draperies, royal blue trimmed in golden cording, carried outside and beaten, then rehung. The air was fresh, though a bit chilly, be-

cause Maisie and Susannah had opened the windows
earlier to clear away the musty smell of disuse. Chairs
had been carried to the small dais at the far end of the
room to accommodate the orchestra. At the time of
Aubrey's arrival, Hawkins and two of the clerks from
the mercantile were busily decorating the walls with
bunting so white that it made Susannah's eyes ache.

Standing beside Aubrey, just inside the towering
double doors, her sewing finished at last, Susannah
pushed a stray tendril of hair back from her forehead.
"Well," she began when he was silent too long, "does it
suit?"

"Nicely," he responded, and turned his head to let his
gaze connect, jarringly, with hers.

"Maisie has worked very hard."

"You are too modest, Miss McKittrick. It would appear that you have done your share, and then some. I
hope you won't be too worn out to dance."

The idea of dancing, of being held in this particular
man's arms, brought a blush to Susannah's face; in her
youth, she had learned the steps of the waltzes and reels
she'd mostly only read about, but she'd long since resigned herself to her place as a wallflower. "I hadn't expected—" she began, and faltered, because it made her
dizzy to imagine whirling about the ballroom in
Aubrey's arms. "The fact is, I don't know how. To—to
dance, I mean."

"Then I'll teach you," Aubrey said, folding his arms.

Her heart was thundering at the base of her throat,
and she felt a need to sit down. She must have swayed,
for Aubrey grasped her elbow and squired her to a
nearby chair.

At his touch, she felt an aching but ever more familiar heat rise within her. She thought of the dress she'd
fashioned, the hopes she cherished against all reason

and right, and knew that her dreams were very much alive, despite their implausibility.

"I am very awkward," she said. Her chin was quivering, and her eyes burned. She wished, as she had done many times before, for Julia's easy grace, her laughing aplomb and seemingly unshakable confidence. Julia had always known what to say, how to charm everyone around her.

He smiled. "Are you?" he responded. For one terrible and infinitely precious moment, she thought he was going to kiss her again. Instead, he laid an index finger briefly to the tip of her nose. "We'll see, won't we?"

"Aubrey—"

Unexpectedly, he took her into his arms and swept her out onto the center of the floor. Holding her right hand in his left, he curved his free arm around her waist and began waltzing her around and around in a graceful, ever-widening circle.

His legs were long, and she scrambled to keep up with him, but soon she had learned to match his pace, and she realized with a breathless soaring of her heart that she was *dancing*, truly dancing, the way other women did. Women with beaux, women with husbands. Women with full, rich lives.

For an interval, she felt less spinsterly than usual, but then she tripped on the hem of her calico gown and stumbled. Aubrey caught her immediately, restored her balance by hauling her hard against him. It was a matter of moments before he released her, and yet it seemed he had seared her to the soul, branded his image upon her very spirit. She looked up at him, blinking and miserable, wishing that she and Victoria were far away and, at the same time, wanting this man with a most unseemly degree of passion.

She pulled out of his embrace and stepped back, and, once again, she nearly fell. Once again, he caught her, this time by the arm, and held her upright, but he did not try to draw her near. His expression, full of laughter and mischief only a heartbeat before, was solemn.

"I—there are things to do—" she muttered, and tugged at her skirts.

He sighed. "Yes," he said, and thrust a hand through his hair.

She took another step back. It was too soon, she told herself. Too soon after her arrival in Seattle, too soon after Julia's death. All the same, the wanting was a great, yawning chasm inside her, and she was teetering on its brink. Turning on one heel, she fled through the dining room and the entryway and up the main staircase.

Victoria was just waking from her nap, but since she seemed contented, Susannah went ahead and ran a bath. Already, the twilight was thickening into darkness, and the street lamps glowed, spilling soft golden light over crusted snow. The dress she had chosen lay across the bed, neatly spread, and even as she admired its lovely, full sleeves, its snugly tailored bodice and flowing skirts, she imagined lying there in its place, with Aubrey leaning over her.

She closed her eyes and bit down hard on her lower lip. Whatever else she did, she must find a way to bring her thoughts and feelings under control. She could not afford such fancies; they could lead only to ruin, since Aubrey had freely professed that he did not love her.

Susannah took her time with her bath, then dried off and generously applied scented powder to her pinkened flesh. Victoria sneezed delicately, then chortled with great good humor. She could not sit up on her own yet, but she was trying hard, so once again Susannah arranged a pillow behind her small back, and the infant peered over the side of the cradle, chattering all the while.

Once she was dressed, Susannah brushed out her damp hair, then wound it carefully into a loose knot at the back of her head, securing it with the two tortoise-shell combs Mrs. Butterfield had given her the Christmas before. It made a soft, pale cloud around her face, which was flushed with excitement at the prospect of the evening ahead. Looking at her reflection in the mirror above the vanity table, Susannah felt almost like Cinderella preparing for the ball. The difference, of course, was that no prince would come tapping at her door with a glass slipper in hand. When this night was over, she would still be exactly what she was right at that moment: a spinster. Passed over. Unchosen.

She sighed and rose from the bench just as Maisie came in, knocking on the inside of the door as an after-thought. Seeing Susannah, she let out a long, low whistle of exclamation.

"Don't you look like somethin' in that there dress!" she cried.

Susannah took note of Maisie's green gown and up-swept hair. "You're a fair sight yourself, my friend," she countered.

Maisie grinned, showing her strong, ivory-colored teeth with their ingenuous gaps. "I ain't never looked this good before," she said in a gruff, embarrassed whisper. "Once we got the ballroom ready, there wasn't much left to do 'cept for feed Jasper and fuss over the way I was decked out." A worried expression sobered her. "Thing is, I don't reckon I have any idea how to dance like fancy folks do. Like as not, I'll mash some gent's toes for him with my big ole feet."

Susannah laughed to hear her own private fears echoed back to her, in a slightly different vernacular from the one she would have used. "I'm sure everyone will come through unscathed," she said.

"Un—?"

"Without getting hurt."

Maisie beamed. "Oh. Well, that's good."

Just then, the sound of carriage wheels rattling over hard ground rose from the street below as the first guests arrived. Susannah stood a little taller, though a part of her longed to take refuge in her room and refuse to come out until everyone had gone. Another part wanted just as fiercely to dance with Aubrey, again and again.

More carriages came, and the sound of jovial voices swelled on the night air. Susannah went to the window, pulled the curtain aside, and looked down to see a woman alighting from a sleek black coach, apparently the sole passenger. The driver bowed to his charge after helping her down.

A light, feathery fall of snowflakes pirouetted in the lamplight and came to rest on the shoulders of the woman's hooded velvet cloak.

"Damnation," Maisie breathed, standing beside her, and Susannah started, because she'd forgotten her friend's presence until that moment. "She's got some gall, comin' here without no invite."

Something tilted inside Susannah, slid, and shattered. The woman just arriving was Delphinia Parker, of course. As though aware that she was being watched, Aubrey's mistress—more precisely, his *former* mistress—lifted her head and looked directly at Susannah. Or, at least, it merely seemed so in that poor light.

"Perhaps she did receive an invitation," Susannah mused, turning away from the window with a hasty motion. "She is a—close friend of Aubrey's, isn't she?"

Maisie made a disdainful sound. "She ain't nobody's friend, 'cept her own. When Mrs. Fairgrieve passed on, she probably figured he was goin' to marry her. The gall."

Susannah moistened her tongue. Inexplicable tears throbbed behind her eyes, but she would not—*would not*—allow them to fall. "It seems unfair to place all the blame on Mrs. Parker," she said. "Aubrey's cooperation was required, after all."

"He was half out of his mind over the missus," Maisie said, gathering up Victoria. "I got to make sure Jasper's eaten his supper. You have yourself a fine time at the party, Susannah, and don't let them old biddies downstairs get to you, no matter what. Ain't a one of 'em fit to pour your tea."

With a soft, nervous laugh, Susannah kissed Maisie's cheek. Then, holding both the other woman's hands in hers, she asked, "What would I do without you?"

Maisie looked mystified by the question. "Why, what you've always done, I reckon," she said. She drew a deep, quivering breath to fortify her courage and let it out in a loud rush. "Well, guess it's time to play fancy," she said with happy resignation.

Susannah squeezed Maisie's hands briefly. "I've never had a friend like you," she said, and it was true. Even Julia, she realized, had never cared a tenth as much about her feelings as this bluff, good-hearted housekeeper did. "I'm so grateful."

Maisie reddened with what must have been a profound embarrassment. "You hurry down there, now," she blustered, opening the door with her free hand and gesturing for Susannah to precede her into the hallway. "Mr. Fairgrieve is lookin' to show you off, and he cuts a fine figure in his own right when he's had some spit and polish, I can tell you. Why, the two of you will set this here town back on its heels."

Susannah followed Maisie's earlier lead and drew a

deep breath, let it out slowly, then repeated the process. She didn't feel much calmer in the end, but she came to terms with the fact that a combination of challenges awaited her and resolved to meet them as bravely as she could.

Squaring her shoulders and tilting her chin upward a notch, she swept past Maisie and along the corridor, the silken skirts of her gown rustling like leaves in a soft breeze as she moved. At the head of the stairs, the swell of conversation and the first, faint strains of the orchestra rose to meet and surround her.

For a moment, she couldn't breathe.

"Go," she heard Maisie whisper somewhere behind her. "Show 'em. Show 'em all. And him, too."

Susannah rested a hand on the banister and took the first step, then a second, then a third. Momentum sustained her through the rest of the descent, although it seemed to take a lifetime with all those people staring up at her. She saw appraisal and suspicion in the eyes of the women, admiration and, yes, desire in those of the men. She thought she might choke on the panic and prayed she wouldn't be called upon to speak before she'd managed to acclimate herself.

Aubrey was waiting at the foot of the stairs, and he offered his arm the instant she was beside him. "My late wife's closest friend," he said, and though he was addressing the crowd gathered in the foyer, he was looking at her. "May I present Miss Susannah McKittrick?"

There were murmurs, desultory handshakes, more curious looks. Susannah recognized various members of the Benevolence Society and figured if Aubrey hadn't been holding on to her, she would have turned and dashed back up the stairs in terror. Nothing in her quiet, simple life at St. Mary's or subsequently on Nantucket had prepared her for so demanding an occasion, and she felt like a swimmer being borne out to sea by a powerful current.

"Breathe," Aubrey urged in a whisper as they entered the ballroom and immediately took the floor. The music seemed to throb behind some barrier, muffled as it was by Susannah's heartbeat.

She took a great gulp of air. Around them, other couples rode the swell of notes from the small orchestra. "I don't belong here," she said.

Miraculously, Aubrey heard her over the din of music and conversation. "But you do," he countered. "You are the loveliest woman in the room."

She was breathless and told herself it was the exercise that caused this affliction, not the strange, sweet madness Aubrey had stirred within her. "You are a flatterer," she accused.

He laughed. "On the contrary," he replied, "I never say anything I don't mean, and I have no propensity whatsoever for flattery."

She had no answer at the ready. Out of the corner of her eye, Susannah caught sight of Mrs. Parker, saw the angry glare on that classically beautiful face. What an odd thing it was, she reflected, that *she*, Susannah McKittrick, should be dancing with the most attractive man in the room, while a woman like Delphinia stood idly on the edge of the festivities. An instant later, Susannah saw Maisie come through a doorway in her wonderful green dress and felt encouraged.

"I plan to announce our marriage tonight," Aubrey said. "Will you humiliate me with a public refusal?"

Susannah's knees turned to water; she stiffened them instantly. The room, filled with noise and candlelight, brightly colored gowns, and the glitter of jewels, became a blur. The music hid itself once again behind a pounding pulse. Her own. "Surely you aren't serious. I've told you—"

"I want you, Susannah. I need you. And I will teach you to want and need me in return."

She heard the words so clearly that she feared all the guests must have done so, too. "You have a great deal of confidence in your own prowess," she said. It was a brazen statement, and she wasn't entirely sure what it meant, but it served a purpose. Aubrey was silent.

All too soon, however, the grin was back, in the company of an insufferable attitude of self-assurance. His hazel eyes glittered with mischief and something Susannah was not quite able—or quite ready—to identify. "One day soon, Susannah," he said, "you will share that confidence."

She might have slapped him if they hadn't been in the center of a crowded room with half of Seattle looking on. If she hadn't wanted so much, so conversely, to surrender to him in every respect.

The music stopped, and she was spared the necessity of an answer, because Mr. Zacharias, God bless him, appeared at her elbow straight away, asking for the next dance. At the first strains of the next piece, she and the lively older man went spinning away from Aubrey.

"I'm so glad to see you," she told her favorite student, and she was in earnest.

He laughed. "Why's that? You looked like you swallered the moon whilst you were dancin' with Fairgrieve. And he was happy as a bear cub dunked in honey."

She couldn't explain that she'd been afraid, minutes before, not of Aubrey but of herself. Her feelings were vast and unfamiliar, and they threatened to overwhelm her good judgment. "He's going to ask me to marry him," she told him, leaning close to speak into his ear.

"Lucky feller," Mr. Zacharias said. "You gonna say yes?"

She wanted desperately to accept Aubrey's proposal, even though she knew it was an empty one. She yearned to share his bed and his life, to bear and rear his children—not just Victoria, whom she already loved as deeply as she would ever love a babe of her own, but half a dozen more besides. What did that say about her? "I don't know what to do," she admitted.

"Then I reckon you ought to bide your time. Till you come to such a place as to be real clear-minded on things."

Her feelings were all too clear, but that was too personal a thing to discuss with Mr. Zacharias or anyone else, except perhaps Maisie or the minister, Johnstone. She bit her lower lip and shook her head once, in frustration rather than denial.

"You sure do look pretty tonight," Zacharias said. His eyes were twinkling, and Susannah wondered how soon it would be proper to introduce him to Maisie. The two of them would make a fine pair, in her opinion. It made her smile to think of Maisie living in the grandeur of that house a few streets away, never wanting for anything again, as long as she might live.

Maybe in the spring, she decided, when the sap was flowing again, even in older trees, weathered by time and hardship.

The next dance was taken by Ethan, who looked splendid in his Sunday clothes. He took her hand when the waltz ended and led her out of the hot press of celebrants and into the shadowy parlor, where it was cooler.

"Sit down," he said, guiding her to a settee. "You look ready to swoon."

She took a seat, grateful for a chance to catch her breath. She leaned back and closed her eyes, humming softly to herself. When she looked again, Ethan had fetched each of them a cup of punch from the refreshment table just inside the ballroom.

"Have you any idea how you've changed things around here?" he asked before drawing up a nearby chair and sitting down. He took a sip of punch while awaiting her answer.

Susannah, taken aback by the question, held her own cup carefully, lest she spill the contents onto her silken skirts. "I don't understand what you mean."

"I think you do," Ethan said in a quiet voice. "That ballroom's been closed up like a tomb since the trouble started between Aubrey and Julia. He never gave two hoots in hell about parties, his own or anybody else's. Now, all of a sudden, he's entertaining half of Seattle and keeping an eye on who you dance with."

Susannah had made a point of not looking to see whom *Aubrey* was dancing with. If Delphinia was waltzing around the ballroom in his arms, she didn't want to know it. "I'm sure he'll keep himself amused," she said lightly.

Ethan's face was in shadow, but she saw his eyebrows rise. "What does that mean?"

She sighed, took another sip from her cup before answering. The taste of the punch was tangy-sweet on her tongue. "Delphinia Parker is here," she said. "Surely you noticed her."

"Ah," Ethan said.

Susannah sat up a little straighter. "Now it's my turn to ask," she said. "What does that mean?"

"Nothing. I just think it's interesting that you're jealous of Delphinia."

"I'm not jealous. Don't be preposterous."

"I'm merely making an observation. A blind man could see that you feel something for my brother. Why are you pretending you don't?"

She set the cup aside, with a hand that trembled slightly, and lowered her head. "Is it so obvious?" she asked.

"Maybe not to everybody," Ethan answered. "But I know my brother, and I'm beginning to form some opinions about you, too."

"Such as?" It was safer asking questions. She could hide behind them—for a while, at least.

"Beneath that piano-teaching maiden-aunt facade of yours, you're a very passionate woman. You like waltzing until you're breathless. You like being kissed, and wearing your hair all soft and loose like that. Am I right?"

Susannah's cheeks burned. "You're rude, that's what you are."

He chuckled. "In case you think I'm about to misbehave, relax. Aubrey has his sights set on you, and, whatever he believes, I'm not about to step over a line like that. I just think you need somebody to talk to, that's all."

She was silent a long time, weighing the matter. Behind her, in the ballroom, the music was spritely and a little too loud. She wondered if Aubrey was smoking in the conservatory with a handful of other men or squiring some woman around the dance floor. Let it be anyone, she thought, besides his former mistress. "How do I know I can trust you?" she asked at long last.

He didn't answer directly; he simply leaned forward in his chair, bracing his elbows on his knees, the glass of punch still in hand. "What do you want most in this life, Susannah? What makes you toss and turn at night?"

She swallowed. It was clear enough what he meant, though the temptation to pretend she didn't understand was strong. "A family," she confessed in a soft, bereft voice. "A husband and children."

"If Aubrey wants to marry you—and I know he does—what are you waiting for?"

Susannah scraped her upper lip with her teeth. "He doesn't love me."

"Love," Ethan repeated, and frowned, sitting back now, pondering the word. "I had that once. Love, I mean. We took too long getting together, and I lost her. You know what, Susannah? If I could go back, I'd marry her right away, no matter what society had to say about it. If she didn't love me back, I'd still take a chance. I'd squeeze all the happiness I could out of every moment."

She felt a chill weave itself along the length of her spine. Oddly enough, it had not occurred to her until that very second that Aubrey was mortal, that he could die, like anyone else. Suppose there was an accident, or he fell ill, and perished or simply went away, as Ethan's Su Lin had done?

"He doesn't love me," she said again, but softly. Brokenly.

"He'll learn to, if he doesn't already. Don't let him go without giving it a lot of thought first, Susannah. He's a rare man, my brother. A good one, too."

Susannah felt tears spring to her eyes and was very glad of the dim light in the parlor. She could neither help nor hinder the slight quaver in her voice, however. "He was unfaithful to Julia. Why should I believe he wouldn't betray me in the same way?"

"Aubrey built and furnished this house for Julia, before he even met her. He went back east especially to find her. She was happy for a few months after they came out here, but then she changed. She did everything she could to torture him. He can be forgiven, I think, for seeking a little comfort somewhere else." He watched her in silence for a little while, and it didn't seem that he expected an answer. A good thing, since Susannah couldn't have spoken just then to save her life. "The hell of it is," Ethan went on, "I think he was supposed to find you when he went looking for a wife, not her."

Susannah had a handkerchief folded beneath the cuff of her right sleeve. She pulled it out, wadded it into a tight ball, and pressed it to her mouth. "That's crazy. How could he be looking for someone he didn't know?"

"He wasn't," Ethan said easily. "He was looking for somebody who was sensible and pretty and good clear through. That's you, Susannah."

She sniffled. "Julia was good," she protested.

"Maybe," he said. "She wasn't the same woman you remember, though, once she'd been here awhile."

"But why?" Susannah asked. "Something specific must have happened. Do you have any idea what it was?"

Ethan shook his head. "Despite what she would have had Aubrey think, Julia and I weren't close. Fact is, we had sharp words once or twice, she and I. I guess that's why she wanted to give the impression that we'd been lovers. She knew Aubrey would hate me if he thought I'd been with her, and who could blame him? A man ought to be able to trust his own brother, if not his wife. When you think about it, it was damned clever—she got back at me and drove Aubrey straight out of his head, all in one masterful stroke."

Susannah felt ill. It would have been a comfort to believe Ethan was mistaken, but she knew he wasn't. There had been something fragile in Julia, something brittle. She had been capable of wicked mischief, even cruelty, when moved to anger or jealousy. Once, when an abandoned kitten had found its way to St. Martha's and adopted Susannah, Julia had set about winning the animal's devotion for herself, cooing to it, stroking it, giving it cream and bits of fish. Later, the kitten had fallen ill and died. Just as well, Julia had said. She'd been tired of looking after the creature anyway.

Now, a surge of resentment swept through Susannah, and she felt silly for the intensity, the terrible magnitude of it. She hadn't thought about that incident in years, but Ethan's words had brought the memory back with all the immediacy of a slap across the face, and she had not had time to brace herself against it.

Susannah stood. "I'd better be getting back to the party," she said, smoothing her skirts. Julia's skirts.

Julia's house, Julia's husband, Julia's baby. Would there never be anything, anyone, to belong only to her?

Chapter

12

~

$\mathcal{T}$he ring was quite modest, really, just a simple band, a narrow circle of gold studded with tiny, glittering stones. And yet it was the most breathtaking thing Susannah had ever seen.

Aubrey took her aside, in the midst of the dancing, to offer it.

There, behind a potted palm that Maisie had dragged in from the main parlor, he put the same question to her as before, but this time he spoke only with his eyes. *Will you marry me, Susannah?*

She looked at the ring, then at his face, remembering what Ethan had said regarding the dangers of waiting too long for love. Perhaps he was right; perhaps love *was* something that could be nurtured and cultivated. She swallowed hard. "It's—it's not really proper, is it? Our getting married, so soon after—after Julia?"

"Whatever Julia and I shared was over long before she died," he said. His voice was low, but he did not seem concerned that others might overhear their conversation. "You'll be happy with me, Susannah. I promise you that."

Her friend hadn't been content, she reflected, for she was possessed of a logical turn of mind, generally speaking. On the other hand, Julia had been—well—*Julia*. She drew a deep breath. "When would—when would this marriage take place?" she asked, and the calm sound of her voice surprised her, for inside she was in a whirling tizzy. "If indeed it *does* take place, I mean."

His face revealed none of what he was feeling. If, for that matter, he happened to be feeling anything at all. The matter of matrimony was mostly one of practicality, as far as he was concerned; he'd made that quite clear from the beginning. As attractive as Aubrey was, in the spiritual and intellectual senses as well as the physical one, and as wealthy, he was for all intents and purposes just another lonely Seattle man. Like Mr. Zacharias and the other members of the parade of suitors posing as aspiring musicians. Her heart softened a little, despite the discouragement this logic caused her, for she certainly knew what it was to long for companionship and tenderness.

"Why, Aubrey?" she asked, honestly puzzled. "Why would you choose me?"

He had taken her hand in his, and he was poised to slide the ring onto the appropriate finger. "I've told you. Because I think you're beautiful. Because it's obvious that you care deeply for Victoria." He paused and sighed mightily. "Because sometimes I think if I have to lie alone in that bed for just one more night, I'm going to go mad."

The mention of his bed was sobering. Susannah, after all, was a virgin. Except for her own turbulent imaginings and the few hints and tidbits Julia had passed along over the years, she knew nothing about matters of intimacy. Color surged up her neck to pulse in her face. "You don't understand. I've never—I've never been with a man before. In—in that way, I mean." She whispered this last, since some of the other dancers were beginning to squint and peer as they passed the potted palm. She would die of mortification if anyone over-heard this most private of conversations.

"And you don't have to be intimate with me. Not be-fore you're ready, in any case." He looked and sounded sincere, very unlike the man Julia had painted as such a scoundrel over the last months of her life. Was he speak-ing the truth, or was he simply another deceitful charmer?

She stared at him after a few moments of close-throated misery. "But you said we would be sharing a bed."

"We would. But I won't force you, Susannah. That's another promise, one you can be sure I'll keep." He sighed once more, and the sound gave her an odd sense of comfort, though she could not have said why. "At whatever cost."

Susannah was once again stricken to silence, and this state of affairs lasted for some moments. She searched her mind and heart desperately for the proper words. When she did speak, it was in a rush of impulse. "Yes. If you'll give me time, then—yes."

He smiled, kissed her forehead, and slid the ring onto her finger. "Then we have an agreement," he said.

It unsettled Susannah a little, his referring to their engagement as an agreement, but she supposed she should have expected him to use formal terms. After all, he considered their marriage to be a business arrange-ment, nothing more. Whatever might be happening within her own heart and spirit, she must not forget the truth of the matter. This was not a romantic match.

"We have an agreement," she said, and immediately wondered when she had become so reckless. The day she boarded the train in Boston to travel all the way to rough-and-tumble Seattle, she decided. That was when she had begun to change. Or was it even earlier, during the first part of Julia's marriage, when she'd written such eloquent letters, brimming with the joys of love? Perhaps it had been then that Susannah's wistfulness had deepened into yearning.

Aubrey gave her his arm. "Smile a lot," he instructed her in a pleasant undertone. "I want people to think you're happy about this."

She *was* happy, truly so, she realized, and in spite of everything. But it would have been too humiliating to admit as much, since he did not share her devotion. She laid a hand on his forearm and raised her chin. No one, she determined, then and there, would ever know by her demeanor that she was the lover but not the beloved. She set her chin at a triumphant angle.

Aubrey swept her onto the dance floor, and the other guests cleared the way for them, smiling. It was as though the beams of a radiant sun were pouring through the roof of that splendid house on that cold autumn night, setting them and them alone ablaze with a golden aura. Susannah felt the warmth of it settling deep, settling forever, into her very bones.

When the music stopped, Susannah was breathless and flushed and happier than she'd ever been before. It seemed so easy then to push thoughts of Julia to the back of her mind.

Aubrey held her left hand in his and raised it for all to see. The engagement ring glittered in the flickering, merry light of the gas lamps. "Much to my delight," he said in a clear voice that carried into every corner of the ballroom, "Miss McKittrick has just agreed to become my wife."

There was a startled pause, or so it seemed to Susannah, then came a spattering of tepid applause, followed by exuberant shouts and whistles of congratulation. Some of the women glared at her from behind painted fans—perhaps they intended to import plain daughters and sisters, aunts and nieces, ripe for the marriage market, to Seattle and had chosen Aubrey, prosperous widower that he was, as a prime candidate for the role of bridegroom. It was the men who showed generous enthusiasm, who came forward first, grumbling good-naturedly even as they offered their felicitations, punching Aubrey in the shoulder or pumping his hand. Maisie, breathless with dancing and beaming at all the attention she'd received, hurried over to hug her.

"I checked on Victoria a little while ago," she confided. "That girl Mr. Fairgrieve brought in is lookin' out for her just fine."

Susannah, who had already visited Victoria several times herself, knew the child was fine. Distracted, she hoped the announcement of impending matrimony would not cut too deeply into her growing clientele of piano students. Marriage or no marriage, she still hoped to earn her own funds and establish some semblance of independence.

She pressed the back of one hand briefly to her forehead, more than a little dizzy. She had agreed to marry a man she barely knew, she marveled. One who had made her closest friend wretchedly unhappy, who had stated frankly that he did not believe in romantic love, let alone feel it for her, Susannah. She wanted very much to sit down, but that was not to be.

The band took up again, playing an energetic tune, and once again Susannah was in Aubrey's arms, spinning round and round. She might have collapsed if he hadn't been holding her so tightly, but, as it was, her feet barely touched the floor, and she felt as though she were dancing on clouds spun of sunshine and silk.

He waltzed with Susannah until there could be no question of his devotion to her and then slipped out into the wintry garden to enjoy a cheroot. Since her arrival, smoking indoors had been tacitly forbidden.

"Do you love her?" The voice was Ethan's. No need to turn around and look to know that. So Aubrey remained where he was, leaning a little, with one shoulder braced against the cold stone wall of his house. It was, he reflected, a mausoleum of a place, a giant crypt. Or, at least, it had been, until Susannah.

"No," he answered. With Ethan, he was usually blunt.

Ethan stood beside him. In the dim, icy light of the moon, Aubrey saw that his younger brother's jawline was hard with irritation. "Then you ought to let her go. She deserves better. She's a woman, with thoughts and hopes and feelings, not some pretty toy."

Aubrey gave a dry chuckle, though he wasn't in the least amused. "My brother, the poet. If you believe in love, why don't you find yourself a woman and start a family? Su Lin's gone, and things probably wouldn't have worked out between the two of you anyway."

The look in Ethan's eyes was hot enough to melt that wintry moon, and Aubrey braced himself to block a punch.

"Damn you, Aubrey, you don't know a blessed thing about how it was with Su Lin and me. I *loved* her. I would have died for her. Unlike you, I can't just pick out another woman and go on as if nothing had happened!"

For a moment, the silence between them was charged. Ethan knotted his fists, unknotted them again, flexing his fingers.

"Is that what you think I'm doing? Going on as if nothing had happened?" Aubrey asked, flinging his cheroot aside into the frosty grass. "Believe me, brother, a night doesn't go by that I don't break out in a cold sweat, thinking it might be like it was with Julia. I'd sooner put a gun to my head than go through that again!"

"Then you're a damn coward," Ethan said, keeping his voice low. "Susannah cares for you. Anybody with two eyes could see that at a glance. Anybody, that is, except you. And the hell of it is, you could care for her, too, if you were willing to take the risk."

Aubrey stared at his brother, amazed and stung to a low, vibrant fury. "Listen to yourself, little brother. I don't see *you* taking any risks. You're stuck like a mule in a mudhole, and you're not even trying to free yourself."

Ethan looked away and sighed. "I shouldn't have let Su Lin go—if I'd insisted—"

Aubrey took his brother's shoulders in a hard grip. "There was nothing you could do," he said. "The way you explained it to me, Su Lin went back to China for a lot of reasons—many of them you'll never understand. She's another man's wife. It's over, Ethan."

The expression in Ethan's eyes was bleak. Distant. "Why didn't I fight for her?"

"Maybe you knew, down deep, that it wouldn't have been good for either of you. Right or wrong, people are still real backward when it comes to things like that."

Ethan drew a snuffling breath and looked away for a moment. "I've been mourning her so long," he said. "It's as if she'd died." Then he shook Aubrey's hand, meeting his gaze squarely. "But damned if you aren't right. It's over." He smiled. "Congratulations on your engagement, brother. For your sake, I hope you know how lucky you are." With that, he took his leave, and Aubrey stood watching until he was out of sight.

Maybe, he thought, it was time both of them moved on, himself *and* Ethan. He'd been stuck for a long while himself, mired in regret, in anger, in guilt.

Tilting his head back, Aubrey searched the frigid,

star-strewn sky, for what he did not know. Then he returned to the engagement party.

She was dancing with John Hollister, and, at the first sight of them together, Susannah smiling, flushed and bright-eyed, up into the Pinkerton man's benign face, he felt a stab of something primal, something territorial. He was still grappling with this most elemental emotion when a slender, bejeweled hand came to rest on his forearm.

He knew the touch, had selected the diamonds and sapphires himself, on various trips to San Francisco. He raised his eyes to meet Delphinia's gaze, but otherwise he didn't move at all.

"Just one dance?" she asked softly.

He spoke in quiet tones, well aware that the exchange was being observed, that any implied intimacy would result in a spate of gossip that might well hurt Susannah and, one day, even Victoria. "You shouldn't be here," he said in a flat voice.

She snapped open the silk and ivory fan she carried, another gift from him, no doubt, though he couldn't rightly recall the purchase, and fluttered it in front of her finely structured face. She was, he thought as analytically as if he'd been judging horseflesh, probably much more beautiful than Susannah, in the classic sense. God knew, he'd enjoyed the pleasures of her bed. Then, too, in a place where almost everybody had a colorful past, he could have taken her for a wife with relative impunity; after the initial social uproar had died down, Delphinia surely would have been taken into the fold, if only because of her money and status.

For all that, he had never once considered marrying her. It was an odd insight, and it caused him to frown.

"You are a fool if you think that little mouse can make you happy," she hissed through lips parted in a winsome smile. "Look at her. She doesn't know the first thing about dancing. As for social graces—"

"Social graces?" Aubrey interrupted. "This is Seattle, not Boston or Paris. Not much call for fancy manners here."

The fan fluttered faster. "Then what is her attraction?"

Aubrey turned and assessed Susannah. "I don't know," he said. "But I mean to marry her, Delphinia, whether you approve or not." He paused, raised an eyebrow. "Didn't we agree, you and I, that you would catch the first available steamer for San Francisco? It would seem that you've missed a few."

Delphinia's cheeks were bright with color; she was the perfect portrait of a woman scorned. "You will regret your treatment of me, Aubrey Fairgrieve," she said in an undertone, and the fancy fan was practically a blur. "You will regret it sorely."

He resisted an uncharitable urge to roll his eyes. "Maybe," he said. "I believe there's a steamer tomorrow afternoon. Maybe if you start packing now, tonight, you could secure a cabin." With that, he walked away, found Susannah on the dance floor in the arms of one of her more energetic piano pupils, and rescued her by taking her hand and pulling her aside.

Looking down into her face, her glowing, innocent, beguiling face, he realized for the first time that Ethan had been right, out there in the garden earlier in the evening. Susannah cared for him. The knowledge caused him a twinge of guilt, but then he consoled himself with the fact that he'd never misled her. Never claimed to feel any of the gentle sentiments for her or any other woman. She was entering this marriage with her eyes open.

"It's like a dream," she said, a little breathless. "The

music, the dancing." She looked down at her dress. "This gown. Have you seen Ethan? I was hoping—"

Aubrey felt his jawline clamp down. He forcibly relaxed, but it was too late; he knew by her expression that she'd seen and comprehended his reaction. "He's gone home, I'm afraid," he said.

She let that pass without comment but made no effort to hide her disappointment in learning that Ethan had already left the party. "Oh," she replied in a dispirited tone.

"One more dance?" he asked.

She nodded, and he took her into his arms, and that was all it took, for that moment, for that night, to make everything all right.

Susannah awakened to a pounding rain and peered through her bedroom window to see that the last dirty rags of snow had been washed away. The cobblestones shimmered in the thin light of day, and the lawn was already brown with mud. She might have been demoralized but for the ring sparkling on her left hand.

She was going to be married! It hardly seemed possible, after so many years as a spinster, and yet here was the proof. Aubrey had given her his pledge and announced their imminent wedding to virtually all of Seattle.

Victoria cooed in her cradle, legs bobbling, grasping at her toes with both hands. Susannah let her forehead rest against the cool, damp glass of the window. "I'll be a good mother to her, Julia," she murmured. "I promise."

A brisk knock at her bedroom door startled her; she jumped and, expecting Maisie, called out, "Come in."

Aubrey stepped over the threshold, looking unreasonably handsome in his starched white linen shirt and well-tailored black trousers. He wore suspenders, too, and shining boots. He grinned, knowing full well that Susannah had not been expecting him. "You should be more careful," he teased. "About whom you invite into your bedchamber, I mean."

Susannah's hand had gone of its own accord to the buttoned collar of her flannel nightgown; she clenched it like a maiden about to be ravished. Amusement flickered in Aubrey's eyes, and she flushed, releasing her hold. "I certainly wouldn't have invited you," she said in belated response.

He chuckled and swept her with his gaze. "Wouldn't you?"

"Of course not. It's improper, your being here. Before our—before our—"

"Wedding?" Aubrey prompted. His hazel eyes were still smiling. He showed no signs of leaving but instead held out a celluloid collar. "Would you mind fastening this thing for me? I can't seem to get it closed without choking myself."

Susannah hesitated. She was still in her nightclothes, after all, and she was naked beneath them. She and Aubrey were alone in the room, perhaps in the house, except for Victoria, who certainly would not suffice as a chaperone. She let out a long breath and stepped closer, accepting the collar.

The air between them seemed to shift and buckle, like the shimmering mirages Susannah had seen over Nantucket waters on hot summer days. A strange ache implanted itself deep within her and set every nerve end to trembling. Her hands shook as she reached up to put the collar around Aubrey's neck.

He smelled of laundering soap and some subtle, spicy cologne, and his chest seemed to exude heat. His brown hair brushed the backs of her fingers, a touch of silk, light as a breeze yet possessed of the power to rock her on the deepest levels of her being.

She fumbled with the buttons at the front of the collar, aware of the man gazing down at her in every tissue and fiber, finally managed to close them.

"Susannah," he said. His voice was pitched low and a little ragged, and all he said was that one word. Just her name. Yet something shifted inside her, and she knew she would never be quite the same again. That he had changed the very shape of her soul once more, as he had done a few days before, with a single, consuming kiss.

She shivered, though the room was warm. Far too warm. She commanded her legs to carry her back a step, then another, until she was out of his reach. Her legs didn't listen. "The baby," she said.

"Let me take you to my bed," Aubrey responded.

Susannah felt herself sway. Squeezed her eyes shut, opened them to find that he had taken a loose hold on her nightgown, bunching the worn flannel in both fists. She was too breathless to speak and would not have trusted herself to reply sensibly in any case.

"Don't you think we should at least seal our engagement with a kiss?" He was so persuasive. He drew her close, by her nightgown, and bent his head to claim her mouth with his own. He was gentle at first, then more demanding, and Susannah's body responded in a most unspinsterly fashion, expanding somehow, opening like an orchid that has been coaxed and nurtured to blossom. She gave a slight moan and parted her lips, allowed him to deepen the kiss.

She was vaguely aware that the nightdress was rising slowly, trailing over her calves, her knees, her thighs, her stomach. She knew she should protest, should at least *want* to protest, but instead she clung to him. When he broke the kiss long enough to pull the gown off over her head and toss it aside, she merely moaned and took him back eagerly when he claimed her mouth again.

He stepped back, his hands weighing her breasts, and

Susannah stood before him proudly, utterly without shame. Unschooled though she was in the ways of men and women, she knew she had a certain power over this strong, confident man, and she reveled in it. Let him look, she thought with gentle defiance, but she gasped softly when he passed the pads of his thumbs over her nipples, causing them to harden and strain.

"So beautiful," he breathed.

"The baby," Susannah reminded him, but weakly. He had, without her knowing it, maneuvered her behind the changing screen that stood in the corner of her room.

"Is a baby," he replied, and bent to take the tip of one breast between his lips.

Susannah made a sobbing sound and grasped the back of his head, plunging her fingers into his hair, holding him tightly lest he pull away. "Oh, God," she whimpered, and he chuckled again and worked her with his tongue.

"Do you want me, Susannah?" He whispered the question while nibbling at the other breast.

"Oh, yes," she choked. "Yes." She waited for him to sweep her up into his arms and carry her down the corridor to his bed, but he did not.

"Good," he replied, and went on enjoying her. Presently, just when Susannah thought she would lose her mind for certain, he slipped one hand between her legs, through the moist hair that sheltered her most private place. She sagged back against the wall, her breathing rapid and shallow.

He caressed her for a time, then, without warning, slipped his fingers inside her, while his thumb lingered outside her body, wreaking havoc of its own. She gasped and closed her eyes, at the same time thrusting her hips forward. Welcoming his attentions, scandalous though they were.

"If you have any doubts that I can keep you happy,"

he said, tracing the length of her neck with the lightest of kisses, "remember this."

Susannah swallowed a lusty groan as he pleasured her; it seemed to her that things progressed at a breathtaking speed and, at the same time, took forever. She did not understand what he was leading her toward, what he was promising, for she had known only vague, fevered yearnings until then. One thing was vividly clear: she would perish if he let her go too soon.

Her hips were busy—they seemed to know what to do, without being told—meeting every thrust of his hand with no sort of restraint, and then it happened, the unexpected, undreamed-of cataclysm, seizing her like the teeth of some great beast and shaking her violently, causing her back to arch spasmodically, over and over again. It was only when she came back inside herself that she realized she'd been shouting her surrender for all the world to hear and that Aubrey had covered her mouth with his own all the while, catching and swallowing her cries.

She started to sink, and he caught her by the waist. Brought her back to her bed. She waited for him to lie down beside her and finish what he'd begun—his erection was obvious, even to a spinster—but instead he simply stood over her, a man engaged in a private struggle. She held out one hand to him, for her wanting was greater now that she had tasted glory.

He shook his head and retreated a step. "No, Susannah. Not yet."

"But why?" she asked, wounded. Aware suddenly of her nakedness, like Eve in the garden, having taken the forbidden fruit, she snatched at the covers in a vain effort to cover herself.

Aubrey took in her body with a slow, hungry gaze. A muscle flexed in his cheek, and his right temple throbbed visibly. "Not because I don't want to," he said. "That's for damn sure."

She simply looked at him, too mortified by his rejection really to comprehend his meaning. "You were only mocking me, then," she accused, near tears but holding firm against them. "When you asked me into your bed, when you—when we were behind the screen—" She felt her face go hot and toppled into wretched silence.

"No," he said, almost growling the word. "I would indeed have taken you to bed, if you'd agreed." He thrust a hand, the same hand that had brought her to release, through his rumpled hair. "But it wouldn't have been right. There will be time enough for that when we're properly married."

She pulled the sheets and blankets up to her chin while Victoria cooed on in her cradle, blessedly oblivious to everything but her own tiny, elusive toes.

"And what just happened?" She could barely force the humiliating words past her throat, but she had to know. "Did that mean anything?"

He had turned his back, gained the door, and stood with the knob in his hand. After a moment, he looked at her over one broad shoulder. His smile was saucy, even impudent. "I hope so," he said. "It sure as hell meant something to me."

A heartbeat later, he was gone, leaving the door ajar, whistling as he made his way down the corridor.

Infuriated, frustrated because Aubrey was leaving and she wanted him to stay, Susannah flung one pillow after him, then another. At the same time, to her great consternation, she was wondering how long she'd have to wait for their next encounter.

In his private bathroom, minutes after the interlude with Susannah, Aubrey stripped off his shirt, ran cold water into the basin, and splashed his face and chest until his teeth chattered. His erection finally went down—out of sympathy for the rest of his body, he supposed—and he stood there dripping, both hands braced against the sink, head lowered. With Julia and Delphinia and every other woman he'd ever known, he'd been able to detach himself from their pleasure, to stand back emotionally and wait until the storm had passed and he could appease himself in good conscience.

With Susannah, it was different. Her delight in their lovemaking was so intertwined with his own satisfaction that he could barely separate the two. He'd come perilously close to taking her, to losing himself inside her. To caring.

He closed his eyes, made himself breathe slowly. Nothing—*nothing* was more dangerous than that.

Aubrey raised his head, met his own gaze in the mirror. Water drizzled from his hair, beaded on his lashes and his skin. Indeed, he looked as though he'd just been baptized by an old-fashioned preacher.

"Coward," he accused, as his brother had done the night before. Then he snatched a towel from the rack and turned his back on his own image.

Susannah did not see Aubrey again that day or the next. She was busy the whole time, looking after Victoria, teaching more piano lessons, and helping Maisie as much as she could with the cooking and laundry. For all that, her thoughts were always chasing off in search of her future husband, like children scrabbling after butterflies.

The afternoon of the second day, she was taking tea in the kitchen while Victoria napped upstairs. The large room was steaming, the windows fogged, because

Maisie, disdaining the fancy washing machine, was boiling Aubrey's white shirts on the stove. She had acquired a permanent helper in the silent, awkward-looking young woman who had looked after Victoria during the party. Ellie was her name, and she listened stoically while Maisie issued orders in her gruff, kindly way.

"Ellie's man done lit out for the gold fields," Maisie confided when the new employee had gone upstairs to gather towels in need of washing. "Poor thing. She really believes he's comin' back."

Susannah set down her tea cup and put aside her own problems. "Maybe he is, Maisie. Maybe he'll return one day, with a bag of gold under each arm, whistling a tune."

Standing there by the stove, minding her laundry, Maisie gave a snort. "You read too many books," she said cheerfully. "She's got any sense, she wouldn't take the rascal back on any account. There's no forgettin' somethin' like that."

Susannah thought of Julia and the hurt Aubrey had suffered at her hands. Once one person's trust in another had been shattered, it might be that there was no mending the damage. The idea filled her with sorrow, because she wanted Aubrey's trust as much as his love, and she knew one could not flourish without the other. "I don't suppose there is."

Chapter

13

〜

$\mathcal{L}$ooking back, Aubrey supposed it shouldn't have surprised him, what happened next, given the fact that Delphinia had threatened him just the night before at the engagement party, and he knew her to be a woman of her word, at least where vengeance was concerned. All the same, he was caught unprepared when, working alone in his office above the store the following evening, long after everyone else had gone home, he saw a flicker of movement in the open doorway. Before he could react or even credit that he had uninvited company, a pistol flared, and he heard the report, heard the lamp at his elbow splinter in a spray of glass. The light folded in on itself, disappeared; ducking behind the desk, he groped for the pistol he'd stopped carrying years before. After all, Seattle was a modern, civilized town by western standards. Few men went about armed.

He might have been blind, for all he could see in that dense gloom; the intruders were all around him, all over him, six or seven of them, small and wiry and fiercely strong. He put up a respectable fight, being a big man and handy with his fists, but he'd lost the battle before it began, and he knew it.

Fists came at him from all sides; it was like standing in the bottom of a rock-lined well while it collapsed, stone by stone. The pain went bone deep and finally wrenched him down and down, into a place where there was nothing but the sound of his own heartbeat.

Ethan reached the store first thing in the morning and was busy selecting various staples for his larder when Hawkins appeared at the top of the stairs, screeching like a monkey with its tail caught, his eyes round as stove lids behind his spectacles and almost bulging out of his head.

"Help!" he yelled. "Good God, somebody help—Mr. Fairgrieve—I think—I think somebody's killed him—"

The item Ethan had been holding crashed to the hardwood floor, and it seemed to him that everyone in the store came running, but he got there first. His boot heels hammered on the steps as he mounted them two at a time, and he shoved the secretary out of his way without breaking his stride.

Aubrey lay sprawled on the floor a few feet behind his desk, and he did indeed look dead. Ethan was on his knees beside his brother before he became aware of himself again, feeling at the base of his brother's throat for a pulse. It was there—he closed his eyes for a moment in abject relief—but just barely, and it was thin as thread.

"Get a doctor," Ethan rasped. "Somebody get a doctor." He glanced back over one shoulder, saw a crowd huddled in the doorway. Hawkins splintered off from the bunch, presumably to bring help. "I need some cold water and clean cloth," he added. "The rest of you had better get back to your work."

The doctor arrived within a few minutes; he was portly and middle-aged, with the smells of whiskey, sweat, and stale tobacco about him. Ethan, who had been cleaning Aubrey's wounds as best he could, sat back on his heels, keeping a close watch while the stranger opened an ancient black bag and brought out a stethoscope.

"Damn near killed him," the older man remarked. He looked Ethan over. "You do this?"

"Hell, no," Ethan snapped. Had the circumstances been more fortuitous, he might have been flattered that anyone thought him capable of taking Aubrey, who was six inches taller and must have outweighed him by seventy pounds.

"Well, it's going to be a while before he can tell us who did," the doctor said with a sigh. He ran capable, if none too clean, hands over Aubrey's ribs, his arms and legs. "I hope he's tough, this feller, 'cause he's got a long, hard road ahead of him, if he makes it at all."

Ethan's stomach pitched itself against the back of his throat. Aubrey couldn't die, he couldn't. There were too many things still unresolved between the two of them, and besides, Aubrey was his brother, damn it. All the family he'd ever had.

"He'll make it," Ethan vowed.

"Well, he belongs in the hospital. We'd better get him up there, soon as we can."

"No," Ethan said. In his mind, hospitals were frightful places where people went to die. Aubrey would go home, to the big house on the hill, where he could be looked after proper. "He'd want to be in his own bed, if he was given the choice. That's where I mean to take him."

The physician shrugged, probably anxious to get back to a card game someplace. "Those ribs have to be bound—"

"You can do that right here, can't you?"

"Well—" The man took out his pocket watch, checked the time. Ethan considered sending him packing and fetching another, better doctor, but he was reluctant to leave Aubrey untended any longer. As it was, he'd probably been lying there unconscious for most of the night.

"Get some sheets from the dry goods shelf," Ethan said to Hawkins, who was hovering in the doorway again. The others had gone back to their usual tasks, as instructed. "I'll need some kind of litter, too."

Hawkins gulped, nodded, and hastened away, obviously glad of an assignment. He returned shortly with a pile of crisp bed linens of the sort that sold for a pretty penny; Ethan didn't hesitate to tear them into wide strips. Then, working together, he and the doctor, who had stated his name as Horace Sutherfield, stripped Aubrey to the waist and bound his ribs. He didn't stir during the process, and while Ethan reckoned that to be a mercy of sorts, he would have preferred to hear a few moans and curses. That would have indicated that Aubrey was nearer to life than to death, but as things stood, there was just no telling.

Presently, two of the sales clerks clambered up the stairs with what looked like the weathered door of an outhouse. Ethan and the doctor put Aubrey onto the slab and strapped him to it with the remaining strips of sheeting. In his condition, a fall might well kill him. Or cripple him, Ethan thought gloomily, if that hadn't happened already.

A boiling rage filled him; he would find the men who had done this, whether they were traveling one by one or running in a pack, and repay them in kind for what they'd done. Maybe he'd throw in a bullet between the eyes, just for good measure.

"I had Simpson bring your wagon around front," Hawkins said as Ethan and the stout German blacksmith summoned from down the street each took one end of the improvised litter. The secretary looked bloodless, and there was still a wild glint of panic in his eye.

"Thanks," Ethan said quietly.

"If there's anything else I can do—"

"Just mind the store. And if you hear anything—"

Hawkins stood a little straighter. "You can be sure I'll send word to you right away, Mr. Fairgrieve."

"Ethan," he corrected in passing. "I suppose the police ought to be told what happened."

"I'll see to that, too," Hawkins promised.

By then, Ethan was concentrating on getting his brother safely down the stairs, through the store, into the back of the wagon waiting outside. The doctor climbed into the box and took the reins without being asked, while Ethan crouched in the wagon bed beside Aubrey's inert, blanket-covered form. The blacksmith rode at the open tailgate, knowing his help would be needed when they reached the big house.

As they jostled and jolted up the steep, rutted road that ran alongside the store, fat, feathery flakes of snow wafted down from a burdened sky.

Susannah was on the porch, bidding an eager piano student farewell for the day, when the wagon appeared. Seeing Ethan kneeling in the back, she knew instantly that something had happened to Aubrey, and she went hurtling down the steps and the long walk, heedless of the slippery stones and the biting chill in the air.

She stood with her heart in her throat while Ethan and a burly man wearing rough clothes and a smithy's apron got out of the wagon at the rear and drew Aubrey after them, strapped to a wooden panel and oblivious to everything and everyone around him. Snow settled on his blood-matted hair, filled the cuts on his face, covered his lashes and his lips. Except for the bruises, he was colorless as a corpse.

"Lead the way," Ethan said, and while he did not speak sharply, his tone was crisp. He expected to be obeyed.

Susannah fled back up the walk and into the house. The piano student, a moderately successful miner who called himself Snakebite Charlie, lingered lest his help be needed. The dissolute-looking man she assumed to be a doctor sent him scuttling with an order to bring back the first constable he came across.

It wasn't until she had thrown back the covers on Aubrey's bed, and Ethan and the doctor and the blacksmith had carefully maneuvered him onto the mattress, that Susannah dared to speak. "Tell me," she demanded.

Ethan looked at her with all the sorrows of mankind showing in his face. "There isn't a whole lot to tell," he answered. "Hawkins found him in his office this morning, pretty much as you see him now."

She squeezed her eyes shut as the images assailed her. She indulged in a moment's shame, for she had listened for Aubrey the night before, had known that he hadn't come home. And she'd lain awake, twisting her engagement ring round and round on her finger, fearing that he was with Delphinia or some other woman of similar repute.

The doctor was working busily over Aubrey, lifting his lids to peer into his eyes, testing reflexes, and shaking his head a great deal. He did not look optimistic.

"Have you any idea who did this?"

Ethan's jawline went rock-hard as he looked down at his brother. "No," he answered without meeting her gaze, "but I have a notion or two about who ordered it done."

Susannah had worked her way from the foot of the bed to Aubrey's side, opposite the doctor. She drew up a chair and took one large, still hand into both her own. "Who?" she wanted to know.

"You needn't concern yourself with that," Ethan said flatly. "I'll see that justice is done."

Something in his voice, in his manner, alarmed Susannah almost as much as his words, though he had spoken quietly and without inflection. "I should think the police will consider that their provenance," she said.

"To hell with the police," Ethan replied, and shoved a hand through his hair.

The doctor looked up from his examination of Aubrey. "The lady is right, Mr. Fairgrieve," he said. "You'd do well to leave this matter to the authorities."

Ethan glowered at the older man. "They're more than welcome to whatever's left of the bastards when I get through." His expression was cold enough to send a shiver skittering up Susannah's spine. The kind of vengeance Ethan was talking about could only lead to his own destruction.

The doctor shook his head and tossed an appealing glance in Susannah's direction. "If you've got any influence over this feller," he said, "use it to talk him out of this foolishness."

Susannah swallowed a throat full of angry, despairing tears. Aubrey lay motionless on the bed, waxen where he wasn't bruised, his features so swollen as to be nearly unrecognizable. She didn't want Ethan to wind up at the end of a rope for taking the law into his own hands, but she understood his desire for revenge. Oh, yes, she understood it full well. "The Fairgrieve men make up their own minds," she murmured in reply, "and from what I've seen, there's no changing them."

Ethan had turned away by that time; he stood at the window, looking out, his broad shoulders rigid beneath his shirt. He wasn't wearing a coat and seemed unaware that smudges of Aubrey's blood marked his hands, his clothes, even his face.

"My name's Sutherfield," the physician said, extending one hand to Susannah. "Horace Sutherfield."

Susannah hesitated, then took the offered hand and shook it. She hated even to look up from Aubrey's face, lest he slip away while she wasn't watching. Intuitively, she knew that her hold on him, like that of the earth itself, was tenuous. "Is he in pain?" she asked, her voice fragile, brittle, like the thinnest glass.

Dr. Sutherfield answered by taking a brown bottle from his medical kit and setting it on the bedside table with a light thump. "Probably, but there isn't much we can do about it until he comes around. When and if he does, give him a dose of this laudanum—not too much, though. Just enough to take the edge off—a drop or two should do the trick—stuff gets hold of some people and doesn't ever let them go."

Susannah nodded, smoothing Aubrey's hair back from his forehead with a gentle pass of her free hand. With the other, she clasped his fingers, still trying to anchor him to that place, that room, that bed.

"Send somebody for me if I'm needed in the night." Sutherfield paused, cleared his throat self-consciously. "I'll be in the card room down at the Silver Eagle," he added. And then he was gone.

Susannah forgot Ethan's presence, forgot everything but the broken man lying so still in the bed he had once urged her to share. She regretted her hesitation now, wished she'd given herself to him, if only that one time. As things stood, he might well die, and she would never know what it was to love him fully, with abandon, unfettered by the restraints of propriety. And never was a very long time.

A hand came to rest on her shoulder, and she remembered Ethan. Dashing a tear from her cheek with the back of one wrist, she straightened her spine and squared her shoulders. "We have to be strong for him," she said.

Ethan gave her shoulder a light squeeze before he

withdrew his hand. "He's a strong man, Susannah," he said hoarsely. "The strongest I've ever known. He might just hang on, if he knows you're with him." He paused, as if weighing his words, then added, "My brother needs you, has for a long while, I reckon. That's why he gave you such a hard time when you got here. It scared him, since he probably figured he'd closed himself off for good."

She raised Aubrey's hand to her mouth, brushed her lips lightly across the backs of his knuckles. "Please—tell Maisie I need for her to look after Victoria. I can't leave him."

Ethan lingered a few moments, and she knew he wanted to say something more, but in the end, he didn't speak, and neither did she. Her gaze, her whole heart and spirit, was fixed on Aubrey.

Ethan kicked open the door of Delphinia Parker's stateroom on the steamer *Pacific*, due to set sail for southerly waters with the morning tide. She was sitting at a vanity table, powdering her face, and she was plainly startled by his arrival. She recovered quickly, though; he had to give her that.

"Why, Ethan," she said, fluttering her fanlike lashes. "You've come to say good-bye. Isn't that sweet?"

It was all he could do not to grab her by the throat and jerk her to her feet. Instead, he stood behind her while she watched his reflection in the mirror. He felt the deck swaying beneath his feet, in time with the waters of Elliott Bay. "It almost worked," he said instead. "You almost killed him."

She rounded her eyes and her skillfully painted mouth, the perfect likeness of innocence itself. One slender, snow-white hand fluttered at her breast. "I declare, Ethan, I don't know what you could be talking about."

Her chair was a swivel affair, like a bar stool. He spun her around and bent down, his face a breath from hers. "I'm talking," he said, "about my brother. You remember him? Aubrey Fairgrieve—the man who's kept you in face paint and gewgaws for the last few months? Thanks to those thugs you sent, he's all but dead."

Except for the slightest twitch at the corner of her mouth, Delphinia didn't react. "You're mistaken," she said coolly. Then, to his utter disbelief, she slid her arms around his neck and tried to draw him close.

He jerked back as if he'd been burned, and she laughed. *Laughed.* Ethan closed his eyes, struggled to control his temper. When he trusted himself to speak, he clutched the harlot's creamy shoulders again. "Who were they?" he demanded. "I want names, Delphinia. And I'll get them if I have to shake them out of you!"

She got nervous then; maybe she'd finally gathered that he meant business. That he hadn't come to bed his brother's former mistress before she sailed on to new horizons. She wet her lips with the tip of her tongue and cringed a little in his grasp. "I didn't tell them to kill him," she said, putting a faint whine to the words. "Just—just rough him up a little."

Again, Ethan did battle with his lesser nature. Again, and it seemed something of a miracle to him, his better judgment prevailed. "Well, they did that, all right. He's unconscious, with one side of his rib cage caved in, and God knows what damage there is to his insides." He took in her silk dressing gown. "Put on your clothes, Delphinia. You and I are going to pay a call on the con-stabulary."

She retreated a step, pale behind her rouge. "I can't afford to get in trouble with the law, Ethan," she fretted.

"I guess you should have thought of that before you had my brother beaten to a bloody pulp," he replied, opening one of the trunks that crowded the small stateroom, jerking out some sort of garment without looking to see what it was, and thrusting it at her. "Get dressed, or I swear to God, I'll take you to the police in that flimsy thing you're wearing now."

She nodded toward a changing screen in the corner of the room. "All right, then, if you insist. But I don't want you looking at me while I change."

He should have been suspicious of her sudden acquiescence, but in point of fact, his mind was on other things. Aubrey, mostly. Susannah and the baby, too. She stepped behind the screen, and when she came out, only an instant later, there was a derringer in her hand.

Ethan felt the bullet rip into his side as he stumbled forward, grabbed the gun, and wrestled it out of her hand. He was leaning against the cabin wall, one hand covering his wound, when two men rushed in. Seeing them, he allowed himself to pass out.

"Ethan is in *jail?*" Susannah echoed in disbelief after a grim Maisie delivered the news. She had vowed not to leave Aubrey's side, and she had kept her word, despite pleas and protests from her friend.

Maisie nodded. "Shot, too. In the side. There was a lot of blood, but I guess he weren't hurt too bad, when it came right down to it."

Susannah felt ill. First Aubrey, now Ethan. She could not shake the feeling that she had somehow brought bad luck to both the Fairgrieve brothers, though she wasn't usually a superstitious person. "Wh-what happened?"

"According to Hawkins—he was the one what brought the news—that Parker woman claims Ethan tried to force himself on her, on-board one of the steamers down at the harbor. She says she shot him to protect her virtue." Maisie gave a disdainful har-rumph.

"Nonsense," Susannah replied. "Ethan wouldn't have done a thing like that. He probably found some connection between her and what happened to Aubrey." The reminder brought fresh tears to her eyes; she took in his injuries once again and wished she could do something more than sit beside him, holding his hand, offering silent prayers and hoping.

"We know that," Maisie agreed, "but I ain't so sure about the police. Folks around here tend to think of Ethan as somethin' of a hell-raiser."

"Why?" Susannah asked, honestly puzzled. He had never behaved in anything but the most gentlemanly fashion in her presence.

"He got into some trouble when he was a boy; no worse than most, though. Then there was that Chinese girl. He wanted to marry her, and to plenty of people, that was reason enough to give up on him for good."

"That's ridiculous," Susannah muttered.

Maisie raised and lowered one bulky shoulder in a shrug. "Be that as it may, that was the way of it. Only thing worse than their bein' torn apart the way they was would have been for them to be together."

Susannah had suspected all along that Maisie knew more than she was letting on, and here was the proof. It was small comfort, given the situations in which Ethan and Aubrey found themselves now. "What happened?"

"Her family sent her back home to China," Maisie said in a gruff whisper. "She married some man over there, I reckon. There was never any word from her."

"Oh, Maisie."

"Ethan ain't been the same since, 'course," Maisie reflected, her gaze resting sorrowfully on Aubrey.

"They've neither one had his rightful share of happiness, neither Aubrey nor Ethan."

Susannah watched as her friend went around the room, moving from one fixture to the next, turning up the gas, setting bluish flames dancing. Dispelling some of the shadows—the outward ones, at least. "And then there was Julia."

"Yes, ma'am," Maisie agreed wearily. "Then there was Julia."

The subject lay between them, a great gulf of secrecy and silence that neither woman wanted to breach just then.

"What will happen to Ethan?" Susannah asked after a long time.

"Hawkins'll get him a lawyer," Maisie answered. "I sure hope he does better than he did when he went to round up that doctor feller."

Alone in his cell, a clean bandage bulging beneath his shirt, Ethan lay stretched out on his cot. The doctor—not Sutherfield but some other stranger—had slipped him a flask full of whiskey after tending to his wounds, and he'd been taking regular drafts from it, but the stuff didn't do much to soothe the throbbing ache in his side. Still, it gave him something to do, and without it he probably would have flung himself against the bars, yelling like a wild Indian, until he collapsed in exhaustion or passed out from the pain. Being behind bars was too much like being shut in the root cellar as a boy—one of his pa's favorite punishments—though at least there was light in the cell and a modicum of fresh air coming in through a high, narrow window.

"Ethan?"

He recognized the voice, looked over to see John Hollister standing on the other side of the bars. Hollister was a family friend, of sorts. He and Aubrey had gone to school together for a short while over in Montana, and they'd had their share of scrapes before and after class, bloodying each other's noses and blackening each other's eyes. While Hollister had read the law, Aubrey had returned to Seattle to seek his fortune.

"Hullo, John," he said, easing himself upright with a painful effort. "What are you doing here?"

"I'm about the closest thing you're going to get to a lawyer," Hollister answered. He cleared his throat, and Ethan saw strain in his face, and sorrow. He sighed. "It's what Aubrey would want," he said, as though reminding himself, dragging up a chair, sitting down, and regarding Ethan through the bars. "What happened on that boat?"

Ethan sat on the edge of his cot, braced his elbows on his knees, and rested his face in his hands. "That should be obvious," he said affably, "even to you. Delphinia shot me." He raised his head. "No more than I deserved, letting her get the drop on me like that."

"She says she did it because you were about to rape her. Is that true?"

"You know damn well it isn't."

"Do I?"

Ethan stood with difficulty and crossed the cell to grasp the bars, taking so tight a hold that his knuckles went white and the joints in his fingers ached. "I went there to find out who she hired to beat my brother half to death. That's *all* I went there for."

Hollister winced at the mention of Aubrey's beating, knew he might not survive. "And what did she say?"

"She admitted she'd hired the thugs but claimed she'd only asked them to rough him up a little. I told her I was bringing her here, to account to the police." He paused, gave a humorless chuckle at the irony of that.

"Then I made the mistake of letting her out of my sight. She got a derringer from somewhere and shot me."

Hollister gave a low whistle. "You've always had a special talent for getting yourself into trouble, Fairgrieve," he said. "Some things just never seem to change. Your brother's bookkeeper, Hawkins, has given me free rein as far as your bail is concerned. Soon as Judge Silvertrees sets an amount, you'll be out of here."

"How is my brother?"

"Holding on," Hollister said with quiet sympathy. "I want your word on something, Ethan. When you're released, you have to stay away from Delphinia Parker and let the police figure out who assaulted Aubrey."

"I can't promise you that," Ethan said with some regret. "If I find those sons-of-bitches, I mean to rip their livers out."

Hollister sighed and gave Ethan's bandaged middle a pointed glance. "In your condition," he said, "you'd lose for sure."

"Just get me out."

"I meant what I said, Ethan. No promise, no bail."

"You are one stubborn bastard."

"So are you," Hollister answered, but he was grinning. "I'll take you to my place when you leave here. We'll talk about what happened and plan your defense over a hot supper. You remember my kid sister Ruby?"

Ethan had a vague recollection of a kid with red pigtails, a face full of freckles, and teeth that were too big for her mouth. If he hadn't found the prospect of a home-cooked meal such a comfort, he would have refused the invitation outright. "I remember," he admitted grudgingly. "How old is she now, anyhow?"

"Eighteen," Hollister answered. "She went to normal school down in San Francisco. Means to teach school awhile, though I reckon she'll be married pretty soon."

Ethan retrieved the whiskey flask. He was largely disinterested in Hollister's little sister's life story, the dull thrumming under his ribs had grown to a pounding ache, and he was worried sick about Aubrey. "That so?"

The jailer arrived with keys.

"You promise or not?" Hollister demanded of Ethan, barring the guard's way when he moved to open the cell. The man could be obstinate as a bulldog when he had his mind set on something.

"Hell," said Ethan. The walls were starting to close in. "All right, damn you, you've got my word."

Hollister grinned and stepped back. "Let him out," he told the jailer.

Chapter

14

~

"I can't get her to leave him, not even to look after the baby." Maisie's worried voice came from the corridor outside Aubrey's bedroom. "She ain't slept a wink, far as I know, and when I brung her a tray a little while back, she wouldn't take so much as a bite of food."

The door opened, and Susannah straightened her spine but did not look around. Reverend Johnstone came to stand beside the bed opposite her, but his attention was fixed on Aubrey. He lay a hand on that still shoulder, and Susannah watched as the older man's lips moved in silent prayer.

Only when his petition had been made did he meet Susannah's eyes. "Child," he said, and the word carried the gentlest of reprimands. But there was tenderness in it, too, and a vast, quiet faith.

Susannah began to cry. "I keep thinking that if I can somehow share my strength with him—"

"Aubrey knows you care for him," the minister counseled, drawing up a chair, sitting with his fingers loosely interlocked, clearly prepared for a vigil of his own. "However, you'll do him no good at all by exhausting yourself. This is a battle only the angels can fight, Susannah."

"But suppose I leave and—and—" *he dies*. She could barely think the words; saying them was beyond her.

"Then God will receive his spirit," the reverend said.

She shook her head, refusing to let go. Another tear slipped down her cheek, and she dashed it away with the back of one hand.

"Susannah," the visitor pressed. "At least go downstairs and have some tea with Maisie. She's in a frenzy, between worrying over Aubrey and fretting about you. I'll sit with our patient here for as long as necessary."

She stood then, her knees wobbly and stiff from sitting through the long night, her lower back and shoulders knotted with tension. Perhaps a cup of tea would restore her a little, and of course she was not indifferent to Maisie's concern. "You'll summon me, if—if I'm needed?"

Reverend Johnstone nodded, took a battered Bible out of his pocket, and began to read from it, under his breath.

Susannah hesitated a moment longer, then forced herself to leave the room, descend the rear stairs, and assemble a shaky smile for Maisie's sake. Her friend was rocking a sleeping Victoria, while Jasper sprawled on the floor on a warm blanket, taking a nap of his own.

Maisie's face quickened with both alarm and hope when she saw Susannah. She raised her eyebrows in question.

"There's been no change," Susannah said softly, to keep from waking the little ones. She envied Jasper and Victoria their peaceful repose as she put water on to boil and measured tea leaves into a crockery pot. Although she was worn out, she thought she might never sleep again.

"Look at you," Maisie scolded in a gruff voice barely above a whisper. "Them eyes of yours look like two burnt holes in a blanket, and you're pale as a haint."

Susannah ignored the remarks, though she knew them to be true. "How is Ethan? Have you heard from him?"

Maisie withheld her answer for a moment, her mouth pressed into a thin line of frustration. Then she took pity on Susannah and relented. "I reckon he would have got out of jail last night if Hawkins found a lawyer. Like as not, he'll show up here in the next little while. If he ain't gone lookin' for whoever it was that hurt Mr. Fairgrieve, that is."

Something quivered in the pit of Susannah's stomach. There had been more than enough tragedy in the Fairgrieve family over the years, without Ethan getting himself hanged or taking another bullet. Doubtless, Aubrey's assailants were better shots than Mrs. Parker; they would aim to kill. Before she could say as much to Maisie, there came a knock at the back door, and Ethan stepped inside, wearing a leather coat lined with sheepskin and a stockman's hat that had seen better days. His pants and boots were those of a working rancher, and his shirt was unbuttoned to the waist, revealing the thick bandages that swathed his middle.

Without a word, he crossed the room, took Susannah by the shoulders, and placed a light, brotherly kiss on her forehead. The tenderness of the gesture made her eyes swim again; she blinked rapidly, sniffled, and raised her chin.

"He's so still," she said, despondent.

Ethan nodded and shrugged out of his coat. With a muttered greeting to Maisie, he hung the garment from a peg beside the door and started toward the back stairs. At their foot, he turned and looked back. "When Aubrey comes to, Susannah, he'll want to find you well.

He'll need you more than he's ever needed anybody. So get some rest, will you?"

She couldn't fight them anymore, couldn't deny the logic of what Maisie, Reverend Johnstone, and now Ethan had all said. "All right," she said, and he nodded again and went upstairs.

Thereafter, Susannah ate the poached egg and toasted bread Ellie made for her, then went up to her own room and flung herself down on the bed, fully clothed. She was asleep almost before she reached the mattress.

Ethan shook her awake at sunset; she sat up, blinking and dazed. Terrified and hopeful.

"Aubrey's come around," Ethan told her with a weary grin. "He's asking for you."

She gave a small, strangled cry of urgency and of desperate joy, bounded off the bed, and raced into the hallway. Sure enough, Aubrey lay with his eyes open, and when he caught sight of her, his swollen mouth formed a semblance of a smile.

"Hello, Susannah." His voice was hardly more than a croak, but the sound of it was infinitely beautiful to her. She approached him slowly, knelt beside the bed, took his hand in hers. That same hand she had held through long, dark hours of despair.

Without speaking, she kissed the backs of his fingers.

The Reverend Johnstone stood, clearing his throat, and Susannah heard both him and Ethan leave the room, closing the door behind them. She was grateful, overwhelmingly grateful, for so very many things.

In a painful motion, Aubrey brushed her cheek with his thumb, their fingers intertwined. His eyes, blackened and practically swollen shut though they were, twinkled. "I may not be able to dance at our wedding," he said.

Susannah made a soblike sound with something in it of both joy and sorrow. "How do you feel?"

He looked at her for a long time, his regard at once curious and tender. "As if I've been stomped by a team of horses and then dragged a half mile over rocky ground," he answered, and it was plain that merely speaking was a great effort. "Even so, I don't see how I could look much worse than you do."

She pretended to be insulted, but she knew her eyes were shining with happy tears. "Such flattering words. Are you trying to seduce me, sir?"

He chortled. "I would love to seduce you, lady, but I'm afraid I'm in no fit condition for it." His expression turned serious, and she knew the pain was gathering momentum. "Lie down beside me, Susannah," he said. "Just lie here, so I know you're close."

She didn't hesitate, although she was careful not to jar him as she took her place next to him on the mattress, fitting her shape to his as closely as she could, her lips and the tip of her nose just brushing his neck.

"Oh, Lord," he groaned. "Suggesting this might have shown poor judgment on my part," he said, and chuckled again. His amusement was immediately followed by another moan of pain.

"I never thought I'd hear you admit to anything less than perfect judgment," Susannah retorted. She was smiling, but her eyes were still stinging with tears. She could not seem to stop crying.

"The Ladies' Benevolence Society would not approve of this," Aubrey said. Perhaps, Susannah thought, talking distracted him from his pain, though it was equally plain that every word came at great cost.

Susannah laid her hand lightly upon his chest, fingers splayed, and felt his heart beating strong and steady, as though rising to meet her touch. She aligned her breathing with his and closed her eyes. "A pox on them," she said cheerfully.

She felt his left hand find and cover her right, lying there over his heart. "For shame," he said. Then they both slept, soundly and without dreams.

There was something different about Ethan, Aubrey reflected, a week after he'd come to and found himself in his own bed, swaddled in sheets like a mummy in some pharaoh's tomb. He was sitting up, plumped pillows supporting his back, and though his ribs were still trussed, his bruises were fading, and the pain was becoming more endurable with every passing day.

His brother stood at the window, his back to the room, light shining around his lean frame like a halo. He smiled at the irony; Ethan was a lot of things, but an angel wasn't one of them.

"Delphinia's long gone," he was saying, "but those thugs she hired are still around someplace, I'd bet the ranch on that."

Aubrey was eating some of Maisie's chicken and dumplings; he took time to chew. Just one more simple, ordinary thing he had to be careful about. *Real* careful, since he'd loosened a few teeth in the fight. "Never mind that," he said impatiently. Delphinia was long gone, and as far as he was concerned, it would be downright greedy to ask for more. "What I want to know is, what's happened to you? You aren't the same man as before."

Ethan rounded in his own good time, regarded his brother with a slightly mysterious grin. He was holding his hat, turning it around slowly by the brim. "Oh, I'm the same, all right."

Aubrey narrowed his eyes, then shook his head. "I guess you'll tell me about it when you're ready," he said. "I had a visit from John Hollister earlier this morning. It seems he's resigned from the Pinkerton agency to take up the law again. I suppose he's tired of traveling so much."

Perhaps it was the mention of the police that made the smile slide off Ethan's face and vanish into thin air. "He'd like to marry Susannah," he said, but the comment sounded like an aside; he was plainly thinking of something else. He made another stab at lightening things up a little. "You'd better get well fast, brother. Half the town's set to court her, should you pass away or remain an invalid."

"Very funny," Aubrey said without a shred of amusement anywhere in his being. "You're in bad trouble over that little set-to with Delphinia, aren't you?"

Ethan shrugged. "Like I said, she's disappeared. Hollister thinks they'll drop the charges eventually, given the fact that I was shot in the scuffle and she's not around to testify." Another fleeting, faltering grin. "Provided I stay out of dutch in the meantime, of course."

"Of course," Aubrey agreed, setting aside what remained of his lunch and lying back against the pillows. "That's good advice, Ethan. You won't accomplish anything by getting yourself sent to prison."

"You want me to just let those sons-of-bitches get away with damn near killing my brother?"

"I'd prefer that to seeing you ruin the rest of your life. Forget what happened, Ethan. It isn't your fight."

"Whose fight is it, then? And don't say the police will handle it. You and I both know they'll chase down a few leads, then give up and close the case for good."

"Did it ever occur to you," Aubrey said, "that it might be *my* fight? I'm the one who took the beating, aren't I?"

Ethan slapped the hat against his thigh, and a muscle pulsed at the edge of his jaw. "You can't even get out of bed. How are you going to track a bunch of wharf rats in and out of every dive on the waterfront?"

"Ah. So you *have* been playing detective. And after you promised Hollister you wouldn't."

This time, the grin was genuine. "All I did was ask a few questions here and there," he said.

"Ethan."

"I'll be careful," came the clipped reply. The strains of some really sorry piano playing began to seep up between the floorboards. "I see Susannah's doing a brisk business teaching music," Ethan said from the door.

Aubrey tilted his head back and closed his eyes. "I don't know how anybody expects me to get well with that racket going on," he complained. When he looked again, Ethan was gone. Grumbling, he reached for the bowl of chicken and dumplings and began to eat again.

The sooner he got his strength back, the sooner he wouldn't have to listen to miners and lumberjacks pounding the ivory. The sooner he could marry Susannah and bring her to his bed, and not merely to lie beside him, though that was a great consolation, to be sure.

It was just that he wanted so much more.

Ruby Hollister was bending over, taking a pan of biscuits from the oven, and even though Ethan tried to look away, he couldn't quite find the will to deprive himself that much. When she turned and smiled at him, blissfully unaware that he'd been thinking lascivious thoughts, he felt some sort of coupling inside, two pieces coming together with a crash and then fusing.

Ruby's heavy hair was pinned up into one of those loose arrangements that made it puff out around her face like a cloud, her eyes were brown and bright with laughter, and her figure was womanly enough to stop a man's heart. She was nothing like Su Lin, and yet he knew his feelings for her were as strong as any he'd ever cherished for his lost lover.

It tore him apart, because he'd sworn, in his grief and his guilt, never to care that way for anyone else. For all that, with one smile, one touch of her hand, Ruby had broken down the barriers he'd guarded for so long and taken over his heart like a conquering general. The paradox was that she probably had no idea what she'd done.

"You'll stay to supper, won't you?" she asked.

He thought of the lonely place, hidden away in a stand of pines and Douglas fir in the meadow above his cabin, where he often went to brood, like a man mourning at a gravesite. His dreams were buried there, where Su Lin had told him good-bye.

"I can't," he said. It was penance, of a sort. Su Lin would never know he'd made the gesture, and yet he had to follow through with it all the same. Not for the first time, he offered a silent prayer that she was happy in China, blessed with children, health, and plenty.

Ruby tried to hide her disappointment as she turned away and began sliding the biscuits into a basket lined with a red and white checkered napkin. "I understand," she said, but she didn't sound as if she did.

He took her gently by the shoulders and, when she put down the baking pan, brought her around to face him. "I'd like to come calling tomorrow, Ruby. If that's all right with you."

Her eyes were wide and guileless, but she was anything but stupid. "Is there someone else, Ethan? Because if there is, I'd just as soon you left me be."

He curved a finger beneath her chin, tempted to kiss her, then brought himself under better control and drew back a little way. "There's nobody else," he said. It was true enough, and yet he felt like a traitor for saying so. "I've got some other things to see to—you know that, Ruby."

A pained expression crossed her face, but she nodded. "I know. There's your poor brother, and that business about your being arrested—"

"Not to mention shot," he reminded her. He was healing fast, but he still liked a measure of feminine sympathy when he could garner it. "As for my 'poor brother,' he's getting ornerier every day. He'll be back in the store bossing everybody around before Christmas."

She smiled, and he was lost. He would have done anything she asked of him in that moment, and he was glad as hell that she didn't know it. "We could borrow John's buggy and go out riding," she said.

He wanted to kiss her, but again he denied himself. "That's a fine idea," he agreed. "I'll see you tomorrow, around four."

She nodded, and he took his leave.

Half an hour later, he stood alone on sacred, grieving ground. There was a chilly wind coming up off the water, and he'd raised the collar of his sheepskin coat against it. The moss-covered stone where he and Su Lin had sat so many times, dreaming, was crusted with fresh snow, and the small brass Buddha she'd left behind had tilted to one side.

Ethan lowered himself to his haunches and cupped his hands in front of his mouth, blowing in an effort to warm them. Then he straightened the Buddha and spent a few moments studying the gray sky. There would be more snow before the day was out, he reckoned. His spirit yearned for the light and warmth of summer.

He was silent a long time, pondering what he would say, shaping the words in his mind, practicing them. "There's a woman, Su Lin," he said finally. "Her name is Ruby—"

Susannah supported much of Aubrey's weight as the two of them made their way slowly back and forth along the length of the Persian rug in his bedroom. Victoria, who had recently learned to sit up on her own, watched curiously from a blanket, simultaneously chewing on the foot of a cloth doll.

"Very good," Susannah said, lest Aubrey should need encouragement. She knew it was hard on his pride, not being able to move about on his own. "You've done a great deal today. Let's rest now."

"Let's rest?" he retorted, frowning down into her upturned face. "Are you tired, Susannah? Because I'm not."

Susannah sighed. The truth, she suspected, was that he was expecting a visit from Mr. Hollister that afternoon, and he wanted to be on his feet for the interview, not lying in bed or stretched out on the Roman couch in the corner in front of the bay windows. Even if it meant he would collapse directly afterward. "All right, go ahead and wear yourself down to a nub, if that's what you want."

"I'm ready to try the stairs," he announced, as though she hadn't spoken at all.

The stairs. Just getting him dressed had been an ordeal for both of them; now he wanted to make his perilous way to the distant study. "Couldn't you receive Mr. Hollister in your sitting room? It's perfectly good—" Not to mention that it was next door to the bedchamber and thus within easy reach.

"I can't hide in this room forever," Aubrey snapped. Then an expression of remorse crossed his face, and his features, iron-hard and pale only a moment before, softened a little. Some of his color came back. "I'm sorry, Susannah. It's just that my life is out there, happening without me."

She smiled and laid a hand to his chest. "Your life is in here," she said. "You carry it with you, wherever you go."

He bent his head, no small accomplishment considering how stiff he was, with his ribs still bound, and placed a kiss on the top of her head. "Ah, Susannah, Susannah. I don't deserve you."

"That's true," she said thoughtfully, then laughed. "Come along, then. If you insist on going downstairs, we'd better get started. Mr. Hollister will be here in an hour."

Aubrey shook his head, and his expression was wry. " 'How sharper than a serpent's tooth,' " he quoted.

Susannah summoned Ellie to look after Victoria, and when the other woman had arrived, she and Aubrey set out on their odyssey. The descent to the first floor was laborious, and she could see that he was paying a high price for his vanity. Still, she reasoned, the choice was undeniably his to make, so she offered no further protest. The look of satisfaction on his face, when at last he was seated behind his desk, was worth the whole struggle, though the strain of sitting upright was soon evident.

Susannah stood behind him and massaged the muscles in his neck. Her fingers were strong from years of playing the piano, and soon he began to relax again. He caught one of her hands in his and kissed it lightly, and, for one brief, impetuous moment, she hoped he might tell her that he loved her. Since he'd been hurt, she'd wanted very much to state her real feelings toward him, but she was afraid that he would call off their marriage if she revealed too much.

"How long do we have to wait?" he asked.

"For what?" She was flustered, entangled in other thoughts.

He pulled her around so that he could look upward into her face. "To be married, Susannah," he said patiently.

She felt color surge up her neck to flood her cheeks and hoped her joy didn't show. "Whenever you feel well enough," she said with a certain shyness, "I'll be ready."

He searched her eyes. "Will you? Be ready, I mean?"

She knew what he was asking. He wanted the marriage to be a real one, in every sense of the word. She wanted that, too, but she had virtually no experience in such matters, and so she was naturally nervous. She opened her mouth to say yes, but before she could get the word out, someone turned the bell at the front door.

She started to move away, knowing Maisie and Ellie were both busy, but Aubrey still had a hold of her hand, and he pulled her back. "Susannah," he said.

"Yes," she blurted, blushing again. "Yes, I'll be ready."

He smiled broadly. "Good, because I already am."

She pulled away. "We have company," she reminded him sternly.

John Hollister was waiting on the front porch, the collar of his overcoat pulled up to protect his ears, his bowler hat dusted with melting snow. She saw a gentle sorrow in his eyes as he regarded her, but he smiled and inclined his head politely. "Miss McKittrick," he said. "I've come to see Aubrey."

She nodded and stepped back to admit him, then took his coat. "Come in, please. It's very cold. Could I bring you something warm to drink?" She was acting like a wife, and she knew he was conscious of that.

"You're very kind," he said with a slight nod. He started toward the stairs, naturally assuming that Aubrey was still confined to his bed, given the fact that only a week had passed since his injuries were sustained. During that time, she'd kept from going insane by packing Julia's things and putting them away in carefully labeled boxes, against the day when Victoria would want her mother's belongings.

Susannah stopped Mr. Hollister's progress with a look. "He's in his study," she said.

"Thank you," Hollister replied, and changed directions. Several minutes later, Susannah entered the room with a tray. On it were a china teapot, three matching cups and saucers, silver spoons, sugar and hot milk, and a platter of Maisie's special lemon-sesame seed cakes. The trio of cups was her way of saying she would not be dismissed after she'd served refreshments, like some nosy housemaid.

"—during my time as a Pinkerton—" Hollister was saying.

It took a moment for the meaning of that to register with Susannah. When it did, she met Aubrey's gaze and found that he was looking at her warily. Mr. Hollister went right on talking, unaware of the sudden strain.

Susannah set the tray down with a force that made the china clatter, but the smile she turned on the visitor was a dazzling one. She saw to that. "You were a detective, Mr. Hollister?" she asked. "I didn't know that."

Hollister's face went ruddy as he realized his error. He looked helplessly at Aubrey, then fell silent. Only belatedly did he remember that she'd put a question to him. "Er—yes—I was employed by the Pinkerton agency for five years. Before that, I read law."

Susannah placed a cup on a saucer and poured tea for the guest. "I see." She glared at Aubrey. She did indeed see. When she'd first arrived in Seattle, and Mr. Hollister had presumably come to court her, he was actually investigating her. And Aubrey had been the one to hire him. "Well, it was stupid of me not to work that out before now, wasn't it?" She slammed another cup down in front of the master of the house, who looked none too commanding at the moment.

"Susannah," Aubrey protested.

She poured his tea, hands trembling with anger. "What did you find out about me, Mr. Hollister?" she asked in a bright and brittle voice. "That I've left a trail of husbands behind me? That I'm a typhoid carrier? A murderess? An embezzler, perhaps?"

"Stop it," Aubrey said. His tone was brisk.

Susannah's eyes stung. She flung an acid look at both men before walking out of the room and slamming the door shut behind her.

Aubrey swore softly.

"Obviously, you didn't tell her about the investigation," Hollister remarked. He was a master of understatement, that Hollister.

"It wasn't a secret," Aubrey replied, a little shortly. "I just never got around to explaining, that's all. I've been a little preoccupied of late."

Hollister gave a snorting laugh. "Indeed you have. Now, what can you tell me about the men who assaulted you?"

Aubrey sat back, repressing a groan. "They were mean as snakes, and there were a lot of them. That's about all I know."

"You didn't see anything?" Hollister took a pad of paper from his pocket, along with a well-used pencil.

"It was dark."

"Your brother says Mrs. Parker admitted to having been involved, at least indirectly."

"So he's told me," Aubrey replied. "She's left Seattle, though, and she'd never again admit to hiring those men anyway, even if you caught up to her. By now, she's probably headed for points south."

"Not east? To New York, maybe? Or Chicago?"

Aubrey shrugged. He didn't give a damn where Delphinia was; it was Susannah he was thinking about. He wondered how long she would be angry with him. "She had an ex-husband in Philadelphia, I think," he said. "An industrialist. There was some kind of scandal, though—I doubt she'd set foot on that side of the Mississippi River."

Hollister shifted in his chair. "Don't you want this case to be solved?" he asked. "It seems fairly obvious that those men meant to kill you. And if Mrs. Parker hired them, then she's as guilty as they are."

Aubrey expelled a sigh. He was hurting in every part of his body, and he could feel the need to sleep sucking him down and down. "Yes. Of course. If only to keep my younger brother from going after them himself."

Chapter

15

~

$\mathscr{A}$s soon as Hollister had finished his largely fruitless interview and left the house, Aubrey hoisted himself to his feet, teeth clenched, eyes squeezed tight shut. He was just thinking what a good thing it was that Susannah couldn't see him when he turned and found her standing in the open doorway, gazing at him. She looked pale, and there was a tightness around her mouth.

"You did it for Victoria," she said.

She was referring to the Pinkerton investigation, of course. Because of Hollister's lack of enthusiasm for the project, it had never really gotten past the initial stages, but he, Aubrey, had hired the man all the same. "Yes," he answered. He stood beside the desk, supporting himself with one hand and hoping he looked casual. "At the time, I planned to settle a fortune on you and let you raise the child wherever you chose. Before I could do that, I had to know you weren't—how did you put it?— oh, yes, a murderess, a typhoid carrier, or an embezzler, wasn't it?"

She offered a tentative, rather reluctant smile. He wanted more than ever to take her to his bed, lay her down and pleasure her until she cried out from it, but it was the middle of the day, and besides, he might kill himself in the attempt. "And?"

"For all I know, you could be any or all of those things. Hollister resigned from the investigation right away, because he wanted to court you. As for me—well, I found myself trusting you, for good or ill."

She took a step toward him, paused, her hands clasping each other. "You were going to allow me to take Victoria away?"

He nodded. "A child needs a mother," he said. "A father, too, of course, when possible. But a mother's love is vital."

He saw tears spring to her eyes and wondered what he'd said to cause her pain. Then she hurried over and put her arms around him, gently, so as not to do him hurt. Maybe it was that that caused him to place his trust in her, her gentle ways. Then there was her courage, her honesty, her humor . . .

"You are a good man," she said with a sniffle, "for all that you try to pretend otherwise."

He caught her chin in his fingers and bent his head, at great cost, to kiss her lightly on that delectable mouth. "Oh, Susannah," he breathed. "How I need you." He thought he saw a flicker of sorrow in her eyes before she smiled, and, once again, he was puzzled.

"Do you, now?" she asked.

When he made no reply, she slipped beneath his shoulder, supporting him as she had done while they descended the stairs. "Come along," she said. "It's time you got back into bed."

Aubrey groaned aloud at the suggestion. And this time, it wasn't just because of the pain.

When Susannah finally got Aubrey up the stairs and into his room, she was breathless from the effort. He was a big man, and he seemed to let himself lean on her more than usual.

"Sit down," she said. "I'll help you off with your boots."

Aubrey sank to the edge of the mattress, and Susannah picked up one of his feet. He drew in a sharp, hissing breath and murmured what she thought must be a curse by its tone. "Stand between my legs," he said, "with your back to me. Otherwise, you're going to kill me."

She did as he told her, though she was mildly suspicious of his motives. When she bent over and he pinched her bottom, she knew she'd been right. She turned to glare at him, her face hot with embarrassment and another sensation she wasn't about to admit to.

He laughed. "Just pull my boots off. I promise to behave myself."

She bent, and he pinched her again. She jerked off the second boot and flung it aside, whirling to look down into his face. The boyish twinkle in his eyes softened her immediately, and when he laid his hands on her waist and drew her close, she couldn't resist him.

He buried his face in her stomach and nuzzled her, and something grabbed inside Susannah, clenching tighter and tighter. She had a very unseemly desire to lean back in his grasp and surrender herself to all the nuzzling he wanted to do.

"What are you doing?" she asked.

"Dreaming," Aubrey answered, his voice muffled by her uncorseted midsection and the heavy fabric of her dress. She was wearing a gown of dark green woolen, not taken from Julia's wardrobe and altered, like most of her other clothes, but bought with her own money, earned by giving piano lessons.

She supposed she should retreat—in fact, she was certain of it—but she couldn't seem to move away, even though she knew he would never hold her against her will. "Aubrey," she protested, but she sounded weak, even to herself.

Slowly, he slid his hands up her rib cage to cup her breasts. Susannah gasped and let her head fall back, though she knew she would have crowned any other man with the nearest blunt object for doing the same thing. With his thumbs, he chafed her nipples to attention, then pinched them ever so lightly through her dress and the camisole beneath.

"Close the door, Susannah," he said, dropping his hands.

She swayed for a moment, half dazed. He steadied her by grasping her hips. Kissed her woman place through the weight of her skirts and instantly set her afire, inside and out. Nerves screaming, flesh ablaze, she stood stupidly in his hold, not trusting her knees to carry her as far as the doorway.

"Throw the bolt, too," he added.

She moved then, like a sleepwalker, to do his bidding. The room seemed to pulse and waver around her, as though it were an illusion, the landscape of some erotic dream. She leaned back against the heavy panel, her hands behind her, gauging the distance between herself and Aubrey Fairgrieve. Between herself and destruction.

"We aren't married yet," she reminded him. Her voice sounded somewhat fitful, it seemed to her.

"No," Aubrey agreed. "That's why I'm not going to take you, Susannah. I'm only going to make you wish to God I would. Come here."

She went to him. Like a fool.

"Help me out of my clothes." He stood, and she obediently pushed his coat back over his shoulders and slid it down his arms. She lowered his suspenders, pulled his shirt tail from inside his trousers, unbuttoned and removed both those garments.

She had never seen Aubrey naked before, or any other man, for that matter, and she would have expected such an intimate look at the masculine anatomy to shock her. Instead, she felt compelled to touch him and closed one hand around the magnificent erection he presented.

"Great Scot," she muttered.

He laughed, but there was a low moan stitched through the sound. His ribs were still bound, but above and below the wrappings curled a glorious mat of maple-colored hair. His shoulders and thigh muscles would have done credit to a statue in some Grecian garden.

"Now, your clothes, Susannah," he prompted, grinning at her. He was all mischief and manhood, standing there, and she had never been more conscious of her own femininity. Nor had she ever been so vulnerable; the moment was terrifying, exhilarating, wildly daring, and she'd been born for it.

Still some shyness remained. She swallowed and shook her head. "I—I can't."

"Then let me." His voice was low, and the sound of it reached inside her to caress her in private places.

She wet her lips with the tip of her tongue in a quick, nervous gesture and then nodded. He let her hair down first, pin by pin, tress by lock, until it tumbled freely to her waist. She was already wishing he would make love to her, and even in her innocence she knew he hadn't really begun to seduce her.

Next, he unfastened the buttons at the front of her gown, teasing each bit of flesh with the light pass of a fingertip as he exposed it. Susannah was trembling by the time he reached her waist.

He tugged the bodice off over her shoulders, took his time easing the long sleeves of the dress down and down her arms. He lifted each wrist, in its turn, to his mouth, and sampled it like some delicacy.

Have me, she wanted to cry out. *Have me now.* But she knew he would refuse, and she still had enough pride left to restrain herself, though she was slipping fast.

At last, the dress fell into a pool at her feet. He unlaced the camisole to free her breasts, and she looked past his shoulder at the snow gliding past the window, knowing that if she met his eyes she would be completely lost. She would beg.

He held her breasts in his hands, caressing and fondling them until he wrung a low moan from her. Then he untied her petticoats and let them fall, to lie forgotten on the floor, along with the dress. He left her drawers till last, instructing her to take off her shoes, posing her in her stockings and pantaloons with one foot on the seat of a chair.

Then he removed a garter from above her knee, rolled down the stocking. Her flesh sang where he bared it, quivering in the wake of his caress. Taking his time, he repeated the whole process with her other limb.

At last, she stood naked before him, not ashamed but proud as a pagan goddess. For the very first time in her life, Susannah felt completely and utterly captivating. She knew she was subject to Aubrey's powers then, but the reverse was equally true. Looking into his eyes, she saw a brazen sort of surrender that affirmed her importance to him in the deepest way.

"Lie down beside me," he said. It was a command, and also a plea.

They lay upon the bed together, side by side, face to face. Aubrey draped one arm loosely across Susannah's waist and kissed her forehead.

"You," he said, "are beautiful."

"So are you," she replied instantly, and blushed.

He chuckled. "Bruises, bindings, and all?"

She traced the outline of one powerful shoulder. "Oh, yes," she said. "Why are we doing this?"

"Because," he answered, kissing her mouth this time, "I'm going to go crazy if we don't do *something*. I've wanted you since I found you standing in that corridor out there, looking at me as though I were the intruder."

Wanting was very different from loving, though she supposed the two generally went together. If only, if only he would say he cared for her.

He ran his fingers from the hollow at the base of her throat, past her collarbone, between her breasts, over her belly. She shuddered when he made a teasing pass over the V of hair between her legs, instinctively parted them a little. And still the wispy snow fell, silent and fragile, past the bay windows across the room from Aubrey's bed.

"Make me want you," she whispered.

And he did as she asked.

"You takin' a fever?" Maisie asked two hours later, when Susannah was bold enough to set foot inside the kitchen. The older woman's tone was serious, but her eyes were smiling.

Susannah poured tea and helped herself to a cookie from the platter on the work table next to the cookstove. Her knees were still wobbly, and her voice was hoarse, even though Aubrey had swallowed all her cries. She had strained and writhed beside him, and she had indeed pleaded with him, but he had kept his word. She was exhausted, she was flushed, and there was a grinding need lodged low in her belly, but she was still a virgin.

"I feel perfectly fine," she croaked in belated answer to Maisie's question, and went red all over again.

"I don't doubt that," Maisie said, and chortled.

"Where are Jasper and Victoria?" Susannah asked, mostly to change the subject. With Maisie in charge, she had no doubt that both children were safe and comfortable.

"Ellie's putting them to bed right about now," she said.

Startled, Susannah glanced at the window. Twilight was gathering beyond the glass, and the snow was still coming down. Where had the time gone?

But of course she knew. She'd spent much of the afternoon learning pleasure, and it was a subject she yearned to explore further.

"Do you suppose the Reverend Johnstone is at home tonight?" she asked.

Maisie shrugged. "I reckon so. Why?"

Susannah drew a deep breath and let it out. "Aubrey and I have decided that it would be—well—prudent to get married."

Maisie chuckled again. "Prudent, is it? Well, that's good news, it surely is."

"Tomorrow," Susannah clarified.

"So that's the way of it."

Susannah lifted her eyes to heaven for a moment. Were there no secrets in this house? "That's the way of it," she said. Maisie had made a hearty beef stew for supper, and she busied herself preparing a tray for Aubrey.

He ate with good appetite.

Summoned by one of the stable hands, Reverend Johnstone came calling in the late evening. Aubrey had already gone to sleep, and both Maisie and Ellie had retired as well. Susannah served her guest fresh coffee, hot stew, and buttered bread at the kitchen table and explained that she and Aubrey wished to be wed the next day, if possible.

"This seems like something of a hasty decision," the minister commented, dabbing at his mouth with one of Maisie's crisply starched table napkins. "Your feelings toward Aubrey have seemed quite—well—unmatrimonial at times, Susannah. If I may say so."

It seemed to Susannah that he had already said so, but she made no comment on that. "I am very much in love with him," she admitted. She had not made that confession aloud until that moment.

"And how does he feel about you?"

Susannah felt her face heat up again and could not quite meet the pastor's wise, gentle gaze. "He—likes me, I think." Then, in a smaller voice, "And wants me."

"I see."

"I'm hoping that—in time—"

Reverend Johnstone reached across the table to pat her hand. "There, now. Plenty of good marriages have started this way. Often, love grows out of companionship, shared objectives and struggles. I should tend to trust that sort far more than the kind that strikes between one moment and the next and leaves a person moonstruck, I think."

Susannah gave a tired sigh, cupping her chin in one hand. "Have you ever been in love, Reverend?" she asked.

He smiled, and there were memories in his eyes. "Oh, yes. Long ago and far away, I had a wife. Her name was Laura. She died of a cancer."

"I'm sorry."

He patted her hand again. "Don't be. We had more happiness in our time together than many people enjoy in all their lives, and I know she's waiting for me in heaven."

Susannah sighed. "Did you have children together, you and Laura?"

"Four sturdy sons."

She braced herself, thinking the reverend would tell her of more tragedy, but he didn't. "Matthew is an attorney in Boston. Mark is vice president of a shipping concern and lives in London. Luke preaches the gospel back in Kansas, and John is still at school, being the youngest. He plans to be a doctor."

"That's wonderful," Susannah said, imagining the minister's sons, far away and busy with their constructive lives. "You must be very proud."

"I am indeed. There were times when I thought they'd all wind up in prison." The old man paused to laugh fondly. "They're good boys, but they were full of the dickens when they were young. Preacher's kids, you know. Always something to prove."

"Don't you miss them?"

"I suppose," he replied gently. "But they are men now, busy with their own pursuits, and all of them have families, except for John, of course. That's as it should be—we train our children not to need us, if we're wise."

Susannah thought of Victoria, imagined her as a woman, and wanted to weep for the sorrow of losing the baby she was, the little girl she would become. Time passed too quickly; lives changed, children grew up, lovers got old, only to be parted by death. She sniffled.

"Here, now," the reverend said, offering a neatly pressed handkerchief. "What's the matter?"

Susannah blew her nose as delicately as she could, wadded the kerchief, and dabbed at her eyes. She'd been doing entirely too much crying lately, for someone who was basically happy. "Life is so precious," she said, and sniffled again.

The minister smiled, and after that they talked of the quiet wedding that was to take place the following afternoon in the main parlor. Although Susannah would have preferred to be married in the church, she knew Aubrey wasn't up to traveling even that small distance.

When Reverend Johnstone took his leave, Susannah made the rounds of the house, turning off gas lanterns, securing doors. At the windows of her own bedroom, where Victoria slept peacefully in the cradle, she stood watching snowflakes dance golden in the light of the street lamps.

It seemed perfectly practical, just then, if not ideal, to marry a man who did not love her.

Ethan adjusted his brother's string tie. "Are you sure about this?" he asked, but he was grinning. "Marriage is a serious undertaking."

"Don't remind me," Aubrey said. He couldn't help thinking of the day he married Julia; how stupidly happy he'd been, how he'd believed in love in much the same way a child might believe in fairies or leprechauns. Now, here he was, making the same leap all over again, except for a few minor changes.

He'd learned the hard way that love was for dreamers and fools. He and Susannah would be partners, in and out of bed, and build a life together on a sound foundation of intelligence, good will, and common interests. All very well, but he was *still* stupidly happy.

"What kind of honeymoon will you have?" Ethan fretted. "Here you are, with your ribs wrapped—"

"I don't expect to use my ribs," Aubrey replied. Ethan was still fiddling with the tie, and he knocked his brother's hands away, impatient. "As for the honeymoon—not that it's any of your damn business—we'll take a trip to Europe next spring."

Ethan whistled through his teeth, obviously impressed. "Does Susannah know about this?"

"Not yet," Aubrey answered, inspecting himself in the mirror over his bureau. He was stiff from the bindings, but most of the bruises were gone, and he looked decent in his best suit. With Ethan's help, he'd shaved, and though he'd tried to slick his hair down with water, it was on the springy side. He frowned. "Have you got the ring?"

"For the fifth time," Ethan answered with a mirthful sigh, "yes." He produced the wide gold band with its large, emerald-cut diamond, having plucked it from his vest pocket with a deft motion of two fingers. "See?"

"Just don't lose the damn thing," Aubrey grumbled.

Ethan laughed. "Listen," he teased, "if you're too fainthearted to go through with this wedding, I'll be glad to step in and marry Susannah for you. She's about as fine-looking a woman as I've ever seen, and smart, too."

"Too smart to hitch herself to the likes of you," Aubrey retorted, but he couldn't help smiling. Although his brother hadn't confided in him yet, Hawkins had brought the excellent news that there was a romance brewing between Ethan and Ruby Hollister, the young sister of his lawyer.

"You ready?" Ethan asked when several ominous chords thundered up from the piano belowstairs.

Aubrey sighed. "I'm ready," he said. He sure as hell hoped it was the truth.

Susannah wore a dress she and Maisie had selected together at the general store just that morning. For all that it was hastily purchased and even more hastily altered, the gown was like something out of a maiden's dream, with yards of ivory silk in the skirts, Irish lace on the bodice and the wide, puffy sleeves. The buttons resembled tiny pearls.

Besides the bride, the nervous groom, and the minister, Ethan, Maisie, and Ellie were present, along with Mr. Zacharias, Mr. Hawkins, and several of Aubrey's other associates. Mr. Hollister and his lovely sister Ruby were also among the guests. One or two wives had joined the party as well, prominent members of the Benevolence Society, and they were watchful, as though they expected either Susannah or Aubrey to bolt before the Lord's will could be done and a sinful situation made right.

Susannah bent her head, lest they see her smile.

"If you'll both take your places here, in front of me," the Reverend Johnstone said, standing with his back to the large fireplace.

Susannah and Aubrey looked at each other, and Aubrey hooked a finger under the front of his collar before stepping forward. Susannah stood next to him, her heart pounding with exhilaration and fear.

"Dearly beloved," the minister began in his rolling voice.

Susannah felt the floor buckle beneath her and stood a little straighter. Catching the motion out of the side of his eye, Aubrey took her elbow in a strong grasp, as if worried that she would faint dead away. She wasn't sure she wouldn't, until the vows had been exchanged and Reverend Johnstone pronounced them man and wife.

Man and wife.

Susannah felt giddy and so was caught by surprise when Aubrey pulled her close for the marriage kiss. Cheers were raised, it went on so long, and when he finally released her, Susannah was pink to the hairline and more than a little disoriented.

"Mr. and Mrs. Aubrey Fairgrieve," the minister said in proud introduction, indicating the newlyweds with a rather grand gesture of one hand.

There followed more hurrahs, a few whistles, and some foot stomping, all of a celebratory nature. The ladies of the Benevolence Society looked at once appalled and morally vindicated. Doubtless, they would report to their cohorts the fact that Aubrey Fairgrieve had taken the unattached female living under his roof to wife, as was only decent and proper.

Maisie had made a white cake with coconut frosting, and she sniffled happily as she served slices of the confection to the wedding guests. Ellie, red-nosed and teary-eyed, poured tea and coffee. Outside, snow fell like a benediction from heaven, turning a gray November vista into a magical place mantled in pristine white and littered with diamonds.

Ethan was the first to offer congratulations, shaking Aubrey's hand and kissing Susannah soundly on the forehead. She watched with interest as he introduced Ruby Hollister, the young woman who had come to the ceremony as his guest. Unless she was sorely mistaken, Susannah thought, there would be another wedding before very long.

After the cake, Mr. Zacharias insisted on taking the place of the church organist at the piano and demonstrating what he'd learned since beginning his lessons. He labored through "Clementine" and was rewarded with a round of exuberant applause, though Susannah wasn't sure whether the audience was genuinely impressed or simply glad that he'd finished.

The wedding supper was served in the dining room. This was a grand meal of baked ham as well as roast turkey, with all the accompanying side dishes. Maisie and Ellie had labored the whole of the day preparing it all, and, as Aubrey stood handsome and tall at the head of the table to raise his champagne glass in a toast to his bride, it seemed to Susannah that she would surely awaken at any moment and find that it was all a mere dream.

It wasn't, though. After they'd eaten and had still more cake, the guests began departing, two and three at a time. Soon there was only Susannah, seated at one end of the long table, and Aubrey, at the other.

He smiled through the candlelight—by then, darkness pressed against the windows—and raised another glass to her.

"To the loveliest bride in the world," he said. He took a sip from the crystal flute and then set it aside.

Susannah felt like dancing around the room, such was her joy, but she was nervous, too. They were alone now, and there were no more barriers between them, honorable or otherwise. She inclined her head, suddenly shy. "Remember your promise," she said, and surprised herself, for the words had not been in her mind a moment before. Her body was still thrumming from his thorough attentions the day before, and she'd lain awake half the night, yearning for him, and here she was trying to put some sort of distance between them.

His eyes burned in the flickering candlelight, but not with anger. "I promised to persuade you," he said. "And I will. Do you remember how you begged me yesterday, Susannah? Shall I repeat what you said?"

Heat surged into her face. "Don't you dare!" she cried in an anguished whisper.

He laughed, though not unkindly, and stood.

Susannah remained in her seat. "You have been injured," she pointed out. "You are certainly not capable—"

He was beside her chair in a matter of moments, holding out one hand, palm up, for hers. "That, my darling wife, is your misapprehension."

She looked up into his face. "I'm afraid," she confessed.

He brought her gently to her feet. "Don't be," he said.

Susannah trembled; as Aubrey held her hand, so he held her heart, too, and all her hopes for the future. He led her out of the dining room, through the entryway, and up the main staircase, and it seemed to her that he moved with his old confidence and strength.

Outside the door of his bedroom, now hers as well, he paused to bend his head and kiss her. "I can't carry you across the threshold, Susannah," he said on a harsh breath when he drew back, "but I think you'll find me more than fit for the duties of a husband."

Chapter

16

~

*A*ubrey bolted the door and took Susannah into his arms without bothering to turn up the gaslights. When he lowered his head to kiss her, tentatively at first and then with a demanding thoroughness, all her nervousness slipped away, was replaced by something new, something conjured from fire and fury. For all Aubrey had taught Susannah to feel, during their earlier, unfinished encounters, she had never known needs and sensations like the ones he ignited within her then.

She could not have guessed how long he held and kissed and caressed her, there in their bedchamber, would not have cared in any case. She was transported, utterly naked, and could not remember shedding her clothes; his bare flesh was hard and warm beneath her exploring palms and fingertips, her mouth—when had he undressed? It didn't matter.

He found his way to a chair near the bed and sat in it; her eyes had adjusted to the darkness, but still he was little more than a moving shadow, sitting down, grasping her lightly by the waist, lowering her to straddle his lap. She groaned in exultation, while a niggling voice in the back of her mind pointed out that she had needed no seducing. Where this man was concerned, she was a shameless wanton, and, worse, she had no aspirations to be otherwise.

He cupped her face in his hands. "Susannah," he said gruffly, "listen to me."

She whimpered; his erection was pressed between them, branding her middle with promises. He had loosed her hair, and it fell down her back, heavy against her skin, like a cloak. She raised her arms to lift its weight off her neck with both arms.

"Listen," Aubrey pleaded, a man in agony. She felt his breath against one of her nipples, squirmed when he circled it with the tip of his tongue. "Damn it, Susannah."

"What?" she asked, without any real interest in the reply. Her hands were still clasped at the back of her head, beneath her hair.

"This is important, Susannah. What we are about to do is irreversible. Once it's done, the marriage will be binding, legally and morally, forever and ever. There'll be no room for second thoughts."

"No—second—thoughts—" Susannah confirmed, already lost.

"It will hurt," he pressed.

She knew that, expected it, but her needs were greater by far than the prospect of pain. And she trusted Aubrey to handle her gently. "Only this once?"

He kissed each of her breasts in turn. "Only this once," he agreed.

"Please," she whispered. "Now."

Aubrey positioned himself at the entrance to her body and waited there; she felt herself expand to receive him, and yet it seemed impossible that she could take something so large as his member inside her. "Dear God," he breathed, and she had the briefest inkling of what a price he was paying for his restraint.

"Now, Aubrey," she pleaded, and arched her back, presenting her breasts to him in all their fullness, a gift of utter vulnerability, of trust and abandon.

With a rasped oath, he took a nipple hard into his mouth and, at one and the same moment, with a single hard thrust of his hips, sheathed himself in Susannah to the depths.

In the first instant, the pain and pleasure were interwoven, one inseparable from the other. She opened her eyes wide and cried out, partly in joy, partly because her maidenhead had been breached. Aubrey continued to take suckle at the breast he'd claimed, and slowly, slowly, he began to guide Susannah up and down along the length of his erection. Gradually, the stinging sensation gave way to a sort of sweet friction, a fullness that was pleasing, while creating a sense of rising tension and a state of the most delicious suspense.

Aubrey made no effort to catch Susannah's cries; soft at first, they grew more lusty as he accelerated their pace, as he strained deeper and deeper within, pushed her further and further toward the outermost regions of her soul. She knew only that she was about to lose herself completely, to transcend physical and spiritual boundaries she had never imagined before.

"Oh," she sobbed, galloping upon him now, shameless and wild. "Oh—Aubrey—please—*please*—"

He tasted her mouth, feverishly, as hungry and breathless as she was, and, gently rolling a well-taught nipple between his thumb and forefinger, sent her shouting and clawing over the brink. She was still flexing upon him, in quick, spasmodic jerks, when he gave a low exclamation, stiffened, and spilled his seed into her. The primitive intimacy of that wrought a final, sharp release in Susannah; she rode it beyond the brink of sensibility itself and then collapsed, gasping, against

Aubrey's shoulder. Had he not been holding her, she probably would have slipped to the floor, for her muscles had turned to sun-warmed honey, and she was wet with perspiration from head to foot.

For a long time, neither of them spoke, though their breaths and heartbeats had at some point aligned themselves, one to the other. To Susannah, the joining had been a profound experience, just as holy, just as sacred, as the marriage ceremony itself, and she did not yet trust herself to assemble thoughts into words.

Aubrey found his voice first; after pushing aside her hair, he leaned a little to kiss the side of her neck, then said, "I knew it would be like that between us. The first time I saw you, I knew it."

Spent though she was, Susannah felt something awaken within her as he tilted her head back and slid his mouth lightly, lightly over the flesh of her throat, finding the pulse. He was still inside her, stirring there, and there was power in him. "I can't—not again—"

"But you will," he said. He was rising, swelling, filling her again. Having her again.

She moaned, pressing her knees into his thighs. "I've nothing left," she said. She'd given it all, taken it all. Hadn't she?

He chuckled against her mouth. "You'll be surprised at yourself," he promised. And he grasped her hips in his strong hands and began to move her smoothly, slowly up and down, reaching deep.

"I'll die," she whimpered, though it felt impossibly good, having him inside her, part of her, hard and hungry and insistent.

He nibbled his way down her jawline, along her neck, over the plump roundness of a breast to the nipple he sought. "Ummm," he said.

It took much longer to complete their journey that

second time. Aubrey showed Susannah the far side of the stars, again and again, and brought her back only when he knew he'd wrung the last quivering climax from her straining, exhausted body. Somehow, they got to the bed, collapsed together onto the sheets, and slept.

When Susannah awakened, with the earliest light of dawn, they were entwined in each other's arms, and Aubrey was still breathing deeply, his eyes closed. She admired him for a while, in tender amusement; he was big, strong as the oxen that dragged great trees down out of the hills for planing in Seattle's busy mills, and probably one of the wealthiest, most powerful men that side of Chicago. The injuries he'd sustained at the hands of his enemies probably would have killed almost anyone else, including herself, but he was already moving beyond the experience, looking to the future. For all those things, there was something endearingly boyish in the way he slept, his lashes longer than she had imagined, his mouth softer in repose than she had ever seen it in wakefulness.

She was still reflecting upon those thoughts and others like them when he opened one eye, then the other. His grin was guileless and would be her ruin, she knew, if she didn't establish some defenses against it.

"Good morning, Mrs. Fairgrieve," he said.

Susannah had not tried out her new name, perhaps because that would have meant thinking about Julia. Acknowledging her friend's prior claim on this man, on his home, his heart, and his child. The other woman actually might have been in the room, standing at the foot of the bed, so keenly did Susannah feel her presence just then. She tried to move away from Aubrey, but he was stronger and drew her close again.

"What is it?" he asked. His voice was low and gentle, and yet it left no room for hedging.

"Julia," Susannah told him miserably.

"What about her?" The question was an impatient one, crisp and a little sharp at the edge. He did not relax his hold on her.

"She was the closest thing I had to family. You were her husband—"

"I was her fool," Aubrey said, matter-of-factly and with resignation rather than bitterness. He leaned over, with an effort that showed in his face, and kissed her temple. "There is nothing wrong in our being together, Susannah. For all her—shortcomings, Julia loved the child. In her own way, at least. Don't you think she'd be glad to know you were here, looking after Victoria?"

Susannah blinked back tears. Aubrey was right, she reasoned. Victoria needed her; even Julia would have had to acknowledge that. She must allow herself this happiness, this gift, she decided, however fleeting, for it was something rare and precious. True, in time her husband might well tire of her—men of his sort and station seemed to keep mistresses almost as a matter of course—but in the meanwhile, she meant to know joy, even ecstasy. God willing, she might even have a child or two, to grow up with Victoria and fill that vast house with mischief and laughter, and there was always her music.

"Susannah?" Aubrey prompted.

"Yes," she answered belatedly. "Yes, I'm sure Julia would want me to look after Victoria."

He lay on his side, facing her, propped up on one elbow. Except for the tight bindings that held his ribs in place, he was completely, gloriously naked. "In the spring, we'll go to Europe. Would you like that?"

She stared at him, stunned. All her life she'd dreamed of crossing the sea, and she'd read about places like Venice and Madrid, Paris and London, but she'd never dared hope actually to visit them. "You don't mean it," she said.

He laughed and touched the tip of her nose with one finger. "Oh, I mean it, all right. You'll enjoy seeing the sights, and I'll enjoy watching you see them."

Susannah had been on the verge of sitting up; after all, the day was well under way, and it wasn't right to lie abed wasting light, but the prospect of such a journey drove all her tasks and plans for the morning right out of her head. "What about Victoria?" she asked. She held her breath for his answer, because if he wanted to leave the baby behind, she would stay in Seattle also. Although a great many people traveled without their children, Susannah had no intention of joining their ranks.

"We'll take her along," Aubrey said easily. "With a nurse, of course."

Susannah knew her eyes must be taking up most of her face. Why, just to imagine it—*Europe.* "How long would we be away?"

"Five or six months, I suppose," Aubrey answered. "No sense going so far if you're not going to take the time to look at every significant fountain, painting, piazza, and castle."

Rome, Susannah thought. Vienna and Austria, perhaps Florence as well, and Provence. "But the store—?"

"Hawkins can run it fine without me. Better, maybe."

Although she had made up her mind not to think about Julia, at least not while she and her husband were lying naked together in their nuptial bed, Susannah could not help recalling letters her friend had written when her marriage to Aubrey had first begun to go sour. *He thinks of nothing but that dreadful shop of his. . . . He has all the money he could ever want or need. . . . He's taken a mistress, Susannah. Why does he want to be with her and not me?*

"Susannah." He arched an eyebrow in challenge. Were her thoughts so plain as that?

"You're different," she said.

His expression was solemn. "In what way?" She tried to avert her gaze, but he took her face in his hand and made her look at him. "Tell me," he said.

She swallowed. "The store meant everything to you once. More even than Julia."

He thrust out a sigh. There was acceptance in the sound and, at the same time, regret. "Things change, Susannah. *People* change."

"Situations do. But people? Not overmuch, in my experience."

He smiled and kissed her forehead. "And it's vast, your experience?" he teased.

She remained serious. "Human beings grow into their identities very early in life, it seems to me—their talents and tendencies, foibles and finer attributes are pretty well set before they learn to read and cipher. Take Victoria, for example. As young as she is, she already shows an independent spirit, and she's stubborn, too. She's smart, and she'll be beautiful when she grows up but perhaps a bit too aware of the fact. Humility will not be her strong point."

Aubrey chuckled. "How can you know all that? You're only guessing." He tugged on the top sheet, revealing her breasts, which he had enjoyed with unabashed enthusiasm the night before. Now, he regarded them with frank admiration and not a little avarice. He pulled the sheet down further, to lie across Susannah's hip bones, and, when she reached for it, seized her hand. "Oh, no you don't," he said. "You're my wife, and I want to look at you."

A hot shiver went through Susannah, leaving a toe-to-hairline blush in its wake as it passed. It was then that she realized that her will was no longer entirely her own; in some very elemental ways, she belonged to Aubrey.

Using just the tip of one index finger, he made a small, feather-light circle on her belly, 'round and 'round her navel. In spite of the grimmest determination not to react, she made a whimpering sound and stretched under his caress.

He chuckled and kissed her, and when that happened, all was lost.

"Delphinia Parker's body washed up on Alki Point, sometime last night," John Hollister announced. He had come to the Fairgrieve house to bring the news in person. Out of the corner of her eye, Susannah saw her husband brace himself for what would inevitably come next. "They've arrested your brother for her murder."

Aubrey closed his eyes against the announcement. Susannah, standing beside his chair behind the desk in his study, laid a hand on his shoulder. "Why Ethan?" he asked.

Hollister sighed. "The two of them had a serious row before she disappeared; there's no doubt of that." He paused and regarded Aubrey for a while. "You might have been a suspect yourself, were it not for your—incapacitation."

"What happened to her? How was she killed, I mean?" Aubrey's flesh was gray; his jawline turned to granite while he awaited Hollister's reply, which was slow in coming. When he spoke, there was no doubt of the reason for his hesitation.

"He used a knife. She was nearly unrecognizable, in fact, but the manager of the Pacific Hotel identified her, all right. Said she'd had a suite in his establishment since—" The detective glanced at Susannah and cleared his throat. "Since you and she became acquainted."

Aubrey let out a long breath. His expression was grim, and little wonder. Whatever his feelings for Delphinia might have been, he wouldn't have wished her dead, especially not in such a horrible way, and neither, of course, would Susannah. "Ethan couldn't do a thing like that. Hell, he'll hardly skin a rabbit or clean a trout."

"She shot him," Hollister pointed out. "Had his only brother beaten within an inch of his life. Accused him of trying to rape her—" Another wary glance at Susannah, followed by an awkward silence.

"I've heard the word *rape* before," Susannah said crisply. "My husband is right. Ethan isn't capable of murder, and I don't believe it would even occur to him to force himself on a woman."

"Especially that one," Aubrey remarked thoughtfully. He turned his gaze back to Hollister's face. "Has bail been set?"

The former Pinkerton man shook his head. His carefully brushed derby hat sat on the table beside his chair, along with a pipe rack and a copy of a very thick book written by a man named Adam Smith, and he reached for it with some relief. "He's considered dangerous," he said. He cleared his throat as he stood. "Fact is, there are those who say he hasn't been right in the head since that Chinese girl left the country. The one he was going to marry."

A sigh of exasperation erupted from Aubrey. "You don't need to explain Su Lin's identity to me, Hollister. I remember her well enough. And yes, Ethan loved the girl, and it tore him up when she went away. He went through hell, and so did she, I'm sure. But he wouldn't have killed Delphinia or anybody else, I know that much."

Hollister looked anxiously in the direction of the entryway. "Somebody killed the woman," he said with a sort of dogged weariness. "And right now, your brother is the most likely candidate."

Aubrey, too, was on his feet. "No," he said.

Susannah suppressed an urge to link her arm with

his. He would not have welcomed any gesture of sympathy just then. "Might we visit Ethan?" she asked.

Aubrey glanced down at her in surprise. "You aren't to go near the police station," he informed her. "It's no place for a woman."

Susannah was willing to overlook this last remark because she knew Aubrey was under great strain and still suffering from his injuries. She left him behind to escort Mr. Hollister to the front door, where he stepped out into a day of cold, blustery winds and bright sunshine. Aubrey, unable to move quite as fast, lingered at the entrance to the study, watching them.

"Has it never occurred to you," Susannah whispered to Mr. Hollister, "that the very people who nearly killed my husband—at Delphinia Parker's behest, may I remind you—might have turned on her in the end? For that matter, *I* might as easily have done the murder as Ethan."

"Hardly," Mr. Hollister said, but he sounded tired and discouraged, and in spite of everything, Susannah found herself feeling a little sorry for him. "Whoever murdered that woman was strong, Mrs. Fairgrieve. Stronger than you're likely to be." He sighed and resettled his fashionable hat. "We're looking for those hooligans she hired, if that's any comfort, but the fact of the matter is, they've probably scattered to the four winds by now."

An icy wind blew up the walk and bit into both Susannah and Mr. Hollister, causing them to shiver. "Is that any reason to settle the blame on Ethan? Because he's close at hand?"

"The police aren't in the business of hanging innocent men," Mr. Hollister informed her. "If your brother-in-law didn't kill Mrs. Parker, then we'll find it out soon enough."

"Will you?" Susannah asked. "I'm afraid I don't

share your confidence. While Ethan is languishing in jail, the real murderers are very likely getting away!"

Hollister set his jaw, touched the brim of his hat. "Good day, Mrs. Fairgrieve," he said. "Perhaps next time I come to call, I might be able to bring better news."

Susannah said nothing, and when Hollister turned to walk away, she closed the door a little too hard.

Aubrey, standing just outside the study only moments before, had vanished. Suspecting the worst, Susannah hurried through the dining room and kitchen, just in time to see him start down the rear walkway leading to the stables.

"Where are you going?" she demanded, bounding after him without even pausing to put on her cloak. She didn't need to look back to know Maisie and Ellie were gawking at them through the kitchen window.

"Now that's a damn fool question if I've ever heard one," Aubrey said, and walked on at his slow, determined pace. "I want to see Ethan."

Susannah had to scramble to keep up, even though Aubrey was much hampered by his cracked ribs, because his legs were so much longer than hers. Once or twice, she nearly stumbled in the hard-crusted snow. "Wait," she pleaded. "Aubrey, please, *wait*—"

He stopped, and he waited, but he didn't look happy about it. Susannah knew she could not dissuade him from saddling a horse or hitching up a buggy and heading for the jailhouse, but she couldn't let him walk away unchallenged. "Let me go with you," she said. That way, she would at least know what was happening.

But Aubrey shook his head, and the expression in his eyes was downright obdurate. She would never allow him to blame Victoria's stubborn nature on Julia; plainly the baby had inherited that particular trait from her father. "No, Susannah. There are very few things I would deny you, but this is one of them. When I said the police station was no place for a decent female, I meant it."

Susannah believed in choosing her battles; she knew if she did not, she would soon be exhausted. She and Aubrey would work out his misconception about where women did and did not belong another time; for now, she was more interested in getting through a crisis with the potential to destroy her new family.

"I won't be the sort of wife who stays meekly at home and waits for her husband to grant her his permission to think," she warned, hugging herself against the bitter cold of that crystalline afternoon. "I am a Fairgrieve now, too, and what happens to you *matters* to me, Aubrey. Ethan's situation matters, too. Let me be a part of this."

He regarded her solemnly, looking gaunt and, at the same time, unshakable. His smile was brief and flimsy, but it warmed her heart all the same. "Believe me, Susannah—I know full well you won't be content to confine yourself to a traditional wifely role. I don't think I'd be happy if you did. But in this particular instance, it's important that you do as I ask."

She subsided a little, stricken and yet seeing the sense in what he said. He needed to consult with Ethan, come up with a plan of action. Perhaps he feared that his own compunction to look after her, should she be present in what he regarded as a dangerous and unsuitable place, would hamper him in those efforts.

"If you aren't back here by sunset, I'm going to decide something terrible has happened and come looking for you," she said.

He laughed and came back to place a quick, light kiss

on the top of her head. "Fair enough," he said. "Now, go back inside before you take a chill. Please?"

She sighed and returned to the house with the greatest reluctance. It was quite impossible for her simply to wait; she needed to be busy, yet Ellie and Maisie had the housework and the children well in hand, and she was too unsettled to play piano or sit down to read.

It was for that reason that she decided to finish the task she had begun while Aubrey was resting—she would sort through the last of Julia's things, putting aside personal items like books, ornaments, and jewelry for Victoria, turning some of the simpler, more practical dresses over to Maisie and Ellie, donating the rest of her friend's extensive wardrobe to Reverend Johnstone for the church's charity work. The baby's furniture would be moved in later that day.

"You aren't overdoin' it now, are you, Mrs. Fairgrieve?" Maisie was standing in the doorway, a troubled expression on her face.

Susannah sighed. "Please, Maisie—don't start addressing me as Mrs. Fairgrieve, as if we were strangers. You and I will not be observing the formalities. We're friends, remember?"

"I ain't likely to forget," Maisie replied.

"Then, please, just call me Susannah, as you always have," came the answer. She surveyed the boxes and other clutter that remained. The weather was mild, so she'd opened a window to air the place out. "I guess the most important things have been done."

Maisie narrowed her eyes. "You ain't thinkin' of movin' in here with the baby, are you?" She slapped one large thigh and chortled, a startling sound. "I'd have sworn things was better'n fine betwixt you and the mister."

Susannah blushed but refrained from comment. What was there to say, after all—that she was very happy in Aubrey's bed? Plainly, Maisie knew that much already. Maybe the whole neighborhood knew. Although inwardly she was smiling, for the Benevolents had come to her mind, she winced at Maisie.

"Don't be consternated now," the older woman advised with a waving gesture meant to dismiss Susannah's embarrassment as unfounded. "It weren't all that much hollerin', really. 'Sides, it showed your man was makin' you happy—nothin' wrong with that."

Susannah closed her eyes for a moment, then turned and busied herself sweeping out the armoire in order to hide her flaming face. It was then that she spotted the drawers in the back, near the floor. Expecting to find special pieces of jewelry and other keepsakes to save for Victoria, Susannah instead discovered stacks of old letters, some written in her own hand, a packet containing photographic likenesses of various subjects and sizes, and a thick leather-bound journal.

Holding belongings so personal to Julia brought the loss of her home to Susannah all over again, and with a cruel clarity. For a moment, it was as though the news of her friend's death had just reached her, fresh and terrible and so very unjust. Her hands shook as she set the letters and the diary on the bureau top and concentrated her attention on the tintypes.

There was an informal wedding picture of Julia and Aubrey, both of them smiling with their eyes, if not their mouths, the bride standing proudly behind the seated groom, as custom dictated, one slender hand resting on his shoulder. She found a very handsome likeness of Ethan, too, and a tattered picture of herself and Julia as children at St. Mary's, taken by an itinerant photographer one Christmas. Parts and pieces of a life ended far too soon.

She sat down on the edge of the bed, all the starch gone out of her knees, and stared blankly into the past for a long time. *Let them go, Julia,* she thought. *Aubrey, Victoria, Ethan. Let them all go.*

Chapter

17

~

$\mathcal{V}$ictoria sat in the midst of a pile of soft pillows, chewing industriously on her doll's foot and watching Susannah's efforts at cleaning and sorting with wide hazel eyes. Aubrey's eyes. The child seemed to find the whole enterprise cause for fascination and mirth.

"Silly bug," Susannah said once in a burst of affection, crouching to kiss the top of the infant's downy head.

Victoria chortled and waved both plump arms and the cloth doll in exuberant emphasis. Susannah laughed and kissed the baby again, then went back to her tasks.

It could have waited, she knew, this final disbursement of a dead woman's dresses and shoes, trinkets and books, but Ethan was in jail, charged with murder, and Aubrey had gone to his aid immediately, despite the fact that he was still dangerously weak. Working kept her from thinking too much.

Three full hours had passed when Aubrey returned to the house by carriage. Susannah watched from the window of the master suite as he climbed gingerly out of the cab. Even from that distance, she could see that her husband was pale, and his powerful shoulders drooped a little under the fabric of his finely made coat.

She held herself in place only by sheer force of will; every instinct bade her dash down the stairs and fling herself upon him, fussing and fidgeting.

He would have hated that, of course.

The door of the carriage remained open behind him, and Susannah was startled to see Ethan climb out, rumpled and a little thinner than usual but otherwise hearty. A smile lit her face, and she scooped Victoria up into her arms and made her way out of the room, along the corridor, and down the main staircase, decorum evident in every step.

In the entryway, she stood on tiptoe to kiss Aubrey's wind-chilled cheek, and he looked down at her with a light in his eyes. Although he was plainly tired, she could see and sense that his strength was returning; he seemed more vigorous every time she encountered him.

"You've escaped," she said to Ethan, kissing him as well.

He laughed somewhat grimly, shrugged out of his jacket, and allowed Aubrey to take it from his hands. "Not exactly," he said, watching as his brother hung the garment beside his own on the massive oak coat tree next to the door. "My dear brother here, with some help from John Hollister, convinced the police that I could be trusted not to jump bail."

"Trust, hell," Aubrey scoffed, already making his way toward his study. "They let you out because I put up everything I have as a guarantee that you'd be here if this thing comes to trial."

Ethan stopped, looking as stunned as if someone had struck him across the belly with the broad side of a plank. "You did what?" he rasped.

Aubrey had reached the double doors of his study, which stood open. He paused on the threshold and turned to meet his brother's narrowed gaze. "You heard me."

The younger brother took a single step toward the elder, stopped. "Suppose I lit out of here one dark night, hit the trail for good, changed my name—"

"You won't," Aubrey said. His voice was calm, and he hadn't moved from his station in the study doorway. "You'd have to leave Ruby behind, unless you wanted to make a fugitive out of her."

Ethan let the comment pass, since there was no refuting it anyway. After an interval of silence had gone by, he spoke again, waving his arms in a gesture that took in not only that grand house but all Aubrey's many and varied interests beyond its walls. "Everything?" he marveled.

Aubrey grinned. "Everything."

"Why?"

"That's a stupid question. Because you're my brother." At that, Aubrey favored Susannah with a wink, turned, and vanished into his private sanctum, leaving Ethan with little choice but to follow. They remained closeted away, the pair of them, talking until long after Susannah had fed Victoria, told her a long, made-up story, and settled her in her cradle, which now occupied a space in the corner of the splendid new nursery.

Maisie thought it was pure foolery, Susannah's habit of talking to the infant, reading to her from books and even newspapers, and relating fairy tales, but it was Susannah's firm opinion that children, the very smallest included, were too often discounted and even ignored by adults. She well remembered what it was like to be looked through, not at, spoken about but not to, as though she were made of mist or smoke rather than solid flesh.

Victoria, she had determined, would grow up with a sturdy sense of herself and of her substance, tangible and otherwise, as a person.

Susannah was pondering this as she descended the staircase and was therefore close at hand when a visitor turned the bell. She opened the door to find Mr. Hollister, now Ethan's legal advisor as well as a family friend, standing on the porch with his sister Ruby at his side. The strain of the day showed plainly in both their faces, and Susannah felt such sympathy that all her discomfort in the man's presence ebbed away.

"Do come in," Susannah said warmly, stepping back to let them pass into the warmth and light of the foyer.

"Mr. Fairgrieve didn't tell you we were coming," Ruby guessed aloud. She was very young, and pretty rather than beautiful, with an air of competence and quiet self-assurance about her that Susannah very much admired.

John smiled. "By Mr. Fairgrieve," he explained, "she means your husband. He invited us to join you for supper. I hope it isn't an imposition."

Susannah laughed and shut the door, pushing against a breeze sweeping uphill from the not-so-distant waters of the bay. "Quite frankly, I haven't given a thought to supper, though I'm sure Maisie has. I'm delighted that you're here."

Ethan came out of the study then, and Susannah's heart practically turned over when she saw the way he looked at Ruby. Aubrey might not believe in love, but it was perfectly plain that his brother was of quite another opinion on the subject.

Ruby crossed the entryway and stood looking up at Ethan, her expression as poignantly eloquent as his had been. Susannah felt a momentary sting of envy and glanced at Aubrey, only to find him watching her in a very thoughtful fashion.

Despite the clouds of trouble that had gathered over them all, supper that night was a pleasant experience, spiced with laughter, good-natured political disagreements, and unspoken hopes. Maisie had cooked up a veritable feast, with help from Ellie, and there were no leftovers when the meal ended and the dishes were whisked away.

"That was delicious," Susannah told the two women as she entered the kitchen, pushing up the sleeves of her dress. She had left their guests in Aubrey's charge, intending to help with the clearing up. "Thank you both."

Maisie accepted the compliment with a grunt, but there was something obstinate in her bearing. "You just run along and chat with your company, now," she said. "Me and Ellie'll take care of these dishes."

Susannah felt shut out, even though she knew the women wanted to do her a favor. She opened her mouth to protest, realized it would be hopeless, and then simply left the room.

Ruby and John took their leave fairly early, and Ethan, who would be staying at the house for the time being, seemed at loose ends after that. He was pacing the front parlor when Aubrey levered himself out of his chair and announced that it was about time he went to bed.

Susannah said good night to Ethan as she took her husband's arm, and they climbed the stairs together. As she had suspected, it turned out that Aubrey was not nearly so tired as he'd made himself out to be.

With the morning came Mr. Zacharias, money in hand, seeking yet another impromptu piano lesson. Susannah did not fail to notice that he lingered in the kitchen, drinking Maisie's fresh-brewed coffee, afterward. Maisie, for her part, was friendly but not forward; after all, she and Mr. Zacharias had just discovered each other. Susannah left them alone and went upstairs to resume the job of going through Julia's things.

Aubrey had left the house directly after breakfast,

taking Ethan with him, and Susannah had not seen either of them since. She hoped they were at the store or meeting with Mr. Hollister regarding Ethan's defense, but she feared something quite different. Both of them believed Mrs. Parker had been murdered by her own hirelings, the same men who had attacked Aubrey in his office. Ethan had referred to them as wharf rats on more than one occasion, and of course the term indicated that they might be found in one of the iniquitous pits along Seattle's busy waterfront. She wouldn't put it past either her husband or her brother-in-law to go poking around down there, amongst people who would sooner slit the visitors' throats than part with any information concerning the killing.

She worked diligently, and Aubrey did not return, and finally there was nothing left but Julia's diary and the letters. With Victoria napping in the next room, Susannah curled up on her and Aubrey's bed and pondered the envelopes first.

There were her own letters to Julia, tattered from much reading and bound together by a faded yellow ribbon. That simple show of caring on her friend's part brought tears to Susannah's eyes, and she blinked them back. She hadn't dreamed, in those innocent days when she was writing to Julia from Nantucket, that they would never see each other again. She'd believed, in fact, that they would be old together, the two of them, looking back over long, productive lives, comparing notes and exchanging memories.

Suddenly, Susannah couldn't bear staying shut up inside that house for another moment. She got to her feet and went in search of Ellie, asking the other woman to look after Victoria while she was out. Then she put on Julia's hooded cloak and set off down the hill, toward the heart of Seattle.

Some of her notices offering piano lessons were still fluttering on poles and the sides of buildings, and Susannah felt a little sad when she saw them. That source of income was almost certain to dry up now that she was married to Aubrey, since most of her students had actually been suitors, not sincere lovers of music, and she regretted that. Not only would she be without funds of her own, but she was certain to miss teaching as well.

She strolled past the store, certain now that Aubrey was not there, and headed toward the waterfront. She could not have explained why the place drew her, but it did, almost irresistibly. Maybe it had all along.

There were ships riding the tide in Elliott Bay, and several were tied up at the various wharves. Giant stevedores, mostly Germans and Scandinavians by their accents, worked alongside impossibly small Chinamen, loading and unloading crates and boxes and baggage of all sorts. Susannah garnered a few looks as she picked her way through the sawdust that served as fill dirt, but she ignored them.

Mashers and rascals, she had read in various periodicals, were best dealt with in just such a fashion. If one paid them any mind at all, they would merely be encouraged in their vices.

She did not see Aubrey, but then, she wasn't looking for him; indeed, he was the last person she wanted to encounter at the moment. Somewhere between the house and the docks, she had decided that the waterfront had important secrets to share, if she would only pay attention. Ethan had had that damning confrontation with Delphinia here, aboard the steamer *Olympia*, and whoever had killed the other woman had thrown her body into these same busy waters. The truth, Susannah knew, was here—somewhere.

The place was loud and foul-smelling, a noxious conflagration of odors including rotted fish, sewage, low tide, and sour sweat, and Susannah held a handkerchief to her nose as she pressed on. She did not know what she was looking for, nor was she under the delusion that she could solve the crime on her own and vindicate her brother-in-law, but she was impelled to proceed nonetheless.

A stench of swear words swirled overhead like a flock of birds as the workmen shouted to one another, but she took no offense, knowing the oaths and curses were not directed at her. She had walked for some distance when she heard shouting up ahead and peered around a huge stack of crates to see Ethan standing with his feet apart and his hands clenched into fists. A Chinaman railed at him.

"White devil!" the smaller man screamed. "Woman spoiler!" A stream of sulphurous abuse followed, accusations so impossibly vicious that Susannah felt as though she'd been eavesdropping at the keyhole of hell.

Ethan did not move, and Susannah knew for certain then, if she had ever truly doubted it, that he had had no part in Mrs. Parker's death, nor had he earned the bullet he'd taken from that woman's derringer for allegedly trying to force himself upon her. Had he done those things, it would have been impossible for him to endure such insults, especially in public, while still holding his temper in check.

A bearded man in a sweat-drenched shirt ceased his dockside labors long enough to take in the scene and demand, "You gonna take that kinda sewer slop, Fairgrieve? I say you ought to drown the little bastard."

This opinion brought a round of cheers from onlookers, and Susannah was frightened by the blithe hatred of the crowd. They were *hoping* for violence.

"Everybody stay back," Ethan said in a clear voice. "This is between Su Wong and me."

The Chinaman spat out Aubrey's name and something about a bank draft.

Susannah was disturbed by the reference, but she had no opportunity to pursue the matter. The Chinaman continued to berate Ethan, spewing his native dialect, broken here and there by fractured English, in shrill, birdlike squawks. She lost track of the content, but Su Wong's tone of voice was eloquence itself.

Ethan closed his eyes for a moment, held up his hands, palms up. "Enough," he said quietly.

It was then that Susannah realized the angry man was probably Su Lin's father, brother, or uncle. She could not judge Su Wong's age by looking at him; he might have been seventeen or fifty. He wore the standard black silk shirt and pants, and a coarse, thin braid dangled far down his back.

Just as Susannah stepped out from behind the crates, the Chinaman shrieked something vehement, again in his own language, then covered his face with both hands and turned away from Ethan, wailing in furious sorrow. The sound stabbed at the pit of Susannah's stomach, and Ethan moved to touch the man's thin shoulder in what appeared to be sympathy, then thought better of the idea and withdrew. It was then that he noticed Susannah.

"Good Lord," he said. Striding toward her, he took her by the elbow. "What are you doing here?"

Susannah shrugged free and patted her hair with both hands in order to stall for time. Then she let out a long breath and met her brother-in-law's gaze. He reminded her a lot, in those moments, of Aubrey, for all their differences, physical and otherwise. "I don't know," she replied, and she was telling the God's truth.

Su Wong had vanished into the throng of workers on

the dock, and the spectators were minding their own business again. Ethan seemed to notice none of this; all his attention was fixed on Susannah. He took a new grip on her arm, and, though it wasn't painful, it was tight as a manacle.

"Let's get out of here," he said, and dragged her among boxes and barrels, wheelbarrows and waiting travelers, toward the street. In one direction was the notorious Skid Road, a long, muddy track, once used to slide timber down from the hills to the waterfront. Now, it was lined with brothels, gaming rooms, and saloons, and Maisie had told Susannah it was the only part of town with a worse reputation than Water Street's.

"That man—" she began.

"Su Lin's father," Ethan replied, dragging her behind him, never looking back. "He blames me for bringing dishonor on his family. Do you realize that if Aubrey sees you down here, he'll have me horsewhipped and lock you up in the attic for a year or two?"

They crossed Water Street, Susannah hurrying to keep up. "Ethan," she gasped, "will you *stop*, please, before my lungs burst?"

He came to a swift halt, and his blue eyes were snapping as he looked down at her. He cocked his thumb toward the bay. "This isn't Nantucket, Mrs. Fairgrieve," he said. "Half those men are cutthroats, and the other half think any unescorted woman who crosses their path can be had for two bits and a shot of whiskey."

Susannah was at the end of her patience. She put her hands on her hips and tapped one foot on the frost-slickened boards of the sidewalk. "I am well aware that this isn't Nantucket, thank you. About that man—"

"What man?"

"Mr. Su."

Ethan looked sick, weary to the very center of his

soul. "I told you. Su Lin was his daughter. I wanted to marry her, and he wanted her to take a Chinese husband. Recently, Su received word from the man he'd chosen—Su Lin was carrying a child. She tried to—to do something about it—on the ship, and died in the process." He put out a hand, braced himself against the brick wall of a building. He breathed deeply for several moments and swallowed. "Are you happy now, or would you like to go out into the country someplace and put a hand into a few snake dens or maybe bait a bull?"

Susannah was shaken, not only by the loud and dangerous encounter on the waterfront but by the implications of what Ethan had just said. Su Lin, the woman he had loved, was dead, and she had perished in an attempt to eliminate a child that was almost certainly his. It was all too overwhelming, too personal to address, particularly in the street.

She spotted Aubrey just then, on foot and coming toward them like a storm made flesh, and felt a sort of rueful gratitude. "I don't think that will be necessary," she replied. "My baiting a bull, I mean."

Ethan followed her gaze and muttered something under his breath. Some of his color was coming back, but he was still leaning against the wall. He would be a long time getting over what he'd learned that day, though she wouldn't have been surprised if he never mentioned it again.

Susannah shivered as another cold wind ruffled the water and then rolled over her like an intangible wave.

"I won't ask what you're doing here," Aubrey said, looking at Susannah, "since it's obvious. You're looking for trouble, as usual, and my guess is, you found some."

Susannah glanced at Ethan, hoping for a word of support, but he was stubbornly silent, his lips pressed together into a thin line. He thrust a hand through his hair and glared at Aubrey, as though all the sorrows of the world were his fault.

Aubrey, meanwhile, shifted his attention from his wife to his brother. "You promised to leave this alone," he said, and Susannah knew he was referring to the inquiry into Mrs. Parker's death. They were on a public street, and passersby nodded in greeting or tipped their hats, their glances avid and curious.

Susannah took Aubrey's arm, then Ethan's. Their breaths made vapor in the cold. "If we must discuss this further," she said, "might we at least do so in private?"

Five minutes later, they were in Aubrey's office over the store. He sat on the edge of his desk, arms folded, while Susannah took a nearby chair and Ethan stood at the window overlooking the street. It wasn't hard to guess what he was thinking about.

Aubrey poured brandy for himself and his brother and produced a mild blackberry cordial for Susannah. She normally did not indulge in spirits, but she was still freezing from her impulsive trek to the waterfront, and poor Su Lin and her child were very much on her mind. Too, now that she was well away from the docks, she was beginning to imagine some of the singular calamities that might have befallen her there.

"Hollister swears the police are questioning every man on the shoreline," Aubrey said, speaking to Ethan's back. "For the time being, brother, that has to be enough."

Ethan turned. "My life is at stake here," he said. "I'm not going to stand by and wait for Hollister or anybody else to solve the problem." His face contorted. "Su Lin is dead," he rasped.

Aubrey and Susannah exchanged glances, but neither one spoke.

Ethan sought and held his brother's gaze. His anger

and pain were palpable. "It's my fault. If I'd married her—"

Susannah set her glass on Aubrey's desk, not trusting herself to hold it steady. Aubrey did not look away from Ethan's face; his shoulders were straight, and he held his head up.

"You can't change the past. Sometimes you just have to walk away from it."

Ethan's smile was terrible to see. "Ironic advice, coming from you," he said.

The silence that followed was lengthy and palpable.

"I'm sorry," Aubrey told his brother. "About Su Lin, I mean."

Ethan's gaze flickered in Susannah's direction as he'd just remembered her presence; she grasped the arms of her chair, her way of saying she wasn't going anywhere. He turned back to the matter at hand. "There's more."

Aubrey poured himself another splash of brandy and sipped from it. Susannah's heart beat faster.

"Yes," Aubrey said, and waited.

"You gave her money. You paid her off."

Aubrey shook his head. "No," he said.

"The draft was drawn on one of your bank accounts," Ethan said. Another dreadful pause ensued. "Why?" the younger brother ground out, agonized. Then he slammed both fists down on the surface of Aubrey's desk. "*Tell me why!*"

The atmosphere in the office seemed charged; Susannah didn't dare move or speak.

"I told you," Aubrey said. "I didn't go near Su Lin."

Ethan leaned forward. "Did you tell her she would bring disgrace on the Fairgrieves, Aubrey? Did you tell her that her children—*my* children—would be outcasts?"

Aubrey's jawline clamped down hard. Susannah could see that his control was stretched to its limits.

She closed her eyes, awaiting the explosion, but it didn't come. When she looked again, Aubrey and Ethan were still well apart, taking each other's measure.

"You bastard," Ethan said at long last.

Aubrey ran the tip of his tongue along the inside of his lower lip, a gesture that Susannah recognized as an effort to hold on to his temper. "Think what you like," he replied.

"I need a drink," Ethan said. Then he turned, without another word, and walked out of the office, slamming the door behind him.

"How could you, Aubrey?" Susannah asked.

He heaved a sigh. "Not you, too."

"You had no right, interfering like that."

"Thank you for your faith in my word, Mrs. Fairgrieve."

"There was mention of a bank draft," Susannah said stubbornly. "I was there, if you will recall."

"I can't explain that," Aubrey said. "You'll just have to trust me." He sighed, staring off into space. "I won't deny that I was afraid for both of them," he confided. "Ethan was eighteen years old at the time, and he thought he could hold off a world full of bigots. Su Lin was sheltered, innocent. The two of them would have suffered beyond anything they could have imagined."

Susannah held her tongue. She had begun to believe Aubrey, even in the face of evidence to the contrary, and she could not bring herself to admit as much.

Aubrey lowered himself into his desk chair—a place, she reasoned, where his authority was absolute. He looked pale and gaunt sitting there but in no way diminished. He was without question the strongest person she had ever known, and yet he had been very nearly destroyed by a single, feckless woman. A sobering measure, that, of his attachment to Julia.

He sat back and gazed up at the ceiling. "Oh, yes," he agreed, having taken the time to absorb her statement regarding Su Lin's tragic death. "She suffered."

"You know what happened on the ship, don't you?"

He sighed again, nodded. "Word got back to me, yes. Su Wong made sure of that."

Susannah sat for a moment with the backs of her fingers resting against her mouth. "I don't understand— why didn't you tell Ethan?"

By then, Aubrey had taken his brother's place at the window; perhaps he could see Ethan walking away from where he stood, perhaps not. "We haven't been on the best of terms lately," he said.

Susannah stared him down.

"All right," he admitted. "I couldn't do it. I tried, but I just couldn't seem to get the words out."

For a long time, neither spoke. Then Aubrey turned to face her again. "Let's go home," he said.

Susannah nodded and got to her feet.

Downstairs, lost in her own thoughts, she perused a selection of fabric while Aubrey spoke with an associate and Mr. Hawkins rushed out to summon the carriage and driver. It startled her a little when Aubrey appeared beside her, placing his hand over hers.

Soon, they were in the carriage, jolting up the hill toward the house. Snow drifted past the windows, but they were warm, sitting close together the way they were.

Susannah drew a deep breath and let it out slowly. "I expected you to lecture me for visiting the waterfront on my own," she ventured to say.

Aubrey chuckled, but there was little humor in the sound. He sat with his head tilted back and his eyes closed. "Would it have done any good?" he asked without looking at her.

"No," Susannah mused, "I don't suppose it would have."

He sighed. "Just don't do it again, please." At last, he turned and met her upraised gaze. "If you must go to the waterfront, the jailhouse, or some equally unsuitable place, have the courtesy not to go alone. Take Ethan. Hell, take Maisie. But for Victoria's sake, as well as your own, please be more careful after this."

Aubrey had spoken calmly, and yet Susannah felt as though she'd been roundly—and justly—scolded. She wanted to explain, all of the sudden, despite her intense pride, but she wasn't exactly sure how to go about it. After all, she didn't know herself what she'd hoped to accomplish by crossing Water Street to the wharves.

"The answer is there somewhere," she said.

Aubrey took her chin in one hand, but gently. "You're right," he said. "But finding it isn't your responsibility, Susannah." He paused, tightened his jaw for a moment, then went on. "My God, if something were to happen to you—"

She waited, her heart in her throat, but Aubrey didn't say he loved her. He just bent his head and kissed her lightly on the mouth.

"Aubrey," she began, fully meaning to tell him how she felt about him, that she loved him as a wife should love a husband, but in the end her courage failed her. Perhaps she had used it all, visiting the waterfront.

"Yes?" he asked in a teasing voice, still tasting her mouth.

"Nothing," she said.

His glance was wry and a little sad. "If you say so," he replied.

Chapter

18

~

The heartbreaking realization brought Susannah shooting straight up out of a sound sleep. She sat blinking, with her back rigid and her heart hammering in the back of her throat. "Aubrey," she gasped, feeling for her husband in the darkness and finding that his side of the bed was empty.

Disappointment seized her, fierce and desperate, and she scrambled out from under the covers to turn up the nearest gas lamp. She was winded, as though she'd just run a great distance, and she needed a few moments to catch her breath. Aubrey was nowhere in sight.

She found her way into the nursery, where Victoria slept peacefully in a spill of moonlight from the windows, but Aubrey was not there, either.

After pulling on a wrapper, Susannah descended the rear stairway into the kitchen. A single light burned on the bureau, and the remains of some midnight repast were on the table. A book lay open beside that, spine up. Stepping closer, she saw that it was Julia's journal.

Leaving plate, crumbs, and book for later, Susannah lit a small lantern and pressed on to the study. At last, here was Aubrey, not seated at his desk but standing at the window, watching snow fall through the darkness, opalescent in the flimsy glow of the street lamps. He was fully dressed, in trousers and a shirt, boots, and even a jacket.

"If we find Su Lin's father," she said, knowing by the stiffening in his broad shoulders that he had either heard or sensed her approach, "we'll find Mrs. Parker's killers. He knows something, Aubrey."

Aubrey turned to look at her. She could not read his expression in the gloom, but his tone of voice revealed a certain skeptical interest. "On what do you base that far-fetched conclusion?" he inquired.

"Think about it. He hates Ethan. He might have thought he had to avenge his daughter's honor in some way."

He sighed and thrust a hand through his hair, already rumpled from previous passes of his fingers. "There are probably others," he said. "My brother is no saint, after all—he has his share of enemies." He paused, reflected upon thoughts of his own, thoughts he did not choose to share. "You know, don't you, that Hollister will probably dismiss the idea out of hand? Su Wong has a grudge against Ethan, no denying that, but he probably didn't even know Delphinia."

Susannah set down the lamp and put her hands on her hips. "Be that as it may, if you won't take me to the police station first thing tomorrow morning, Mr. Fairgrieve, I shall go on my own."

She saw his jaw work as he suppressed his irritation. "You might be just foolish enough to mean that," he answered. "Given that you went wandering along the waterfront today. We'll talk to Hollister together." He paused. "Susannah—where did this notion come from?"

"Call it intuition," she replied. "I've been working the situation over and over in my mind, waking and sleeping. A little while ago, the answer woke me up." The answer and something else. She was not ready to speak of the private and shattering decision she'd made, not yet.

He crossed the room to kiss her forehead. "Go back to bed," he said. "The matter can wait."

She didn't move. "You've been reading Julia's journal. I saw it on the kitchen table."

Aubrey sighed. His hands lay lightly on her shoulders; she liked his touching her, even in so mundane and ordinary a way, and couldn't hold back a soft crooning sound as, with the pads of his thumbs, he rubbed the tense muscles supporting her collarbone.

"I found the diary by accident," he said. "And I was curious. There are those, you know, who would maintain that I have every right, given the fact that Julia was once my wife."

"What were you hoping to find?"

He pulled her close and, for a moment, rested his chin on the crown of her head. "It was more a question of what I was hoping *not* to find," he answered. "I was disappointed."

Susannah lifted both hands and rested them gently against either side of his face. "Not Ethan?" she asked, barely breathing the words.

He shook his head. "Not Ethan," he answered. "She made it all up, Susannah. There were no other men. She believed I was unfaithful and wanted to torment me for it. Inventing a flock of lovers must have seemed a viable means of revenge to her." His eyes were dark with remembered pain as he looked down at Susannah. "Because of that, I broke vows made before God and man, Susannah. I made her accusations true."

She put her arms around his waist, careful not to put pressure on his mending ribs. "There is no changing any of that now," she reasoned quietly. "Let it go, Aubrey."

"Why didn't I see how unhappy she was? Why didn't I think, even once, that she might need my help?"

Although Aubrey's words were laudable, they were painful to hear. After all, if Julia had lived, and the two of them had built a happy life together, Susannah would still be a lonely spinster with only the sea, her music, and books for company. She looked deep into her own heart and found guilt festering there, along with sorrow and a vast, endless love for the man standing now in her embrace. Was it also a hopeless love?

He did not give her time to reply but instead hooked a finger under her chin and raised her face for his kiss. "Let us return to our marriage bed, Mrs. Fairgrieve," he said hoarsely. "I have need of your singular comforts."

She stepped back, her earlier vow to shed no more tears forgotten as her vision blurred. "Do you pretend that I am Julia? When we—we lie together?"

He looked as stunned as if she'd drawn back her hand and slapped him. "Good God, Susannah," he rasped. "No." He buried his fingers in her hair, which fell loose around her shoulders and breasts to tumble past her waist. "*No*," he repeated.

She freed herself, an easy matter, since he did not attempt to restrain her. "I can't do this," she whispered, awash in misery. "I thought I could—I thought it was enough that I love you—"

He took hold of her shoulders when she would have fled. "Susannah, what are you talking about?"

She gave an inelegant sniffle and wiped her face with one sleeve of her wrapper. "I love you," she repeated, with more force and more desolation than before. "I thought I could live as your wife—give myself to you— that my loving you would be enough—"

"You're not making sense." He spoke gently, even tenderly.

"That's the very worst of it. All my life, everything I've done has been sensible. Julia was the flighty one, the pretty one, the one men fell in love with and wanted to marry. I can't live out the rest of my years as her substitute, Aubrey. That's what I'm trying to say. Let me take Victoria. Let me leave Seattle."

"And me?" The question was almost inaudible.

"Can you say that you love me? Truthfully, I mean?"

He rubbed the back of his neck with one hand. "Susannah—"

"Don't say anything more," she interrupted. Now that she had begun, she could not seem to stop the torrent of words spilling from her broken heart. "*Don't* say you don't believe in love. You adored Julia, at first, anyway, and you care very deeply for Victoria and for Ethan, as well. I was a fool—*such* a fool—to think you would ever change, ever come to feel devotion toward me."

He encircled her loosely in his arms. "Susannah. Stop this. I—"

She jerked away, half wild with humiliation and regret. Why, why had she put herself in this position, when she'd known his truest feelings all along? He'd made no secret of his philosophy where human emotions were concerned. He wanted a companion, a partner, a mother for his children, and Susannah longed to be those things to him, but it simply wasn't enough. Since she'd seen the way Ethan and Ruby looked at each other, she'd known that, God help her, it wasn't enough.

She needed passion from Aubrey, fire and frenzy. She wanted to be loved, wildly and richly and without reservation, she wanted to be cherished. And she would rather live without those things than merely pretend to have them.

"What do you want?" he demanded. His eyes glittered, and the taut flesh along his jawline grew pale.

"You know," she told him, squaring her shoulders and raising her chin. If he didn't let her take Victoria, she would have nothing and no one in all the world, all the more reason to hold on to the last shreds of her pride.

"A lie, Susannah? Is that what you want? Shall I tell you a pretty lie? Good God, you are too smart, too fine to live like that!"

"I want Victoria, and a reasonable living allowance," she said. "That's all."

"My daughter? You expect me to let you take *my daughter* from this house? Have you forgotten, *Mrs.* Fairgrieve, that you are legally my wife and therefore subject to my command?"

She barely kept herself from kicking him, and the immediate regret she saw in his eyes did nothing to stem her indignation. "Your *command*? You are no sort of king, *Mr.* Fairgrieve, and I am most certainly not yours to govern! It was a mistake, our marriage, one we can still rectify—"

"You're not going anywhere," he interrupted. "And neither is Victoria."

"You cannot force me to stay!"

"I *can* force you to stay. I *won't* force you to share my bed, however. Oh, no, Mrs. Fairgrieve. When you want my tender attentions—and you will—you will have to ask for them!"

She stared up at him in outraged amazement. "We would do better," she found the breath to say, "discussing this in the morning. Good night, Aubrey." Having delivered this tart farewell, she turned and started toward the doors, but he immediately took an inescapable hold on her arm and pulled her back. They collided briefly, from the force of it, but there was no pain. Not the physical sort, at least.

"Not so fast," he said, fingers encircling her wrist. "I want to know what brought this on. Just yesterday—

even this evening—we understood each other. Now, all of the sudden, marriage to me doesn't suit you. What happened, Susannah?"

She swallowed a healthy chunk of her pride. "I didn't listen to my own instincts, and I've come to regret it. That's what happened."

At long last, he released her. "Sleep well, Susannah," he said. "I assure you, I shall not."

"You may have your bed," she said, with what dignity she had managed to hold on to. "I'll use my old room."

"Do as you like," he said with icy dispatch.

She said nothing in reply, merely turned from him, walked away and out of that room, across the broad entryway, and mounted the stairs a different person from the one who had descended them only minutes before. Yes, she still loved Aubrey, and yes, what remained of her life looked bleak indeed without him in it, but she was strong in her resolution to find a place for herself, put down roots, and thrive. For Victoria's sake, for her own, she would only get stronger.

She did not sleep that night but instead sat upright in the chair in Julia's old room, where the baby slumbered contentedly, blessedly oblivious to all that had transpired, and was still transpiring, in that household. When she heard Aubrey stirring about, she stood, smoothed her nightgown, and made for the wardrobe in the spare room, where she had hung a few of Julia's simpler dresses. That day, she felt no reticence about wearing one of her friend's gowns; she chose an un-Julia-like frock of indigo woolen, piped with silk of an even darker blue, and was waiting in the kitchen when Aubrey came down in search of coffee.

As his gaze fell on Susannah, she saw his eyes widen slightly; she marked the reaction down to the dress being one he remembered, although he'd given no indication that he'd noticed it. In one hand, he carried the familiar volume, Julia's journal; he needed barbering, and his suit looked to be the same one he'd worn the day before.

"Here," he said, thrusting the volume toward her. "Here's a little remembrance of your beloved childhood friend. Should scatter a few illusions—I know it did that for me."

Susannah wanted to defy him, but her hand reached out for the journal of its own accord. Anything she might have said was shut away behind the hard dryness at the back of her throat.

Maisie was upstairs by then, looking after Victoria, but Ellie was there in the kitchen, casting sidelong glances at "the mister." Certainly, he must look odd to her, in this unkempt state, as he did to Susannah, for it was not like him to take so little care with his appearance.

"You be wantin' any breakfast, either one of you?" Ellie asked. She looked ready to bolt and run when the first note of discord sounded.

Susannah merely shook her head in answer to the question; Aubrey made a raspy sound, no doubt intended as a chuckle.

"No, thank you," he said.

Ellie looked from one to the other of them again and made for the back stairs. "I'll just see if Maisie's needin' any help, then," she said, and was soon gone.

"Did you think I would go to the police without you?" Aubrey asked, at last letting his gaze drift over her clothing. He looked ghastly, like a man striving without hope to assimilate some deadly poison of the soul.

Susannah merely nodded. Julia's journal felt heavy in her hands; for a moment, she wanted only to stuff it into the cookstove and let it burn. She might have done that, if she'd thought the past described therein might be consumed with it, in the hungry heat of those frosted-morning flames.

"Well," he said, "you were wrong. I've asked one of the stable hands to hitch up the coach and bring it around. They ought to be out in front right about now, waiting." He made a gesture with one hand, a sweeping motion inviting her to precede him, which she did, pausing only to collect her cloak. He took the garment from her, secured it around her shoulders, and opened the front door.

Mr. Hollister, as it happened, had taken a small office in one of several rabbit holes above the jailhouse; every surface in the place was piled high with books, various bills advertising for stolen horses, wagons, wives, and daughters, wanted posters from all over the United States, and handwritten reports. He did not look surprised to see the Fairgrieves, although Susannah thought his eyes narrowed slightly upon their entrance and concluded that he had guessed what the situation was between herself and Aubrey. Perhaps it was obvious, though, requiring no particular discernment on the part of an intelligent observer.

"Well," he said, and rose from his chair, executing a half bow in Susannah's honor before putting out a hand to Aubrey, who shook it firmly. "How may I help you this cold morning?" To emphasize his question, he shivered a little and went to the potbellied stove in the corner of the room to feed in a chunk of wood. A comforting, snapping sound ensued, entwined with the pleasant scent of burning cedar.

"Susannah has a theory," Aubrey announced, clearing a chair for his wife but remaining on his feet. "Would you like to explain it, my dear?"

In the bright light of day, the idea that Su Lin's father had had some part in Delphinia Parker's death seemed less feasible than it had in the night, when she'd wandered endlessly among the fragments of her shattered heart. Beneath her doubts, however, intuition pulsed like another heartbeat, insistent and sure.

Briefly, she outlined what she knew of Ethan's involvement with Su Lin and the lasting fury their ill-fated association had engendered in the girl's father. "Seeing the man on the waterfront must have triggered the idea in my mind. There's more to Su Lin's story than Ethan knows, I'm sure of it. And I believe the beating Aubrey suffered led up to Mrs. Parker's murder somehow."

Hollister sat back in his chair, tenting his fingers and regarding Susannah as though she were some ancient slate that must be deciphered. Then he put the question she dreaded. "Have you any proof to present, Mrs. Fairgrieve?"

She ran her teeth over her lower lip. "As much as the police had when they charged my brother-in-law with murder," she replied.

Hollister leaned forward, causing the chair to creak, and glanced up at Aubrey before meeting Susannah's unwavering gaze again. The air in the small room was beginning to feel hot and close; she imagined opening the single window and drew a modicum of consolation from that. Smiled at the mental image of papers fluttering about like confused birds.

"I'll find the man if I can," he said. "Talk with him. That's all I can promise, of course."

"That's all I'm asking," Susannah replied, and rose stiffly from her chair. "Good day to you, Mr. Hollister, and thank you for your time."

The former detective stood, nodding confirmation to Susannah, but he looked puzzled, and his gaze kept straying to Aubrey, who had remained silent and still throughout most of the interview.

"This Su Wong—what do you know about him? Anything?"

Aubrey thrust his hands into the pockets of his coat,

which needed pressing. "Just that he was Su Lin's father and that he works on the waterfront."

"I'll ask the police to put a man on him, find out what we can," Hollister said, and it irritated Susannah to no small degree that he directed these remarks to Aubrey. She had been the one, after all, to steer the inquiry in this new direction.

She bristled but said nothing, and when Aubrey offered her his arm, she took it with only the briefest hesitation. Whatever her regrets, whatever her plans for the future, he was still her husband, and it wasn't entirely his fault that he didn't, *couldn't* love her. He had never misled her, never declared himself, and she had gone into the marriage with open eyes, thinking his feelings would change in time.

Fool, she chided herself.

He escorted her out of Hollister's office and down a staircase crowded with policemen and criminals alike, with a few newspaper reporters added in for good measure. Two of the writers pursued them, calling out questions about Ethan and about Mrs. Parker, but the carriage was waiting nearby, and they were inside before any of the journalists could catch up with them.

This time, they sat facing each other, knee to knee, instead of side by side. Aubrey growled some deprecation under his breath, tilted his head back, and closed his eyes. He did not speak again until they were in front of the house once more and alighting from the coach.

"Read the journal, Susannah," he said. "You'll find it enlightening."

Yet another early snow was falling, the flakes fat as chicken feathers drifting down from a dark sky. "What are you planning to do?" she asked, feeling suspicious. Perhaps it was because Aubrey had made no move toward the house but stood instead beside the carriage, the door still gaping open behind him.

"I'm going to find Ethan, for a start. Then I'll probably go back to the store. I'm supposed to be the proprietor, if you remember."

It was cold outside; the wind bit at Susannah's cheeks. "Very well," she said, and turned from him, proceeding toward the house. In the middle of the walk, she paused and looked back, allowing her gaze to link with his. "Please take care."

"Are you worried about me, Mrs. Fairgrieve?" There was a soft smile curving one corner of his mouth, but he looked forlorn somehow.

She said nothing. He knew that she loved him, and she would be damned if she would declare her affection again, in full view and hearing of the carriage driver. After lingering a moment, she continued toward the house and entered without looking back.

She was not ready to face Maisie, nor did she wish to fret and pace over Aubrey, suspecting as she did that he meant to go in search of the Chinaman himself once he'd found Ethan. Victoria was happily knocking down toy blocks as Jasper stacked them, both children overseen by Ellie, and any piano pupils remaining to Susannah had yet to appear.

She recovered the journal from the pocket of the prim navy dress, carried it into the rear parlor, where the piano stood like a lonely monument, sat down in an overstuffed chair, and opened to the first page.

At first, the diary was a cheerful account of meeting Aubrey in Boston, falling in love, marrying, and traveling west. Julia had been impressed with the house when she'd first seen it, and with the store, though less so with Seattle. The city was, she had written, a "noisy, messy place, fraught with ruffians." She rhapsodized over the clothes and jewelry Aubrey bought for her, looked forward to a promised tour of Europe with great excitement. Susannah felt a pang at the mention of the trip, for Aubrey had made the same promise to her, though now it probably would never come to pass.

Eventually, Julia's happiness had given way to a growing dissatisfaction with life "on the frontier." There were no real social occasions, she complained. One could expect only the most asinine forms of entertainment, and fine music was such a rarity that she had nearly forgotten the sound of it. Furthermore, she had begun to suspect that Aubrey was keeping a mistress, an older woman, more sophisticated, more experienced than she was.

Susannah felt rising despair as she read on; it was as though some inner shadow had fallen across Julia's spirit. Instead of passing with time, as such private demons will in most people, Julia's gloom had only deepened. She took to sipping sherry well before teatime and then added laudanum to the ritual.

Gradually, she began to speak of an ardent "love," growing between herself and Ethan. Although her brother-in-law had not avowed to such feelings in so many words, she confessed, he had let her know that he cared for her in a variety of telling ways. He smiled at her. He instigated conversations. He was always unfailingly polite.

Susannah closed her eyes for a moment, full of sorrow. Ethan had merely been kind to Julia, that was obvious, but she'd been so hungry for affection and approval, so lonely and far from home, that she had misinterpreted his attentions. Pregnancy surely had caused her to be even more emotionally volatile than usual, and then there was Aubrey, believing that she'd been false to their marriage vows, caught in the throes of his own pain and disillusionment. What had he said and done to make matters worse?

She shifted positions in her chair and continued to read. She had nearly reached the end of the tragic account when she read the most devastating part, the one Aubrey surely had been referring to when he had first handed her the book that morning in the kitchen.

Julia had visited Su Lin before she went away. She'd found the girl alone and weeping; she must go away, Su Lin had told Julia, because she could bring no joy to Ethan, no honor, but only trouble and disgrace and the worst sort of suffering. She was to marry a Chinese merchant, chosen for her by her father, and she dared not defy the decree, for she would be beaten, perhaps even killed, if she did.

None of that mattered so much, Su Lin had confided, as the terrible secret she was keeping. In a flood of tears, the girl had told Julia that she believed she was carrying Ethan's child. There was a Chinese woman living near the waterfront who could provide a potion that would cause her womb to empty itself, thus sparing her father and future husband in China the shame of a white infant.

Julia made a few sympathetic noises, according to her own account, and then offered to pay Su Lin to take her to the woman.

"Oh, dear God," Susannah whispered, stricken, her stomach doing a slow roll as she realized the meaning of that request. Tears burned her eyes. Sweet, precious Victoria . . . had Julia truly valued her unborn infant so little?

She wept awhile and then dried her face, blew her nose, and took up the journal again. Su Lin had refused Julia's demands, and Julia had instantly become angry. She had raged at the girl, in fact, and told her that she loved Ethan, and he loved her in return. All that ever stood between them, she had said, was Su Lin herself and, of course, the baby. Aubrey's baby.

Su Lin had been distraught, and when Julia offered her a bank draft, signed that morning by Aubrey's own hand—he'd thought he was paying a bill sent by Julia's dressmaker in San Francisco—she had accepted it in silence.

That night, Ethan had come to the house in a frenzy of grief and despair. Su Lin was gone. She'd boarded a ship headed south to San Francisco; from there, she would set sail for China. Julia had pretended to sympathize, but inside, she'd gloated, and she'd said nothing of the girl's pregnancy. Ethan might have gone after her if he'd known the truth.

It was all too vivid in Susannah's mind; she hugged herself and rocked back and forth for a few moments, trying to absorb the tragedy, when it would not be put from her, making it a part of her own soul.

Julia had fully expected Ethan to turn to her at last. She would give him solace, and in time, he was sure to forget Su Lin. They would run away together, she raved, her handwriting odd and erratic. If it became necessary, she intended to persuade him that the baby she carried was his. It shouldn't be so difficult, she speculated; she had already succeeded in convincing Aubrey of that same thing, hadn't she?

Subsequently, she had continued a diligent, if discreet, search for the mysterious Chinese medicine woman who could help her to miscarry. Finally, she had found her. She wasn't ready to bear a child, she'd said. She was afraid, and Su Lin had told her the old woman could solve the problem. She must promise, however, that she would never tell Maisie, Mr. Fairgrieve, or anyone else what had happened.

After a few days, a messenger had brought her a

packet of some loose, strange-smelling tea, along with instructions. Julia had immediately brewed herself a dose of the stuff, and it *had* brought on cramps and even some bleeding, but in the end the child did not leave her.

In the last entry, Julia was nearing her time. She was terrified—of the pain, of the damage that might have been done to the baby when she was trying to end her pregnancy, of death itself. So many women perished bearing children, she wrote. How she wished she had never left Boston, never married at all, but instead become a spinster, like dear Susannah.

Susannah closed the volume, and when she looked up, Maisie was standing in the parlor doorway, her eyes sunken, her flesh pale.

"It's that Chinaman," she said. "They've found him."

Chapter

19

~

It's that Chinaman. They've found him. Susannah stared at her friend as the words echoed through her, settling like a cold weight in the pit of her stomach. Laying the journal aside, she rose slowly, shakily to her feet, crossed the parlor, and took Maisie's work-roughened hands into her own.

"There's more, isn't there?" Susannah urged.

Maisie nodded. "They think it was Ethan that done it."

Susannah swayed slightly, and it was Maisie who held her up. "Dear God." Of course, the police would blame Ethan. And dozens of witnesses could attest to the fact that he and Mr. Su had exchanged angry words only a few days before on the wharf.

"He's been through enough, Ethan has," Maisie said, and her expression was bleak, her normally florid flesh gray and drawn. Clutching the hem of her long apron in one hand, she pressed it to her mouth. The Fairgrieves were her family, perhaps the only semblance she'd ever known. It was certainly that way for Susannah.

"Somebody knifed him," she repeated, almost inaudibly this time, and with a haunted sort of horror. "That Su Wong feller, I mean."

Before Susannah was pressed to say anything further, Mr. Hollister stepped into the parlor, having followed Maisie, no doubt. He was accompanied by a man in a constable's uniform, and while he seemed abashed at having had to deliver more bad news, as he looked at Susannah, she saw a new respect in his eyes, as well as certain reservations.

"It appears that your theory might be right, Mrs. Fairgrieve," he said after clearing his throat. He glanced at Maisie and cleared his throat again. Susannah dropped into a chair. The constable paced slowly back and forth in front of a window.

Would it never end, Susannah wondered, the darkness and sorrow that plagued this house?

"Maybe you'd like to see Reverend Johnstone," Maisie said, laying her hand on Susannah's shoulder. "I could send Ellie for him right away—"

"I suppose he'll get word soon enough and come around on his own," Susannah said numbly.

Maisie stooped to kiss her cheek. "I'll look after Victoria as long as need be," she said.

Susannah nodded, full of gratitude.

Mr. Hollister was polite enough to hold his tongue until the door had closed behind Maisie, but no longer. "I hope we're not intruding," he said. He indicated the nervous constable. "This is Officer Fitzsimmons."

Susannah did not reply directly, nor did she acknowledge the policeman, except with a glance. She was still absorbing Mr. Hollister's recent decision to practice law instead of serving as a Pinkerton man. "Do sit down," she said, and if she sounded somewhat stiff, well, it couldn't be helped. She wished Aubrey would return from wherever he'd gone, for the presence of Mr. Fitzsimmons, coupled with Mr. Hollister's odd manner, troubled her very much.

The lawyer sat in a wing-backed chair next to the hearth, where a small fire burned, while Fitzsimmons preferred to stand, and Susannah remained where she was, intertwining her fingers in her lap in a vain and belated effort to hide her near panic. She knew right away that the tactic had not been successful, for the policeman's gaze dropped, briefly but immediately, to her hands. So, she noticed, did Mr. Hollister's.

"Did Ethan kill that man?" Mr. Hollister asked. "Did Aubrey?"

"Ethan is a handy scapegoat," she said, with a pointed look at Mr. Fitzsimmons. "However, I fail to see how anybody could suspect Aubrey." Now, she focused her full attention on the young and obviously flustered officer. "Have you forgotten that he was beaten so severely that he almost died? Or do you think, perhaps, that he hired his own assailants?"

The parlor doors swung wide before either Fitzsimmons or Hollister could form a reply, and Aubrey strode in, the power of his presence preceding him like a strong wind, filling the room. He had shed his coat, but his skin was ruddy with cold, and there were snowflakes in his hair. Ethan came in behind him.

"Well, Hollister?" Aubrey prompted, ignoring the policeman. "Are you going to answer my wife's questions?" He went to a side table, where several decanters stood, along with whiskey glasses.

Hollister sighed. "Mrs. Parker was your—friend," he said with as much delicacy as possible, though Susannah knew he would have made no such attempt if she had not been present. "It might have served your purposes to be rid of her."

"Whiskey?" Aubrey inquired hospitably, offering a shot glass to his interrogator. His accuser.

Hollister hesitated, then accepted the drink. "You

wouldn't have been the first man to set the scene for an alibi, either," he went on after a bracing sip. "Taking a battering compares favorably to hanging for murder, any way you look at it, and there's always the possibility that the fellows you engaged just got a little carried away with the task at hand."

Aubrey regarded the other man with an expression of benign thoughtfulness, though Ethan looked wrathful. Susannah could empathize with that point of view, being furious herself.

"You really want me to be guilty of this," Aubrey said, puzzled. "Why is that?"

"I can tell you why," Ethan interceded after one hot glance at Susannah, who sat rigidly in her chair.

Without looking at Ethan, Aubrey held up one hand to stay his brother's diatribe. His gaze did not stray from Hollister's face, which was growing progressively redder. After a long moment, the former Pinkerton man rose to his feet, his glass in hand. He studiously avoided looking at Susannah.

"It is quite true," he said with immense dignity, "that I hoped to win Mrs. Fairgrieve's affections for myself prior to your marriage, but I am not a vindictive man, and I do not allow my personal feelings to affect my work."

Susannah was embarrassed by this declaration, and Ethan's expression revealed outright skepticism, but Aubrey seemed to feel a certain sympathy for Mr. Hollister, despite what anyone else would have viewed as a betrayal of their friendship. He patted the other man's shoulder.

"My brother and I have a plan," he said. "If you're interested in hearing it, sit down, and I'll get you another whiskey."

Mr. Hollister seemed undecided at first, but after a

few moments, he took his chair again, emptied his glass in a single gulp, and handed it to Aubrey. The policeman declined a drink of his own.

Aubrey turned his attention on Susannah while he poured. "I believe Maisie could use a hand with the baby," he said, and though his tone was mild, the statement was a pointed one, and irrefutable.

The last thing Susannah wanted to do was leave the room, especially then, but Aubrey had cornered her neatly, and there was nothing else to be done. She did feel a need to look in on Victoria, even though Maisie was with her, and make sure she was all right. Too, Ellie was probably overwhelmed with the housework and would need both women's assistance.

She stood, straightened her skirts and her shoulders, and swept out of the room, favoring Ethan and Mr. Hollister with a nod as she passed them and narrowing her eyes at Fitzsimmons. The look she gave Aubrey was hardly more cordial.

Aubrey merely smiled, well aware that he'd bested her in their small, secret skirmish, and raised his glass in an impudent gesture of triumph.

Susannah closed the doors crisply behind her and made for the kitchen, where she found Ellie rolling out dough for biscuits. Jasper, quiet and well behaved, was sitting on the floor, over by the cookstove, playing with a set of wooden blocks.

Maisie, of course, would be upstairs in the nursery.

Susannah mounted the rear stairway and moved along the corridor to the door.

"Maisie?"

The answer was nearly toneless. "Come in."

Heaving a sigh of relief, Susannah opened the door and stepped into the nursery. Maisie sat in a rocking chair, Victoria in her arms, both of them covered with a quilt. Even in the dim light of a bleak winter day, Susannah could see that the other woman's eyes were red-rimmed.

Susannah went to stand beside Maisie's chair, laying a hand on her shoulder.

"You mean to leave Seattle," Maisie ventured after a long time. "You and the baby here."

Susannah offered no denial.

Maisie hugged little Victoria so close that the child fidgeted. "I heard you talkin', you and Mr. Fairgrieve."

Susannah nodded. "I'm sorry, Maisie. I thought I could live with a husband who didn't love me, but—"

"Hush," Maisie complained. "He does love you. It's just that his heart hasn't told his head the whole truth of things, that's all."

That, Susannah thought, was too much to hope for—a lovely fantasy. She shifted her thoughts from her own problems, her own heartbreak. She was needed in this household, at least until the latest crisis had passed. She drew up a hassock and sat down near Maisie's chair. "Never mind about Aubrey and me," she said gently. "Right now, we have to think of other matters."

Maisie sat up a little straighter, her expression faintly hopeful as she peered through the gloom. She sniffled. "Turn up the lights, will you?"

Susannah rose and reached for the key on the nearest wall fixture. The flame leaped to life, spilling a soft glow down the wall and over the quilt, the baby, and Maisie's tear-stained face.

"You need to eat something if you can," Susannah said. "Or at least have a cup of tea."

The answer was a negative shake of the head. Maisie stared off into the ether, her gaze fixed, as though seeing a specter in the near distance. "She cursed us all, you know. Mrs. Fairgrieve, I mean. Lyin' there on her death bed, she damned every last one of us to hell. Seems like she's got her way."

The revelation startled Susannah more than a little, though she tried not to let on. "I don't believe in curses," she said after a time with quiet conviction. "Besides, Julia must have been out of her head. She didn't know what she was saying."

Maisie's brow was furrowed, but some of her color was coming back. "It was the medicine Mrs. Fairgrieve took," she murmured. "It made her crazy."

Susannah's heart raced. "Medicine?"

"Laudanum. When the doctor wouldn't give it to her no more, she'd go down to some place on the waterfront." She met Susannah's gaze, looking ashamed. "I wanted to tell Mr. Fairgrieve. I should have. But she said she'd see me and Jasper turned out onto the street if I said anything."

Susannah waited, barely breathing. Good God, she thought, what had become of the Julia she'd known, the sunny, feckless creature, always laughing or spinning some happy scheme?

This information gave her a place to start, though, in making sense of things, something to tell Aubrey and, of course, the police. She had no illusions, after her experience of the wharf, that she could navigate the area on her own.

"There was one feller came around to the back door with a package sometimes—real short and mean-lookin', he was." Maisie shuddered slightly. "He and Mrs. Fairgrieve, they always talked real earnest like, and she would give him money."

Susannah wondered if Maisie knew about the herbal concoction Julia had taken in an effort to bring on an abortion. After a moment's consideration, she decided to let the subject lie, at least for the time being.

"You look all done in, Maisie," she said instead. "You go to your room and rest. I'll bring you a supper tray and some tea."

Maisie nodded and sat back in the rocking chair, staring blindly up at the ceiling.

Within half an hour, Ellie had taken charge of Victoria, and Susannah had helped Maisie to her room, settling her gently on the bed. She served the promised tea, and Jasper, no doubt sensing his mother's sadness and exhaustion, stretched out beside her, trying to encircle her with his little arms.

Susannah kept a vigil of sorts, standing at the window and gazing outward as a new snow began to fall.

"Is that policeman still here?" Maisie asked in a hoarse whisper when some time had gone by.

"I suppose he might be," she said, "if he hasn't taken Ethan to jail."

Jasper stirred fitfully beside his mother but didn't awaken.

"You reckon he knows, little as he is?" Maisie asked. "What's happenin' to all of us, I mean?"

"Probably not," Susannah answered at some length, gazing wistfully at the child. "I'm sure he senses that something is wrong, though. He'll need an extra measure of attention, I suppose—more holding, more soft words and loving touches." When she looked at Maisie again after a long while, she was surprised to find the other woman smiling at her.

"You know a lot about motherin' for a spinster," she said.

Susannah assumed a pose of mild offense. "I am not a spinster," she pointed out. No, indeed, she thought, with a certain sharp grimness. She was neither an old maid nor a bride, for all that she'd entered into the folly of a loveless marriage and given herself to Aubrey with abandon. Her passion for him might well be the ruin of her entire life.

She stood and collected the tray, ready to leave.

It was plain that Maisie could see more in Susannah's

face than she had ever wanted to reveal. She smiled a little, though her countenance was one of sadness. "You're
full of love, Susannah Fairgrieve," she said. "Burstin' with
it. Don't you give up on that man out there, you hear
me? He's a lot of trouble, but he's good right down to
the marrow in his bones, and you could look the whole
world over without findin' a better husband."

Susannah paused in the doorway. "He doesn't love
me," she said, all misery, and was immediately chagrined
for bringing up such a petty problem when Ethan, or even
Aubrey, might be facing imprisonment and hanging.

Maisie waved a hand, dismissing the comment. "He's
like one of them trees out there," she said, apparently referring to the far-reaching timber rising around Seattle
like a green mantle. "He's been in shallow ground, without enough sunshine or water neither one. You turn some
of that love on him, missy, and watch what happens."

"Sometimes," Susannah said, after a moment spent
scrambling for her tongue, "you amaze me."

"Turn out this here light before you go," Maisie said,
settling in for a sound sleep. "I'd do it myself, but I feel
plumb tuckered."

With a small smile, Susannah went back, set the tray
on the bureau top, and reached up to turn down the gas.
Maisie was snoring before she reached the door.

Leaving Maisie and Jasper's room, Susannah found
that Mr. Hollister and the policeman had gone, taking
Ethan with them. Aubrey was there in the kitchen, lifting
pot lids and peering beneath them, evidently in search of
supper. There was no sign of Ellie or of little Victoria.

She took two plates from the shelf and set them on
the table, then added napkins and cutlery. The food—
stewed meat of some sort, dumplings, and corn kernels
from a tin—had cooled and had begun to congeal. Susannah served it exactly as it was, pots, kettles, and all.

Aubrey surveyed the repast with a sort of rueful amusement. While Susannah took the chair opposite, he remained standing, prodding at the brown, stringy meat with a fork. "What is this?" he asked, clearly mystified.

"I have no idea," Susannah answered. "Sit down, Aubrey. I'm hungry."

"You must be," he retorted easily, but he sat and served himself generous portions of Ellie's cooking.

All of the sudden, she was bursting to tell him what she'd learned about the man who had sold Julia laudanum, but she knew his energies were depleted and he needed sustenance. His brother had just been arrested for the second time, he might be taken into custody himself very soon, and it had not been long, after all, since he'd sustained severe injuries.

"You look," he observed between bites, "as if you're about to shoot out of that chair like a Chinese rocket, spilling sparks on your way to the sky. What, pray tell, is on your mind, Mrs. Fairgrieve?"

Unlike her husband, eating heartily now, she found the food unpalatable and pushed her plate away. "Maisie told me that Julia used to go to a place on the waterfront," she confided, leaning forward slightly. "She encountered a man there—"

Aubrey's jaw tightened at this observation, but he did not interrupt. She felt like a traitor to her friend's memory, but she went on anyway. "Maisie said he came to the house several times, with—with laudanum. She described him as small and cruel-looking."

"And?"

Susannah felt her face go warm with conviction and shame, though she couldn't quite pinpoint the source of the latter. "Don't you see? If Mr. Su was murdered because of something he knew—well, isn't it possible that he was acquainted with the people involved in Mrs. Parker's killing as well as your beating?"

"That's quite a leap," Aubrey remarked, pondering the unnamed meat, then opting for a second helping of dumplings instead. "I don't suppose I need to tell you what Hollister is going to say—that Ethan and I—even you, for that matter—all had viable reasons to commit the crime."

"Well, we didn't," Susannah said, "and that's the point. I think this man Maisie told me about might know something. Mr. Hollister has got to find him."

"Hollister has his hands full as it is. I'll find him myself. Did Maisie have a name?"

Susannah shook her head. "Ethan—Ethan's gone back to jail?"

"No," Aubrey said, surprising her. "He's in John Hollister's custody for the time being."

"Is he all right?" She wondered how Ethan's discovery about Su Lin would affect his tender alliance with Ruby.

Aubrey's mood darkened slightly; he looked grim and not a little discouraged. "No," he answered with a shake of his head. "He will be, in time, I think. In the meantime, we've managed to strike an uneasy truce, he and I. Ethan has a long memory where my transgressions—be they real or imagined—are concerned."

Susannah took a breath, let it out. "Not so long ago," she began, "you were the one holding the grudge, remember? You thought Ethan and Julia had been intimate."

Finished with his meal, Aubrey stood, without responding, and pushed his chair back into place with one hand. In the other, he held his plate, which he carried to the sink.

"It's time there was peace in this family," Susannah said gently. "And happiness."

Aubrey's eyes were solemn when he looked at her. "I agree," he said. "Perhaps you can tell me how to achieve those worthy objectives?"

She sighed but made no answer, for she had none.

Aubrey came to her, bent, and placed a gentle kiss on top of her head. "I won't be out late," he told her, and then, as simply as that, he was gone.

They came in the depths of the night, the men who had killed Delphinia and attacked Aubrey in his office over the store; Susannah heard them on the stairs, in the corridor. For one brief, desperate moment, she thought she was merely dreaming, but when she opened her eyes, the sounds did not stop.

She reached out automatically, reached for Aubrey, but his side of the bed was empty, and the covers had not been disturbed at all. Worse still, Victoria was nearby, in the nursery, and the intruders were sure to find her.

That thought galvanized Susannah, broke the paralysis of fear that had held her pressed to the mattress, her hands clenching the blankets. Heart pounding at the base of her throat, she rolled out of bed onto her feet and made her way toward the child. The murmur in the hall intensified, shaped itself into the occasional word or a low chuckle. Plainly, these outlaws did not fear discovery, and the implications of that scared Susannah almost as much as the situation itself.

If only she'd locked the bedroom door, she thought frantically, uselessly, as she groped her way through the darkness, arms extended before her like a sleepwalker in a melodrama, she might have gained a few minutes in which to save Victoria and herself. Because Aubrey had been out when she retired, because, right or wrong, she had wanted him to lie beside her, to hold her, it would not have occurred to her to turn the key.

Using the passage adjoining the master suite to the nursery, she rushed to the crib and gathered Victoria, a warm and solid bundle, into her arms and dashed back into her own room and Aubrey's just as the door sprang open. She clutched the baby against her chest, brushed her lips across the small, downy head, and prayed silently. There was no way out, no place to hide.

Two men entered the master chamber, shadows in the gloom, and one of them turned up the gaslights.

"He ain't here," sputtered the smaller of the pair, glaring around him until his gaze fell on Susannah and Victoria. If he wasn't the person Maisie had seen at the back door with Julia, he certainly resembled him. He had small, colorless eyes, pitted skin, and a hard mouth, thin as the slash of a knife.

The other stared at Susannah. "But she is," he said, and smiled.

A searing chill rushed through Susannah. "Don't come any closer," she warned, all bravado. They were armed; both carried a pistol, and the little one had a blade thrust beneath his belt. She had no weapons at all except her instincts. Her concerns had all boiled down to one, in just an instant: she had to protect Victoria.

"Pretty little thing, all right," the second man mused, as though she hadn't spoken. He let his gaze drift over Susannah's trailing hair and practical flannel nightgown with slow impudence. "I'm going to enjoy this."

Susannah had never in her life been so frightened or, conversely, so deadly calm. She held Victoria more tightly, and the child began to cry. There were others in the hall; she heard their footfalls, heard a curse and the crash of a vase falling to the floor.

Where was Aubrey? Dear God, Susannah thought, don't let him be dead.

The tall man took a step toward her.

"Stay back," Susannah warned. Victoria began to scream.

"Do something with that kid," the short one commanded.

Susannah bounced the child in her arms and patted her back, trying hard to comfort her. "What do you want?"

The ringleader merely smiled at her, sending another chill skittering along the length of her spine. Then, incomprehensibly, he started making his way around the room, turning up the gaslights. It was then that Susannah smelled the first fumes, just beginning to roll in from the hallway.

The little man pulled a bandanna out of his pants pocket and pressed it to his face, then went to the door and shouted, "Send that woman in here to get this kid— my eardrums is about to split wide open!"

Maisie, Susannah thought in despair. Were she and Jasper safe in their room, undiscovered? Or had they already been asphyxiated by the escaping gas? How long could Victoria breathe the stuff without being overcome?

Ellie stumbled over the threshold, looking more sullen than surprised, and Susannah realized with a shock that the woman knew these men. She was fully dressed, and she did not meet Susannah's gaze as she crossed to her and reached for the squalling baby.

"Let me take her," she mumbled. "I promise she'll come to no harm."

Susannah had little choice, given the fact that the leader had begun to retrace his steps from one light fixture to another, calmly blowing out each flame without turning off the lethal vapors. "I swear by all that's holy," she vowed in an angry whisper, surrendering the precious child with the greatest reluctance, "if any harm comes to this child, I will find you, and I will kill you with my own hands." By then, Susannah was coughing intermittently, and her eyes burned. She wondered how long she could remain conscious.

"Why are you doing this?" she demanded of the two men.

"Tie her up, and let's get out of here before the place blows," urged the leader.

His partner was standing directly in front of Susannah now. He clasped her chin hard and forced her to look up at him. "It's a shame," he mused, ignoring his partner's insistent plea. "A damn shame." Then, without further warning, he raised one hand and struck Susannah with such violence that the very darkness itself came inside her, entering through every pore, snuffing out all conscious thought.

The smell of gas struck Aubrey like a cudgel the moment he opened the front door. "Jesus God," he gasped, and, pulling a handkerchief from the inside pocket of his coat, covered his nose and mouth.

"Get Susannah and the baby," Ethan said, coming in behind him. "I'll look for Maisie and Jasper."

Aubrey was already taking the stairs two and three at a time. "For God's sake, hurry!" he yelled over one shoulder. "And be careful!" The house was as black as the inside of the devil's heart, but he dared not strike a match, of course; he felt his way along the corridor, cursing himself for a fool as he went and, at the same time, begging God's mercy for his wife and child.

Stumbling into the bedroom at last, already choking on the poisonous air, he went to the bed first, found it empty. Then he saw her, because of the whiteness of her nightgown, lying on the floor near the hearth. He did not bother to feel for a pulse but simply draped her limp and motionless frame over one shoulder.

The crib in the next room was empty, a fact that terrified him; he deliberated for a few moments, then set Susannah on her feet, holding her by the shoulders, and shook her hard, shouting her name. Her head lolled.

"Susannah!" he bellowed. "Where's the baby?"

Miraculously, she answered, murmuring like someone talking in her sleep. "Gone—Ellie took her—gone—"

The relief was so great that it nearly crushed him; Susannah was alive, his daughter was safe with the housemaid; for the moment, he could think no further than that. He lifted his wife into his arms and rushed out of the room, along the corridor, and down the rear staircase to the lawn. They had barely reached the grass, crisp with frost, before a thunderous explosion hurled them both forward onto the ground. Another blast followed, and another, and debris and hot ash rained down upon them, an apocalyptic baptism in fire and fear.

Aubrey sheltered his wife with his body as best he could, and Susannah, only half conscious, whimpered beneath him. He did not need to look back to know that the house was gone, utterly destroyed—and he didn't give a damn about that pile of brick and wood anyway. The tears on his face were for Maisie, for Jasper, for Ethan. Dear God, Ethan. Had he gotten out before the place went up? And where had Ellie taken Victoria?

He became aware, gradually, of the pain in his ribs, the burns on his hands and back, the distant clanging of bells. The fire department, he thought, and gave a shout of bitter, ironic laughter. Then he levered himself to his feet and pulled Susannah after him, farther and farther from the blazing ruins of his house.

"Aubrey!" At first, the sound was just part of the cacophony that surrounded him; a moment or so passed before it sorted itself out as his name. "Aubrey!"

The voice was Ethan's. He dragged a soot-covered arm across his face and called back a reply. "Over here!"

Ethan materialized out of the fiery gloom, fair hair singed, clothes in tatters, and his whole face about to disappear behind a jubilant grin. "Thank God," he said.

The two brothers embraced.

"Susannah?" Ethan asked hoarsely. "The baby?"

"Susannah is back there, in the gazebo," Aubrey said. "My daughter—" He choked on the words, had to stop and begin again. "Ellie took her. If they got out in time, they're both safe."

"We'll find them," Ethan said. His own eyes were glittering, and he laid a reassuring hand to Aubrey's shoulder.

"Maisie and Jasper?"

"Safe, except for a hell of a scare and a few minor burns," Ethan assured him. "I took them to the stable."

"What about you?"

Ethan grinned again. "I reckon I'm doing about as well as you are, brother. No better, no worse." With that, he went into the gazebo and collected Susannah, lifting her easily into his arms. Since his ribs felt as though they were about to spring out of his skin, Aubrey didn't protest the liberty.

When Susannah opened her eyes, she had a thundering headache, and she was lying in a bed of loose, fragrant straw, covered with a horse blanket. Aubrey knelt beside her, and, seeing him, she let out a sob of relief and flung her arms around his neck.

"Shh," he said. "It's over now. You're safe."

"Victoria—"

He kissed her forehead. "Ellie left her with Reverend Johnstone. She's all right, Susannah. So are Maisie and Jasper."

She heard the noise then, smelled the dense, acrid smoke. "The house?"

"Gone," Aubrey said. "Don't fret, Susannah. We don't need it."

We? She clung to him. Was there something different in the way he'd used that word, the tone he'd given it, or was she imagining things?

He smoothed her tangled hair back from her face, kissed her lightly, chastely on the mouth. "I love you, Susannah," he said, quietly but clearly. "Stay with me. Please."

Tears of joy stung her eyes; exultation was violent within her, like a storm. "You love me?" she echoed in disbelief.

He nodded and kissed her again, this time on the forehead. "Come on, Mrs. Fairgrieve," he said, getting to his feet and pulling her with him. "Let's get you to Reverend Johnstone. He's going to put you and Maisie and Jasper up for the night."

"What about you?" She saw her brother-in-law out of the corner of her eye. "And Ethan?"

"We'll be all right," Aubrey insisted, but tenderly.

"Wait," Susannah said when he took her hand to lead her out of the stable, under the orange and crimson sky.

"What?" He sounded a little impatient.

"I love you, too," Susannah told him. "I just wanted to say it out loud."

He chuckled. "And I wanted to hear it," he said. Only then did she realize that she was wearing his coat, that there were burn holes in his shirt and probably in his flesh as well.

She looked sorrowfully at the house, now an inferno, beyond saving. "What will we do now?" she asked.

He smiled. "We're going to start over, Mrs. Fairgrieve. From the beginning."

Chapter

20

~

 The once-grand mansion lay in ruins under a winter-cool sun, and as Susannah stood gazing at the rubble, she thought about new beginnings. Aubrey, beside her, put an arm around her waist. Victoria was still at the parsonage, under Maisie's care.

"I'm sorry, Susannah," he said.

She looked up at him in surprise. "Sorry?"

"You're a bride. You should be living in a house. Instead, you and I and Victoria are going to be residing above the store for a year or so while we build the new place."

She smiled, let him hold her close against his side. "I don't care where we live, as long as we're together," she said.

He brushed his lips lightly across her temple; she felt his breath move through her in a warm shiver. "I'll make it bigger, better—"

She looked up at him. "The house?"

He nodded, plainly baffled by the expression on her face, which must have mirrored the doubts she felt. "Isn't that what you want?"

She searched his eyes, saw that he genuinely wanted to please her. And she shook her head. "We'll need plenty of space," she said with a slight blush, "because there are bound to be more children. But I'd prefer something far simpler and more—well, *homey*. Couldn't we just have a modest stone house?"

He smiled. "No ballroom?"

She laughed softly. "No ballroom. I will require a piano, however."

He kissed her temple again, squeezed her close. Then he chuckled. "As long as your students understand that your courting days are over." He watched her responding smile with real pleasure, like a man basking in spring sunshine. It touched her heart. "Let's get in out of this cold before we freeze to death," he said practically.

He helped her into the buggy waiting at the curb, climbed up beside her, and gathered the reins in one hand. Then he looked down at her solemnly. "I love you, Susannah," he said.

The words made her heart sing. "And I love you," she replied, cuddling close. Aubrey had taken a room for the three of them at the Union Hotel, while a makeshift apartment was being set up above the general store. "What's going to happen to Ethan?" she asked when they were on their way.

"He's been cleared of all charges," Aubrey said. "According to the police, those men who broke in last night were part of the gang that killed both Su Wong and Delphinia."

"How were they connected?"

"They were partners in a smuggling ring. Opium. Like wolves in a pack, they turned on each other in the end."

Susannah sat still on the buggy seat, taking it all in, or trying to, at least. "Mr. Su and Delphinia were part of the ring, then? What about Ellie?"

"It turns out that Su Wong was the head of the whole operation. Delphinia liked plenty of money, so it's not hard to imagine how she got involved. And, of course, there was an element of revenge—Su wanted to get back at Ethan, and Delphinia wanted to bring me down any way she could. As for Ellie, well, I think she was forced to cooperate."

Susannah sighed, then set her thoughts on a more cheerful path. "Maisie and Mr. Zacharias are sweet on each other, you know."

Aubrey laughed. "That they are. I'm afraid we'll be looking for a new housekeeper, once we get settled in someplace permanent." He was quiet for a few moments, enjoying some vision in his mind. A moment later, Susannah knew what it was. "Just imagine how the members of the Benevolence Society are going to spit and sputter when they see Maisie as mistress of Zach's house, dripping diamonds and swathed in silk."

It was a delicious thought. "And Ethan," Susannah speculated after some moments, "will be married to Ruby Hollister by spring."

Aubrey nodded. "Guess you and I aren't the only ones getting a fresh start," he said. There was a wicked glint in his eyes as he looked down at her. "In the meantime," he said, "everyone is safe and sound. Victoria is with Maisie. I say you and I take a trip to San Francisco, have a real honeymoon. We'll go to Europe in the spring."

Susannah's eyes widened. "Could we go to the opera? In San Francisco, I mean?"

He kissed the tip of her nose. "Anything for you, Mrs. Fairgrieve," he said. "Now," he went on, "let's go back to the hotel and get to know each other a little better."

Susannah's face throbbed with heat. "What about the store?"

He gave the reins a light snap to hurry the horse pulling the rig. "The store can wait," he said. "I can't."

Visit Linda Lael Miller on her Web site:

www.lindalaelmiller.com

**POCKET BOOKS PROUDLY
PRESENTS**

Springwater Wedding
Linda Lael Miller

**Coming Soon in Hardcover from
Pocket Books**

**Turn the page for a preview of
Springwater Wedding. . . .**

Maggie jammed the woody stems of a cloud of white lilacs into a gallon jar, and some of the water spilled over onto the counter in the kitchenette of her parents' guest house. "J. T. Wainwright," she said, with typical McCaffrey conviction, "is a whole new twelve-step program, looking for a place to happen. I don't need that kind of trouble."

Daphne Hargreaves, her best friend since Miss Filbert's kindergarten class at the old schoolhouse, now a historical monument, like the Brimstone Saloon across the street from it, watched with a wry and twinkly smile as Maggie took a sponge from the sink to wipe up the overflow. "Just as I suspected," she mused, sounding pleased.

"What?" Maggie snapped, setting the jar of lilacs in the middle of her grandmother's round oak table, the thump muffled by a lace doily.

"After all these years, you're still interested," Daphne replied, and she was damnably smug about it. "In J.T., I mean." She sighed, and her silver-gray eyes took on a dreamy glint. "It was so romantic, the way he showed up at your wedding and everything—"

"You need therapy," Maggie said, fussing with the lilacs. "It wasn't 'romantic,' it was downright awful." She closed her eyes, and the memory of that day, a decade before, loomed in her mind in three distinct dimensions and glorious Technicolor. She even heard the minister's voice, as clearly as if he'd been standing right there in the guest house.

If anyone here can show just cause why these two should not be joined together in holy matrimony, let him speak now or forever hold his peace.

Right on cue, J.T. had squealed into the driveway behind the wheel of his rusted-out pickup truck, jumped out, leaving the motor roaring, the door gaping, and the radio blaring a somebody-done-me-wrong song, and vaulted over the picket fence to storm right up the petal-strewn strip of cloth serving as an aisle. His ebony hair glinted in the late-spring sunshine, and he was wearing jeans, scuffed boots, and a black T-shirt that had seen better days.

Maggie stood watching his approach from the steps of the gazebo, herself resplendent in mail-order lace and satin, her bridegroom clench-fisted at her side. The guests rose of one accord from their rented folding chairs to murmur and stare, and Maggie's brothers, Simon and Wes, edged toward the intruder from either side. Reece, Maggie's father, had risen to his feet as well, though the expression in his eyes as he gazed at J.T. had been one of compassion, not anger.

"You can't do this, Maggie," J.T. rasped, as Simon and Wes closed in, handsome and grim in their tuxedos, each grasping one of his arms. He shook them off, his gaze a dark, furious fire that seared Maggie's heart, then and now. "Damn it, you *know* it's wrong!"

He'd been right, that was the worst of it. Marrying Connor *had* been a mistake; she knew it now, and she'd known it then, deep down. She'd gone ahead with the wedding anyway and, having acted in haste, she had indeed repented at leisure.

Daphne snapped her fingers. "Mags?"

Maggie made a face, but a grin was tugging at the corners of her mouth. She'd missed Daphne, she'd missed Springwater, and, though she wasn't ready to admit as much, even to her closest friend, she'd missed J. T. Wainwright.

"Sooner or later, you're going to have to face him, you know," Daphne observed, opening the refrigerator and peering inside. She brought out a pitcher of iced tea, jingling with fresh ice cubes, and plundered the cupboards for a glass. "Springwater is a small town, after all."

Maggie drew back a chair at the table and sank into it. "Why did he have to come back here?" she asked, not really expecting an answer. J.T. had been seriously injured in some kind of shoot-out, everyone in Springwater knew that, and though he'd recovered within a few months, he'd turned in his badge and returned to Montana to run the long-neglected ranch that had been in his family for well over a century.

Daphne came through with a reply, as she filled a glass for herself and then, at Maggie's nod, another. "Same reason you did, I suppose," she said. "It's home."

"Home," Maggie reflected, somewhat sadly. To her, the term covered far more territory than just the big, wonderful old house on the other side of the long gravel driveway; it meant Reece and Kathleen McCaffrey, her mom and dad. And after nearly forty years together, after three children and five grandchildren, they were sleeping in separate bedrooms and, when they spoke at all, discussing the division of property.

Daphne sat down, then reached out to squeeze Maggie's hand. Her fingers were cool and moist from the chilled glasses. "Home," she repeated, with gentle emphasis. "Everything's going to be all right, Mags. You'll see."

Maggie attempted a smile, took up her iced tea, and clinked her glass against Daphne's. "I guess that depends on how you define 'all right,' " she said, and sipped.

"J.T. looks good," Daphne observed, never one to waste time and verbiage bridging one subject with another. "*Really* good."

Maggie narrowed her eyes. "There you go again," she accused, losing patience. "What is it with you and J.T., anyway? You're fixated or something."

Daphne ran one perfectly manicured fingertip around the rim of her glass, her gaze lowered. In that solemn, thoughtful pose, with her dark hair upswept, she resembled the portrait of her great-great grandmother, Rachel English Hargreaves, even more closely than usual. Maggie glimpsed her own gamine-like reflection in the polished glass of the china cabinet and noted the contrast. She was thirty years old, with short brown hair and large blue eyes, and outside of Springwater, people still asked for ID when she ordered wine with her dinner.

"Daph?" Maggie prompted, when her friend failed to bat the conversational ball back over the net. Daphne was planning to marry Greg Young, whose father owned the only automobile dealership within fifty miles, in less than a month, and she'd seemed distracted lately. She'd booked the church, sent the invitations, chosen the flowers, shopped for the dress. All of the sudden, it seemed she had a lot more to say about J.T. than her fiancé. "Is there something you want to tell me?"

Daphne met Maggie's eyes and shook her head. Her smile looked slightly flimsy, and sure enough, it fell away in an instant. "I'm not in love with J.T., if that's what you're thinking," she said. "I can't help wondering, though, what it would be like to be the object of the sort of passion he felt for you."

Maggie bit her lower lip. She'd been troubled by Daphne's mood ever since she'd moved back to Springwater less than a week before, having sold her condo in Chicago and given up her job there, planning to turn the old Springwater stagecoach station into a bed-and-breakfast, but she hadn't found the words to express her concern. Now she simply took the plunge. "Daph, maybe you're not ready—to get married, I mean. Maybe you need some time to think things through."

Daphne's hand trembled a little, Maggie thought, as she raised her glass to her mouth and tasted the sun-brewed tea. "I love Greg," she said, a few moments later. She glanced down at the doorknob-sized diamond on her left-hand ring finger and frowned as it caught the afternoon light. If someone onboard the *Titanic* had been wearing that ring, they could have summoned help at the first sign of trouble. "What's there to think about?"

Maggie didn't answer. With a failed marriage behind her, and a couple of dead-end love affairs into the bargain, she wasn't exactly an authority on relationships.

"We're going to start a family right away," Daphne said. She'd told Maggie that a number of times already, first by long-distance telephone, then e-mail, and finally face-to-face, but Maggie pretended it was news.

"That's wonderful," she said. Again.

"Do you ever wish you and Connor had had a child?" Daphne ventured.

Maggie prodded the lilacs with one finger, bestirring their luscious scent. "We were only married two years, Daph."

"That's not an answer," Daphne pointed out.

Maggie shrugged ruefully and hoisted her glass in a second salute. "Yes and no," she replied. "Yes, I would love to have a child, and no, I don't wish Connor and I had had one together." A part of her, a part she'd never shared with anyone, not even her dear friend, wished something altogether different—that she'd left Connor at the altar that long-ago summer day, climbed into that battered old truck beside J.T., and sped away. Though she couldn't rightly say how such an action would ultimately have affected J.T., there could be little doubt that she and Connor would both have been better off.

"Do you realize that every woman from our graduating class—every last one of them, besides us—is married, and a mother?" Daphne sounded a little desperate, in Maggie's opinion. "Even Virginia Abbott."

"There were only six of us," Maggie pointed out, but the truth was, she was a little stung by the comparison. Okay, she'd married the wrong man. Instead of kids, she had Sadie, a spoiled beagle now snoring on the hooked rug in the living room, with all four feet in the air. In general, though, Maggie had done pretty well in life. Good grades in college, a fine job afterward, with profit-sharing and a 401K big enough to choke the proverbial horse, the enthusiasm and confidence to get a new business up and running. She was healthy, with a family and lots of friends, and happy, too, though in truth there were nights when she lay awake, staring at the ceiling and feeling like a traveler who's just missed the last boat to the land of milk and honey.

"Virginia Abbott," Daphne marveled, sounding mildly disgusted. Sometimes it wasn't enough for Daphne to merely make a point; she had to write it on the wall in a spray of bullet holes. "Good Lord. A stretch in reform school and the world's worst case of acne, and she *still* ended up happily married."

Maggie resigned herself to a long diatribe, settling back in her chair and taking another long sip from her iced tea.

"And Polly Herrick," Daphne went on. "Look at her. President of the P.T.A.!"

Maggie hid a smile.

"I'll bet she's put on fifty pounds since high school," Daphne raved, "and her husband treats her like a goddess." A slight flush blossomed on her cheeks. "If I gain an ounce, Greg orders some new piece of exercise equipment off an infomercial and keeps track of my workouts on a chart on the kitchen wall."

A low growl rose within Maggie, but she held it back. She'd never been especially fond of Greg Young the boy, a classmate of her elder brother Simon's, and the more she learned about Greg Young the man, the less she liked him. He was good-looking, in a self-conscious, flashy sort of way, and always "on," like a motivational speaker run amok. Worse, he had two ex-wives, both of whom hated his guts, and he'd once come close to suing his own sister over a trust fund set up by their grandmother. Since Daphne was no idiot, Maggie had to assume that Greg's best qualities were subtle ones.

All of a sudden, Daphne ran out of steam. She flung out her hands and gave a laughing sigh. "Listen to me running on," she said. Then, with a glance at her watch, she got to her feet, rinsed her iced tea glass at the sink, and popped it into the top rack of the dishwasher. "I've got shopping to do. Greg is barbequing steaks tonight, and then we're going to watch *The Best Years of Our Lives* on video."

There you have it, Maggie thought. Any man who likes classic movies can't be all bad. "See you tomorrow?"

Daphne smiled. Now that school was out, she was on hiatus from teaching, and despite being up to her elbows in wedding plans, she insisted on helping Maggie with the heavy work over at the Springwater Station. They'd done the worst of the cleaning—the place had been closed up for several years—and for the past few days, they'd been sorting through the contents of trunks, crates, and boxes, looking for old linens and other antiques that could be used to lend authenticity. "Bright and early. We've going to that estate auction over in Maple Creek, right?"

Maggie nodded. "I'll pick you up at six sharp. We can have breakfast on the way."

Daphne rolled her eyes. "Six sharp," she confirmed, with a notable lack of enthusiasm. "See you then."

With that, she was gone.

Sadie got up off the rug, stretched methodically in all directions, one leg at a time, and ambled into the kitchen area to check out her food bowl. Finding nothing there but half a dog biscuit and the remains of that morning's breakfast, she raised baleful brown eyes to Maggie's face and gave a despondent little whimper.

"Did you know," Maggie said, already headed toward the tiny laundry room at the back of the cottage, where she stored kibble, dog dish in hand, "that the typical beagle gets way too much to eat on account of Sad-eyes Syndrome?"

Sadie panted, wagging at warp speed. *Great*, she seemed to be saying. *It's working.*

Maggie laughed, shook her head, and gave Sadie an early supper. While the dog ate, Maggie stepped out onto the back step, watching the sun set behind the gazebo. The structure was all but swallowed up in climbing rose vines just beginning to bud, and it was not only innocuous but beautiful, in a misty Thomas Kinkade sort of way. In the ten years since her wedding day, she had returned to Springwater many times for holidays and short vacations and rarely if ever associated the gazebo with any unhappy memory. Now, after her conversation with Daphne, it seemed that she couldn't get J.T. out of her mind, couldn't forget the way he'd looked in the golden light of that spring afternoon long ago—not just angry, but earnest and confounded and, worst of all, betrayed.

"I'm sorry," she told his ghost, and turned to go back into the guest house.

J.T. gestured, in mid-stride, toward the barn, with its sagging roof and leaning walls. The whole ranch was a disgrace; Scully and Evangeline, the first Springwater Wainwrights and his great-great-grandparents, must have been turning over in their graves in the years since he'd turned his back on the land to play homicide cop in the Big Apple.

"Purvis," he said to the older man double-stepping along beside him, "look at this place. I'd like to help you out. I really would. But I don't have *time* to take on another job."

Purvis Digg, a friend and contemporary of J.T.'s late father, Jack Wainwright, had served in Viet Nam, and though he apparently didn't suffer from flashbacks or delayed-stress like many of his fellow veterans, he'd somehow gotten stuck in the 60s just the same. He wore his salt-and-pepper hair long, even though it was thinning on top, and bound back with a leather boot-lace. Sometimes, he added a headband, Indian-style, though J.T. had yet to see a feather. He sported a fringed buckskin jacket bought second-hand during the Johnson administration, combat boots, and thrift-store jeans embellished with everything from star-and-moon-shaped patches and old Boy Scout badges to grease stains.

"But you're a cop," Purvis argued.

Reaching the corral gate, which was falling apart like everything else in J.T.'s life, he stopped, one hand on the rusty latch. "I *was* a cop," he corrected his old friend.

"Once a cop, always a cop," Purvis said.

J.T. thrust splayed fingers through his dark hair. He'd taken a bullet himself, and lost his partner to a punk who would probably be back out on the street in another eighteen months, and while he'd recovered physically, he wasn't sure he'd ever get over the memory of seeing Murphy fall. Then there was the funeral, with full honors, the brave, baffled face of the dead man's widow, the plaintive wail of sorrow from his teenage daughter. "Look, Purvis—"

"Feel pretty damn sorry for yourself, don't you?" Purvis broke in, reddening a little at the base of his jaw. Like most everybody else in and around Spring-water, he knew all about what had happened in that warehouse, six months back. "Well, here's a flash for you, Junior: you're not the first guy who ever lost a buddy. Your dad was the best friend I ever had, and one fine day somebody shot him right out of the sad-dle, if you recall."

Grief and exasperation made J.T.'s sigh sound the way it felt: raw. "Damn it, Purvis, that's a low blow. Of course I 'recall'!"

"Then you probably recollect that nobody ever rounded up the shooter."

J.T. clenched and unclenched his left fist. He could not, would not, hit a skinny old man, but the temptation was no less compelling. "I recollect, all right. I still have nightmares about it."

Purvis slapped him on the shoulder in an expression of manly commiseration. "Me, too. How old were you when Jack was murdered? Fourteen?"

"Thirteen," J.T. said, averting his eyes for a moment, in order to gather his composure. His father had ridden in from the range that afternoon, on the first hot breath of a summer thunderstorm, so drenched in blood that it was hard to tell where the man stopped and the horse began.

J.T., working in the corral, with a two-year-old gelding on a lead-line, had vaulted over the fence and run toward his father. Jack had fallen from his paint stallion the same way Murphy had gone down in the warehouse, in an excruciatingly slow, rolling motion. And like Murphy, Jack Wainwright had most likely been dead before he struck the ground. J.T. had still been kneeling in the dirt, rocking Jack's body in his arms, when Purvis had shown up in the squad car and radioed for an ambulance. It had been too late for J.T.'s dad.

"I didn't bring that up just for the hell of it," Purvis said, in his gruff way. "And maybe it was a little below the belt. The thing is, J.T., that wasn't an isolated incident. A lot of the same things that were going on back then are going on now—the ranchers around here are losing livestock to theft and poison just like they were before. Just last month, somebody took a shot at Ben Knox while he was out looking for strays. I got me a crazy feeling that we're dealing with the same outfit."

J.T.'s next instinct was to grasp Purvis by the lapels of his campy jacket and wrench him onto the balls of his feet, but he restrained himself. "Are you telling me you think these are the same people who killed my dad?"

Purvis swallowed, then nodded. "Yup."

"You got any proof of that?"

"No," Purvis admitted. "Just an ache in my gut that says history is repeating itself." He paused. "J.T., this situation ain't gonna go away by itself. I ain't as young as I used to be, and I can't run these bastards down without some help. If I *don't* get them, the ranchers are going to have my badge, and you know as well as I do that once I'm gone they'll be up in arms like a bunch of yahoos out of some black-and-white western. We'll have the Feds crawling all over the valley after that, but not before a few more people get hurt or killed."

"There must be somebody else," J.T. breathed. He was weakening, and Purvis surely knew it.

"There's nobody else," Purvis insisted. "Oh, I could come up with a pack of hot-headed rednecks, call 'em a posse. But you're the only professional around here, besides me. You're a cop. You can ride and shoot. Besides that, you're a rancher, just like them, and you're Jack Wainwright's son. You've got a stake in this, too."

J.T. was silent. Purvis might be a hick lawman from a hick town smack in the middle of no place, but he had the tenacity of a pit-bull, and he could argue like a big-city lawyer.

Purvis came in for the kill. "What do you figure Jack would do if he were in your place?"

J.T. closed his eyes, opened them again. The first seismic stirrings of a headache made tremors at the base of his skull. "All right," he said. *"All right."*

Purvis grinned. "Judge Calloway can swear you in tomorrow," he said.

"I'm going to an auction in the morning," J.T. replied. There was an estate being liquidated over in the next county, household goods and livestock, and he intended to bid on a couple of quarter horses and maybe a beef or two. Then he'd be able to call this pitiful place a ranch again with a semi-straight face.

The marshal of Springwater could afford to be generous; he'd gotten what he wanted. "All right. We'll have supper together tomorrow night, then, over at the Stagecoach Café. You, me, and the judge. Be there by six."

J.T. gave a rueful chuckle and shook his head. "You got it, Pilgrim."

Purvis laughed, administered another resounding shoulder slap, and turned to head back to his beat-up, mud-splattered Jeep. Halfway there, he turned. "Say," he added as a jovial afterthought. "Maggie McCaffrey's back in town. Going to spit-shine the old Springwater Station and make one of them fancy little hotels out of it."

J.T. knew all about Maggie's return to Springwater; uncannily, her homecoming had very nearly coincided with his own, though they'd managed to avoid running into each other so far. He hadn't seen Maggie since the day he'd tried, without success, to keep her from marrying Connor Bartholomew, her big brother Simon's friend from medical school. He'd made an ass of himself, and even after all this time, he wasn't anxious to face her, and not just because he wasn't good at apologizing. He'd been married, fathered a son, gotten divorced, and dated dozens of women, before and after his ex-wife, Annie, but somewhere down deep, he'd always had a thing for Maggie. He'd known it and so, unfortunately, had Annie.

"I'll have to stop by and say hello," he said, as lightly as he could. "The Station's been sitting empty for a long time. It's good to know somebody is going to restore it."

Purvis nodded. "A McCaffrey, too," he agreed, pleased. "It'll be almost like the old days, when Jacob and June-bug was runnin' the place."

J.T. might have laughed if he hadn't just been roped into signing on for an indefinite stretch as Purvis's deputy. The way the marshal talked, Jacob and June-bug McCaffrey might have been happily retired and cruising the country in an RV, instead of dead and buried well over a century. "Almost," he agreed.

Purvis lifted a hand in farewell, climbed into his Jeep, and started up the engine. J.T. watched until the aging lawman had turned around and headed down the long dirt road leading to the highway.

"Shit," J.T. said aloud. He gave the gate latch a pull, and the whole thing fell apart at his feet.

He hoped it wasn't an omen.